My Keeper

My Keeper

$\mathcal{D}$*edication*

Writing a book is a solitary endeavor, getting it published is not.

This book is dedicated to my brother-in-law Vince (so happy to call him that at last). He was the first to read this book in its rawest state, but he loved it anyway. Vince has helped me get it published and always encourages me to continue my writing. His friendship and love have lifted me up countless times.

And to his husband, my very dear and loving and handsome (need I go on) brother John, who pushed me and assisted me in getting this book out there. I love you both.

To my beloved husband, Arnolfo, who always supports me. He helped with many confusing choices, cover design, Web page... and endless other details.

Also want to say thank you to my friend Kathy who read My Keeper in 24 hours. She immediately asked for the next installment, pushing me to complete Our Master.

My Keeper

Prologue

Dark, almost black, but for the bits of light that stream into the cracks of the small windows. I do not like the light, but know it will not harm me. Although, now I would bless the light if I could only be in it.

Trapped, captured, isolated as I am. I don't know how long I have been here. I cannot understand time, a moment feels like forever, a week a day. In and out of reality, and yet I know no reality.

I am wild with a dark hunger. Such a hunger; impossible. Not a core emptiness, held within my abdomen, but an emptiness aching in every limb, every organ.

I think I know what I am, when I can think. Most of the time my brain feels like it's melting inside my head. Lava. I have become something that is me, nonetheless not me. An inconceivable being. Need is all I know now, though in the recesses of my mind I sense there is more. It has no intelligence now, just nagging fragments. Impossible to fully pull out of my burning mind. As forgotten lyrics from a song you know too well, yet somehow cannot sing.

I wait until he comes. The one who keeps me in chains, feeds me and then when I quiet attempts to hold me. I am in chains, cannot resist his touch, his intimate kiss. He woos my heat until I concede begrudgingly to his efforts. This strange one who's captured me, feeds me, and rapes me.

I am sure now he aims to tame me for his pleasure. The dark man who keeps me hidden in his basement, my dungeon. He is a handsome human, loose dark messy waves, long, over broad shoulders. Little more than average height but a body no human or immortal could ignore.

If it were not for these chains, I would make him my slave; or better yet drink him dead.

I have little idea who I am. I remember some things that were me but few. Most are so confused and scattered. All I really know now is my need for blood. In my bindings I struggle, I hunger. Who I may have been before, a whisper in my mind. There, but fleeting and unimportant.

So I find myself a new immortal, a vampire. As unlikely as that may seem, what else could I be? This happening, I have no memory of. Not even a glimmer of being turned into this incomprehensible thing. Woken to chains, confused, full of rage and dark hungers I could not comprehend. No immortal master but a human master at my side. One who could never understand my desires, my needs. Somehow still trying to serve me while making me go mad at the same time.

I have no idea who he is.

Hear soft steps on the floors above me. Hear them approach the cellar. Like the sound in an old horror movie, the door slowly creaks open.

He brings no good food for me tonight, like always. Just a dog, big and black. A, a... can't remember. I know what kind of dog it is but the name will not coalesce in my mind.

Still it lays unmoving at my feet. Without thought I grab it and sink my teeth into its furry neck, feel the rush of warm blood flowing into me. Life still there; know it is life to me.

As I drink the last of the animal, I feel the lava cool slightly. As if a mist of water has touched the molten surface yet still runs hot underneath. My temperament tames a bit as well. Though not nearly enough for his intentions. He knows this, tightens my bindings so I have little chain, confining any movement. He adds more straps on my arms, tightening them to the wall behind me until I cannot move but a fraction. My legs are bound apart with chains leading off where I lay into the darkness.

I do nothing but hiss and cry. Who I was before reduced to a hissing animal. Still somewhere deep inside there is a human who cries. Captured.

I see him undress and come to my bed with thick harness. I dread what I know will be next.

He takes no time to caress me. Growling I try to bite at him. I seem to have no words of protest, only bawling rage and pain. Even as I try to pursue my desire he keeps his neck, his blood, well away from me. Mounts me, pushing into my dryness slowly with great control, hurting me with the thickness of his manhood. I fight, but my bindings do not give me much to work with. Arms over my head, legs open, I have no recourse. He takes his time, or just takes. Depends on his mood. I can't do a thing about it.

Pushing himself into me over and over. Not a word just his shameless moaning and grabbing at me until he is done. He gives a wet kiss to my breast. Lingering for only a moment and then he is gone. Leaving me alone again in his dark basement, only the shadows of civilization seeping through the windows.

I lie aching, burning inside until I see the light creeping into the windows. Feeling weaker as each ray grows stronger across the cement floor. Hear him get up, walk about, door, car, and he disappears for the day. That is all I know of the day, his day. Just soft sounds in the back of my exhausted mind.

Chapter One

"Margret, wake up." The window is black but for the false light of the neighborhood above. He pokes me. "Wake up."

My burning and confusion is always strongest as I wake. "I thirst!" I yell, realizing my own voice. A shadow of a smile crosses his lips. Oddly pleased at my outburst. I try to free myself, only to rattle the thick chains that bind me.

"Yes, I know, but finding appropriate humans is not so easy. Especially with the way you are now."

He glares at me, curiously, watching me struggle to free myself. His pet, he hates, he wants. What does he want from me?

"I will go out this evening and try to find you more suitable food," he says calmly, sounding as if he is going to the market to pick up milk.

I am burning inside! I want HIM. He is "suitable" food. His nearness when he rapes me only makes me hunger for his blood more. I feel the very thing I lust for so near, rushing by me like a train that can't be caught. I cannot reach him or anything I want now.

"What is an appropriate human?" I angrily hiss at him.

What a scornful look and a painfully long pause; staring into me with his dark eyes.

"You are not much more than an animal at the moment. Uncontrollable. You would take the innocent, kill anyone." He shakes his head in disapproval. "I cannot tolerate that. I will give you what I find and what is at least stomach-able to me."

How I hate him, hate that I am at his mercy. Give me human blood, give me yours! My mouth waters and lusts just at his presence.

My thoughts run wild; a dog gets me by but does not really quench my thirst. Not for long anyway. I am in constant burning hunger. He has fed me only animals, but I know from his nearness that is not what I truly desire. I want him, human blood. Can smell it, nearly taste it in the air when he is close to me. Only human blood will cool the burn raging inside me.

"I am going. I may or may not bring you what you want, but…" He trails off into his thoughts.

The light from the bulb in the wood rafters obscures his face. My eyes hurt as I try to read him, I can't see him clearly.

"You have no concept of my needs!" I screech at him. "Nor do you care! You care nothing for me, you care only for your own fucking desires!" Meant that most literally. He turns back to face me, scowling.

"I will bring you what you need, that is all I can do, and I do know what you need! You will get it only from me, Margret!" How I hate it when he says my name aloud. Hate the sound of it in my ears even as it is the only thing I recognize as me.

Then you will have what you need, I think as he stomps up the stairs. His only intention and my only intention conflict wildly.

Lie for hours, strapped and unable to move. Like a rabid dog I rattle my chains. I can hear people coming and going in their cars. Wonder did I live that life before? I must have. Can't remember any details but feel like it was once mine, a real human life.

I have been this thing for weeks, or is it days, months? Time is difficult for me. My memory so veiled and obscure. I know it's there, time, yet I seem to have no tracking of it. Cannot seem to connect with myself as I was, even as I am. Now I am empty, wild with hunger, full of aggression and want.

Finally he comes home. Detect the hot fragrance of wet human blood as he walks down the stairs. Though even as I am lustful in my need, what he brings gives me pause.

He lays her gently at my feet like a gift to a mad goddess.

"She is just a child!"

"She is young, but not a child." His eyes so dark, cold. He hates feeding me, clearly. Maybe even the dogs. Who can blame him, this human who endeavors to feed the insane vampire he has chained up in his basement?

Still, I will take anything brought my way so great is my thirst.

Her face is pretty, yet so thin and frail. Innocent.

"Why do you bring me a child?" I scream at him. How my heart fills with hate for what I am, what I want. At the same time I know that I need her.

His eyes full of distaste. Is it me, or that he brings me a child to feed on? Is he more hateful of the beast I am or the beast he is?

Do I really care? Not really, just one of many thoughts that go so quickly through my fluid mind.

"What has she done to deserve this?" He brings her closer to me. She is hurt, a gash on her head, out cold, yet not cold. The aroma of her blood swirls in the air, causing me to dizzy with desire. Need her.

"What does it matter to you what she is? I could bring you anyone and you would feed, even if reluctantly. I alone control what you have for your food." He seems angered by my questions. My reluctance.

He frees some of the chains on my arms so I can reach her. My eyes are transfixed on the young girl, barely noticing him. Still he keeps his distance as he lets several lengths loose.

He is correct. My need, the smell of blood, and finally the feeling of my hand on her warm living flesh. Her powerful pulse rushes under my fingertips as I run them over her pale skin; the small streams inside her a powerful river rushing under my caress. Too much for another thought of whether she deserves this death. It is hers, and she is mine.

This, the first human he has given me; most likely I have not tamed enough for him. Beast to the beast.

"Feed!" he furiously barks before making his way quickly to the stairs. Disappearing.

As soon as I hear the door slam behind him, I grab her. Her white neck, soft and sweet. Tentatively run my mouth over it. A cheap vanilla perfume conceals a darker smell, somewhat familiar to me. Yet it is the blood that moves under it that fills my nostrils. Crazed with hunger, I sink my teeth deep into her vein.

To my shock the blood gushes into my mouth. I swallow, scarcely keeping up with the flow. Not like a dog at all. Thick and full of an excitement like nothing he has ever given me. Feel her blood moving into me, through me. Penetrating every cell, organ, limb with life. Taking her life and making it mine.

Beautiful colors bleed into the blackness behind my lids. Smoke-like wisps engulf each other, making whole new colors as they blend.

Hate him! Hate me! Cannot, will not stop! I drink until I hear the beating inside her chest slow, cease. She is dead. Cold. I release her. Her sweet face rolls back in my arms, white and lifeless like a frightening china doll.

Wish I could cry for her but I have no time for remorse in this moment. I feel so alive. Strong and powerful! The relentless burning in my head has greatly lessened. I try to break the chains he has put on me. Struggle and pull at them with all I have. The chains stir, maybe strain a bit more than before. Still do not even threaten to break.

I can't remember feeling so good since I woke to this nightmare. Life is throbbing in my veins, soothing the hot rage in my head.

I pull again with all my might at my bindings. Nothing breaks, except maybe my spirit.

Will I ever be free of them, of him?

He is the devil, I suppose. So am I.

Again I hear his footsteps approach, the door to my dungeon timidly opening.

Gradually he comes down the stairs. Caution, fear? Until he is sure I have finished her, he stays on the last step, peering around like a shy boy spying on me. My sweet young feed still draped over me, in death's arms. I stare at my captor with a new loathing.

Dark shadows his face and then slowly the light as he walks over to me.
"Have you had your fill?" Somewhat scornfully.

"Yes," I hiss, "but she did not deserve this death. She was not evil, you are!"
He looks at me a bit confused.

"I will not be your toy!" I scream at him.

Laughter, soft and condescending.

"Really, my toy? It is you that is confused, Margret," he says with
sharp breath.

He turns to look at the soft light showing in the basement window,
beckoning his thoughts away for a while. Away from her, away from me.

I try to read what he may be thinking. My eyes roam over his figure. Just
the dim light in the room highlights the curves of his slim black jeans. His
muscular arms and chest hugged tightly by a simple white tee shirt. Why
am I noticing this now? No matter the great physical attributes he may
have. He is my captor and I despise him!

"You have no choice to what food I bring you. You would drink everyone
within your reach if I did not have control of you." His face becomes sad
as he looks down at the girl. "Because of her, you are stronger already."

He pulls a blanket off the mattress I lie on, lays it out on the cold basement floor. Takes the dead girl softly up into his arms, slowly placing her
on it. Handling her delicately, as if she was still alive. Folding her arms
properly over her chest as she would be if in a coffin. One she will never
lie in. He wraps her in the shroud, tucking gingerly around her until at last
he covers her thin lifeless face.

Then he reaches over to pick up a new folded black tarp, stands, shakes
it open over her. Quickly she is enclosed in it. Ripping long strips with his
teeth, he secures it with gray duct tape. Wrapping it tightly around the
slight frame of her body.

Not sure what horrifies me more. That I gave her death or the way he seam-
lessly moves from gentleness to serial killer without a moment's hesitation.

Well, I am not impressed, I just killed a child! Suppose I would have killed many innocent humans by now if I were not in his chains. Still, force feed. I want to make my own choice as to who will have my death. Not what he wants; what I want!

He lifts her up, she weighs nothing to him, takes her to the dark side of the basement. The other side of the staircase I can't see beyond. I only hear the crinkling of the tarp as it drops slowly to the floor.

When he returns the sadness I perceived on his face before seems gone. He looks blank, lost.

Finally he says, "You are well fed, even if you are still hungry, which I am sure you always are." Sits down, crossing his legs over each other close to me, glaring. "You know I am your only source of food?"

I know where this is going, and he is right. He is. If I will ever be strong enough to break these bindings, overtake him, it is not now. Not tonight.

"Now you will give me what I need." Raises his brow. "If not, you will have at best a dog."

Though he is trying hard to exhibit his dominion over me, I still sense conflict in him.

I feel like, well a slave. He quickly undresses, tossing his shirt and jeans near the foot of the mattress.

He tightens the bindings over my head once again so my arms are no longer a threat. Pulls the thin black cotton robe I have as my only defense away.

He whispers softly, sweetly, belying the monster he is. "I need you right now, Margret."

He moves to kiss me. Not on my mouth, which would be, even as I am well fed, very foolish. Where he thinks I may forget for a moment how much I hate him.

He opens me, finds my heat and goes to it first with his fingers, rubbing it firmly. Quickly follows with his engulfing warm mouth. Still I am forbidding him. Struggling in my chains, fighting him. He holds tight to my hips, restricting my only real movements further. He is very strong, restrains my struggles with little effort. After some minutes of his precise attentions, he brings me to wetness against my will. He arrogantly has to acknowledge the forbidden fruit he has drawn from me.

"Yes, Margret." Mumbles over my ripening, going deeper to the source, taking it in with his ardent kisses. "You're so wet...so hot." The warmth of his breath over me with every word, every moan, exciting me further. All the time I desperately try to fight him the only way I really can. Filling my head with as much hatred and rage as possible.

I feel weak, guilty for giving him what he seems to want so badly. Continue to resist what he is doing to me.

The more he persuades my body, the more pleased he is, the more intensely he kisses me. Drawing me harder into his mouth, inducing me to concede to his desires. Although I am angry with myself, he knows well how to make a woman ready for him. Obviously he doesn't want just ready, he wants defeat. I have no idea of time, but I am sure he took much of it on me. Never feeling like he was anything but eager, wanting, not a performance, desire.

I choked back my pleasure, fought it as hard as I could but his deep kiss was too hot to resist any longer, even as I wished to. My body begrudgingly gives him what he forces from it. I stifle my release into his needy mouth.

He knew I had climaxed, although I did my best to silence any note of it. His fingers were deep inside me. I doubt my contractions could have eluded him. Even if I was begging, fighting him the whole time. I was begging, but for what? At the end all I could utter was 'please.'

He took his time, relishing it, my defeat. His needy kiss not slowing much even after I succumbed. How I hate him for this. Forcing me to give him...anything!

"Just do it!" I scream at him. Not sure if I sounded as hateful as I aspired.

"Just a few more," moans into my dripping, "moments." His words nearly lost in my flesh. His success giving him as much pleasure as it was giving me shame. Endlessly sucking my wetness greedily into his mouth. As hungry for me as I am for him. Though what I really desire is his blood.

Although.

I can't move away from him, hit him, bite him, do anything. He finally moves himself over me. He is so thick, hard. His flesh hot, damp with sweat. Enthusiastically enters me. Not my most intense desire, but he seems to be trying to make it my second.

I despise him for making me want this, but after the long time he spent making me ready, even without the chains I may well have conceded. Suppose it may have been the human blood I needed to feel more of the desire he does. I find myself moaning at the long, slow, deep strokes without realizing. Clamp my mouth shut. Again he needs to take notice. Mumbling into my neck.

"It's all right, Margret. It feels good. Just relax, let me love you."

After his thrusts forcefully quicken, he loudly climaxes. He slows, sweetly embraces me, comforting me. Tenderly kissing my neck and shoulders. His hands move over my body with lulling caresses. Never loosening his hard lock inside me. Strokes me tenderly, as if to calm my anger with him. Almost like he really cares for me. I do eventually calm, and even quiet with his soothing.

Abruptly he lets go of me, falls between my restrained legs, encircling my hips in his arms. Lifting me to his eager mouth. Pressing his tongue deep inside me, drawing out his release within mine. Vehemently sucking them from me.

"It tastes so hot," moaning over my wetness, "us."

It will be a long night. I cannot resist. My body is revealing much more than I want him to know.

How I hate this mortal man. Want to drink him until he lies dead in my arms. Pale and cold like the innocent girl he seduced me to take. I am so confused, unsure and afraid of everything I am feeling now.

Seduction is his sword; he wields it flawlessly.

The morning is coming. I can almost feel the sun as it breaks over the horizon. Filling the trees with morning glow. Even as I cannot see it, I sense its arrival. Feel very tired, in my head and my body, as it approaches.

He still lies half over me, head below my breast, arm and leg draped over me.

"I wish you could take me..." He looks innocently up at me, like he is not a murdering rapist. Just a man. "I know you can't, won't, yet. I hope soon..."

"You mean suck you?" I bite at him in warning.

"NO, take me in your arms," correcting me. He is fully awake now, a bit mad. On his hands and knees over me, staring me right in the eyes. "Yes, I do want that but, I want you to willingly hold me, very much." His face goes from a weak anger to wicked. Smiles razing his brow. "You used to do both, quite well."

"Really?" I say with as much anger and sarcasm as I can muster in my drowsy state.

He falls back over me. "Yes, you did." Embraces me with his arms and strong legs, his head cuddles under my arm, suckling at the side of my breast. How can he be so dammed content while I am chained up like an animal underneath him?

Soon after he falls asleep again. Eventually I too sleep, but not before I ponder what he said. Do both, willingly? That can't be, I don't know him. I hate him!

I am covered, his warmth draped around me like the old quilt. A vampire and a chained whore, but at this moment as he holds me, his breath warm, sleepy. Well, content in my binding, for the moment. What the hell am I feeling? Don't know, I am too f'in tired to think about it now. Just let the damn human with the passionate kisses hold me until...

I sleep another day away.

Chapter Two

What a cursed thing I am. I feel much stronger today, yet the burning is still there, haunting me, reminding me. Feel more myself, whoever that is. I wish I could escape this endless nightmare. Though I know even if I break myself free of these chains, this nightmare will follow me wherever I go. And what if I do gain my freedom? I will be alone.

So I lie in my chains and don't even try. Why? Who can know, I just don't. I wait, and think.

I know I am no longer human; no human could have the dark lusts that drive me now. Clearly I still have human feelings, desires.

Who is he? This man who is so cruel, evil, lustful? Much like me now.

I silently cried my every waking moment, unwilling to let him hear a sound of my remorse, my guilt. Remorse for the innocent life I took. Guilt for the pleasures he gave me, took from me last night.

There is no stench from the young girl in the room. I suppose he moved her away while I slept. Where could he have taken her? Hate to think of her wrapped in plastic, dumped alone somewhere with no one to mourn her but the evil woman who put her there.

I hear his car pull into the driveway, its headlights moving across the dark windows announcing his arrival. The keys in the back door, his steps on the floor above.

"I'll be down soon." Words seeping down through the rafters to me. His life above, my life beneath.

I hear too much now. Things I know I should not hear from my place far below. Food, shower. I wait; for what I am not sure. Still I wait, and want.

"I'm here, Margret." Announcing himself meekly as the door to the basement opens.

"You cannot continue to leave me here, alone and bound all day and night while you live your life!" I yell as he approaches. All the anger I have nurtured throughout the day comes out of my mouth quickly. Well before his face arrives before me.

He looks sympathetically at me. "That is not my intention. It's however the way it needs to be for now. Not that you understand that or anything yet." Comes to sit next to me, looking at his captured beast indifferently. "Best for you, me, and, frankly, everyone else."

He kisses me sweetly on the forehead. Smiling, somehow actually looking boyish and innocent. He is neither. He has modest dimples, his smile one the devil would have a hard time resisting. His almond-shaped eyes are a rich brown, specked like an egg with black. Thick lashes, to a woman's envy. Ample mouth, his bottom lip seemingly always in a pout unless his smile is broad. Overall rather handsome, even so. Hate that. Why does he kiss me so tenderly?

Lying next to me, he rests his head on my chest, wraps his arms affectionately around me. Seductively tender his embrace.

Why does he tempt me to want more from him than his blood?

"If I could, I would let you go. I can't. Not yet." With warm lips pressed to my ear, he whispers, "You need to be tamed, to know who you are before...it's safe to free you. I know you are confused, afraid but it will be OK soon, Margret."

His insincere empathies, deceitful affections. I fill with anger, turn my face away. "You care nothing for me, or for anyone I would take! You want only..."

My word fade as he kisses my neck, my shoulders, sliding his hot mouth to open over my breast. Slowly, gently. Ignoring my anger completely. Makes me even more pissed off. I will not let myself feel this!

"Stop it!" My demands go unanswered; he continues as if I hadn't uttered a word.

Well, he can afford to do anything he wishes. I am in chains and straps and any damned thing he has to restrain me. Just go ahead; what the hell can I do about it?

He takes his tee shirt over his head and slips out of his pants and comes back to me. I despise it, how his warm flesh is starting to feel like comfort, strong arms like safety. My internal fight becoming one not only with him but with myself.

He succeeds in calming me after many long minutes. His sweet caresses work way too well tonight, overwhelmingly so. My anger withering, even my need for blood. His or anyone's. His mouth slowly travels from his lustful sucking at my breasts to licking slowly over my stomach. Finally settling at my crest. Moves his arms underneath me. Lifting me with his shoulders, runs warm hands up and down my thighs. Locks his mouth into me, full of hunger. If I was not lost a minute before, I am now.

He knows too well how to calm me. His kisses no matter where they are so full, so passionate. I am consumed with strange and conflicting emotions. I want to resist him yet my body is unwilling to surrender to the conviction of my mind's refusal.

Endless searing kisses. I forget everything but them. Is it the human blood he gave me last night or is he succeeding in his task of taming me?

Too quickly he brings me to reluctant climax. His mount so quick and forceful it causes me pain. Still convulsing, tight and he is, well, not average. I gasp at his invasion. Gratified with his dominion over me, a content moan hotly breathes out of him.

He moves inside me much slower and sweeter than ever before. I lay bound to him, deeper than the thick links of chain that forbid me from movement. Our joining lasts for a long time before he can no longer suppress his passions. I feel the rush of heat burst inside me. His loud groans as he climaxes.

He stays inside me yet unmoving. Breathing hard into my neck, calms himself. After a while he curls up next to me his face cuddled on my shoulder, legs around me. He finds sleep. I lie awake, so full of conflict, anger, pain and need.

How he can sleep his mortal sleep so innocently? My head bursting! Most notably my guilt for killing an innocent child. Ripened now by hours of remorse. Her white face everywhere my mind turns. Making any thought excluding her nearly impossible.

Though I can think more clearly than I have in weeks, my thoughts are like wild horses. Unbridled, powerfully running through my mind, almost impossible to capture. Save this one.

Yell at him with all my regret. "Why? Why her?" Try to toss him off me with the little mobility I have. "She was so young!" All I can do is twist my body from left to right with all the angry force I have. Manage to break his embrace. He takes a second or two to read the situation.

"Quiet, Margret! Please let me…" rubbing his hands over his sleepy eyes, "explain," he says weakly.

Slides his fingers slowly back into his messy waves, finally resting them on the back of his neck. Curling his elbows over his face. He is hiding. So quiet, except for his harsh breaths. I wait, feel the intensity in the air, hold my tongue with much effort. His dark retreating figure somehow frightens me. It is several minutes before he speaks, muffled into his arms. A human most likely would not have heard him but I hear him clearly.

"The dogs, cats, and fat raccoons I have brought you have sustained you, woken you a little but they weren't enough to give you the strength or the insight you need."

Shit, I drank a raccoon? Gross, don't remember any raccoons. Undeniably I don't have much memory of anything. Do remember the name of the dog he brought me, a black lab. No clear memory before the night I took its life.

I wait for his next words.

"You don't understand anything now, remember anything. I know that."

His tone becomes forceful. "But I do know, I do understand what is happing to you." Takes a sharp breath.

"I am in charge of your care."

Sighs so harshly it lifts his shoulders. He looks up, seems unsure. After a moment's pause he continues.

"OK, Margret, here it is," glaring very deeply, very seriously in to my eyes. "My name is Eric. Eric Campbell, and I am your keeper."

Spring my confusion at him. "What do you mean my keeper?"

"I take care of you; help bring you back to yourself."

"How are you supposed to do that? I am a vampire, right?" I snap angrily.

"Yes. Yes, you are, but you can come back to most of yourself, your humanity. With time and controlled feedings." This Eric, my keeper, continues to explain himself to me. "You needed to have a lot of human blood to bring you back from the wild thing you became when you were transformed."

I ponder this. I have been wild, dark, confused. I recognize my name, bits and pieces. Blurred images at best.

"I couldn't wait any longer to give you strength. Still, I could not risk your insatiable hunger. You are, were, much too uncontrollable to feed just a small amount from a human. I had to find someone," clears his throat uncomfortably, "someone you could drink freely from."

Pauses, looking rather sad. "She was very sick, dying in fact. She was older than she looked; 18, I think. Nevertheless, yes, too young. She had cancer, fought with it for years. She wanted to kill herself, wanted to end it."

Shrinking, returns to his cocoon. "I brought her to you. She would have been dead in a few months at best, but she was done with the pain. I have never had to do that before. If my master took someone like that, I wasn't there, certainly did not have to bring them to him." Almost angry with me for his actions.

Find it hard to understand what he is saying. How did he know her, know she longed for death? I could see he was displeased he gave her to me, no matter his reasons or his rationalizations.

Master...what? Who was that, the one who made me as I am?

"My... a keeper's duty is to take care of you. Give you what you need, what you desire."

"What I need is answers!" I bite quickly. "How did you know her, how could you know she wanted to die?"

Again he looks up from his arms.

"I met her at the cancer center in the city. I volunteer there some days while you sleep. We became friends, I talked to her, got to know her." His words labored, trying to control his emotions. Not sure I am able to read any of them clearly. They shift before I have a firm grasp on them.

He looks off at the small window for a bit, lost in memory, I suppose.

"She was a very sweet girl, but there was no hope left and she knew it." Weariness. "Jennifer." He turns, looks straight at me as if I would recognize her name. "That was her name, Jennifer, but liked to be called Jen." Eyes full of curiosity, as if waiting for me to comment.

"Jen was plotting to jump from the top of the hospital. Very dramatic, silly really, but that was her current plan. She had a few of them." He almost laughs. "Escape plans, she called them. I visited her as much as I could, made her laugh, talked to her, she confided in me." He waits a bit before he continues. "You were still, well, not yourself, wild and uncontrollable. I had to do something. I knew it was time, so I brought her to you."

Looking at me as if I had something to add to this confession. "Go on, tell me."

"I convinced Jen I would help her do it. She eagerly agreed to my plans. So the other night I snuck her out of the hospital, got her into my car and then...." Seems reluctant to go on.

"I didn't want her to have any more fear, or be afraid of you. She did not expect it." Again a marked pause before he was able to continue.

"She was quite happy with our covert mission to gain her release from the hospital. It was kinda fun for her. Sneaking around, hiding. The whole time giggling." Whispers, pained.

"She was feeling pretty good that night, stronger. Made it...harder, for me." Not sure he wants to continue, reluctantly does.

"Anyway we took secret elevators, snuck down dark hallways until we got down to the garage and my car. She knew nothing but good feelings... I knocked her out."

He rushed that last part as if I wouldn't catch it. The gash on her head served a double purpose. Once I smelled her blood, saw it, I had little reservation left.

I see now it was a painful task for him. Odd I did not read this much feeling that night. Although he did quickly leave me when I took her, and the way he covered her. I am nothing if not about myself in my current crazed condition. Not so odd I wouldn't have noticed anything but my lust for her. I did feel guilt for killing her after I had time to think and feel. After the powerful blood lust abated.

"Why are you so upset? I'm the one..." I can't even say it aloud. Drank her blood until she had none. Killed her.

"Margret, please don't feel bad, you had to do it. She wanted to die. You are much stronger, closer to yourself now. You have no idea how much I needed ..." Cut him off.

"You mean couldn't have seduced me, force me to give you..." My anger choking my words back, "without her blood?" Remembering how successful he was in gaining my body's permission that night.

"Margret, you don't understand yet. You needed the strength to connect with your human self. The only way was to drink more than an animal. You had to have a full human to break through. I had to find you someone..."

He goes to a children's hospital to find me, as he called it, 'appropriate food'? Defenseless sick children. Searching for someone I could drain? Most likely so he can 'tame' me further for his sick pleasures. Insane as I am.

"You volunteer there so you can bring me food?" I am thoroughly disgusted with him, repulsed.

He yells back at me, "No, Margret!" Apparently appalled at my insinuation. Glares at me.

"I volunteer there because I want to! It was serendipitous that she was dedicated to killing herself!" His voice lowers by many degrees. "It is, however, where I met you."

Blaring light rushes into my head. Like opening a curtain to brilliant sunlight after hours in complete darkness.

"I was a nurse! I remember it!" Comes back to me as if his words were the missing link in the invisible chain that is my past. This link replaced now, this part of me enlightened.

We both sit in silence for long minutes. Eric looks only to the dark window, or into himself. Resting his chin on his crossed arms.

I start to read the memories. They are only of the hospital. I see coworkers, remember some of their names. Patients, doctors. The fourth floor nurses station where I worked, all the rooms. All coming back; fragmented, but slowly coming.

He sits in silence. Knowing by my expression memories are returning to me. Does not want to disturb them.

More...I work with children, remember many of their sweet faces, some names. I fill with wonder at the strength and ability for joy I see in all the pain. All new, yet mine, part my life!

Oh, I oversee the volunteer program! Searching the newly opened space, still I see no Eric here. He is a liar!

"Why don't I remember you if I met you there?" I say spitefully.

"Your memories that are nearest to your changing will be some of the last to come back to you."

"Convenient." Again spiteful.

Unexpectedly I feel something crushing my heart. A memory so hard to accept. Just as I was finding some small peace in them, my memories turn sharp, painful. Jen; I remember Jen! I fill with rage so quickly it overwhelms me.

Hatefully my eyes burn into him. "I knew her! How could you be so cruel to bring her to me? To have me kill her! Why would you do such a vile thing?" I scream with all the painful force of this new revelation.

I must look like a rabid dog because he moves quickly away from me, eyes dripping with fear.

I am trying with all my might to hit him but he is out of my reach. Thrash about so full of madness. Inconceivable that I could be possessed with the fierceness of this anger.

He looks mortified. "Yes, yes! You knew her!' he confesses. "She was a patient of yours for years, one of your favorites."

I wail; scream every hateful word I know at him. Eventually Eric gets so exasperated with me, he throws me back on my pillows. Thrust me down with all his might.

Yelling at the top of his lungs. "Margret!" He looks at me square, eyes full of anger. "Calm down and let me explain! You can hate me with all your heart after, but just let me talk to you!"

He takes several labored breaths, flushing hot anger out with each. I try to calm; still it is several minutes before I quiet enough for him to speak. He is very strong; eventually I give up struggling with him.

"Margret, I was seeing you for months before this happened to you." Curtly adds. "We were lovers." Roughly lets me go, sits, waiting for my reaction.

No! No! That can't be true!

"Lovers? How can that be when I despise you so?" He looks rather hurt, but I don't care. I want to hurt him! So I add for good measure. "You're evil, a killer! A disgusting rapist and I fucking hate you!" I cry in anger. "I would never be with someone like you. Never!"

Hurt, angry, minutes. He visibly composes himself before he speaks again. Calmly.

"I was with you before you turned. Over two months we were lovers. Though I knew you, worked with you, for five months altogether. You may not remember that now, but I was." Again he waits for me to process this new and rather disgusting information.

"I know full well how you felt about Jen. I saw you with her many times, you spoke of her often. Her long painful struggles with leukemia, her many relapse. Her cancer, spreading everywhere. Nothing could be done, she was dying, in so much pain." As if he saw it too.

"One of the reasons I became so close to her was because we were friends. Jen knew about us, she was the only one who did." Somewhat contritely adding. "She loved you, trusted you; she trusted me as well."

Finally he stands straight and tall over me. Looking not at me but in my direction, down to the gray quilt. Eyes not meeting, as he wishes.

"Obviously you are the wrong person to trust." I hatefully bite.

"Enough of this! I am not happy about what I did but I did what I had to do. For the both of you! It's done!" Guilt, anger written over his face. Eric throws the quilt harshly over me and nearly runs up the stairs. Doors slamming, car leaving. Silence.

HE LEAVES ME ALONE FOR DAYS.

Chapter Three

Once again I wake alone, hungry. Does he really think he can tame me, change me like this?

Where has he been? Not even a footstep above me for two days and one endlessly lonely night. As evening finally takes over the windows for the second time, I dread another dark night alone. Not even my tormentor for company.

I have nothing but my thoughts. Puzzling over all he told me. Remembering Jen, the hospital, being a nurse.

I was torn about giving death to the hopeless, euthanasia. Eric may have known these feelings? My feeling of sorrow for her? I remember how hard it got for me after many years of working at the children's cancer center. I loved the children dearly but it grew so hard to see too many of them die in such pain.

Do remember Jen had expressed more than once her wish for it to be over. The treatments, the pills, everything. Her anger that medicine kept her going long after she wished to go on. I always dismissed it and tried to reassure her she would get better, even though we both knew that it wasn't true. My heart ached for her struggles. Still to take her, give her death when I loved her.

I was glad she was unaware that it was me, her angel of death. I would not have wanted to cause her any more pain. As he said, rightfully.

I still have no memory of him.

I am missing Eric, growing to need even his vile company. I would still bleed him in a second if he let me out of these chains. His confessions were hard to hear. Only further confuse me, enrage me, soften me. I hate him, yet somehow feel a shadow of something more pulling at me.

Confused by every strange need, every thought, every feeling I have now.

Thank God I am dead, or I would have to piss. Undead I suppose is the right word. Just that realization is enough to get my head around without all the strangely distracting Eric crap.

Hours and hours alone. Watching shadows move over the gray cement floors. I have nothing else to do but struggle to remember my past. My memories are bits of shattered glass. Endeavor to put the pieces back together again, not many cohere. Working at the hospital, making a simple dinner, folding clothes. Daily things, intuitive memories. Fragments of gatherings, Thanksgiving, Christmas. Dull, foggy memories. Eric seems to think he was so important to me. Still don't see him in any of the pieces that come to me.

Why? My thoughts are still so confused. Was he really a part of my past life? Is he deceiving me? Manipulating me so he can have his way with me?

It is late and my head is beyond its ability to comprehend all the agonizing thoughts that race inside it. I want only to rest now. It's near morning. Two days, two nights alone.

Before I shut my eyes, I hear his car well before the headlights invade the dark windows like a ghost moving over them. At last he is home. Though I hate him, my isolation is still harder to bear. Even his company is better than this lonely dark basement. Inhuman, I belong to nothing but these chains and him for now.

I regret my relief.

The basement door opens. He comes down, carrying in his strong arms the limp body of a full grown man. Lays him in my lap. No eye contact, just this offering to me.

"There," gruffly whispered. He stands at the foot of my bed, looking at the floor.

"Who is he?" Whoever he is he is filthy and stinks to high heaven!

"I don't know. A drunk, a drug addict. Just eat!" Seems he is still angry as he refuses to look at me.

Hard to tell my feed's age, scruffy beard, lightly peppered with gray, long tangled hair. Stained red plaid jacket buttoned up to his neck. Who knows how long he has been uncared for. Forgotten.

"Where did you find him?"

"Where the hell does it smell like, Margret?" Snaps at me. "Just feed."

I can't reach him as my arms are tight over my head. Eric doesn't want to notice me or my lack of capability. His distaste painfully clear.

"I can't get to him, Eric." I say his name aloud for this first time, not very nicely either. He kneels down between my chained legs and lifts my feed to my face. Unwilling to let my restraints loose even to feed. I turn away. "His neck is so filthy," I groan.

"Fine." Annoyed with me he drops the poor man back on my lap; he moans a bit. Eric goes to the other side of the stairway. I can hear a faucet turn on, water, off. He returns with a dripping wash rag and wipes impatiently at his neck.

"Will I kill him?" I ask sheepishly.

"NO! You will not!" he yells at me, and for the first time looks me straight in the eye. Albeit only for a second. "I will let you take more than you should, but NO killing. He is already such a mess." Looks sympathetically at the dirty body on my lap.

"After you feed I will drop him at the emergency room closest to where I found him. They will most likely have seen him before and will not be surprised to see him again in this condition." Shoves him to my face.

He smells of ancient sweet, alcohol and all types of trash. Still I can smell the blood. I bite into the thick vein and all smell is forgotten. Eric turns his head away; not sure if he is avoiding looking at me feed or just avoiding looking at me. Think it may be the latter.

I perceive only a few short moments of hot rushing blood flowing into my mouth. Filling my body with soothing life before he barks, "Enough. Stop now."

I don't.

"Margret!" I cling harder to the life flowing into my mouth. The beautiful colors overtaking my dark mind. "Stop!" I feel the fullness of Eric's hand pushing hard on my forehead, the other pushing down on my jaw. Eric is very strong, forces me to release my teeth.

He says nothing' just lifts the man up and starts for the stairs.

"Will you come back to me after?" I really don't want him; don't want to be left alone again either.

"I don't know, I'll see."

That is all I see of him until the next evening.

When the door to my basement finally opens. He slowly descends, stands in front of me just beyond my bed. "Margret." Curt, soft. Unwilling to look at me.

"You sadomasochist shit, you left me alone for days!" I thrash about, wild with anger.

"Margret, calm down!" Anger. Quickly composes himself. "Please, calm down." Soft, controlled, pleading. "I need to explain some things to you now that you have fed well; now that you are more yourself and can understand me."

"You left me alone!" I repeated. He pays no attention. Eric is full of thought.

Why can't I remember him? No matter how I try to pull him out of my memory, I see nothing of him. Yet the sound of his name somehow makes me feel safe. I am so disoriented, the shattered bits, the raging hunger, the confused lusts... Eric.

"I don't know you..." I pause to say his name with as much distaste as I can muster, "Eric."

He looks at me in a way that is hard to express—fatherly, brotherly, sexually... is that possible? Sense them all in his glance.

"You do know me, well. I was there when this to happened, when you were changed. You are part of something...it's impossible to explain it all now. We are," kneeling between my legs, "connected in ways that you can't understand, believe now."

A dizzy feeling overtakes me. Like getting off a roller-coaster, finally putting your feet on solid ground. For just a moment the ground seems foreign, the wild ride still raging inside you. Life so near me, Eric's handsome figure confusing me. Rushing, heat, blood.

I fear and want him. Hate and need him.

"You may think I am a regular mortal man. I assure you I am not."

He removes the covers from me. Softly kisses my leg from ankle to thigh, lingers, nibbling at the inside, whispers into it.

"A mortal man, but very different." Feel his need, hate his need.

"STOP IT!" I yell at the top of my voice. "Please stop, I can't...I need to know more, talk to me."

The kissing clutters my mind, distracts me. As always he pays no mind to my outburst.

His probing mouth traverses long between my legs, merely touching my heat. Reaching my belly button, he sinks his tongue into it. Wet over my stomach, nibbling at my ribs. Licks under my full breasts, sliding from the dark beneath to the waiting fullness. Covers my breast, sucking, running his veiled tongue over my nipple, making it hard under its tight maneuvers. Finally he crouches over me, brings his lips to touch my ear. Hot whispers.

"I know you won't believe this now but I love you, Margret. I am sorry that you hate me, as well you should, but..." exhales, the heat of a fire over me, "unfortunately, this is the only way. You have to be controlled."

His seduction working. My body is on fire. Still I gather hatred from every corner of my mind. Trample the last of his lies. "Bull Shit! Love me? You've imprisoned me, raped me, that is NOT love!" I pull myself as far away from his face as my restraints will allow me. So angry but still the passion, feel it growing. Shit!

He turns my face back to him with a strong hand, eyes just an inch from mine. The black specks that pepper his brown eyes seem to expand, nearly overtaking them. Holding my chin firmly so I cannot look away.

"I am sorry for my passions, for these chains, sorry for all you don't yet understand. As I have told you many times, it is as it has to be for now, Margret." Releasing me from his grip, he pulls the fat gray quilt back over me. "You must be cold, I will not be here to warm you tonight." Such arrogance.

"Why, you can't possibly have had enough?" My retort full with sarcasm.

"No. I need to go out tonight, I have… errands."

"Will you bring me something?" I ask hopefully.

"I will try, but it is not for your dinner that I go out." Disgust in his tone.

Disappears quickly up the stairs. His steps loud across the floor above me.

"You are leaving me again!" I yell after him. No response, just the back door, his car. Alone again, now throbbing from his deliberate teasing, I lie chained in his cold prison. Only my endless questions and disconcerting lusts to befriend me.

What did he mean, not a regular mortal man? He is not as I am. Is he some other kind of immortal? If he was dead, would I want to drink him so badly? Well, I am new; I may want him anyway. No, no, he is not a vampire. Maybe different, but still full of heat and human life. He has been close to me with both. He is not like me.

Though I can't really know anything for sure right now. Still I ponder all of it over and over. Lie and wait for long hours, trying to make some sense of this. Try to remember him until my brain feels like it is bleeding inside my head. Hope he will come to me soon.

The sunlight is coming and I have grown so tired that even my questions cannot keep me awake.

Darkness, sleep.

Chapter Four

I hear him come home. He comes down the stairs very quietly, as if I am still sleeping. I have no idea what the time is, still day, but not early in it.

He stands before me, tight black jeans, red dress shirt. Beautiful, frightening, confusing to me. Eric looks very tired this evening, his eyes lined in red. He has a small wooden chest in his hands, takes it into the receding light sitting it most carefully on the gray basement floor.

"I have waited long enough for this, Margret." Softly spoken under his breath. His back still turned to me. Nothing more than a shadow at the foot of my bed. The shadow stands but still does not look on me. "I have kept you safe, fed you, pleased you." His whispers becoming pretentious.

I hiss at him, strain at my bindings with all my strength. Nothing, but lost energy.

"PLEASED ME? You arrogant asshole! I hate you!" Eric approaches me. I stare into him, trying very hard to look and be most imposing...in my chains. Eric is unaffected by my display. Suppose he knew I would react like that. Well, it was no shock, no matter the effect I had in mind.

"Don't deny it," he says quite calmly and confidently. "I know I have pleased you...many times. And you don't really hate me, Margret, you know you don't."

Can only watch as he begins to undress himself. Why does he have to be so handsome? It would be so much easier to reject him if he was not.

Eric's hard breast, tight stomach rippling down into sharp hips. The thick muscles of his thighs, an imposing hardness the centerpiece. How I despise his attributes and the effect they have on me!

He comes to me, leans over me, his mouth touching my ear. A gentle kiss and a fevered whisper over my neck.

"You will do this, and I will not be concerned if you will bite, hurt me, or fail to perform."

A gentle kiss disproportionate to the arrogance in his tone.

"You understand, don't you?"

Spoken softly, though each word full of malicious confidence.

He kneels over me, legs on either side of my chest. I know what he expects from me. There is no question, his resolution.

Looking down at me over his thick pillar. "Margret." His tone concern, or pleading?

"Please do this for me. I know you can. Just forget everything, try to love me as I have loved you."

His heartfelt request only enrages me.

"Loved me! Fuck you! I can't love you! I hate you!" Turn my face away from him, from it.

Unexpectedly he slaps my face. He never hit me before. It stings though not nearly as hotly as it would have when I was human. The pain is there but it is gone just as quickly. If I was human, I would be in tears from the continued pain from a slap so hard. As I am now, the pain dissolves as if it never happened. Still it makes me angry and, yes, surprisingly a bit hurt.

Eric bends to me, cradles my face in his hands. Again, soft whispers, kisses seeking pardon.

"I am so sorry. So sorry I didn't mean to hurt you, never," Near tears. Eric runs his open mouth tenderly over the skin that should be inflamed by his outburst. Caresses me for a few moments.

Then his temperament switches again.

"I don't really care if you love me right now. I just need to feel like you do."

Aggressively grabs the back of my head and pulls it up to him.

"Just do it like you care for me, or maybe like your life depends on it, because it does, Margret. If you cannot be mine, tame, and in control." Though his words are full of commitment, there is still something damaged in them.

He wanders off into silence, brings himself to my lips. I am not sure if that is anger or need on his face. However I am sure he is most earnest in his desire.

He instructs. "Just kiss and lick first, don't rush."

Our eyes meet, lust in his. I am in no position to refuse his demands so I timidly begin. Small open mouth kisses over him, lingering as he instructed.

A moan so deep escapes him, like he has waited a lifetime for this pleasure. Although I am very sure he has had plenty of it in his life time.

I lick the full length, suck over his head, kiss over him. He is very encouraging and grateful for my efforts. After a long while, his arousal is more than enough; he makes my mouth full. Gently thrusts, careful with his movements. Somehow, sometime, while giving him what he desires, it becomes what I desire as well. Eric senses this switch from forced to want in my performance. He pulls himself away and bends over to kiss me, so sweet and deep on my mouth. "I love you." Smiles sweetly at me. Why does he keep saying that to me? His chained whore.

It weakens me.

Back to his knees, pulling me up by the back of my neck, lacing his fingers into my hair. I know he is near his limit, close. Taste the bitter drops. I work in earnest to bring him his full pleasure. Hear his moans intensify. Feel my own passion rise from just the sound of them. I take all of his release, swallow it.

He falls over me, gratefully kissing my neck, shoulders, breasts...there he lingers, caressing and suckling them tenderly. Why can't I hate him, well, more?

He lies next to me, holds me close with arms and legs. I still feel the hunger for blood, but somehow it has lessened. Eric's intense body heat surrounding me. So soothing, and strong. I cannot hold him but he holds tightly to me.

I feel his thick hardness pressed to my hip. I squirm unintentionally with desire for it.

"You want me inside you?" Biting at my neck, pushing himself harder against me.

"No!" Try to pull myself away, taking the temptation from me, but Eric pulls me under him. Groaning, pleading.

"Yes, just say yes." Grinding himself on me, pressing, teasing.

Again, I try with more anger. "Get off me, I don't want you!" I turn my face away from him, can't bear to look at him. Ashamed at myself.

Using his hand to guide his hardness over my soft flesh, just pressing himself between my legs. Rubbing himself where he well knows I will become weakened. There can be no hiding how wet with desire I am as he is saturating himself in it. He has brought me to this heat before, though not without great effort on his part.

Hotly whispers over my ear, "You say no, but your body says yes." Moaning, unceasingly advancing into me yet only enough to cover his head. "Quite loudly."

Finally he thrusts all of himself into me. I moan; as hard as I try to hold it inside, it escapes. I bite down hard on my lip, trying to forbid another revealing sound.

Full of hubris from my self-betrayal, he whispers, "Admit it, Margret; you want me.

I want you to. I need you to." The passion in his voice, his clinging, his hunger for me.

Dammit yes, I do want him!

He takes his time, being most gentle with me before he can hold back no longer. He quickens, his passion erupts. Exploding deep inside me as I have never felt it.

After his fervent lovemaking, he pulls the heavy quilt over us. I am bound like the beast I am; he is free to caress me.

"I do love you, Margret." Sighs, whispers. "So much."

Somehow I feel as if my human heart woke; it aches. Impossible! Why does he say that to me? My captor, my rapist, the man I hate? 'I love you' over and over as if he really means it?

Why am I feeling this way? Am I starting to believe him?

Someday he must release me. Will I hold to him as he does to me now, or kill him as I so often want to do? He deserves that death, surely.

But not right now. My heart is beating loudly, my hunger quieted. I relax in his embrace, no fight left.

It takes all I have to lie there for hours, his neck so close. So trusting, nestled in my own. Still I could not drink him. No matter the need I felt for the blood so close to my hunger. I could not.

Was it fear that I couldn't get out of these bindings? Would not be fed, or make my way alone?

My head and heart pained, my mouth watered and struggled. At dawn as I heard him stir towards wakefulness, after hours of agonizing I knew it was not fear that kept me from taking him. I knew but was not nearly done with my anger. As I would soon see.

As he wakes he kisses softly over my lips. We have never really kissed, deeply kissed, obviously. Though after his great success last night it seems he is sure we can. Unfortunately he forgot that he failed to bring me even a rodent to feed on. Suppose he was distracted and it just slipped his mind?

So as his lips opened over my eager mouth, all seemed well.

I think only of him for a while. How I want to kiss him, and I do really want his kiss…for a bit. Our mouths hot and needy for each other. I feel like maybe I am still a bit human. Yet he is so excited, blood spiked with adrenaline, his flesh hot, heart drumming much too loudly in my ears.

I feel his blood surging through him. Burning into me. I feel his hardness pushing against me.

After he presses himself into my mouth for what seems to be endless minutes, my thoughts turn to his blood not the kisses. I do not mean to, really, but I lose myself. I grab hold of his invading tongue with my teeth.

Blood so sweet like nothing I have tasted before! Passion again, different passion, and yet so much the same. I let go, fairly quickly, but not before his blood is mine. Moaning, I swallow, cherishing my stolen drops.

He pulls away. I think he will be angry with me but he just smiles. Harshly grabs the hair at the nape of my neck, tilting my head back.

"You are quite the deep kisser, my love." His voice deep and sensuous.

He roughly kisses my neck, biting, excited. Moves to touch my lips, only this time just a shadow of a kiss over mine. Over and over, tormenting me. He denies me access to the fullness of his mouth with his grip on my hair.

"Stop! I want blood, you!"

I turn my face away from him. I don't know what I feel. Heat everywhere, need. What am I supposed to feel? Everything is crashing into me at the same time. I am glad to be bound; I have no control over myself. Though I know he will control me, do what he wishes with me.

"What do you want more, me or blood?"

What an ass!

"You have not fed me, what the hell do you think?" I bite.

Softly kisses my neck, the bones of my shoulders, the crest of my breasts before he answers. Undeterred as always by my anger.

"I am sorry for your struggles last night, Margret. You loved me well."

I may not need to breathe, still his words took my breath away, painfully. Took it more completely than death. For a moment I had none. No breath, no words.

"I struggled... I..." As much as I could get out. Silently we both acknowledge my conflict, and my yielding to him.

Eric wraps the quilt, and himself, tighter around me. "I am sorry I have not been able to give the best of myself to you. You are just starting to be tame enough to understand, to remember."

I want to concentrate on his words and the warm feelings inside me. However, a unique hunger is growing stronger with each passing second. His words become lost, his touch torment.

"PLEASE!" I scream, pleading with him. I turn my body as best as I can away from him. "I need, I hunger." I am in agonizing need, yet not sure exactly what it is I am needing. Blood or Eric?

"I know, I know." Runs his hand soothingly over my hair. "I will give you what you are desiring of."

He sits up, turns to the wall on his knees. His dimpled ass a bit distracting. Can't see what he is doing at the edge of my bed. As he turns back, I see a gash on his forearm, blood seeping quickly out of it. Immediately I start to pant like a wild dog, smell blood, my captor's, flush in the air.

It is as intensely hot as his sex, and I want it more than anything I have ever wanted. Craving him with a whole new level of desire. "Give it to me!" I yank harshly at my chains with all the force I have. "Now! Please, Eric!"

Not even when he raped me, starved me, made me so angry I could have killed him have I ever wanted to be out of these chains more. Just the smell of his blood. My nostrils fill with the beautiful crimson dripping down his thick arm. I am so wet, and so dry.

He looks surprised by my fierce reactions.

"Lie back, Margret!" Blood dripping, mouth watering, I try to do as he wishes but I still writhe back and forth wildly. Unable to force quiet over myself. He pauses, with his right hand holding tightly to the gash, restraining the flow. Clearly thinking something, maybe that this was a bad idea?

Eric gets up and rushes over to the dark side of the basement beyond the stairs, the side I can't see. An overhead light goes on, then fumbling, looking for...

"Just a second, Margret, I need..." He trails off, searching.

Seems like hours until he returns to the light, to me. Just seeing Eric's beautiful body distracts my mind from the blood. Fully naked, red hard. I am out of my mind with an all-consuming lust I could never have imagined.

"Give it to me, Eric! Don't tease me so!" He looks down at me with a bit of exasperation, coming hard to his knees next to me.

"Margret, I am sorry I have to use this but it seems it is the only way I can control you."

He opens his left hand; in it a silver chain. Like a long necklace. Considering the heavy chains and leather straps he has me in, this does not really seem to be very threatening. Somehow he still looks concerned.

He drapes it over my neck and I immediately fall back. It burns like a hot iron. I cannot raise my head from the pillow below it. My neck is on fire, useless.

"What the hell are you doing? It burns!" He does not answer, just brings his bleeding arm finally to my lips. Even in my pain, I take it with vigor. Quickly forgetting everything, knowing nothing but the sweetness of his blood flowing into me. I understand now why he put me in the silver. I could not get enough of it, his blood. Sucking it into me with such need not even full starvation could inspire. Nothing, no human or beast as sweet or quenched my thirst so completely. Cooled the hot rage in my head. I took me many moments of feeding to realize, and only because Eric's trusts became so forceful, that he was inside me.

Once my mind adapted to this, I had too few moments of his hardness and his blood at the same time. Sucking and thrusting. All of him moving inside me. These the best moments of my life. Never have I felt so perfectly contented and loved. So hot and alive. Saturated. Too soon he pulls his lovely blood away. I could not move my head even an inch to pursue it. Silver was the only way. I did not lose his hardness, I was very thankful for that. He came so fiercely it felt as a fire burst inside me. I quickly followed with more intensity than I had ever experienced, even with him. Both saturating my whole body in such unbelievable pleasure.

Full of Eric's passion, Eric's blood. He quiets his thrusts, but not from lack of ability.

"How do you feel, Margret?"

I am unable to answer right away, or even open my eyes from the bliss I see behind them. I feel pleasantly drunk. He removes the strand of silver from my neck and tosses it. I come to myself after long moments, hearing only his hard breathing, feeling only his hot skin, his hard cock still one with me.

"Why have you withheld this from me?" I try to sound mad, yet am so content I'm almost moaning the words. "You must know how you taste to me. You do, yes?" I squirm and moan and long for more.

He gives me a few final soft thrust and pulls himself out then off me. I groan sadly at being released. Eric lies back next to me and wraps a cloth tightly on his arm. It is not bleeding as hard as it should be, but a trickle still seeps from his wound.

I lust for it. Lust, lust, lust for it!

He turns to his side, bends his elbow, rests his head in his palm. How Eric manages to look like a sweet boy after that I do not know. He just does. I try to focus my eyes, my mind. His blood still in the air, in me.

"Yes, I know. I withheld it because I want to live."

"What does that mean? You are in complete control," I snap although nothing I say comes out sounding like much more than half-hearted attempt. I am too satisfied.

"Margret, you were not in control enough, or ready for me, not able to appreciate it. Our bonding."

I cut him off. "I am sure I would have appreciated that weeks ago!" Do sound a bit angry now, I suppose.

"You don't even remember the first week or so you were here. I am sure of that. You didn't speak a single word for the first, just hissed and growled like an animal. It was so bad I was sure the neighbors would hear you; thankfully, the soundproof windows and your 'bedroom' here helped with that."

There are new walls tight around my bed, ones that don't look like the other brick ones at the far end of the basement, and I guess other side of the stairs would the same. Just regular gray basement walls. My three 'bedroom' walls are white and new. Most likely thick.

"You had this done for me?"

"Markus and I prepared this space for your turning and, well, training for lack of a better word."

"Training?" I ask with more than a note of contempt. "And who is Markus?" His face grows sad and he looks away from me off to the ceiling.

"He was my master, the one who made you as you are now."

"Where is this Markus, and why didn't he take care of me instead of you, a human?" I sounded more spiteful than I intended. I could see my attitude after what we just shared hurt him more than a little.

Eric sits up, pulls the cover over his still hard member and looks rather insulted.

"Wow, Margret, have I been so bad a keeper, a companion? Considering I am trying to care for, tame, an insane new vampire?"

A day or two ago, I would have had a very hateful retort. Now I am stronger, and now I am starting to understand in some small way what is happening. Most importantly I have his blood inside me. His blood brings me a calmness that I haven't felt in a very long time, and yes, admittedly his sex.

"Sorry, Eric." I lean and twist, trying to get him to look at me; he doesn't. "I didn't mean it like that. I mean wouldn't he be able to control me better, train me better?"

Looks at me with great annoyance. "He, my master Markus, is no longer. He is full dead and gone." Eric turns from me. "That is enough for tonight; you will know more soon."

I have upset him, and I genuinely feel bad about it. We were just so lovingly content and now I have, with my bitchy mouth, ruined it. He goes to get up and, I know, leave me alone here again.

"Eric, please, I need to tell you something." He reluctantly settles back down.

"What?" Annoyed with me.

"I have never felt so beautiful, so happy as before," I confess, "when I had you fully inside me, your blood and your..." I smile at him shyly. That manages to bring the sweet little dimples reluctantly out. He makes a happy little snort, shaking his head at me.

"Margret, what am I to do with you when you can twist my heart so easily?" He leans over to kiss my forehead. "I do need to rest now. Being near you does not lend itself well to rest. I am very tired and have not..." Unspoken thoughts trail off into silence. I have never seen him look this tired. Have I taken too much from him?

He gets off my bed, his back to me, pulls on his jeans, stuffing himself into them.

"Are you always stiff, Eric?"

Eyes glimmer over his shoulder at me; he shyly smiles. "Only when I am near you, my love."

Have to admit I like being called 'my love.' I see him so differently in this moment; my captor has become beautiful to me.

Eric is off up the stairs to rest.

When the morning comes, I need my rest. As always I hear Eric shower, leave in his car. I know not what he does with his day until he comes back to me. So I try to sleep the day away and wait for his return.

Chapter Five

I've grown angry again at the hours alone and these damn chains. I can only sleep for so long. Then I am awake, alone, enchained. I hear his footsteps above me; still he does not come down for a long while.

I am oddly anxious. At last I hear the door, his footsteps on the stairs.

He is more beautiful to me tonight than ever. Stone-washed blue denim jeans, a fine white dress shirt, untucked and loose over him, sleeves rolled half way up his arms. The dark waves that cover his head resting on shoulders of crisp white. No shoes or socks, like most times, bare feet. I don't want to stop hating him, but know I am well beyond that now.

"When will you trust me? I want to hold you, why can't you let me hold you? Let me go!"

I plead with my captor, undeniably my lover, a little overly dramatically.

Eric, my sweet tormentor, smirks. "Very nice performance, most convincing."

"You're an ass hole!"

"Thought that was behind us, Margret! Really?"

He sits next to me. "I hunger, although..." I stop myself.

"Although what?" Brow raised in question.

"Nothing!" I snap back at him. I am unwilling to confess how completely he quenched my thirst. How our joining made me feel more human, more loved, just more. Stubbornly holding on to my hate.

Truly I am just trying to be a bitch. It maddens me that he is winning this battle. That he has managed to turn rape into lovemaking. That he leaves me alone and I actually miss him. That I still feel his blood flowing inside me, satisfying me. He does not need to know any of that just yet.

"Margret?" Sighs, impatiently waiting for my reply. "Although what?" Eric insists.

I say nothing, just look blankly at him.

"Women, 'nothing' when they mean everything."

"I will tell you in my own time!" Much more pissy than I am feeling.

Eric ignores my anger as he often does. He grabs my shoulders, shaking them a bit like he is excited. "I have something for you, but you must promise me to play along and listen to me." Eric's eyes widen and he makes quite the stern dad-like expression. "Do as I tell you!" He shakes me again, this time harder, but playfully.

"What is that supposed to mean?"

"You have to trust me, Margret, that is what that means. Please. I am here to take care of you, protect you..."

I break him off in mid-sentence with a howl of anger. "What about feed me?"

He looks deep into my eyes, does not break his grip on them. "YES. Feed you, and I will.

But to insure you are...well, behaved." Exasperated with me again. "You get who and how I give for good reason." He is getting very impatient with my games. "Just trust me! I am your teacher, your master...." Again he trails off to silence. Rubbing his forehead. His eyes turn to mine. "Just as you soon will be mine."

What is that supposed to mean? Nearly everything he says confuses me.

A quick kiss to my lips and he rises, disappears swiftly up the stairs. I sit in my cushions and pillows, steam and want.

Then I hear him opening the front door, talking to someone. Two sets of feet above, two voices. Two. Two? Never had company before. Who, and why now?

I would soon find out.

I could not hear exactly what they were saying but I did perceive they moved from the front room to the kitchen after a while, and that it was a male voice with Eric.

After about an hour or so, the talking becomes louder, interspersed with laughter. Suppose they were drinking heavily. When the door to the basement finally opens, I hear them both quite clearly.

"She is cool with this?" A male voice, bewilderment in his tone. They walk down the stairs.

"I promise she just wants to watch. I will take care of her, and you, don't worry." Eric so sweetly convincing, and the young man is so easily seduced by him. I get that. Eric is beautiful.

They are both soon at the foot of my bed. Eric turns on a small light. Not the one over me but a few feet away, nestled in the wood rafter of the ceiling above them. It casts just enough light for seeing, but not too much for romance, I guess.

"Wow, she likes this?" Shocked as the light casts itself over me. Full in my chains, wrists bound to the wall above me, legs spread, chains trailing off my 'bed' to the stone floor beyond it. I only in the very loosely wrapped robe, exposing what it will.

Eric meets my eye and winks, smiling. "Yes, it's a game we play. Like I said, I'll take care of you both, no worries." That seems to be quite enough reassurance for this stud. He glares full of want over Eric's frame.

Food; think I may be getting some human blood tonight.

He is rather tall, and thin, but looks to be muscular as well. Bleached blond short hair with a finely close cut beard. Rather handsome young man, maybe 23.

My thoughts turn quickly to feeding with much excitement. Eric and Blondie start to caress each other. Chest, backs, backsides, fat full jeans before zippers are undone. Then hands start moving over each other's hardness. Both impressive.

Not much kissing really, just groping, stroking each other with eager hands. OK, nice, but lay him down by me, give him to me. PLEASE! I am too full of blood hunger to be as astounded at what I was seeing as I would have been before, when I was human.

I am amazed at how I can sense the blood flowing in them, smell the heat of them in the air. I am wet with passion but so thirsty. My mouth and throat feel dry, like coarse sand. My thoughts wander for a bit to feeding wildly on them both. Fantasize that I am free to hold and take all I want from them. Feeding where and how I wish. After a few moments lost in my dream, I return to focus.

Eric and Blondie are fully undressed. I have never witnessed anything like this before, ever. Eric is on his knees. He is taking the blond boy's cock quite willingly and aggressively into his mouth. Blondie is holding the back of Eric's head with both hands. Fingers full of Eric's dark curls, pulling him back and forth over him. Eric's hands softly on Blondie's ass, accepting him as he deeply as he wished. Suppose what woke me from blood lust were the loud moans of pleasure from Blondie.

Eric forcibly breaks away and coaxes him to lie down next to me. He rests under my arm, next to my breast, looking up at Eric with much desire. Eric lies over both of us. He meets my eyes for only a second.

His mouth sucks at my breast, his body over the young man's. They grind their hardness against each other. Blondie is quite excited, thrusting himself up to Eric, stroking his ass and balls vigorously.

Well, I have to admit, this is amusing, even hot. However, my thirst is greatly exacerbated now that they are so near.

"Eric," I moan. Still Eric continued to engage our friend with his hand until he makes Blondie orgasm. Finally my pleading will be noticed.

In my ear I feel his breath, his kiss, hear his voice clearly, even in blood lust, and yes, just lust.

"You have to behave, my love, take only what you need, and not what will kill. Feed gently. I will help you."

Eric kisses me quickly on my lips with a hot open mouth. Didn't know what he was up to just yet but understood I was to feed soon. Eric turns the boy over and lays him across my breasts. Neck near my waiting, salivating mouth.

I hear Blondie moan, then jerk roughly forward, it brings him even closer to my lips. Eric's hand presses on his shoulder, forcing him hard to me. My teeth find him and bite in. He cries out but he does not fight or struggle for release. I feed. His blood full of heat, of life and the willingness is good as well. I feel him move forward and fall back. It is not me that makes his movement; it is Eric. No matter how great the thrusts, my teeth hold firm to his fat vein. My lips surrounding his neck as if to disguise the evil feeding hiding under their wet embrace. Serene, my eyes close, beautiful colors flow into the darkness like liquid clouds.

I want to be out of these chains, to embrace them both with my arms, my legs as well as my bite. All eager and needing. Still, even as I contently feed, I feel the need to have Eric inside me. How can this be in moments full of blood lust? Yet it is. My writhing must have communicated this to Eric because he releases himself from his lover. He forcefully thrusts himself into me as I continue my feed. I climax so fiercely I want to cry out, but I am unable, or rather unwilling, to release my teeth from this sweet hot neck.

Finally Eric pulls my food from my grip and lays him next to us. His focus now only on me. He kisses my bloody mouth with great passion. His thrusts long, over and over, pulling out, slowly returning all of himself into me. After a short time, I crest again from his restraint, only then with a deep groan into my neck does Eric allow himself release.

Panting as if he just ran miles. After he regains his breath, Eric looks at me and smiles with those irresistible dimples. Like a dark angel. "We will have this many times, over many nights ahead, my love." Falling, exhausted, over me.

They sleep for a while, the two humans, content from their orgasms. I rest in a swoon of blood, warm human flesh and, yes, orgasms. Though I, only for a bit.

Try to wake Eric who is still lying partially over me. Kiss the top of his head, nipping and pulling at his long dark hair with my teeth.

"Eric, please release me. I want to be able to hold you, please." Begging him for release.

"Stop, stop," he says sleepily. Pushing my nipping mouth away from him.

He looks up from the place he has rested. "I would love to give that to you, and me. But my love, I am not sure that would be a good idea just yet."

I try to look full of sincerity, my voice gentle, pleading. "You feed me well, I am fine." I gingerly insist.

"You think?" A sweet yet sarcastic smile. He kisses my eyes and then he moves his lips over my face until his mouth locks with mine. We kiss deeply for a few minutes before he stops and asks me.

"Margret, where is your heat most strong?" His dark eyes so close, so curious. His fingers press between my folds, find their way deeper and deeper until they are inside me. Rubbing them deep inside my walls. He is driving me mad!

"Here, my love?" he whispers, pressing harder inside me as if to annunciate the question further, "or in your blood lust?"

Not sure, not sure, not sure! Need both.

Is that what he wants, or what I am supposed to be? I don't know, but for right now, him, Eric. I had enough blood to quiet that thought for the moment, but not rid myself of it. I was very sure I would never rid myself of it completely.

"You, want you more right now," I say breathlessly. I think I hate myself for admitting this to him, but no other words could come out of my mouth.

"I cannot yet free you completely, but will free your legs and one arm, just enough to make sure I can constrain you again if need be," he says quite seriously.

He covers my breasts with hard kisses, soft bites. His arms strong around my back, pulling me firmly up to him.

"I am much stronger then you may think, Margret. I can still restrain you." His words full of confidence. I am sure he means what he says, and I have no intention to test his will or physical strength now.

He lets my legs free first. It feels good to move them, to be unchained finally. Bend my knees back and forth, stretch them out a few times just enjoying the movement and freedom. They ache a bit, but it quickly dissipates.

Reaches up to remove the bindings from my right arm. Not without giving me a last stern glance. Trying hard to look like the mean Eric that will overtake me if I tried anything. Not sure he really could but...

"Be good." Oddly fatherly.

My arm is finally free. Immediately grab him, pull him down to me, driving my fingers through his long dark hair as I have longed to do.

I surprise him for a moment; he stiffens. "I want you." Demand in a whisper.

When I insist on his deep kiss, he understands I will not harm him. "Not just to feed on, inside me."

I confess much too eagerly. Eric pulls away from my fervid kiss with much effort. He smiles so tenderly.

"I am so happy, Margret. Soon you will be free and then I will be yours." My fingers run through the mess of waves, pulling him into my mouth. Free to kiss, free to hold and touch him.

"Do you want him as well?" He shrugs his head toward our resting blond lover.

Again, confused, unsure of new myself.

"Both of you? But..." I pause look into his dark brown eyes so close to mine. See only love in them now. I do not fear myself, or him for once.

"Yes, Margret, what is your 'but'?" So beautiful to me now, melting my heart.

"Just you now, like you love me..." My words trail off.

He buries his face in my neck. "It is not LIKE I love you Margret, it is that I DO love you." He moves to lie over me. I spread myself open and for once I can wrap my legs around him and I pull him to me, into me. I choose to have him, freely. Eric groans, happy with the pleasure of my new desire for him. My grip on him tells him all I will not yet say aloud. I cannot hide my surrender to him, my need for him any longer.

⚜

Our lover, well, I may have taken a bit much from him. He slept for quite a while. That was fine; I had Eric a few times before he returned to us. Groggy and lost. It was near morning when he woke. Eric took him most caringly into his arms and got him to his feet. Helped him dress. His kindness and maybe guilt guiding Eric to be most sympathetic of his lack of mobility. I think our Blondie believed he was still drunk, possibly was a bit, but his weakness was from my feeding. I did take more than I should have. Eric let me feed too much but not kill, as is his charge to do. I was glad to see him go alive, drained but alive. Blondie would recover in a week or so from it. Eric gave me a last glance.

"I'll drive him home and be back soon." Gingerly helped him up the stairs and out front to his car. In the silence of the dawn, I hear it start and drive off.

Again I sit alone to think. Now my thoughts are much changed from even a few days ago. Now I know what I am, and who I need. Eric, my keeper.

The sun rising, as is my need for rest. Don't hear Eric come home. Sleep as soundly as I had in many weeks.

The day is near gone before I wake.

Chapter Six

Hear him walking about upstairs. The sun in the window has grown very dim. No clock, no time. I try to wait for him to come down but grow irritated and call up to him.

"Eric! I am awake now." I wait; hear nothing. I yell even louder. "Where are you?"

"Coming, Margret, just a sec."

It was much more like ten minutes but who's counting?

He has a long thick button-down gray sweater on over his shirt and jeans. A tall glass of ice water in his hand. He sits down, legs crossed, next to me and smiles "I am here now, my love." Weak but content smile.

I am happy now. He is back.

Eric looks rather washed-out, exhausted. Wonder if he is ill, or did I weaken him? I am reluctant to say anything because I seem to be quite adept at aggravating him. But I can't hold back.

"You look so tired. Did I take too much, ask too much?" He drinks down the whole of his glass and places it on a ledge by my bed. Notice the silver chain lies close by.

Sighing deeply. "Well, yes and no." He lowers his head, brings knees up, wrapping his arms around himself as if he were cold. "It is just that I have not..." marked pause, "fed for nearly six weeks now."

"Fed? On me?" I ask, shocked. Didn't know he did that. Not a vampire like me so why would he?

"Yes, on you!" As if I am silly to think otherwise. Looks up at me with a mischievous glint in his eyes. "Margret, how do you think I can be 97 years old and still look this dashing?" Attempts a laugh.

"What? Ninety-seven! No way. Really? That is..." I trail off, shaking my head in disbelief and confusion, "not possible."

"It is, and I am."

"Tell me then, how?" I demand.

"There is so much to explain." Deeply fills his lungs, exhales loudly. Ready for his tale, he continues.

"As I have told you, I am your keeper. That is what we, I, am called. I watch over you, help you feed, not be a wild uncontrolled vampire. Be your human companion and, lover." Those dimples. How is it a man who I am sure has had as much sex as half the planet still manages to look shy and innocent about it?

"Keep your connection to your human side. Things like that." He shrugs.

"Anyway, Markus made me his keeper, and don't ask me about that tonight, it's a story of its own. We'll get to that some other time. I was 29 at the time, and I have been, until six weeks ago, his for 67 years."

He stops for a second and looks at me, trying to read my face, I suppose.

"Wow, that's crazy. I had no idea." He does look amazingly hot for 97. Really looks about just about that, 29, 30ish still. Un-aged.

"Go on," I insist.

"I stay like this, young, because I feed. Not a lot, Margret," he says reassuringly.

"Once, maybe twice a week, just enough to keep me healing myself. Your blood keeps me young and strong, and, well, my prowess that comes from feeding here."

Eric runs the back of his hand over my robe, over my sex. Devilish grin the whole time. He gets too easily distracted. Feels like electric tingles when he touches me, even this little bit. Although if I had use of my arms, I would have slapped it. Instead I thrust myself up and away from him, curling my free legs up close. Forbidding him access.

"Eric! Don't get distracted, I want to know more, understand it. How often do you feed from me? Do you bite me? Tell me?" Rambling in my amazement.

Grunts unhappily and shakes his head to clear it. He gets up, walks over to the wooden trunk he brought home the other day and sat down in the shadows. Takes out his keys, fumbling for the right one; finding it, he opens the box. Looks to be a small book. He brings it over, sits. Then he looks up at my bindings.

The stern look appears.

"You will behave." Not a question; a firm statement. He releases my right hand only and sits back down, book in his lap. I reach over to softly run my hand over his tired face. Move my fingers through the dark waves. How I love his long waves. He looks up at me, bewildered.

"I hate to see you look so tired and drawn."

Eric smiles weakly, takes my hand from his hair, kisses the palm of it before he hands me the book. I have never had his hand in mine before, so warm. I hold to it before I take the book. He seems pleased by my affection.

It is not old, a journal you could buy at any bookstore. Fine black leather cover, not cheap. It is tied with a thick red bow, a tag and a ring hang from it. I place it on my lap. He is watching me quite closely. I turn over the tag to read the writing on it. Almost calligraphy the hand, beautiful. It reads.

> *'For Margret*
> *Your maker,*
> *Markus'*

The ring that is attached is beautiful, yet odd. Gold filigree in a kind of Celtic design, but it has like a fingernail off the top of it. It's pointed, very sharp and curves a bit inward. I roll it around in my fingers, examining it. My attention goes back to the tag after long minutes. He says nothing, just watches me as I touch and think.

It is odd to think someone, a vampire I do not know, well, remember, wrote this, prepared it for this moment. For me. I wonder if he was as beautiful as his writing, or as beautiful as his keeper. Now mine, my Eric.

Finally I look from the gift I hold and our eyes meet. He not only looks weary, but sorrowful as well.

"This is for me, he wrote it for me?"

"Yes, Margret. It is full of things he wanted to tell you. Things you need to know to help you grow strong and confident. He wrote it before...he left us." A sad sigh escapes him.

There is no disguising how Eric feels about his master Markus. Looks a lot like love. Well, 67 years, that is a long time to be with someone. I do not pursue the many questions I have about him and Markus. Eric did say that was a story for another time. I have plenty of that now.

"I was very well instructed on my responsibilities. Markus told me how to take care of you as you changed. How to feed you and, well, break you." 'Break you' he said with a bit of distaste, but I did understand what he meant and took no offense by it.

"All right, you can tell me more later," I say sympathetically. "Right now just tell me how I fix this weariness, how I bring your smile and heat back to you."

Shakes his head in amazement. "Margret, you have NO idea how I have longed for this. Your affection, caring for me. It was not easy to see you as you were, wild and angry. Not yourself for so long. I was always fearful I could not, did not, have the strength to return you to yourself. To hear you say 'I hate you' and know that you did. You will never know how it hurt me to be the one you hated," nods, "rightfully so. I am relieved that you are starting to be the woman I knew before. My Margret."

Every time he speaks tonight, it raises more and more questions in me. They are getting to be miles high and wide. Nevertheless I want to relieve Eric's weakness most. I will not drag this out with my questions. Like I said, I have tons of time to hear about it all after he is well.

If he is supposed to drink once or twice a week, he is far behind his quota. Did he not say I have been with him for six weeks? Eric must be in much need by now.

"Eric, tell me, show me how to feed you." Then a vexing thought pops into my mind. My emotions shift so quickly it makes my own head spin. "Why didn't you just take it from me as you needed it? Why would you wait so long?" I am in anger again.

"The blood has to be given, not taken," he insists.

I cannot seem to control myself. A rage rises from inside me, from a place I do not know. It is fierce and must have its release.

"Not taken?" I yell. "What? It's OK to rape me over and over but not to bleed me? Shit, Eric, you could do, and did do, anything you fucking pleased!" His face grows red with anger and hurt at the same time. He visibly tries to control himself before he speaks.

Rubbing clenched fists hard over his forehead. "Margret, I needed you, and had to wake your human side as well. I would be lying to you if I said it was completely not for my pleasure that I took you. Nonetheless I had to continue our bonds, whether you were willing or NOT!" Silence full of anger from us both.

Minutes pass with nothing but heat in the air. Both of us waiting for it to cool.

"You were nothing more than a mindless thing for weeks. When you were at least calm enough to be near, not only did I have to start to wake your heart, your desire, but by that time my needs were so great for you... well, it gave me the motivation I needed to take you that way!" He yells at me. So full of ire, maybe at his deeds more than me.

"You have no idea what I had been through, or how I hurt seeing you like that. I needed you!"

He looks away from me; still the darkness around his eyes reminding me of his state. Notice they are wet as well.

"I am sorry you still feel that it was rape, and I suppose it was." Regret saturating his words. "I assure you it was not only to aid in your change, but because honestly I could not have gone any longer without..." Frustrated, adds, "I had to love you."

He groans in exhaustion. "I know you don't remember, but I do! I was before, still am, very much in love with you, Margret."

That's it, anger done...'in love with you'; ouch. My arms burn to hold him, my lips need him, my heat throbs. Still I am in his chains, his slave.

I know he wants me to tell him the same, but can't bring myself to do it. Not just yet. Understanding, maybe even forgiving, are very different things than love. I don't remember loving him in my mind but my heart and my body seem to.

I must deal with this situation, his health now.

"Please, forget that, my, our anger; leave it for it for another time. I still feel the blood you gave me, stronger, sweeter, than any flowing inside me. I do know I need you, Eric." I smile as sweetly as I can at my keeper. Softly touch his face. "And I do want you, I do." I wait for his reaction.

Roughly shakes his head. "You bounce my heart around like a ball. Up, down, over and over again. I know you have been very confused, and even though I know what is going on, well, you confuse me as well." He seems lost.

I ignore his comments. "Show me." I take his hand in mine, hold it to my heart.

He takes the book from my lap and unties the bow from it, the ring falls into his waiting hand.

"Markus wore this on his index finger, but I suppose it will fit on the tip of your thumb." He reaches to take my hand again in his. I grab and squeeze his tightly before he places the ring over my thumb. It fits well, just over the nail as I think it should. Eric places the book carefully on the ledge. Turns his attention to me.

"You use this to cut yourself so I can drink from you. It is mostly done while bonding, sex. Though maybe, as this is our first time, we should just let me feed." Think Eric doesn't want to overwhelm me with both.

"You never did this with me before, not when you made me or...?"

"No, my last feed was from Markus before he..." Doesn't want to finish his thought.

"OK, but where shall I cut?" It is so clearly a ring made to cut. I see that now.

"Anywhere you wish; it's your gift to me."

Confused with all this new information, feelings. "I don't know. Tell me where you would like me to?" Can't make a decision or have a precise thought.

He pulls my robe open a little, exposing my breast. Running the back of his fingers across it gently, then turns it to rub softly at my nipple until it's hard. "Here?"

"There?" EEK! "Will it hurt?"

"You do feel pain, not as harshly as a human. Quickly disappearing. Plus, when I start..."

Deep breaths full of anticipation. Obvious desire. "Well, it will be very intense; not just for me, but for you as well."

"Do it for me. I'm unsure and afraid of the pain," I plead desperately. "I don't know how..."

"I cannot do it for you," he insists. "You must give it to me."

"I can't, you must help me." Persisting. "Please," I implore him.

He thinks for a moment. "All right. I will help you, but I will lose my mind quickly when it starts." Bit testy. "I can't feed too much from you, that would be bad. You heal pretty fast, as it needs to be, so..."

"What does 'that would be bad' mean? What is too much?" I question him.

"Too much can hurt me. I'm sure Markus wrote all about it. You'll understand after you read it. Please, now, my love?" He looks at me with such longing. I nod my head. "Ready?" His eyebrows raise in question.

Ready as I will ever be. "Yes Eric. Just help me," I ask again uncertainly.

"I will." His commitment to me full in his words.

He cups my hand with the giving ring on it in his. Brings it to his lips and kisses it sweetly. Caressing it with his mouth so lovingly it makes me forget my apprehension. As I am sure he knew it would, his tenderness.

Keeping his soft grip on me, he lies full at my side. Eric brings my hand to my breast. Even in need he cannot resist making me rub my hand over myself, guiding it over my fullness, hardening my nipple. I watch him focused on it. I throb, grow wet at just this simple passion for me. He is a devil.

Finally he takes firm hold of my thumb, bringing the sharp point of my new ring to the place where my white flesh meets the dark pink of my nipple. Pushes the sharp tip hard into my skin. Pierces me, sharp pain. Then, when it is deep enough to bring full blood, he pulls it to make a small gash at the top of my nipple. It is quite painful at first. Yet when he takes my breast into his eager mouth and begins to suck hard in hunger for it, I orgasm almost immediately. It feels as if he is drawing the yearning between my legs from my nipple. Pulling my throbbing desire through me into him. I groan lustfully, grip him harder to me. I want him.

Hope Eric can breathe because I cannot seem to get him close enough or have his need draw me into his mouth hard enough. Grab his hair in desperation. His arms tight around me, pulling me off the bed to his salacious hunger.

Was it minute that has passed? I feel myself heal much too quickly. He does not stop affections but he loses some of the vigor he had as I bleed in his mouth.

No! I want more!

I manage to reach around his head, still licking at my hard nipple to my other breast and with no hesitation cut a deep gash as near my nipple as I can manage. He breaks his bond and looks at me with crazed eyes.

"Margret." Chastising me. Panting. "I can't drink too much."

Take hold of his head, forcing it over my bleeding breast. Eric gives no resistance. Consumes it with as much passion as he did the other.

"You have been starved, just a bit more," I moan breathlessly.

Eric moves on top of me; I feel him struggle to free himself from his jeans. I can only assist by opening my legs wide, giving him the access he needs. His mouth is drawing me in so hard, I swoon. Sill I hold him to it. When at last I feel him push inside me, I let out a profound cry, true ecstasy. The thrusts are as powerful as is his devouring need. Again I climax. Feel his warmth explode inside me. Still I am not yet healed, Eric's thrusts continue as if he had not. Again his release bursts inside me.

Feel the blood flow cease almost as if I was taking it into my own mouth. He does not move himself off me, take himself outside me. Just slowly runs his hands over my thighs, gratefully pulling, needing me to remain close to him. My legs are so tightly wrapped around him, doubt he could move even if he wished to. Soft kisses, grateful licks over my nipple for many moments after my blood stops. He brings his mouth to cover mine full of need. We satisfy our affections for each other in long blissful kisses.

He eventually looks to me, still locked hard into me. I am glad to see the light back in his eyes and the weariness gone. Only beauty and dimpled smiles.

I manage to speak. "That, unbelievably, was as amazing as when I took your blood in my mouth, being one with you." I admit. "Even more so."

He is breathing so hard, I feel his chest rise and fall with each. "It was very beautiful, Margret, thank you." A last great sigh escapes him; his body falls, relaxes.

"We are fully bonded." Relieved.

"I'm so happy you feel it, Margret." There is no attempt, or ability to hide the great pleasure he gave me. Eric knows how completely he pleasures me. As I do him.

I look at him, still lying over me. His sweet face rests between my breasts, cupping them softly to his kiss. Like a hot child, comfort and desire.

He gets up unexpectedly. Removes the last of my bonds and falls back eagerly into my arms. One arm goes to my thigh, making sure my leg is again securely around him, the other cradling my shoulder to his face resting there. Now I am able to have both my legs and arms holding him to me. Such contentment, such love and warmth.

I sigh, still reluctant. Though I know it to be true.

"Eric." Whisper timidly.

"Yes?" Tranquil, yet sleepy.

"I love you."

I hear a tender sob. Eric squeezes me tighter. Soon feel a tear that quietly escaped, it pools in my neck. I relish the feeling of it. Eric's tear, loving, warm as it rests on me. It weeps over my shoulder, seeping into my pillow, disappears. "I love you, Margret. More than you will ever know."

***

After a long while just being in each other's arms, we both fell into fitful sleep.

For hours, no matter how or where we move in our rest, we are always touching, holding. Arms, legs, hands. Darkly grasping for each other. When the morning comes, I feel a consuming bliss. His body, his heart, and now his blood he professes to be mine. All are incomparably beautiful to me. A love deeper than even my grandest fantasy is mine. It seems as implausible as me being a vampire. Yet both are true.

I have kept Eric from deep sleep most of the night. Now he rests soundly.

He lies on his side next to me but even in his deep slumber insists on my hand in his, his leg over me. His head near my shoulder, resting on a pillow tucked to me. I look at him, fill with desire. Yet feel guilt to wake him. The waves of his hair nearly cover his face. I so love the mess it is. Don't want to disturb him but want to run my hand through it. It's so full and soft. I hear a sleepy content moan as I touch it. Eric's sleep not as deep as I thought.

"Is the sun up, Margret?" Weariness in his words.

"Yes." He turns over, pulling me over with him. I am free, on top. I feel his sleepy hands run over my legs, over my butt and up my back, over and over. Caressing me with eyes closed to wakefulness. I lie fully on top of him, my head on his chest. Listen to his strong heart. Eric is half, at best, awake. Still wanting and hard under me. I kiss his neck, want to feed. Still, he has only just regained his strength. I resist the need and try to focus on my freedom to touch him. I am free to run my hands over the hardness of his muscles, arms, chest, legs. I do not leave him but touch him as best I can from my close rest. Eric's body is a place full of lust and comfort for me. I suck at his nipples, bite and kiss his chest. Sleepy moans responding to each.

He reads me too well. From behind me, he presses his fingers into me. I bite softly at his shoulder in between my kisses. He knows.

"Feed if you want."

"You are not yet strong enough for me to feed on you." Hungrily kissing and sucking where ever my mouth wanders. The need I have for his flesh, manhood, his blood, voracious.

He puts both hands firmly on my hips and lifts me over his hardness, pulling me down on it. He is strong, moving me like I am nearly weightless. Somehow he knows once I have him inside me, I will weaken in my other lust for him. Both seemingly insatiable.

"Take me, Margret," he says, groggy.

I resist. Slowly ride him for a few minutes, enjoying my freedom and my superior position too well. He still seems sleepy, but I know it is now passion. His moans strong and full. His grip firm on my hips, pulling me hard to him every time I rise and release too much. I am loving this, him. His face so full of desire, eyes still closed, head rolled back, and those sweet fat lips moaning and gasping for breath. Just to see him in this state overwhelms my heart. Beautiful, he is so beautiful to me!

I bend over, giving up. Sink my teeth into his shoulder, filling myself with all of him. His hardness inside me, the flowing gift of his blood. I cannot describe the beauty of it, the passion, the need, even as it is being fully satisfied. I want more, need more. He thrusts himself up to meet me, not letting me go. I climax several times as I continue my feed.

How I wish I could say that I had enough control, clear thought to stop this, but I didn't. Who could stop such complete ecstasy? Only when I feel him weaken in his passions do I break myself from him. Like an alarm. I cannot kill my keeper, my beloved Eric! Though I know I could.

I desperately embrace him, kiss over his peaceful face. I am so afraid I took too much. "Eric, Eric, are you all right?" Nearly frantic.

"OK, yes, OK," he weakly answers.

"I am so sorry, I was so lost in you. I have not hurt you too badly, have I?"

"I'm all right, just need to rest now." I hear the need for sleep clear in his voice. Eric strokes me, trying to soothe my anxiety. Still I fear I have drained him too much in my selfishness.

"Are you sure I have not hurt you, Eric? I would die without you."

He pulls my face to weakly kiss my lips. "Not the first time I have been taken..." he is falling. "a bit too much." Nearly inaudible.

Our bonding is very powerful, addicting. I need to be careful because without him, his love, his blood, I would be truly lost to myself. I know a loneliness I have never felt would overtake me. Just the thought...

I spend the rest of the day with my ear to his chest, his arms gently around me. Listening to his heart, praying it still beats strong.

Chapter Seven

I wake near evening from the look of the sun in my window. He is not here. I am covered in the warmth of the quilt. I do still feel the cold, though it does not affect me like it used to. Makes me shiver and such, but still feel it. Much prefer the warmth.

My arms are back in my bonds.

Although he left me a full length of chain so that I could move freely, they are secured. This angers me more than a little bit. Does he think that I can't just remove the leather straps around my wrists and free myself from the wall? That I will be a good girl and stay locked up? Screw that!

I investigate them like I had never before. My mind clear enough to do so now.

The leather is thick and inlaid with decorative chain, it has a large interlocking silver clasp, also elaborately engraved. Rather pretty, like girly punk bracelets. I want to be free of them, so I try to undo the clasp.

"Shit!" I yelp. I forgot. Silver! It burns like putting my fingers on a hot stove, and for some reason the burn makes a fat welt on the fingers that touched the metal. Well, they did think of everything, didn't they?

I take a deep exasperated breath and wonder what I am to do with myself. Flopping my hands into my lap in frustration and pain, my chains rattle.

Then I see the journal lying on the quilt. A piece of white note paper folded in half on top. I open it. It is not in the handwriting on the tag, but is nonetheless fine cursive.

Margret,

First, I am sorry about the bindings, but you are not strong enough to be set free just yet.'

He means he can't trust me.

'Don't try them they are silver and it will burn you! If you already have tried, well, in that case, sorry again. I had to go out to get groceries (remember I eat) and run some errands. I will be home well before nightfall. Read some of the writings Markus left for you if you'd like.

I love you,

Eric'

I run my still red fingers over the writing; Eric's writing. The paper smells of him. I miss him. So much has changed in just a few days. I hated and feared him, now I love and crave him.

I pick up the book, hating the sound my chains make every time I move. It's a journal-sized book, embossed with a paisley design. I open it and see the same fine hand that was on the tag; Markus's hand. There are no pale blue lines to guide the writer. Just fine white paper. Yet all the script is straight as if guided by an invisible rule. It's rather beautiful, and to see my name written in such lovely penmanship makes me feel rather special. I settle myself on my pillows to read it.

Dearest Margret,

Welcome to your new life. I hope you are at a place now that you have accepted who you are and embrace it.

I am, as you know, your maker, Markus.

Because you are reading this, my beloved Eric must believe you to be back to yourself enough for some understanding. I will do the best I can to help you have more of it.

You are, as I'm sure you must know by now, a vampire. As unlikely as this may seem, we do exist. As long as man has, from what I have gleaned over my years. We keep our numbers few, scattered throughout every corner of this earth. We are transient creatures, imposing ourselves for short years in one place. Rarely killing our feeds, everything about us serves to hide our existence from mortals.

It may appear to you as a curse now as you are changing. I know you are confused and maybe even tormented by your new situation. I assure you this is not as awful as the nightmares of childhood or the many ignorant movies about our kind. If you will only attempt to embrace the new being you have become, I promise you will find peace, and even joy, from it.

Much of that peace relies on your acceptance of your keeper, Eric.

Our close relationship with mortals is limited mostly to our keepers. However, it is the most important relationship we have. Without them our survival would be at best questionable. They keep, remind, prevent.

By this I mean they keep us, close to our humanity, lost mortality by conveying their own to us.

A keeper reminds us of our human selves. Once we were as they are, living mortal lives.

They prevent us from doing too much harm to our mortal brother and sisters.

I do not know, but hope that you have already fully bonded with Eric. Nevertheless as the giving ring is attached to this journal, you have surely talked about this. I will speak more about the importance and caution of giving a bit later in my writings. If you have not yet done so, fully bonded, I encourage you to do so. Not only because it will, I assure you, give you great pleasure, but more importantly, Eric will by this time be most weakened and need your assistance to regain himself. I am however confident he has given himself to you or you would not be well enough to have received these writings.

You know by now Eric's blood tastes like no other to you. Satisfies you, excites you in ways you cannot understand. This is for good reason; his was the first human blood you drank as you woke to your new self. Forever Eric's blood will be the flavor of life to you. I am sure he was inside you as you fed on him. This is your bonding to him. Much the same, when Eric feeds *and joins with you, that is his bonding to you. Both are equally important to your happiness and stability. Most importantly to Eric's continued health and longevity.*

As you know, Eric is yours, your keeper, as our kind lovingly call them.

His duty is to protect you, love you and connect you back to yourself. A vampire without a human keeper can become a wild soulless being. Killing indiscriminately. In all my years, I have seen very few of this kind, but you must believe me when I tell you, YOU do not want to be a soulless vampire. Eric will ensure you have subsistence. You drink only what will sustain you and not kill. Have no doubt you assuredly would kill! Everyone you plunge your teeth into would find death. Even as old and strong as I am now, he has had to remind me to stop. To bring me out of blood lust. Although not often, sometimes a particularly savory human can still lead even me to forgetfulness.

DO NOT FEED without him.

You could of course feed without him, kill. Soon you will be able to do anything you wish. Be forewarned— taking a single human life eventually brings remorse, and taking many fills our hearts with darkness.

Choose wisely.

Eric chose you. (After many exhausting months of searching and court-ing.) He wanted you not only for your physical beauty but for your kind and delicate heart, your heart's purity. So my new child, killing would be particularly bad for you. It is not in your true self to do so. It would bring you much unhappiness. If you embrace Eric, and I pray you do, he will fill you not only with life's blood but contentment.

It is very difficult to bring death to humans when you are sharing your life, your bed, your blood, and most importantly your love with one. Without a keeper humans can quickly become only food. Not beautiful warm creatures full of life, their own, and life to you.

You must fully trust Eric, and again, I pray you will love him.

Even though this is the first of my writings you read, it is the last thing I ever write. Soon I will be full dead, and my dear Eric will be alone until you come back to him. You will not be exactly as you were, your thoughts and experiences will open outward to embrace and feel many new things. If you both succeed in your turning, this will be a very wonderful time for you and you will regain, with time, yourself.

Eric worries so that he will not be able to do this alone. I have full confidence he can and will. He is a strong and noble man. I will wait no longer, I want death; even my lusts have waned. I am eager to go on so I will not stay to assist him in the many difficult weeks ahead.

My sweet Eric as I write this is lying next to me in a ball. He is beside himself with grief and worry. You, Margret, are chained and hissing like a wild cat in the basement below. You will have no memory of it, thankfully. I must admit I underestimated Eric's ability to see you like this. He feels much empathy for you. I have never, no matter what challenges or difficulties we have been through, seen him look so distraught. You have little of your true beauty at the moment and none of your true self. He fears so for you, and his ability to bring you back from your turning. I suppose this pain is greatly exasperated by his last task for me. One I wanted to be done already, but I could not bring myself to leave him this way. To ask any more of him today. So I will wait another full night until the sun is high to ask his assistance.

I can't read fast enough, I want to know all of it. Like the best novel I've ever read, I can't put it down. I hear Eric coming in the back door, he yells down to me.

"Home, Margaret. I'll be down in a few."

"Yea, OK." I think I said it aloud. Much too engrossed in Markus's writings. Vaguely hear cupboard doors and the refrigerator opening and closing. Putting away his food.

The door opens. "You OK?" he calls down to me.

"I am fine, just reading." Distractingly reply.

"All right. I am going to take a shower then."

"OK." Returning to my reading.

I chose Eric 67 years ago now. For all those years he has been my keeper, human companion, friend and lover. I do love him most dearly so his continued happiness is of utmost importance to me.

When I met him, Eric was a fine handsome gentleman with the heart of a sweet child and the inner strength of a bull. His selfless gentle nature and strong heart were the reasons I had to have him. He was a unique man. Unlike the other keepers I've had over my years, Eric was drafted. Had no choice. I knew even then he would be my last. Unwilling to take a refusal, one I knew he would wholeheartedly give me. I selfishly took him. I so often regret this and the long months it took me to break him. It was very unpleasant and, well, if he wishes he can tell you the hell I put him through to make him mine.

He is my beloved, the best of all I have had the honor of loving. So that eases much of my regret.

It is important that you understand why and who to enlist as a keeper. I have already told you much of the why, but in a nutshell your keeper keeps you as near your humanity as is possible.

The who, well, much of that depends on what you find appealing in another. You will know that instinctively. It is other qualities you must look for that are the most important to have a successful attachment to your keeper. Qualities where our vampiric nature is somewhat deficient. Compassion, tenderness, empathy.

Most especially a desire to give of themselves to others, to serve. These are the characteristics that will keep the best of your human side alive. As well as ensuring your keeper's content and strong enough to endure all that you will ask of them.

A lover can be trained, but you cannot train a person to be kindhearted and loving. Eric is both of these.

You may wonder why as you are new and have barely begun your time with Eric I tell you this. You must understand Eric may not want, or be able to live forever, and I know he will not be changed over. I offered many times after I expressed my desire for true death, and over the year he searched for a new master. It is not in his nature to be as we are, Margret. He is a care giver. That is why I chose him; that is why he was the greatest of all.

Yet as I am done with life, Eric is not yet. So he looked for you. Someone to care for and love.

Some of my previous keepers eventually wanted death— I gave it to them, or let them go on to find death naturally. Two wished to become immortal, I gave them immortality. Two died from too much of me.

I have had seven Keepers in my lifetime, all of them dear to me, few still walk as I am. The rest are gone, save Eric."

I cannot bear to read this. Eric cannot leave me, in death or in any way! I fall into uncontrollable sobbing.

"Margret, what is wrong?" He is sitting on the last step. I must have been so occupied with my reading, I didn't notice him come down. He comes over, wanting to embrace me, his face full of worry.

"NO! NO! Unchain me now!" Push him away and yank at my chains with all my force.

"Margret. calm down. What is wrong?"

"Please unchain me!" Sobbing and pleading.

"If you calm down, I may, but the state you are in does not lend me any confidence to do so."

He is trying to hold me but I want full freedom to take him into my arms. I try to settle myself without much success.

"Eric, please I need to be free. Please," I beg.

He relents, frees one wrist, then the other. I immediately grab him, widely embrace him, pulling at his hair. Generally a clinging mess of sobs. He holds me the best he can, kisses me, tries to calm me.

"Margret, what is it? What has upset you so?"

"I missed you." Darkly press my face into the warmth of him.

"You are not this upset over a few hours without me. What?" He pulls my face back, out of his neck to look at me directly. I feel my tears rolling back, falling over my temples, wetting my hair. They are still coming fast. I can't speak, just look at the dim light above me. He kisses my tears, brushes wet hair from my face, and wraps his legs tightly around my waist. Pulling me close to him. We sit intertwined until I calm enough to speak without inconsolable sobbing.

"I was reading," I manage to squeak out, "and he said…" I fall again into tears that choke my words back. What the hell is happening to me? Why am I so full of overwhelming sadness? He waits for my next words, soon realizing I can't utter any sound save my sobbing. Sweet kisses on my tearstained face. I cling to him.

"What could Markus have written that would be so upsetting to you? You already know you're a vampire. You withstood weeks of my cruelties, hours of loneliness. Never have I seen you so distressed or cry so hard. What? Tell me," he insists.

Still I don't want to express aloud the idea of him dying or leaving me. "Read it," I whimper.

"No, that book is for you. Tell me."

"No! You read it." He frees his arm, reaches for the book I tossed aside in my fit.

"Where, show me the part that upset you so." I take it from him, find the page, and point to the words. He reads the few paragraphs carefully. Shakes his head, confused. "What? I am not leaving you, I am right here," whispers, confused.

"But he says you may want to die or leave me alone." I start to sob again.

"Please, Margret. Why do you worry so? I don't want to die, I want to live. That's why I asked Markus to turn you for me. To love you and live with you."

"But you may want to someday and I cannot have another. I will NOT have another keeper!" I sound like a spoiled child.

"Come lie down with me." He lays us both on our sides, tucks me into his arms and pulls the quilt over us. "If I ever did want to die, it would not be for a very, very long time. If nothing else you have made me want to live more, as long as you want me."

"Want?" I say, bewildered. "I had no idea what the word truly meant before you. I will always want you!"

Eric kisses my head and softly strokes my back. I feel a bit of calm returning to me in his embrace.

"What if you tire of me and wish leave me?" I weep.

"That is the silliest thing I have ever heard, Margret, really! You still have no concept of my love for you or how deeply we are bonded together." He pushes his full jeans against me when he says deeply. I look up to that devilish smile. Seduce anyone with that smile.

He takes hold of my jaw and brings my face to him. Kissing my mouth over and over, teasing my lips with his tongue yet not giving me his full kiss. How he knows how to torment me. Every time I move forward wanting, he pulls back. Too many moments. I am unable to endure another second. I grasp the back of his head, sinking my fingers into his hair, and pull him roughly to my needs. Finally his full mouth is mine. He moves on top of me. Other than his soft strokes over me, he makes no move to do anything more than embrace and give me passionate kisses. Each reassures and brings me calm. Though the hardness pushing in between my legs quickly becomes my central focus. I need it. Need our connection more than ever.

"I want you. Undress and be close to me," I ask, shyly demanding. My heat is just as strong as my blood lust when I am in his arms now. I do feel hunger as always, but want him more.

"As you wish." Eric stands over me and begins to undress. I only have my robe to pull from myself, so I watch with excitement as he undresses, unzips his pants. When the zipper is completely down, his hardness bursts out.

I have never seen a cock that aroused me so, I wanted so much. As soon as he comes near me, I ravage it with hard kisses, quickly sucking all of him into my mouth. I must have been too rough because he pulls away from me.

"Margaret, slow down." He leans over me, takes my face into his gentle hands, kisses me softly.

"I am sorry, did I hurt you?" His eyes close to mine. Smiles sweetly at me, shaking his head.

"No. I am very pleased that you are so willing, and so eager, but no rushing. Make love to me."

He lies on his back, spreading his legs, revealing all of himself to me. Beckons to me to come closer with his hand. I am wild for every bit of him. With some difficulty I hold myself.

"I'm sorry, my crazy feelings, fear of losing you, my lusts." I take a breath so deep, yet only needed by my human heart. "I am overwhelmed by desire and need."

Eric strokes my hair, holds me to him as I rest my head on his hip. "I understand. You have been through so much, Margret. I hope you understand now, I am here to love and please you, nothing more." Rest his head back on the pillows. "And we have nothing but time, my love."

I go to him again, taking his hardness into my hand. This time I show him the love I feel in lingering kisses and long slow licks between his legs. Giving him all my lustful affections in each kiss. Suck places I have never desired before; nothing is beyond my desire now. His moans only encourage my new adventures.

I kiss him, all of his sex for a long time. Every part of him seems new and wildly arousing to me. His legs wrapped around me, my mouth moving over him with a hot need I had never felt before. Mouthing him, kissing him, makes me drip with heat.

When I have loved and teased him to his limit, he begs me. "Take me, please."

His groaning grows louder as I pull him fully into my mouth, lovingly take his climax, relish it before I swallow him.

Still I greedily suck the last drops. Eric forcibly pulls me from under my arms up to his chest. Encircling me with his legs and arms. I lie there, full of contentment, hearing his heart beating rapidly, breath trying to calm.

Honestly, I don't know what this is but I know what my heart and body are telling me. It is as strong and as loud as my need for blood; neither can be ignored. Clearly I can't resist my need for him any longer. Shamefully don't even want to. Eric is all I have, his arms, his lusts, now my only pleasure.

The night is as endless as his desire for me. As dawn approaches I feel my need for blood grow strong and ask him to bind me, find me someone, something to feed on. He offers himself to me and even though it is like refusing water after days of thirst, I refuse him. I do not want to weaken him so soon after he has recovered from weeks of need. I am thinking of only him, even in blood lust. That is, well...love.

Eric promises to bring me something quickly and then try to find someone for the evening. I get a dog and sleep, waiting for better.

Chapter Eight

I hear nothing above me. Eric must be gone already. My arms are loosely strapped, my legs free. The more I feed, the more I come to some semblance of my human self, the more conflicted my feelings become. Not nearly as conflicted as they should be, I suppose, considering. Still, I find myself somewhat agitated as I wake. Unsure what exactly has me feeling this way.

My own thoughts and feelings unwanted, I decide to read more of Markus's journal. Maybe his words will bring me some understanding of my new self.

Now about giving. It is just that, your gift to your keeper. You of course do not have to give, bleed for them. Two things will happen if you choose to withhold yourself. One, your keepers will not have the small degree of immorality it gives them. I say degree of immorality because they are still very much mortal. They can and do die. The blood we give greatly slows aging by healing the human body as it starts to fail, age. It saves them from some sickness and gives them increased physical strength. If a keeper is denied blood for an extended time, their body will start to age. If they never have it again, they will continue to age much like normal from that point on. keepers do age, but very slowly. They can be hurt, broken and such but will heal faster than a normal human. Though not near the rapid healing you now possess. So they are similar, but not immortal.

I knew a rogue vampire many years ago. Unfortunately he became as he was because his long- held and much loved keeper was killed. Far beyond any healing, in a car accident. Long ago when automobiles were fairly new, and often a death trap. He was so distraught at this sudden loss. Refused to take another keeper. Eventually he lost his humanity. It was very sad, but these things happen, and if they do, you must go on and find another. For your own happiness and, more importantly, for the safety of others.

Secondly if you don't give, your bonds to your keeper will be much lessened. Sharing blood is much like the sharing of body, just much more powerful. It binds you together and along with physical joining, well, I hope you already know this from your own experiences with Eric, but in case you have not. Blood and sex will give you both such intense pleasure as no two humans could ever possibly reach. It is the most beautiful and fulfilling experience. You will never tire of it, you will however crave it. So my next words are of great caution.

You may drink your keeper dry of course, if you wish. Too much of their blood will only cause them harm, or bring them death, not you. Conversely, if a keeper drinks too often, too much from a vampire, it will kill them.

I am not a scientist but I will explain to the best of my knowledge and abilities.

Let us start with a very simple explanation of what happens when you create a vampire. Fairly simple, really. All you need do is drain a human until death occurs, then quickly give your life blood to them. The organs inside will be rapidly dying after they are drained. A vampire's blood renews these organs, changes them over. Our blood brings new life.

On the contrary, if a living healthy human drinks too much vampire blood, it will still seek to transform the organs. However, as they are healthy organs not dying, this effort becomes fatal. Instead of healing, too much destroys. I suppose in an attempt to make the living immortal. I hope that makes some sense to you.

I found this out the hard way, twice. It was most heartbreaking for me. The first time I had no idea what happened. My keeper became sickly, and I so ignorant gave him more of my blood, hoping to make him well. Only sealing his fate and expediting it. I was warned not to give too much, but I was a young vampire and had no concept of what too much was. Coupled with the intense sexual benefits, I could not resist. Gave too often, selfishly really. Still, I did not know that was the cause of his passing. Not until I had it happen again with my especially needy female keeper, Melissa. She was quite the beauty— dark, sad eyes, and knew very well how to plead with them.

Forgive me, I digress into memory. After she passed I investigated the cause as best I could. I found all organs inside her to be black and rotting. I alone killed them both from my selfishness and ignorance. I will hopefully save you this great regret.

As I have said, giving coupled with the beautiful sexual experience it is very hard, for both, to resist. I warn you, no matter how your keeper may beg or plead, no matter how dearly you love them... Do Not let your keeper drink more than twice a week, and only from one bleed! Your healing assures Eric will never drink too much. I have found once a week is the safest. I Gave to Eric once a week, unless I had taken too much or too often from him, in that case I would give to him twice. Be careful, and you will have intense and pleasureful givings together over many, many years.

I have also cautioned, warned and scolded Eric on this, to his great annoyance. As you are a female, well, I may be showing my age, but I feel you will have an even greater ability to seduce him— tears. No gentleman wishes to cause the woman he loves a single tear, though we cause many.

There, call me a chauvinist!

Chapter Nine

We are lying together as the sun fills the basement windows. He is trying to wake himself, but as I have again kept him awake most of the night, he struggles. I have no bindings on me as Eric is here with me, but if he is away, he binds just my arms with full lengths of chain. He still feels I am not ready.

"Morning, Margret." He kisses my cheek and struggles to stand up. "Come here." Reaching his hand out, beckoning me to stand on the floor with him outside my 'bedroom.'

I stand and for the first time place my feet on the cold tile floor beyond my bed. Wonder what he is up to. Eric brushes my hair off my face and embraces me. "How would you like to take a proper shower with me this morning?"

He has a few times wiped me off with a wash cloth but... "I must be starting to smell," I respond, embarrassed.

"Not really. You don't really sweat, but I sweat all over you. It will feel good to you, nonetheless."

"All right." It is me that now has sleep in my voice. He smiles and turns, walking to the stair. When I reach the first step, I stop. Looking up at the closed wood door above, the dark stairs leading to it. I have a very strange feeling. Like I am a creature of this room and should not go above.

Do I deserve to be above ground? I am dead, bring death.

Eric turns, noticing my hesitation. "What is it, Margret? Come on." Again he reaches his hand out for me to take it, I do but I do not move.

"Are you sure you can trust me? That I will not try to run away from you?"

Snickering. "Well, considering what you did to me last night, it seems that you no longer want to run away from me." He smiles reassuringly. "Come; it is full light so even if you wanted to run off in your little robe, you would not get far before I overtook you."

I slowly take one step at a time until we are at the door. Always holding tightly to his hand. I feel so strange and somehow out of place. Well, out of my place I have been for such a long time.

Eric opens the door; searing bright light fills my eyes. It blinds me for a second and I waver.

"Here, I've got you." He puts a strong arm around my back and helps me into the kitchen. I blink, try to get used to the light. "Sorry, I forgot you have been it that dim basement for so long. Can you see OK now?"

Harshly rub my eyes, adjusting to it. "Yea, OK. It will not hurt me, right?" I find myself clinging to his arm like a frightened child. Eric rubs my arm and gives me a kiss to my forehead.

"Of course it will not hurt you. Do you think I would spend all that time and energy regaining your love only to bring you into the sunlight to burn? This is not a movie. It does make you weak, not pleasant, but it is not your natural time. Vampires were made to hunt in the dark of night, so you are not at your strongest, but no burning to a crisp either." Smiling down at me as I rub my face into his shoulder. I really am acting like a child, but he seems to enjoy my clinging to him.

"I've got you, Margret." He slips the arm I am holding to around my waist and starts out of the kitchen into the dining room. It's not a very big room. Full windows along the front wall, thankfully the dark blue drapes are drawn. A rather cheap looking round dining table and chairs, matching buffet and bad print art above it. A few candles and nick nacks along the buffet. It looks nothing like anything I thought he would own. We only pause before he takes me around the archway into the front room. I note the front door and the many bolts on it briefly. There is a decent sized fireplace on the far wall, redbrick, simple wood mantel. A very large TV above it. Rather tacky. In front of it a long brown leather couch flanked by matching armchairs, coffee table, again bland and not at all Eric.

"This is nice; not what I expected, but nice."

Full laughter bursts from him. I have never heard him laugh so boisterously. It sounds so wonderful to me. I am afraid I have said something stupid but laugh because he is laughing. We are both laughing, like real people!

"Margret, this is just my guy trap for you." Again he laughs, squeezing my hand, brings it to his kiss.

"Whatever do you mean?" I say, all proper. Playing along.

"I needed, one, a home close to where you were, the hospital, your house. And two, I had to look like just a plain old bachelor with little money for fine things."

He is still chuckling a bit as he confesses his schemes.

"When I finally got you, I had to have a place that looked like the sweet guy who volunteers at the hospital and watches hockey. A place to seduce you and all that dating stuff. I was only here when you were here with me and of course now that you are changing."

I admit to him. "You know nearly every word you say brings a thousand questions to my mind!"

"I'm sorry." Still happy. "I know there are so many blanks yet. I will do my best to help you, just not all at once."

"You and I were here, in this room?" I ask.

He leads me over to sit on the couch and put his arm classically date-like around my shoulders.

"I made out with you in this very spot, Margret. I managed to get to second base and after a few frustrating weeks got you to go upstairs to make love to me."

"Wait. I am married. I do remember that."

"Yes, you were, and that was a very big problem."

"It was?"

He pulls my legs over his lap and rests his feet on the coffee table. "Yes, it was. You are a good woman, even though your husband was an ass and never appreciated the great beauty you are, you would not leave him, or for that matter cheat. So I had more than my work cut out for me."

"How did you get me here if I was so difficult?" Sassy.

"I, as I told you before, met you at the hospital. From the first time I saw you, I was very attracted to you. You became a real possibility; still, I had to know who you were inside. So I made sure I knew your work schedule, volunteered when you were on shift. Made myself impossible to miss, as I was there much of the time you were. I talked to you, did nice things, things I would have done maybe anyway, but knew they would help with winning your friendship. Maybe endear me to you."

"Like what things?" He kinda laughs.

"Like bringing in fat-free cookies from this great bakery I know. They were awesome. Sometimes I would bring in a big bouquet of wild flowers to the nurses station, chocolates, of course. I swear I had every nurse there in love with me, but not you; you were tough. The nicer I was, the more you ran the other way."

"So what did you do to gain my trust?"

"Well I kept after you, tried to be your friend. I went out with you and a few of the other nurses for drinks and dancing a few times. Got to know you better. You drank vodka tonics in case you forgot."

I nod. "Yes, I did."

"One time I think I really got to you was when I was visiting Jen." He pauses, remembering, smiling with his remembrance. "We were drawing and talking, she loved to do both. You walked in and were doing your nurse thing and from nowhere Jen blurted out, 'Eric thinks you're beautiful.' At first I was embarrassed, but by the look on your face realized how badly you needed to hear that. Shy, yet glowing with the compliment. I pretended to scold Jen, said she shouldn't tell secrets. And then you looked right at me with that sweet smile of yours. I acted as if I was still talking to Jen, but I was looking straight at you. Then I said, 'Nurse Margret is very beautiful, inside and out.' I think that may have been the moment I got into your heart."

"Did you mean it or were you just trying to...?" I don't finish, not sure what I am asking. Eric turns my face to him and lets out a sigh.

"Of course I meant it, then and now. I already knew before a hand holding or a single kiss that you, well, I cared for you. I courted you, fell in love with you, waited for you, finally won you. Now you are here with me."

"You didn't just want...?" Again I don't finish my thought. I am so unsure what I am wanting to know.

"Margret, I am NOT trying to boast here but I don't have much trouble getting women, or men for that matter, into bed with me. I am not bragging really, but if that was all I wanted, I could have picked someone much, much easier to get in bed with. I wanted to be in love, with you, for you to love me. A beautiful person inside and out."

I grab his face and kiss it all over. Resting finally on his lips. "I have come to realize, my sweet Eric, you are impossible to resist."

His smile widens, then he asks, "You want to make out for a while," raises his eyebrows, "before we take our shower?"

"Yes, I do. Though now I will let you have any base you wish, and as many home runs as you can manage."

"You may be sorry for that last part."

"Doubt that."

We kiss for a long time before he takes me upstairs. Again, a simple room, king-sized bed, plain gray quilt and crisp white pillows. Another huge TV over the wood dresser.

"You watch a lot of TV?" I ask. Eric is distracted, pawing me all over, slipping hands into my robe. I am out for the first time and am a bit more curious than in need. I know I will have him as much as I wish.

I am in no rush, but he...

"Didn't have much to do with my time there for a few weeks but chase wild dogs, catch raccoons in the yard, and feed you. Yes, then I watched a lot but not normally."

"Eric, did we make love in that bed?" I find it so strange that I remember nothing of it. Any of it.

"Yes, many times," he says, buried in the back of my neck, biting at it. His hand moves inside my robe to my heat, going for the base he left off at while we were making out on his couch. I push it away.

"Eric!" I scold, "I want to know more."

"Now?" he says, impatient with me. He releases me a little. "What? What do you want to know?"

"How many times was I here with you? Weeks, months?"

"As I told you before, we were together for about nine weeks, but knew you for five months all together. You didn't come over here for a week after our first kiss. You were fighting it, me. Then it took about, well, maybe another two weeks before I bedded you."

Cocky smile on his face.

"Bedded me?" I laugh.

"I could only see you a few times a week at best, besides at the hospital, because of your husband thing. I must say, after I made love to you," says it with such fake bravado, "well, you made as much time in your schedule to be with me as you could." He smiles rather proudly.

Dear God. Men.

"You were made in that bed." Turns me holding my shoulders, backs me over to it. I sit on the soft quilt, like velvet, but not velvet. He sits down next to me. "How far are you in that journal Markus left you? Has he written about your turning at all?"

"Not really, not in any details, he is mostly talking about giving to you and stuff like that."

"Oh." He looks down, thinking. "I don't want to overwhelm you with too much all at once."

"Too much for me or you? You only want to get me in the shower."

"Yes, and I had no idea how long it was going to take to get you in it."
Smiles at me. "Should have taken you on the couch." Mumbling to himself.

"Eric, please."

"Can I tell it to you in a short story for now, and not the novel? I think
it might upset you too much in detail." He looks up over his brow at me.

"Yes, fine, short story."

Not happy, but I am trying to trust that Eric knows best for me now. I
don't want to be a bitch on my first day out of the basement, and free to
walk around as well. Not to mention his jeans are still full from our affections and he is wanting.

"Well, let's just say Markus and I were with you, he drained you, fed
you and then we chained you in the basement until you became more of
yourself again." Falls silent.

"That is NOT even a short story, Eric, it's barely a paragraph!" Again more
questions rise with every word.

"Margret, please. It may disturb you if I tell you too much."

"Answer me this, what do you mean Markus and I were with you, in this
bed? Was I was making love to you when he took me or...?"

Deep sigh. "Not exactly, more like we were making love to you."

"What?" I yell, shocked.

He had brought Blondie to me, but I never had him, Eric did. My blood
letting was too much and he just slept after. I did not have them both, and
I was feeding. A vampire.

"Both of you? I had sex with Markus?" Dubious to say the least.

"Sort of..." He trails off shyly, waiting for me to react.

"How did you get me to let Markus into our bed when it took you so
long just to do it yourself? As I recall I had no other lovers, just you and
my husband. None."

"It wasn't easy. You met Markus a few times before. Knew he was my
best friend. Markus was a handsome and very charming man. Irresistibly
attractive to almost everyone. We partied a bit that night..."

I snap at him, "You mean you got me drunk!" Now I am staring to get upset, again.

"No! You weren't drunk, a bit tipsy, but not without sense. You needed to be coaxed for sure, but you were willing, after some effort from us both."

"Effort?" I question sarcastically. "You mean you seduced me!"

"Margret, why are you making me tell you all this now? You need time to adjust and remember yourself slowly. Not have me tell you every detail. It's upsetting for you when I tell you things you can't remember yourself, like they are untrue to you."

"I am not looking for every detail, just need to know what happened and how. That's all."

"OK, I told you. Markus was there, while I made love to you. He was my master and lover for many years. I wanted to have you both. Give his … approval."

"What? His approval of my lovemaking? Shit, Eric." I fling myself back arms first on the bed in exasperation and stare at the ceiling. Not go to that enraged crazy Margret place. Takes all I have not to.

"No, of my choice. He met you, as I said, well twice before that night. Once we had lunch together, that was shortly after our first kiss, and here for a couple hours. He was most enamored with you. Still, I needed to know that you were going to be strong enough, love me enough to undergo this huge transformation. And yes, selfishly I wanted to make love to you both."

"I think I understand, I guess. I am not angry, well not much, still. I will want more details someday."

"Hopefully you will just remember them and I will not have to go through telling them to you," he says.

"Are they that horrible?"

"Well, I am not sure if horrible is the right word, but to you it will mean something different, maybe very different, than it meant to me. For me it was the best night I had ever had, to have you both. Believe me, I have had plenty to compare it to."

He is still sitting but now bent over, rather defeated. I wonder if he can possibly still be hard. Why am I thinking that? I am so strange to my own self. Even as I am just now remembering myself.

"It was the best because I loved the two of you so much." He nearly whimpers. "Then it became the hardest, most painful, worst time of my life. Ever."

Eric refused to talk about it. He was happy and did not want to be reminded of painful things. Though he promised to tell me more later if I didn't remember it on my own.

He swooped me up in his arms, stood me in the shower, no discussion.

Feels like forever since I've felt warm water flowing over my skin. Eric begins to wash my hair. It's relaxing to feel his hands rubbing my scalp, running through my hair. So relaxing I nearly lose my legs, but he has me firm in his strong embrace. Washes me completely, spending extra time in places he wishes.

When he is finished, I do the same for him. Really I am just loving him with my soapy hands. Eric's body is beautiful. Soap his strong muscular legs, moving up to his tight dimpled ass. I spend some time there with groping hands and kisses. Seems Eric likes that very much. Finally I turn him around to passionately kiss the hard flesh that seduced me, tormented me. Now I want all of it, crave it.

Our shower beautiful, relaxing, certainly hot. It feels as if I have never felt anything like this before. Maybe I haven't.

Eric takes me by the hand, dries me off. Insists, will not let me do a thing. He takes such care of me, as if I were an invalid. When I am all dry, he wraps me in large white towel. Thankfully puts one around his hips as well. Then he lifts me up to sit on the counter between two sinks. Turns me around to brush my hair. I sit cross-legged and look into the mirror. This is the first time seeing myself, my new self. Eric is occupied, trying to get a brush through my thick brown hair. My hair is long, below my shoulder blades, one length, straight as a pin. I gaze, most intrigued by my new reflection. I recognize it to be me, yet somehow foreign. My eyes are also brown, rather oval. Suppose I am pretty. Eric talks as if I am a goddess. Happy I am to him, but not much more than just pretty really.

I touch my new lighter skin; it seems flawless to me. Not a pimple, pore or scar to be seen. Can't remember where they were exactly, but know I had them. Open my mouth wide to investigate my new teeth curiously. He notices my interest in my reflection.

"You are much the same beauty as before, Margret. Your skin smoother, paler, your eyes a bit darker brown than they were, but still my Margret." Smoothing his hand over my hair, looking over my right shoulder at me in the mirror.

"My teeth." I press my finger to my new improved canines. "They are not as, well, big and frightening as I thought they'd be." Eric chuckles.

"No. Just better for biting."

They are sharp, if you press on them, but not like a razor blade or anything.

In my curiosity I press a bit too hard and draw blood from my finger. Immediately Eric goes to take it in his mouth but I take hold of his wrist, crossly say, "No!"

"What, Margret? It is way too precious to let even a drop go." He gets his way, seems he is still stronger than me. Sensually sucks my fingertip, truly only getting a drop or two before it heals.

"I don't want to overfeed you!" I insist.

"I see Markus has put the fear of God into you about that, as he did me. A drop will not kill me." He takes me by my hips and flips me around to face him. The maneuver pulls my towel open.

"The last time you were right here, you were mortal." Dropping his towel to the floor, he pulls me by my lower back right to the edge of the vanity.

"You had me right here, just like this?" I purr at him.

"Yes, and I had never heard you moan and groan so." His eyes sparkle with that endless heat he seems to have for me.

I look up shyly. "Why did I moan so?"

"Let me show you." Opens my thighs, lifting them around his hips.

Eric presses his hard cock to me, not entering, just pressing. Still a little harder, his head enters, pulls back. Never leaving me completely, never giving me much more than a few inches of him. He does this repeatedly. Slowly breaking into me, spreading me, teasing me. Giving me pleasure with just his shallow penetrations, over and over. Never knew that just this part could feel so amazingly good. It's always over and done before you can really feel it, enjoy it.

Eric is so controlled. Making sure I am getting as much pleasure from entering me as he can give me. Eventually he gives me all of him, but again very slowly. Only to pull back after he reaches his full depth to do it again. I am moaning as promised. My breath wild. Struggle to open my eyes. I find he is intensely watching me, and our joining.

"Please tell me you are loving this as much as I..." Literally moan out every syllable, barely able to speak. Dimples, dark seductive eyes. Eric pulls me fully into his arms, bringing all of his hardness deep into me with the embrace.

"I am not sure what is more exciting to me, loving you so slowly or listening to your sweet moans..." He kisses me hard on my mouth, it is needy hot. "Maybe the moans."

He has no more control nor do I.

***

Like a doomed bride, Eric carries me downstairs to my basement chamber. Lays me still naked in my bed, covers me carefully, tucking me in. I am truly as tired as I can ever remember being. Full sun now. My whole body feels like a sack of wet cement. When he starts to put the leather around my wrists, I struggle.

"What are you doing? Stop, stop!" I weakly protest.

"You are not yet able to be free, you will have full use of your arms."

I am so out of it I can hardly do anything, futilely try to fight. His powerful grip overcomes me and I am back in my bindings.

"Shit, Eric." I can't muster much anger; it is midday, the relaxing shower, the lovemaking. I am spent. Eric's loving kisses and hugs before he releases me.

"I am sorry, but if I leave you alone, and I must, and you got free ...well, I can't chance it. You may feel better, but you are not there yet." Tenderly kisses my forehead and then my lips briefly.

"I must go. I am already going to be late."

"Late for what?" I ask, near unconscious.

"The hospital. I'm on shift today."

"You still go?"

"Yes. Sleep now, we'll talk more tonight."

Don't even hear the car leave. I am well gone to rest before he is out the door.

Chapter Ten

I wake to warm hands cupping my breast and gentle nibbles on the back of my neck.

"Wake up, Margret." I turn to my back and look at my clock, the window. It is full dark. Wow, I was out the rest of the day and into the evening.

"Hi," I say, still groggy.

"How would you like to go out for dinner tonight?" He smiles wide at me. Sit straight up, I am awake now. "Really, out, outside?"

"Yes, out. I hope I am not rushing this, but you have been so good and patient." He sits up as well, taking something from his jacket pocket. Looks like silver bracelets.

"For me? How thoughtful, silver!" I say sarcastically. He had to spoil my mood so quickly?

"Watch." He puts it over his wrist and pushes, it goes on quickly, like hand cuffs, just prettier.

"I will be able to restrain you if you start to lose it. You may feel much more yourself, but being here with just me and maybe one other human is much different from being in a room full of them." He releases the cuff and puts it back into his pocket. "Sorry for the threat, but I can't take any chances. You will be with me the whole time so that will help to calm you I hope, but still. Do you feel OK? Are you very hungry?"

I think yes, but am not going to ruin my chance to leave the house, so I tell him I am fine. He removes my restraints. Again I get to go upstairs to the bedroom.

Laid out on the bed is a dark red dress, matching red heels, black bra and panties. All the girl things I need. He pulls me to the bath. The counter is full of makeup, eye shadow palette, mascara, blush, probably need that the most.

"You get ready and then we'll go. Take your time." He moves to leave. I grab hold of his hand before he gets away.

"Where are we going?"

"Well, I eat first, there is a small Italian place I love. Then after dinner I thought we would go dancing." My face lights up. "My Margret, you love dance, don't you?" Grinning wide, happy to be making me happy.

"Yes! I love to but never get to."

"I know, asshole never took you out, even to dinner, let alone dancing. That all changes now. You and I will dance all night if you wish."

"When will I feed?"

"I will find you someone at the bar, don't worry. I got this. OK? Just have fun getting ready and I will go change."

"K." I turn my attention to all the makeup he bought me. I didn't really use a lot, I remember, but that was the old Margret. "I am all new now," I say aloud to myself.

I spend quite a while trying to do my best at the dark sexy smoky eye look. A few failed attempts, glad to see makeup remover on the counter. I used it a few times. Again. Third time I think I got it. I try applying blush in moderation, don't need base make up, my skin is rather flawless now. Overall it looks good, for a novice. Time to put on my dress.

He is not in the bedroom. I put on the bra and underpants, slip the dress over my head. It is tight, just above my knee and so low cut my bra is showing. I try to pull it and cover myself more but there is not enough dress to do it. He comes in while I am playing with my modesty.

"What are you doing?" Fussing.

"My bra is showing and..." Focusing on covering my cleavage.

"Here, let me help." He quickly pulls the straps of my dress down over my shoulders and undoes my bra, tosses it aside and returns the dress to my shoulders. "There, perfect!"

Cleavage, below cleavage! I am a bit out of my comfort level. Though Eric is happy, sliding his hand inside my dress, cupping my breast. "Very perfect," he moans, content with the ease of access.

I finally look at him. He is very well dressed, like I have never seen him before. A black brocade jacket, very thin collar, rather long, ending well below his hips. Underneath a fine white shirt untucked with straight hem. Black tight straight leg dress pants and boots. He looks so handsome, hot. I can't resist running my hands over his jacket; the fabric is expensive, clearly custom made for him. Nothing a simple volunteer, hockey-loving guy would ever think to wear. Eric is much more then I know, but he is giving me, as always, slow pieces of him.

"You look beautiful, Margret, very sexy." I realize he has been ogling me as I was him.

"As do you, Eric. You're dressed so, well, fancy."

"Glad you like. Do you like your dress?"

"Well, yes. It is a bit immodest, tight."

"No more modest. You are a beautiful strong vampire now. Not an un-appreciated housewife. Put on your shoes and we'll get going." I sit on the bed and wonder if I will be able to walk in these heels.

"OK, ready."

At the back door I have that same feeling I had going upstairs for the first time. Out of place, a bit frightened at the outside world, at myself. Eric is once again aware of my feelings. Takes my hand and guides me tucked into his back to the passenger seat. Reassuring me as he buckles me in. Kisses my forehead and says something about all will be well.

My anxiety rises more every mile we go away from the house. He puts on some familiar music.

"Who is that?" I ask. He laughs.

"It is your iPod, you should know." I look at it, yes, that is mine. I recognize the cover full of pink hearts.

"Dave Matthews, you love him. He makes you happy. Every time you were upset or stressed, you would play him."

"Yes. Yes, I do. I remember, it seems to be working again." I look over at Eric, his attention on the road; something seems very familiar about this. Like déjà vu, but no real concrete memory comes, just a feeling.

We arrive at a corner restaurant, Luigi's. I am starting to get concerned again. What if I lose it in front of a bunch of people? Even my temper is so easily aroused these days. Or maybe I'll have a nice crying fit in the middle of his dinner? He seems to read my mind, or is there terror on my face?

"Margret, you'll be OK. Just hold close to me. I will take care of you, promise."

"What if I..." I trail off, the what if's too many to list. He reaches into his pocket and brings out the silver cuffs.

"These will quickly change anything you may be doing."

"They'll burn me and I will scream, making an even bigger scene!"

"You don't need to worry, I will take you outside and it will be nothing to anyone but a lovers' quarrel or something." Always such tender understanding. It gives me confidence. I see it in him even as I don't see it in me. He opens his door and comes around to open mine, extending his hand for me.

"Trust me, Margret. It will be OK." I do, so I take his hand and we walk inside the restaurant, my arm holding tightly to his. "Reservation for Campbell," he says politely.

"Yes, the table near the windows," the hostess says, leading us over to a cozy table for two. Eric pulls out the chair nestled in the corner for me to sit. He sits closer to me than one normally would do. Arm around the back of my chair. I am quite locked in, my back to a wall, to my left tall windows facing the street. Eric blocking me from the rest of the restaurant, the blood rushing in it.

"OK, Margret?" I don't have chance to answer as the waitress is already here.

"Welcome to Luigi's, my name is Susan and I will be your server for tonight." She puts down the menus and goes into the specials. Eric orders two glasses of Merlot.

"I can't drink that can I?"

"No. Well, you could but too much would just, well come up on you." He grimaces.

"It looks good if you have one too," he winks, "and, well, they are both for me."

The wine arrives promptly and he wastes no time drinking. I sigh heavily.

"I am sorry it must bug you that I can and you…"

"No, not really, just wish I could join you out of, I don't know, sharing."

"We SHARE much, Margret, just not this." He gives me a half-hearted wink. The waitress arrives again to take our orders, Eric orders for me and himself. Cheese ravioli meat sauces, and carbonara, both come with a salad. He refuses his.

"Did we ever eat here before?" I ask, looking around at the restaurant, trying to recognize something.

"No, no way." He is shaking his head. "You would never, except for lunch, go out alone in public with me. You were much too afraid you might run into someone you knew and we'd be found out." He takes another drink of his wine.

"We ordered food for takeout and went to my place, watched movies, danced in the front room. Other than the few times we went out in a group of people from the hospital." The salad arrives before me he picks at it from my plate, switches our wine glasses as his is almost empty, already.

"By the way, the women at the hospital, are they worried about me, I mean where I went?'

He is busy eating the last of my salad. "Yes, they are very concerned. Cassie is worried sick."

Yes, my friend Cassie. She would be my best friend. I feel bad she doesn't know I am OK.

"Everyone knew we were friends. I very much doubt you told anyone, even Cassie, that we were more than that. Still I have had more than a few questions about where I think you are and what could have happened to you. Just tell them I am as worried as they are and try to avoid the subject."

"Does my husband have like the police looking for me or anything?"

"Well, no." What an asshole!

"Not even a missing person report?" I say, shocked.

"I may have given him the impression you left him."

"How did you do that?"

"The morning after you were made, I took your house keys, waited till he was gone to work and went in. Snatched a few of your things, made a mess of your drawers. Found your iPod, laptop and left. So he may be under the impression..." Does not finish, just smiles sheepishly at me. "Sorry, I had to do something to make it seem like you left willingly."

"Oh, I see. Still, you'd think after six years of marriage he would look for me. He was a dick though."

Eric laughs. "Yes, he is." The waitress removes the plate and asks if I want another drink, I look at Eric as I don't know the answer, finally saying no, I am fine, but would like a glass of water. I look out the windows to the endless cars driving by, stopping at the near light. A few groups of people walking by, some coming in the front door of Luigis's. I feel odd; all so familiar, all so strange.

Our waitress returns with our dinners and my water. All conversation stops when the plates hit the table. He eats like a teenage boy, ravaging the carbonara. Once in a while, he takes ravioli off my plate, devouring it whole. It is rather amusing to see him eat so much. I watch in silence for a bit.

"Wow, you have quite the appetite!" Finally he looks from the food to me, that boyish grin.

"Sorry, Margret, I have a very fast metabolism. It takes a lot to keep me going."

"I see we will have no problem covering up that I am not eating." I laugh at him.

"Not a problem." Eric eats our dinners without pause. Sits back relaxing, burps accordingly.

"Sorry, ate too fast."

I smile, feel almost normal for the moment. "That's OK, you seem to make even that kinda endearing." We both laugh.

We sit for a bit after dinner is over and plates are cleared, just talking. I realize that as long as he is near, I feel OK. He makes me calm.

"I need to use the restroom. You OK for that?" Me alone? I think I can.

"Yea, go ahead, I'll be fine." Not convinced, but he has to go, so...

He squeezes my hand and gives me a quick kiss to my cheek. "I'll be quick," he says, getting up, walking away rather fast. Does he have to go that bad, or is he just trying to return to me as soon as possible?

The space next to me seems very large now without Eric. His force no longer blocking me from all the life in the room, I quickly start to feel it in the air, life. Living warm humans everywhere. I pray that the waitress doesn't come back while he is gone. Rather not have a human and my freedom in such close proximity. Luckily I see him making his way back to me. He sits and takes my hand. "You OK?"

"Yes, OK, but nearly as soon as you left, I did feel, well, the life in the room."

"You did great, it will get easier with time. Promise." He is so reassuring and gentle with me. The bill arrives and is paid. Then we are off to the next adventure. Dancing.

When we arrive at the club, he asks if I want to feed a bit from him. I am rather reluctant because I know what that does to me, and sex in the car on a very busy city street doesn't seem like a good idea. I say no; should have rethought that.

After a short walk down the busy streets, we arrive at the bar. There is a wide set of cement stairs leading up the club. The tall double wood doors are flanked by six Greek Corinthian columns, three on each side. Above on the cornice engraved in a Greek style text: Chicago State Bank. Hanging below that, looking most out of place, a great neon sign reading Club Excalibur. It's a big old bank turned night club, cool.

It is very loud, and intimidating. People are rushing in all around us. Eric holds me close around my waist as we walk up the stairs to the doors.

As soon as the doors open, a great rush is unleashed. Noise, music, air thick with alcohol and loud conversations. Like a blast from fire storm. As we go a bit further inside, I am taken back by the humans, the smell, sweat, their heart beats louder to me than the music. I can't focus and start to pull back. Eric looks at me with great concern.

"You all right?"

"No, it's too much. I can't take it." Whimper.

I see Eric frantically look around. Spies someplace to take me, and moves me quickly to it. I close my eyes tight and let Eric's strong hand guide me. We are moving down a hallway? I only feel the blood heat in the air, not my feet on the ground. We stop. It's a dimly lit utility closet, smells of industrial cleaners and moist musty mops.

"Margret, Margret!" Holds my face, gently shaking me out of my blood lust. "I knew I should have fed you before we came in." Upset with himself. Takes off his jacket, unbuttons his shirt, pulling it off his left shoulder.

"Eric, I can't, not without..." He lets out a deep sigh.

"All right, that's all right," he says, reassuring me. "It's OK, Margret."

There is a long table covered with buckets and cleaning supplies. He swipes his forearm across it, wiping most to the floor. Clearing a space for me to sit. Eric swiftly takes off my underpants and opens his trousers. He brings me to the edge of the table, offers me his neck. No conversation or foreplay. He is ready as am I.

He penetrates me as I penetrate him. Immediately I am gone. My mouth and my sex covet him. Time lost in him. Nothing but pretty colors and powerful heat rising inside me. No club or loud music, no people, just Eric. I climax, but not even that will make me release my grip on him. I feel his climax moments after. Still lost in the rush, I refuse to let go. His hand pulls at my hair, trying to gain release, but I still need and hold quick to him. Then I feel the burn. I scream, letting go of his neck to do so. Once free, Eric quickly takes the burning silver off my wrist. Kissing the welts over and over, saying, "I'm sorry" the whole time. I am trying to catch my breath, recover. Sex, blood, burning.

"It's OK now," I insist. I grab his hair, pulling him up from his healing kisses to my wrist.

"I am OK." He kisses my face softly, holds me in both arms.

"I should have made you feed before we came in. The first time I take you out and I have already failed you." So angry with himself.

"No! I failed to know my own needs. It is I who is at fault, not you." I kiss him, try to comfort him.

"You are not strong enough to know your limits just yet. It won't happen again," he says with much commitment. Hands me my underwear, rights himself as I put them on.

"Shall we go home, or do you feel like you can handle this now?"

"You, just you, calm me. Your love and blood together, I am great now, really." Convincing, I hope. "I swear if I feel just a bit, I will tell you right way." I look pleadingly at him, his face softens.

"You swear!"

"YES, I swear!" My eyes pleading.

By the time we are back in the main room, I know that I will be fine, for a while anyway. I can hear the music now and although I still sense the blood and heart beats, smell the sweat, it is much lessened. I feel the music calling me now. Eric orders a Guinness and drinks half in his first swig.

"Are you all right? I didn't take too much, did I?"

"No, I am fine." He judges me briefly. "But you look like you want to dance." He seems much relieved. I realize I am dancing in place.

"I do!" Yelling over the noise. Grab his arm as he is trying to drink the last of his beer before he leaves the bar.

Finally we are off to the dance floor.

Every song seems to be one I love even if I don't recognize it. One I must dance to. I am so happy, full of freedom, and my Eric's loving blood still flowing inside me. We stay on the floor song after song. We dance well together. He moves with the songs but stays close, touching me no matter how fast the beat, even if it is just his hand touching mine. I know why he does it; it still feels nice.

We break only for Eric to get another beer. He insists he is fine, just thirsty and then we dance again. Only once we danced to a slow song. The way he held me to him, moved his hands over me excited me so. I was worried I would drop him to the floor and take him right there without a thought. When another slow one came on, I pull him, most unwillingly, off the dance floor.

"That was a good song," he complains.

"I know, but you make me hot when you hold me like that." He smiles wide. It is wonderful to see him happy, enjoying himself.

"Are you ready to feed? It's getting late and there should be someone easy..." He looks around the still crowed room.

"Yes, you lead." He does, taking me back towards the front doors. Only then do I see the dark stairs leading down off the front lobby. A small red neon sign blinks creepy on and off above the doorway. The Dungeon.

"Wait." I hold him back from his decent. People are squeezing and pushing by us to get in, out, up or down. The lobby is very crowded. A rush of humans.

"What, Margret?"

"I just got out of my dungeon." He laughs and takes my hand firmly in his.

"I assure you, this is not as pleasant as the one you just left. You'll see."

There is a long hall, obnoxious strobe lights along the walls. The music is even louder than upstairs, metal, I think they call it. Not my cup of tea. People are yelling at each other in conversations that make no sense at all because no one can hear what the other is saying.

Several rooms line the hallway. I smell pot and cigarettes, stale beer, humans. As I walk by, I notice the dimly lit interiors, beaten old couches and large armchairs, each full of people doing all sorts of wild things, making out, smoking weed, believe a few were doing coke in one room. None looked appealing, even to a dead woman. Just old filth. We near the end of the hall, even darker here as the strobe light is out, thankfully. I don't know if it is the human scent, blood rushing in the air that is making me sick or those damn strobe lights. But I am quickly getting to the place I was when we first arrived. I squeeze Eric's hand and tug. Eyes pleading.

"I know, I know. Just a sec." The last room has only a few people in it. Most notably two girls sitting on a big grayish tattered couch. Eric gives me a look, nodding over in their direction. Knowing no human could hear him in this noise, he speaks in a normal tone of voice.

"That one is really drunk, I'll distract her friend and you feed on the blonde. Be careful, keep focused as much as you can on where and what you are doing. When you feel me tug or pinch you, you have to stop!" I nod in agreement and we make our way to the couch. I think I can stop myself as Eric is still running in my veins, cooling my hunger.

Eric smiles, engaging the semi-coherent one with ease. The scraggly blonde is bent over, scarcely holding a beer in hand. Swaying from side to side, like she's on a ship somewhere in very rough seas. I sit down, squeezing myself between the two girls. Eric sits at the end of the couch next to the girl with the bright red hair. In this light her hair almost glows. The girls are both dressed much the same way. Short short skirts, camies, multi-colored tennies. Odd; they have exchanged one shoe with each other. The redhead has a neon-pink flowered shoe on her right foot, black, red and green design on the left. Her friend has the opposite arrangement. Must be a new girlfriend thing.

The blonde girl is pretty much incoherent; she thinks I am her redhead friend for a moment. Then realizes I am not and inarticulately mumbles something about 'who the fuck are you?' Eric has laid on his full charm and has the redhead's full attention. After a few minutes, he says, "Go on, Margret." I hear him clearly, but the redhead thinks Eric is talking to her. Repeats "What, what did you say?" over and over loudly in his ear.

I feel oddly nervous, my first feed in public. I lean over the blonde and even though she tries weakly to brush me off, I get my teeth into her neck without much difficulty, and no one seems to notice. Suppose we just looked like two girls making out, nothing to turn any heads down here. I feed, the music fades into the distance, lost in the liquid. It seems like just seconds that I have had her in my grip but sense Eric pinching my thigh. Time, I have noticed, is not so good for me when I feed. I don't let go right away, but feel the pressure increase dramatically. Painfully. I let her go reluctantly, but I do it on my own. I lay my head back for a second or two, recovering myself. Stare at the black ceiling. The colors I see in the black behind my closed eyes are oddly flowing into the ceiling, fading.

Then I notice Eric is hotly frenching the redhead. His hand up her skirt, rubbing her ass. She's wrapped herself around him, lustful grinding. I am not happy! I take hold of his hand and pull him off her with all my force. He stumbles off the couch and looks at me, shocked.

"Margret?" His eyes full of questions. I grab, most indelicately, his crotch; he is rock hard. Now I am really pissed off!

"Let's go! Now!" I yell at him. He makes some excuse to the redhead about pissing off his girlfriend; she calls me a bitch. By this time I am out the doorway. He is quickly chasing after me, calling me and begging me to slow down. I knock more than a few off their drunken feet as I make my way to the stairs. Eric is trying desperately to catch up to me over the bodies I have left in my wake.

I am outside in the fresh air well before him. I walk quickly, almost running down the street to the car, wait for him to arrive.

"Shit, Margret! What the hell is wrong with you? Don't ever run away from me like that!" He is mad, confused, out of breath.

"Just take me home," I demand.

He unlocks the car and opens the door for me to get in. I push his hand away. "I've got it." Slam the door behind me. Not sure how I could go from blood contentment to this rage so rapidly. I am quite sure he is wondering the same. Eric gets in; looks much confused, shaking his head.

"Margret, please tell me what the hell that was all about?"

"You were making out with her!" I yell as pissy as I can. He starts to laugh, but thinks better of it, stifles it.

"That is called distracting her, so YOU could FEED, Margret!" Still he is just holding back his amusement.

"Your cock was hard!" I bite back.

"Holy shit." Still has a smirk on his face and the longer it's there, the more my anger rises. He finds my distress entertaining? "Sorry." He slams himself back in the seat, quite irritated. Then he leans over and shakes his head in disbelief. "Amazing! It's OK for me do a guy so you can feed but I can't kiss a girl for a minute so you can. Seriously, Margret?" He may be right, but somehow it just doesn't seem the same to me. She made me jealous, that guy made me hot, hungry. Besides that was before, before I feel this way about him.

"Just take me home." Stare out the window at the drunk people walking by, wait for him to start the car.

"Fine!" Roughly turns the ignition, grinds to a start. He drives like a maniac all the way back to the house. Each mile spent in heated silence. The trip home seems longer than the one into the city, even though he is driving much faster.

When we finally turn up our driveway, I leap out of the car, demanding entry to the house. I stomp down to my dungeon well before he has even taken the key out of the back door. Tear my dress and shoes off, tossing them into the dark. Fall into bed, wrapping myself in the grey quilt. Eric comes down timidly, stands before me, looks like he doesn't know what to say. So he says nothing.

"Put my binding on!" I demand.

"No, I am here. You don't need them."

"Put them on." Insisting. He gets it. I don't want him here. He looks sad for a split second then quickly back to angry.

"Fine," he snaps. "Really, Margret, it was just a stupid kiss." He puts on my leather straps. Sighs. "Markus warned me about taking a woman." Angrily.

"What the fuck is that supposed to mean!" I shout at him.

"It means…" He stops, thinks. "Let's talk tomorrow when you wake, that is what that means!" He kisses me uncaringly on my check. "I love only you, Margret, you should understand at least that much by now," he says sadly.

As soon as he's gone I regret sending him off, nearly call up to him, but it is very late. He must need to rest by now, besides I am not willing to concede. So I will try to sleep as well. Fuming and crying at the same time.

Chapter Eleven

I sleep most of the day undisturbed. Think its Saturday. Yes? When I wake it looks to be late afternoon. Still Eric is not here. I sit up, arrange my cushions and chains. Notice my iPod, headphones and my laptop are lying at the foot of my bed. Also a note. A charge card falls out when I unfold it.

Margret,

We will talk when I get home. Here is your music and computer. If you like, shop online, you are in need of new clothes, shoes, whatever you want. You can read Markus's journal as well, but think a break from that would do you well.

> *See you soon,*
> *Eric.*

Wow, no love, just, nothing. I really pissed him off. He pissed me off first!

I decide to shop, I can do that. It will keep my mind off his absence and the way I lost it on him, again. I turn on my laptop and start to browse. Victoria's Secret seems a good place to start. An hour or so passes. I am looking at all the nice online stores, buying everything that takes my fancy, and a few things I don't really like but know Eric would. All express shipping. Spent tons of money. Pass time shopping, listening to music, and trying to not to think. Manage to have one recurring thought; in retrospect I am ashamed of my behavior.

I see the lights of his car pulling up the drive. My stomach goes into knots. Wonder what he is going to say; is he still very angry with me? I take off my headphones and wait. Hear him in the kitchen, opening the fridge, then the basement door. Every step he takes fills me with anxiety.

Simply "Evening, Margret." Eric sits at the foot of the bed, back to me.

"Hi." Try to smile, not sure how well it came off. Eric cannot see it no matter how unconvincing it was.

Minutes of silence. Both of us waiting for the other to start.

"I am sorry, Eric, I don't know what's wrong with me. I overreacted, freaked out on you. I just can't seem to control my emotions." I wait for his reply. "I ended an amazing evening by going ballistic."

Eric comes to sit up next to me, puts his arm lightly around my shoulders. "Your emotions are still all over the place, and, well, I am not used to..." Doesn't seem to want to finish his thought.

"Not used to what?" I ask.

"Well, things like that would never have been an issue when I was with Markus. Men think differently about that stuff. That is what I meant by he warned me. Women are different. It's been a very very long time since I was in a real relationship with a woman, well just you, before. I forget." Seems unsure of himself, but quickly recovers. "Nevertheless, like I said, it was just a distraction, I can't help it if my body reacted. You have to be able to separate sex from our connection. They are not comparable." Firm, but not so mad.

"I do, just I...like you being with that guy was different, it made me hot, for sure, but I didn't feel, well, threatened by another man. Not sure why, I just didn't."

He pulls my legs over his, finally really holding me in his arms. Feels good to back in his warm embrace.

"I think I do." Eric waits, thinking before he speaks. "Let's just say you didn't have much of an ego, Margret. Your husband only made it worse. You mentioned to me more than once how he would flirt and fawn over other women right in front of you. To the point you were embarrassed by him. Didn't pay much attention to you either. He is an asshole. Treated you more like property than the woman he loved. You were insecure, especially around him."

I remember that now, and wonder why I stayed with Joe for so long. Suppose it helped that we didn't see each other much. I had the afternoon shift three or four times a week, and he worked construction, often gone most of the weekend. Then Joe would go out with the guys after work, leaving me alone much of the time.

The years go by too quickly.

"I will try to control my temper." I kiss him apologetically on his cheek.

I wait, unsure that I should tell him how I am feeling, but decide to anyway.

"Eric, I'm sure you are used to having whoever you like, but...no women, well, not here in our bed."

Wait for a reaction, thinking maybe he'll be angry. Just listens.

"I would be afraid you'd want her more, or find her more attractive than me." I look shyly up at him.

"Margret, I do, or don't do, what you want, what makes you happy. If you don't want to have sex with another woman, I will not bring a woman to our bed. Or a man, for that matter. But you can't be picky when it comes to feeding. If I need to use my, whatever, to distract for you to safely feed, well, you'll just have to get used to it. It means nothing. Understand?"

"I understand that. I just feel..." I stop. Eric takes my head, turns to face him.

"As for me finding another woman more, well, more anything, Margret, not happening. No woman is more beautiful or desirable to me. No one ever could give me the pleasure you do. You know what pleasure you give me? No competition possible, from anyone." He pulls my head back, our foreheads touching. "I love you. Got it?"

"Yes," I mumble over his mouth. Take it. I break our kisses, curious. "Why did you pick a woman? A man would have been easier, less emotional."

"Women are my preference," he opens my robe, "although I have learned to enjoy men as well, but that is just..." He holds my breasts over his face, kissing, sucking them hotly. "Nothing can replace the comfort of a woman's arms." I can hardly discern what he's said as Eric's smothering his face, his words lost in my breasts. I laugh aloud.

"Those are not my arms, Eric." I feel his smile on my skin.

His hand moves up the inside of my thigh, rubs fingers into the wet folds and presses them inside me. Thrust slowly in and out a few times, adds. "Neither is this but I want both."

Think we are going to have great makeup sex now.

Chapter Twelve

The next week went along rather uneventfully. I was out of my bindings most of the time. Eric left me alone very little. Although if he was gone, Eric still thought it best. My cravings could be unexpected. I would feel all right and then suddenly I thirsted more than I could ignore. So I know he is right. I need to be stronger still. Oddly I still spent most of my time in my 'room' with my laptop and music. Only going up when he prompted me to watch a movie or just have a fire. It feels womb-like to me now. Three walls tight around the big bed, all the cushions, pillows, quilts, hiding me. Maybe when I am completely free of my bindings, I will feel differently, but for now the vampire likes her dungeon.

I bleed Eric twice. His blood satisfies me longer than anyone's. Our love-making as intense as the first time. I drank from another homeless person mid-week. I think Eric felt he may have rushed taking me out to feed a bit and now was being rather delicate with me. Honestly, although I had a lot of fun that night, my emotions and food swings are hard to predict so small controlled doses are good for me now as well.

Eric brought the homeless man to me on Wednesday, late evening. That's where he must have been all afternoon, I suppose, finding me someone. He came down only to take off my bindings and give me a quick kiss. Just saying he had to go back upstairs. For about an hour, I heard them in the kitchen, not much talking, just cooking and eating. I could smell eggs and bacon. When they finally came down, Eric was all but carrying him. Seems Eric not only fed him, but gave him drink as well. He was conscious, unsteady, and rather placid when I took him in my arms.

I felt a bit more in control of the feed. Yes, Eric had to prompt me to stop, but only once. Let's just say it was a very strong prompt. Afterwards, Eric gave him a blanket and took him back to the underpass where he'd found him.

Our homeless friend was well fed, warmer, and, yes, a few pints lower when Eric left him.

We went out to 'linner' as we called it a few times. Linner is after lunch, before dinner. There were fewer people for me to deal with that way. I was slowly getting more comfortable being around people. Depending on my hunger, their heart beats, hot scent, was either there, annoying, or almost all there was. As always he ate his meal and mine with great vigor.

Packages from my online shopping spree were arriving most every day. Eric would bring them down to me after I woke and enjoyed seeing what I'd purchased; some surprised him, like the black knee-high lace-up platform boots, thought they were very hot. Nothing the old Margret would have worn. I got a few negligees, which he liked very much. Said they were unnecessary as I didn't need to seduce him and would not be on long enough to enjoy them.

When Saturday arrived, he asked if I feel good enough to go out to feed again. I do. "You know, those boots you bought gave me an idea."

"I am sure I know what idea that was." I smirk at him. Eric is lying next to me, arms laced behind his head, looking at the ceiling of my cubby.

"No, well, yes, but that is not what I meant. I think I know where I want to take you tonight, but I have to do something first." He sits up. I know what that means.

"Will you be gone long?" Putting the bindings on my wrists, again. It is late afternoon, I have only been up for a few, and now he's off on some errand.

"No, not long. Do you have your charger?"

"Yea, right here, I'll be fine."

"Good. When I get back, you come up and get ready to go out, K?"

"You sure?" He kisses my forehead sweetly as he likes to do.

"Sure I'm sure." Does he sound sure?

Rushes off, in his car and gone in less than a minute. What's the rush?

I sit, arms and legs folded together, looking like a grumpy little girl, I suppose. I just wake and he leaves me. Think to read some of Markus's writing, but find it a little heavy reading for me sometimes. I opt for a movie on my laptop till he gets home. Swing Time with Fred and Ginger. Music and dance; that should take my mind off anything.

I am halfway through when I hear the back door open. He rushes right down, bags in hand but will not show me what he has bought. Releases me. "Come upstairs when you're ready." I finish watching an amazing dance number and shut off my laptop. Want to see what Eric has been up to.

When I get to the bedroom, the first thing I see is the boots standing quite well on their own in front of the bed.

"Margret?" he calls from the bathroom.

"Yes, I'm here." Like last week my outfit is laid out on the bed. Black jeans, a white lace tank and a leather jacket. I pick up the jeans as he comes in. "Don't you think these are going to be too small for me?"

"Nope, your size, just tight." Smiles, he is a bad man. "Just get dressed; do your eyes dark like you did last week, only darker." Kisses my cheek softly. "You looked hot."

"Oh, OK. you dress me now?"

"Sorry, don't mean to be bossy, but we are going to a biker bar and you have to fit in. Although you will never look like any woman that goes to a biker bar, but you will have the eye, and the neck, of every guy in there." See what he is up to now.

"Did you eat?"

"Went to a drive-through on my way back from shopping."

I sigh, go to the bath to get all made up like a hot biker chick. I don't really want to get dressed. I have become accustomed to being naked except for my robes. The tight jeans look very uncomfortable to me. Oh, well. To my surprise they are not that bad, stretchy fabric. Eric must be downstairs waiting, so I put on the killer boots and make my way to him.

He is sitting at the island in the kitchen, keys in hand when I walk in. "WOW, Margret, you look hot, so bad!"

Eric is wearing much the same as me, tight black jeans, boots, black tee and a leather jacket. He has slicked all his hair back into a pony tail. Very handsome, too handsome. I roughly pull him by the collar of his leather, picking him up off the chair as I do. Give him a deep hot kiss. He goes for my backside, pulling my leg up around his waist, holds me tight to him.

"Those boots make me," he grinds his full jeans into me, "well, you'll pay for them later." He bites my neck and growls playfully. "We should get going; it is a bit of a drive."

"How far is it?"

"About 45, no good biker bar near the city. Mostly freeway though."

We take off, listening to his iPod as he has heavy rock and metal, wants to get in the mood. I try to ignore it and look out the window at the passing view. Mostly freeway, as Eric said. When we finally get off, we are in a small town, looks to be, well, not the rich part of town. Walmart is the centerpiece. We drive out a bit more from there. He is following his GPS closely now, turning down one badly lit street after another.

Finally slowing to a crawl when we near a clearing in the roadside brush. That must be it. Not much better than an oversized shack, gravel parking lot. Choppers—what an original name for a biker bar.

"Really?" I look over to him, put off. "I would not have been caught dead in a place like that, ever!"

Eric laughs. "Well then, Margret, guess it is good that you are because we're going in."

Reaches over and releases my belt, kissing my cheek as he does. "It will be fun. Just stick close to me. At least for the first part of the evening. After we get a few guys drunk enough, you'll have your dinner. K?"

"Why can't you just bring me someone? Why the biker bar?" I moan, irritated.

"It will be an experience for you, something you would never have done before. Markus and I used to go and they can be real crazy, fun. Besides, you won't run into anyone you know here. Just trust me and follow my lead."

"OK, but I don't like this." Reluctantly I get out and we go in, Eric nearly pulling me across the lot.

When we walk in, the whole place comes to a stop. Everyone looks at us as if we were two green aliens invading their space. I wrap both arms around Eric, trying not to look terrified. All the men look mean; so do the woman for that matter.

"Margret, loosen up." Under his breath.

"Where did you find this place?" I whisper to him, forcing a smile.

"Google." He pulls my arms off and takes my hand, walks confidently to the long bar to our right. The bartender waiting for us.

"Two tap lites, tall, thanks." Acts as if he fits right in. We don't. No amount of leather could make us look like we really belong here. Still he exudes confidence. Everyone still looking at us although now they are pretending not to. Resuming some soft chatter, most I hear. 'Who the hell are they?' and 'City assholes'; stuff like that. The beers arrive and Eric more than pays for them in cash. "Keep it." Takes a huge slug then asks the bartender, "How much for darts?"

"Three a game." Eric slaps a 20 on the bar.

"That should cover a few." The bartender slips it into his pocket as he goes to the other side of the bar. Returns with two set of darts.

"Have at it," he says.

Eric downs more of his beer. I feel so out of place, I decide to drink mine. Uck, tastes like shit.

"Margret, take it easy, you'll puke."

Coughing. "Just want to look like, well, normal."

He laughs at my failed attempt to fit in. "You'll look like a lightweight if you puke after one sip." He takes my hand, leading me to the dart board at the back of the bar.

There are a few round tables across from the bar then a pool table; the darts are all the way in back. I feel like a specimen under glass, everyone watching as we walk by. There are four guys playing pool. Stop their game, stare suspiciously as we make our way passed them.

I know I am a vampire, strong and deadly, though at the moment all I feel is intimidated. Not Eric, he walks tall, giving them a polite nod.

"OK, you know how to play this?" Handing my darts over.

"Sort of. I played a few times in college, but not well."

"Just hit the numbers on the chalk board, you know 20's, 19's." He goes over and puts an M on one side and E on the other. "Try not to play too well, Margret."

"Not a problem," I mumble.

"Your eyesight and aim will be much better than before. Stand here." He points down at a worn and dirty piece of duct tape on the floor. I line up my shot, just trying to hit the board really. Toss it; bulls eye! "Crap!" he grumbles.

"Lucky shot?" Shrugging my shoulders.

"Try harder to miss, Margret, don't want to look like pros."

We play for a while. I keep getting good shots, basically creaming him. Eric is a bit teed off. I take to squinting my eyes nearly shut, that works better. Eric drinks my beer and his.

"I'll be right back." Returning to the bar for two more.

The pool game is over and two of the four pool players come near to watch us play; the other two guys sit at the end of the bar.

Eric takes his shot, wraps up the game winning by a hair. Only because I let him mind you.

"I promise I'll play worse next game."

"Please." He gives me a kiss on my cheek and goes to erase our scores.

The two pool guys are still standing nearby. Eric asks without even looking at them if they would like a game. The skinny tall one jumps on it with a resounding, "Ya!" Scraggliest beard and long dirty blond hair to match. The other one is a big guy, just big. Yes, overweight, beer belly, but broad and tall, clean shaven with thin short hair. Both have on band tees with faded designs, black well-worn leathers, faded blue jeans. Eric introduces us. Mark is the big one, and Kevin the scraggy. Eric goes to the bar and returns with more darts and two beers for our new friends.

"On me," Eric says, quickly getting in their good graces. Swear he could charm a snake.

I play a few games, making sure I aim for the wall, occasionally trying to hit the board. They are both real good, must play here a lot. Mark seems to have the best game. Eric is feeding them drinks and shots the whole while. After a few games, I bow out and sit by a ledge on the back wall scattered with their drinks and empties. Waiting for mine. I am starting to feel the hunger that is too strong to push aside.

"You doing OK?" Eric asks me.

"OK for now, but soon."

Whispering in my ear, "Start flirting with Kevin more."

Both of them are talking to me, flirting increasing with every drink. I encourage it and Eric pretends not to notice. Although I know he is paying close attention. He drank, but for every one Eric had, they had two, shots interspersed. They were all best buddies, swearing and hitting backs when they got a good shot. I can't pay much attention to their conversation. My thoughts center on feeding now. When and how, knew who.

They are starting yet another game; Eric gives me an 'I'm sorry' look. Finally Kevin says he has to hit the head. The bathrooms are down a hallway right next to us between the end of the bar and the back room where we were. Kevin slams down the last of his beer and staggers toward the hall. Eric comes over quickly.

"Don't you have to go by now?" Winks.

Mark is about to shoot and I announce that I am 'going to take a piss.'

Thought that sounded more authentic than ladies room. It only made Eric laugh, Mark paid no attention, his eyes trying to focus on his shot. I make my way down the hall just in time to catch Kevin coming out of the john. Give him a sexy smile.

"Hey, you play a real good game," lay on more faux sex, "don't you?"

He moves in closer, not doing too well at standing. "I do, I do, pretty lady."

If not for my hunger, his nearness and touch would have had me running in the other direction. As it is, all I really notice are heart beats and salty human flesh, both very appealing. Slip my arms lightly around his neck and pull him in, kissing his sweaty neck a few times for good measure. I nearly have to support him; my kiss seems to have put him over the edge.

I tighten my arms around him, bite in, I feel little resistance. Now I have to hold him up. I am really hungry. My thoughts go into clouds immediately.

If Eric was supposed to come and stop me, he didn't get a chance. Big Mark takes a hold of my shoulder, pulling me out of my feed. Kevin staggers. I lean him on the wall.

"Hey, sweetheart, got some of that for me?" I turn around, making sure to wipe my mouth just in case. I look over Mark's shoulder to see Eric near the doorway to the hall. I don't think he means for me to take on this goliath but I look inquisitively at him.

"Hey, what the hell is going on here?" He rushes towards us, angrily yelling. Pushes past Mark knocking him into the wall. Grabs my arm. I get it, mad boyfriend. "Fuck, I can't take you out anywhere!" Yelling at me, he drags me towards the bar. "You are such a whore, we're leaving!" Roughly pulling me through the bar and out the front door.

I soon wish we had parked closer to it.

Eric starts laughing at his display. We are not even half way across the gravel lot when from behind us Mark bellows, "HEY, asshole, that's no way to treat a lady!"

He is right behind us. Instead of trying to defuse things, Eric gets right in Mark's face, shouting back at him, "It's none of your fucking business! Stay out of it!"

That doesn't help. Things escalate quickly. What starts out as a big boy shoving match rapidly turns into a fist fight. Eric, although not as big as Mark, is a good fighter, seems to be handling himself well. Fists are flying, sometimes hitting their target, sometimes missing. Almost right away the two other men that were playing pool rush out of the bar, seemingly excited that there is a fight. Skinny Kevin is notably missing.

One of them goes to join in, the other stays closer to the bar to watch. I can't stand here without helping; that's two against one! Eric catches my eye. I must have looked wild, ready to attack because Eric screams at me, "Margret, stay out of this!" His eyes dark, warning. I stand still, arms folded across my chest, fuming.

Even as the second guy joins in trying to take Eric down, he is still holding his own. He is fast, strong, and not nearly as drunk as the others. Eric avoids getting grabbed from behind by the new guy; instead turns just in time to hit his chin, knocking him back long enough for Eric to return his attentions to Mark.

Eric is getting hit way too much for my taste; each time I feel it. I can smell Eric's blood hit the air at the first cut. It's taking all I have to just stand here when all I want to do is rip into some necks.

Out of my peripheral vision, I see the fat biker guy near the bar moving toward the three of them. Eric is still in control of the fight and he wasn't going to stand for that. Well, I am not going to stand for this. I can't control my anger, don't even try. I leap onto his shoulders just as he passes by me. Wrapping my arms tightly around his neck, choking him, I sink my teeth right into his jugular. Fuck a slower bleed, I want him down.

He tries to reach behind to pull me off. I encircle his hips as best I can with my legs squeezing hard. He doesn't have a chance.

Blood rushes into my mouth like never before. Adrenalin making the flow faster, helping me bring him quickly to his knees. Still I hold tight with limbs and teeth. Even in my blood lust, I hear Eric's voice. Like a lighthouse in deep fog, it breaks through.

"MARGRET STOP!" he yells over and over until I let go. Drop my feed into the gravel. Still a beating heart, but slow. I try to clear my head. Shake it off. I look over to the fight.

Eric is face down in the gravel. Mark is kicking him repeatedly in the ribs. Shit, I can hear his bones cracking! Eric's painful cries drive me to such madness, I can't hold it.

I rise. With all my power, I run at the asshole. With both hands I shove his chest, pushing him away from Eric. Surprising even me, Mark flies across the lot, only stopping when he hits the line of Harleys parked several feet away. Eric already took care of the other guy; he is staggering around in a bloody daze. Looks like a broken nose.

Trying to pick Eric up with care, I slip myself under his right arm, lifting him to his feet. I have to take most of his weight as I walk him over as quickly as I can manage to the car. Eric makes painful groans with every step.

"Margret, did you kill him?" He can hardly talk, he can hardly breathe. Wheezing, broken ribs? I heard them cracking.

"No, but drank him well," I say spitefully.

I take the keys out of his jacket and open the passenger door. Help him in as gently as I can, but everything I do, every movement, results in a painful cry.

Briefly scan the lot as I walk around the car, no man standing. A few more people have come out of the bar to assist the beaten. I get in and take off as fast as I can. Dust clouds and gravel flinging behind us.

"You know how to get home?"

"Home?" I shout at him. "You need to go to the hospital. God knows how many broken ribs you have, and a ton of bad gashes. You're in pretty bad shape, Eric."

"No. Margret, home." He tries to sound forceful but can't do much more than groan his demand.

"No a hospital, that's..." Cuts me off, managing to raise his voice this time.

"Margret, you're a freaking nurse! Just go home, please." The last of his energy spent, Eric closes his eyes, drifts off painfully.

I make my way back to the freeway, surprised that I remember the way. At 95mph I manage to get us back home in under 25 minutes.

Roll into the drive a bit too fast, nearly taking out the mailbox. Pull up as close to the side door as possible.

"What key is the house key?" I ask, holding them out for him to look at. Eric tries to open his eyes; one is already nearly swollen shut. He fumbles through them, picking a gold square top one. I notice his hand is riddled with cuts. I open the door first then go around to help him out of the car. More pain, but I have to get him inside. Much like before, I put his arm over my shoulders and lift him.

"Your room. The first aid stuff is down by the washer." Every word difficult.

Slowly, one by one I take him down the steps and lay him on the bed. I quickly go to the other side of the stairs, turn on the overhead bulb. The washer and dryer are along the wall adjacent to my bed, above that, shelves with towels, tarps, and yes, a big first aid kit. Grab a few wash cloths and go to the utility sink to wet them, returning to him as fast as I could.

He is out of it. I am afraid for him.

"Eric, Eric."

Moans, "Yea, I'm still here."

"I need to wash and dress your wounds. Sorry if I hurt you but..."

"Margret, you need to give to me first. It will help me heal faster."

"Oh, yea. OK. Good idea."

Find the giving ring on the small ledge and put it on. I sit carefully next to him, put my wrist near his lips, and cut into it. Raising his head, he drinks. I would like to say in this horrible moment, with Eric in such pain, I did not react, but I did. I feel my heat throbbing the whole time he feeds. Squeeze my eyes shut, my legs clench together in a fruitless effort to lessen the desire. I do nothing about these feelings, of course. It took a long time after he stopped feeding before it did.

Still I go into full nurse mode. Make an ice pack for his left eye. He holds it weakly while I wash the cuts on his face and forehead. A few needed butterfly bandages as they are rather deep. The kit is good, has most everything I needed.

Now the ribs. I lift him to take off the jacket, prompting a fresh round of painful groans. I decided to cut off his tee shirt rather than try to get it over his head. As I remove it, it reveals black and blue marks, cuts everywhere. That ass had serious biker boots on and they did a real number on Eric.

I feel as gently as I can at his ribs. Maybe two broken, a few more fractured? Bruised for sure. Without an X-ray I can't be sure. Still, I don't like the sound of his breathing; if he's punctured a lung, it could collapse. That would be very bad. I wish I had a stethoscope so I could hear if both lungs are taking in air normally or if one sounds weaker. Then I remember my hearing is vastly improved. May not be a stethoscope, but better than nothing.

"Eric, I have to listen to your lungs. I'll press as softly as I can."

He smiles down at me, weakly, "K."

I lay my ear to his chest, moving around, trying to discern if the wheezing is from the bruising or a puncture. I did hit a few bad spots and he let me know it.

"Ouch Margret!" Snaps at me.

"Sorry, I have to hear." Not sure, doesn't sound like a puncture. I will have to keep close watch on his breathing for a few days at least. With much effort he runs his hand over my cheek. It's freezing cold from holding the ice pack.

"You are my angel, Margret." Eric looks at me with such love. I take the hand on my face and kiss the cool palm, turn it over, kissing each battered knuckle tenderly. I do the same for the other hand. I taste his blood on my lips though it makes me feel sad, not wild with need and passion like it always does.

Need to wrap his ribs now.

"OK, hard part," I say, sitting up and getting the ace bandages out of the kit.

"The other parts weren't?" Eric whines.

"I'll be as careful as I can." He is exhausted and I know he just wants to sleep, but lets me hold him, lifting him to a sitting position. I wrap the bandages around his ribs tight, but not too tight. Sill he complains the whole time.

"All done."

"Great. Can I sleep now?"

"Do you have any pain killers in here?" I ask, rummaging around the kit.

"No. And why didn't you think of that before you put me through all this?"

I look up from my search, shrug. "Sorry, I got kind of distracted when you..." I don't finish. He knows.

"Sorry about that, promise to make it up to you. Did you have trouble with my blood all over?"

"I could smell it even as you fought, but the taste just now made me sad." I finally start to cry. "I can't stand to see you hurt." Think I have been holding the tears back the whole time. Eric wipes a tear away but can't hold his focus long. I shake it off, need to get him something for the pain.

"Advil?"

"Upstairs, left kitchen cabinet, near window." I cover him with the quilt and run up to get the bottle and some water.

I stand before the kitchen window, drawn to the dark. Advil in one hand, empty glass in other. Just these few moments away from him and anger starts to take hold of all my thoughts. I can feel it boiling inside my chest. The darkness carries me off. I begin to plot.

Could I take off in the car, go back to the bar, maybe he is still there? How could I find Mark? I would love to drink that asshole dry.

"Margret?"

Crap! Eric's call wakes me. Not only have I made him wait with my little revenge fantasy but made him yell up to me. That hurt, I know. I fill his glass from the fridge and speed down the stairs.

"Sorry, I got distracted.' I hand him six. He looks at me, questioning my count. "It's OK, just like taking prescription strength." Help him take them, two at a time, and drink his water.

"Sleep with me." Whispers.

I take off my boots, clothes, crawl under the quilt next to him.

"Spread them," he says, touching my leg.

"Eric, you can't be serious!"

"Oh, I wish I was able. No, just want to lie between your legs, on you."

"Oh, OK." Carefully swing my right leg over his head and around to his back. putting one of the small throw pillows on my hip. He lays his head and painfully snuggles to me. Eric's hair is still pulled back, I pull it out and run my hand through, freeing it. For once this evening a soft moan of comfort escapes him.

I curl both legs up, careful not to hurt him, cradling him in them. I feel like a tender but fierce mother protecting him; at the same time, he lies so close to my heat. Feels like when you get butterflies in your stomach, I tingle there. Didn't think it possible to feel both so powerfully, yet here I am looking at him finally asleep, overwhelmed by them.

I try to rest, but my mind will not let me.

After a few hours of sitting awake, my rage rises to such a level I can hardly contain it. That asshole Mark did this to my Eric. I wanted so to run, and run until I find him and beat him like he did Eric. Then when he is bloody, feed until he goes cold. Every wheeze, every cough, from Eric only enrages me more.

I could drive back to the bar, somehow track him down. Maybe I could smell Mark's blood and like a hound track it. I go over and over what happened. Visualizing the whole fight in my mind. Repeatedly coming up with another silly, yet at the time plausible, way to find him, kill him.

By the time morning is showing in the window, I am ready to leap out of my skin. Only then do I realize why Eric wanted to be lying where he is, now flipped on his other side, tucked between my legs, my thigh his pillow. If I were to move, to leave, it would not be without disturbing him.

Such a clever keeper, my Eric.

Chapter Thirteen

I was very worried. Eric slept half the day away, as did I. When he woke, he woke me as well.

"Margret, have any more of the Advil?" I am groggy but slide carefully out from under him, get more water and give him six more. Propping him up a bit to take them. He is still in a lot of pain. I don't know with his accelerated healing just how long he will be in this shape. A normal human would take weeks to recover from a beating like this, especially if he has broken ribs. I lay my ear on his chest, moving my head around and listen to his lungs.

"What are you doing?" I look up at him and am happy to see his smile.

"Just checking your lungs."

Now looking at the cuts and swelling around his eye. Looks much the same as it did last night; normally a black eye the day after looks worse as the hemorrhaging spreads. Same with the cuts, not much better but not any worse. I wanted to inspect the bruising on his ribs but that would mean removing the bandages—too painful. Decide to look at them later.

"You still look like hell." Inspecting the long scrape on his chin.

"Thanks, love you too." I smile and kiss his chin.

"I do love you, just wish you wouldn't get yourself in such trouble." He tries to laugh, only it hurts and comes out as a coughing sound.

"I could have handled it. They got the jump on me when I saw you on that guy, your teeth in his neck. I thought you were going to kill him."

"I wanted to," I interjected.

"When I turned to go for you, to stop you, Mark kicked me, hard, in my back and I went down, face first." Now he rubs the scrape in his chin. "After that he just kept kicking like a mad man. I couldn't get up."

"I'm sorry but that guy was going to join in the fight. You can't handle three guys and I was not going to stand there and do nothing...so I did what I knew." I smile innocently at him. Eric takes my hand and kisses it.

"Well then, you saved my ass. And shit, Margret, you were a wild thing." He seems most pleased at my aggression. "You were crouched down letting go of the guy you were feeding on, but then you looked over at me. Shit, your eyes were black as night. Then you leaped like a freaking panther. Knocked that asshole across the lot, landing him in the bikes... It was crazy." He is smiling and shaking his head in disbelief.

"You seem proud of me, thought you might be mad."

"No, no, you did, like you said, what came naturally to you. You protected me. Thank you." He tries to lean over to kiss me but it only makes him groan and sit back. I kneel, place my hands on either side of him, tilt my head up for his kiss. It is soft, full of love.

"Should I give to you again?" I ask, reluctant. Not sure I can give again without, well, fully bonding. Still feel the unanswered need.

"No, not yet let's wait a bit, when I am stronger." Again I feel like he is reading my mind.

"Was it hard for you?" he simply adds.

"Yea, a bit. I didn't think... I was so upset and worried about you, I didn't expect to need you so badly. Sorry."

"Don't apologize, that is part of the feelings that come with giving. For you and me it's very strong. I won't put you through that again without loving you, OK? We'll wait. You may need to be on top but." That mischievous look he gets when he says anything about sex all over his battered face."

"I will assist you any way I can, Eric." I kiss him on his forehead like he always does to me.

"You should rest more, OK?"

"K, I am already tired."

"You know how long it will take you to feel better? I mean, if you were just a regular person, this would take a couple of weeks, maybe more." Eric is settling back down to rest, pulls me to his side.

"Not exactly, probably half the time it would normally." I snuggle up to him, trying not to touch anything that hurts. There isn't much. "But you can, well, soon I will be OK enough." I know what he means, but say nothing.

It was good that I fed so well on the biker boys because another night is here and Eric is still in no condition to bring me food. I know he will not allow me to hunt on my own, so I am stuck. I know he will let me take from him if I need, but that seems a bit self-defeating as it will further weaken him, possibly hindering his recovery. We will do what we have to. Still I am checking his breathing regularly, happy it is getting stronger.

Chapter Fourteen

"Margret?" Eric turns over, relieved to see me still by his side.

"How do you feel?"

"Better, still not a hundred percent, but better." His eye and some of the smaller cuts look better tonight. I think if I give to him, it would make him stronger still, but I will not ask. I worry that just the intensity of our joining will cause him more pain than pleasure right now. He wants to sit up. I help him, propping as many pillows as I have around him.

"There, OK?"

"All good, thanks." Not sure exactly what look he is giving me, grateful maybe? "Margret, you will need to feed soon, and yes, you may, and should, take from me. I make you feel better than anyone can..." He stops and looks at me, brushing his hand over my face. "But in order for you to have me, I need to have you." He shrugs his shoulders. "Sounds silly, but you can speed up my healing. You know, then I will be better able to take care of you."

"Yes, it does sound silly, but I know what you mean." I wonder. "Could we just, feed from each other at the same time? Or wouldn't that work right?" Curious.

"Hell no, that is too dangerous!" Eric sternly says, shaking his head. "No way. Not together."

His reaction much more serious than I expected.

"Why? I don't understand. What would be so dangerous, so bad about that?"

"Margret, think." Almost like he is talking to a child. "Think of how it feels when I feed from you." Waits. "K? Now think of how it feels when you feed from me." I nod. Yes, I know the intensity of each. Just the thoughts are making me throb with desire. "Now put them together, and you'll get a dead, yes very, very happy, but dead Eric. We would be so lost in each other nothing could stop you. I would be in such a state, and you...well, not a good idea. Although it may sound fantastic in theory, reality would be much different."

"What, you never did it with Markus, ever?" Jealousy clear in my tone.

He gives me that impatient look, the 'Eric knows best so why are you questioning me' look.

Reluctant sigh. "Yes, we did," quickly adding, "very few times though."

Somehow I find it hard to believe him.

"Markus was much older, stronger, more in control. With you it's, well, different; even more intimate, powerful. More so than it was with Markus."

I smile, glad that I have the upper hand, even on his memory. "What do you mean, more than it was with Markus? How?"

"Most likely because I am your first blood. That is the main reason it is so intense for you."

I remember what Markus wrote: 'Eric will always be the taste of life to you.' Eric does taste very different than feeding on anyone else, and, well, my feelings are wild and hot. Nothing like anyone else.

"OK, I get that, but for you, is it different?" Swear Eric almost sobs. Holds tight to me.

"You, Margret, are everything beautiful and sweet to me. I crave you, need you. Never before and never again will I..." pulls me on top of him, my knees on either side. I feel his hands move up the back of my legs, drawing me close, crushing his face into my chest, "love someone like I do you."

Eric sucks gently at my breasts, just wanting the comfort of them. I love him.

After a long time in each other's arms, I pull away. "Eric, you should." He looks up at me, takes me by my neck and gives me hard kiss.

"Yes Margret, please give to me." I move off him, crawl to the ledge. An empty glass, the silver chain, the journal from Markus, the giving ring. As I place it on my thumb, I hope I can control myself. It has been a few days for just sex, more for giving.

I return to my position, sitting over him. Eric has removed the quilt from his lap. I see he is more than ready for me.

"You're sure you are strong enough for this?" Already has me in his battered hands, moving me over him. I slip my robe off. Eric's eyes move over me, full of desire.

"Yes, I am, but even if I wasn't, I want you too much to stop now." I bring myself down, pushing his hardness into me. Just a few days without him and it feels like I have been missing him forever. I move slowly, carefully over him. Happy his moans sound like pleasure, not discomfort. Eric looks up, his eyes ask, now. I push the ring into my breast, where Eric likes. Drawing blood, I drag the sharp tip to make a deep cut. I can barely get my hand away before he is on me. Consuming my breast in his greedy mouth. I fear I will strangle Eric in my embrace. Try to remember to ride him, but my mind is in such a beautiful fog. I only feel his mouth and the fullness inside me. Nevertheless Eric wants, needs. I feel him take control, guiding my movements over him. My thighs gripped in his strong hands.

Giving to Eric is sweeter even than taking from him. Not by much. I think maybe it's how acutely aware of his passions for me I am when we are joined this way. Or maybe because I am always the taker from others, from him, this I give.

I orgasm just as I feel my blood stopping. Neither affect Eric much, his hold on me is still strong, his hardness pushing inside me, harder now. He releases me from his mouth, tilting his head back with a final thrust, moans. Run my hands through his hair, kiss his bruised eyes. His breath is labored, but he still breathing. I didn't squeeze the life out of him.

I rest on his shoulder, careful not to put any weight on him, still endeavoring to hold him close somehow. After a while my mind starts to wonder, tripping over many unanswered questions.

"Eric, you never told me...about the days after." I know he is wide awake, my blood rushing inside him. His heart beats fast, strong. Even if his weakness returns, for a while after bleeding me, he will feel its power inside him.

"After what?" He is playing dumb, hear it in his tone. Another discussion he wants to avoid.

"After I turned, you know what happened to..." I let the sentence finish in his head. He knows what I want to know. Silence. I have to prompt him more.

"You said it was the most painful time of your life. I would like to hear about it." He takes a deep breath, it causes him some discomfort. Pulls himself up to sit higher in the pillows. I sit facing him as near as I can. I see he is reluctant but with a final irritated look begins.

"Well, after he made you, you fed from me. Like I had never been fed from before. You were rather uncontrolled. Still I stayed, with you."

Wasn't sure what he meant by that, didn't get a chance to ask.

"You became very violent as soon as we separated. You were crazed, wanted more. Even as strong as we both were, it took a lot of effort to contain you and get you downstairs.

"You changed so radically, nothing was left of you. I tried to talk to you, comfort you. Markus said I was wasting my breath. I was. Nothing affected your temperament, you no longer knew me. Nothing I could say..." He reaches over to touch my face. "You were no longer you." Shakes his head, bewildered.

"You were thrashing, kicking, biting at anything that got near you. Finally we managed to get you into the constraints. I wanted to feed you more, but Markus forbid me. Said you would rip my neck open. Knew by the looks of you he was right. Still he had to drag me upstairs. I didn't want to leave you that way. You were violently yanking on your chains. Hissing and groaning like a wounded animal when he closed the door."

Eric looks over my bed and the walls, even to the chains above his head. Remembering that night.

"It was horrid. I have done many things I am not proud of, but turning you; I regretted it immediately. I was so afraid you would never be the same again. Terrified you would never love me again, forgive me." He stops to take a deep breath. He can't look at me.

"Markus tried to comfort me, said it's all normal, nothing to worry about. You would be fine, come back to me in time. Still, I had never seen anything like the wild thing you became. I was a mess. Markus held me, kissed me. For a long time I was inconsolable. Still heard you alone in the dark basement. hissing and crying."

I take his hand, hold it in both of mine. Eric forces a sad smile.

"Over and over I begged to go to you. He knew I wouldn't be stopped if he didn't keep my attention. Forced me to stay with him. Talked to me, comforted me. Eventually we made love, the last time. I knew it was our last time; still I couldn't stop thinking about you. Markus felt my distraction, made great efforts to take my mind off you. Many tender affections to bring my mind from you to him. Markus's tenderness, his love for me, only made me sadder."

Eric's eyes grow wet. He holds them unblinking, pulling the tears back into him. I feel sad for him, even for the evil thing he made me that night. I am glad I have no memory of it, of being that uncontrollable monster.

"Anyway Markus stayed the whole next day with us, helped me feed you for the first times. It was Markus who found the animals for you. I was still in no real condition to be, well, of much help. All day long he instructed me again on your care. How to go on without him. Repeatedly told me that I was a good, loving keeper. Assured me everything would be fine.

"Your condition was unchanged, still wild and unaware of anything around you. Only blood grabbed your attention. You stayed that way pretty much for two weeks." He runs his hand thoughtfully over my cheek.

"Anyway, by the next night, I finally grew so tired I slept, even though I didn't want to. Couldn't keep my eyes open. I was so worried about you, and then..." He stops, holds his breath for a long moment. Releases it with a great sigh. I can see he is growing tired.

"I had to do what Markus wanted. His final demand of me. True death." Eric's head rolls back and his eyes close. I am afraid he will fall to sleep before I have heard the last of his tale. Though it is his reluctance to bring the memories back that gives him pause. Softly he continues.

"The next day we got ready to go, feed you, made sure you were secured. Markus fed you when he turned you way more than he needed to. He was weak from that and the full sun, as he wanted it, but he drove anyway. Mostly because I was still fighting with him, didn't want to go, didn't want to kill him. He was very patient with me, even though he was the one going to his death.

"He had found this place well before we were ready to use it. Saved me the anxiety of preparing for it. It was a couple of hours' south, big state park. All I had to think about was you, and the horrible state you were in or bringing Markus' true death. So I curled up in a ball and stared blankly out the window, trying to just go asleep. It was a very long quiet couple of hours.

"When we got to the park, he drove around it until we came to an old service road. He took it, went a long way into the woods. After a while it became more of a trail so we got out and walked, and walked, and walked. Didn't talk except for him asking me if I was OK. I remember biting back at him with, 'Yea, great.' I wasn't very nice, but...

There was a clearing in the trees, not big enough to be a valley or anything like that, just a clearing. I saw a post driven deep into the soil; I knew we were there. I had brought silver shackles as Markus instructed to hold him to the post. Knowing between his weakness and the silver he was consigned, couldn't..."

Tried not to interrupt him but had to ask. "Eric, if Markus wanted true death, then why the shackles and the silver? He did want it, right?"

"Yes, he did. Still Markus had taken many humans over the years that wanted death. He told me often at the last moments they struggled to free themselves. Changed their minds as soon as death was near. He thought he might change his mind if fear overtook him. He was resolute, didn't want to change his mind.

"I know Markus gave true death to his maker. Years after they had parted ways, his master lost his keeper. He was very old, think Markus said around 600. Anyway, he came back to Markus, asking for his assistance. Think he had me do it the same way he had done it."

As always I am full of questions. All of Eric's stories surprise me. He hides so much behind those soft dimples.

"Well, how did you...do it?" I ask shyly. Again I sense his reluctance to go on.

"I bound him with the silver to the post, as he wished. I remember kissing him over and over, pleading one final time to change his mind. Then I begged to be relieved of the task. Even tried to seduce him...nothing but his sympathy for me and his assurance that this was what he wanted. Markus finally grew tired of my stalling."

His eyes grow wet again, now Eric does nothing to restrict them.

"Said he was sorry to have to ask this of me, but I was the only one who could... .Spoke of you, as I remember Markus said, 'You have a new charge, one you MUST take care of. If you do not she, the one we made, will wreak hell on everyone.' By this time I was bent over him, holding his face close to mine. Then Markus reminded me." Deep breath, repeating the words Markus spoke. "'Beloved, she is yours now, you must love her with all the dedication, passion and humanity you have given me.' Then I remembered you alone in the house, how deeply I loved you, missed you."

Eric shakes his head. "Nothing more I could say. I kissed him goodbye. Gathered myself, knew what I had to do... I slit his wrist up his forearm, inside his thighs as well. He told me to..."

Eric's words trail off, fighting saying them aloud.

"What? Asked you to do what?"

"Cut his throat as well. Said he would suffer less if it was fast. I held him until he bled out."

His face grows very dark.

"There was nothing left of him but a skeleton with loose flesh draped over it. I didn't look at him again, just buried what was left of him and left. I don't even remember how I got home."

Eric looks regretfully to me.

"I took you that night for the first time, the hissing animal you were. Still needed to have you, but you were not... Margret. You bit at me, struggled to free yourself. I did it anyway, I felt so alone. Though I found no comfort, it only made me feel worse. It was a while before I approached you again."

My clouded memories of our first encounter much opposed to his remembrance.

Eric is truly exhausted, not from anything more than the painful memories. My blood should have kept him well much longer.

He wants to rest his mind and body.

"No more now, I am too tired." I feel bad, but I need to know, understand. I do understand much more now. Still have questions but nothing that can't wait.

Take him gently into my arms, tucking him into the quilt. Kiss his head resting on my chest, whisper into his ear, "I love you."

Soon he is gone from reality into fitful sleep.

Chapter Fifteen

It was a few more days until Eric is at all better. I forced him to rest, sleeping most of Tuesday and Wednesday. I took care of him diligently, fed him, nursed him. Think he loved that, my babying and nursing him.

I enjoyed cooking for him. I felt very normal cooking. Not the crazy emotional mess I have been for so long, just normal. The only times I felt near normal lately was in his arms, lost in lovemaking. Making dinner was a normal human thing as well, even if I couldn't eat it.

As to my hunger, I refused to feed from him. He offered, insisted, and once nearly took the giving ring to his arm, knowing full well if I saw his blood, smelled it, I wouldn't be able to resist him. I stopped him before he could cut himself. If I bled him, he would be weakened and I did not want to do that. Not yet.

I did wait till my hunger was strong, maybe a bit too strong. Thursday afternoon I told Eric my need was getting to the point it was nearly all I could think about. Of course he chastised me for waiting so long, for refusing to feed from him. I was stubborn. I knew how much my giving took out of him. Eric slept for many hours after the last. If I drank he would need to make love to me. I know he would hurt himself doing so.

Seeing I was resolved in waiting to feed from him, Eric suggested going for a late night walk in the park.

"How is a walk going to help? I am well beyond being distracted from my hunger."

"I know that. But in the park you can hunt. It will be late, most likely no people will be around, unless we are lucky enough to come across some vagrant. You can feed from a deer. There are plenty of them there. They breed like crazy, people feed them so they never starve, the park is nearly overrun by them."

A deer. I have had dog, and a raccoon I hear, but they are small animals; a deer would be, well, interesting.

"Questions," I ask meekly. He smiles patiently.

"Yes, I knew you'd have a few."

"Will I be able to catch a deer? They are fast. You can't overpower a deer for me, not yet anyway. Will it quench my thirst? Will it taste bad?" I ramble, stop, think that's all I need to know. Eric waits until he is sure I have finished my questions.

"Done?" I nod yes. "OK. Yes, you will be able to catch a deer. You will be able, especially in the quiet of the night, hear it, much like a human heart, locate it, and quietly, I stress the quietly part, sneak up on it and pounce. Like you did to that guy in the parking lot. Fast. Once you have it in your grip, just hold tight and bite. As to its taste, no, it will not taste bad. Markus would take large animals often to cut back on his thirst. He said it was like humans are fine gourmet food, animals are like just plain food. OK, but not the best. Plus a deer will be a lot of blood, more than taking a human; it will get you by for a while. Your thirst may not feel as satisfied as it would with a human, but good enough. Understand?"

"Yes, I get it. I think."

We wait till around 2 a.m. Eric dresses in a heavy dark blue sweater and blue jeans. I am in my tight black jeans and a black tank, all dark. Discovered I had a pair of black high tops, thought they would be good for running, unlike the rest of my new shoes. It is near fall and the night air is cool. Tonight is very windy, making it feel even cooler. He puts on his leather as well. I am happy to see he is starting to look much better, bruises and cuts are fading. Although his ribs are still quite sensitive. I found out by hugging him a bit too tightly today.

We walk several blocks, hand in hand. I am glad to be outside again.

We turn left at the end of our block. "A few more blocks down this way." Sounds to be tiring already.

"You doing OK, Eric?"

"Yea, haven't had any exercise in a while, seems I am still not myself." He smiles reassuringly at me. "I'll be OK. Here." He takes his leather off, placing it over my shoulders. I don't need it. Like I said, feel the cold but am not really affected by it. I am just about to refuse it but realize Eric understands this, he is just being a gentleman. So I just say thanks. "Only till you hunt; don't want any mud or deer blood on my good leather." He chuckles.

I know there must be more to Eric than he is showing me, telling me. This simple suburb of Chicago, the plain house in a nice suburban neighborhood. They are not Eric, or Markus, his previous master. Regardless they are all familiar and comfortable to me.

"Eric."

"Yeess, Margret. What are you questioning now?" He squeezes my hand.

"You said this house was for me. How did you put it— your guy trap. Markus and you didn't live here together, did you? I feel like there is a lot you are not telling me, about the real you. Am I right?"

"This is the real me. Not good enough for you?" I squeeze his arm, shaking my head.

"No, you are wonderful. I just think, this is not all you are. You hold things back from me."

"Just a block now." Pointing to where the street lights end in a wealth of darkness. "Margret, you have to adjust to what you are now. Who I am to you. Adjust to a lot of strange new experiences. So things that are simple, surroundings that are familiar serve to comfort you. Like your cubby, as you call it now. You still stay there much of the time even when you don't need to. You could come upstairs without me asking you, yes? It's your comfort zone for the time being. If I dragged you off to the penthouse in

Chicago, it may be too much for you. You have enough to get used to right now. Plus, I can better control you here. Hopefully not for much longer."

"Penthouse, in Chicago! You have a penthouse?" Squeal, excited.

"Calm down. Yes." By the look on his face I am sure he absentmindedly let that bit slip.

"It was Markus's and now it's mine." He stops and turns to face me. "It is ours, all of his belongings, of which there are many."

"Shit, I can't believe it. A penthouse, in Chicago! When can I see it?"

He shakes me softly by my shoulders. "Margret, not now. Soon enough, but not now. OK? You need to focus on hunting now. Just quiet yourself." Eric embraces me, kisses me sweetly on my head several times. How easily he distracts me now. "Hunt now. OK?"

I take several long deep breaths, clearing my head.

"Focus on heart beats. You will be able to tell if they are human or animal. Deer's hearts sound different, louder."

"How do you know..."

He covers my mouth with his hand. Giving the parental look. "Shush, no questions, just concentrate! Close your eyes and listen."

I do as he asks. Eric takes my hands in his. Slowly pulling me deeper into the park, into the woods. I keep my eyes closed fully, trusting him to guide me. Taking away all thoughts, just listening. I hear something, stop in my tracks. Eric releases my hands, removes the jacket from my shoulders, and waits silently.

His mouth presses to my ear, as softly as he can he says, "If you feel it, follow it."

Instinctively I move toward the heartbeat. Sometimes it gets softer then I change direction until it grows louder again.

Think I am getting the hang of this tracking thing. I move slowly through the brush, trying not to make a sound.

Even louder... strong heartbeats nearby. Finally I see it in the brush, just a few feet from me. Large, female. Beautiful in the dim moon light. Eyes glowing black saucers in the darkness. She does not see me.

I try to remember just how far I jumped onto that biker. Seems this is closer, although in a lot of brush. I should be able to jump on it before it's alerted to me. The wind is blowing away from me; that works in my favor. My hunger is talking very loudly to me now. It takes over; I jump before I make the conscious decision to do so. I make it easily on the deer's back. Quickly wrap both arms tight around its huge neck. It bolts, me strapped to its back. Feels like a wild bull ride.

For a moment I forget what I am supposed to be doing, my mind lost in the feeling of the powerful muscular deer moving under me. I regain my head and with some effort I bite in to her tough skin.

The deer tries desperately to get me off her back, ultimately falling over in the effort. Still I hold tight. She is very strong, furiously fighting for her freedom.

The blood flows fast, hot. It is good; different, but good.

I don't have the colorful dreams I do when taking a human though a pleasureful soothing comes over me. I feel unencumbered and free. I drink it in, it seems endless. As she gives up the fight, but not yet its life, I feel a strange connection to the animal. I lie with it in the brush until there is no more life to give me. Until we both are perfectly still.

The moon is not quite half full, only a few bright stars glow in the city sky. I lie on my back, waiting for my head to clear. Waiting for Eric. I feel strange, alone, calm. It's beautiful.

By the time a full week passed since the horrible fight at the bar, Eric seemed much better. The walk to the park on Thursday seemed to set him back a bit though.

I bled him on Saturday evening and, as expected, he was a wild man.

Between the fact that we were not having sex near as often as we normally do, and not completely joining with him for so long, he had no restraint, regardless of any discomfort he was in. I did try to just pleasure him a few times during the week, but that was never enough. Even after I gave him a long oral loving, Eric would soon be hard again, beg to be inside me. Though a reassuring sign he was regaining his strength, I still forced him into submission. Sat over him, taking charge so he was not moving around too much. I knew his ribs were not yet healed, so little movement on his part was best.

When I finally bled Eric, his pain, well, let's say it didn't detract from his performance much. The sounds he made as he thrust himself inside me were clearly pain and pleasure well mixed. He ignored the pain part. As I knew he would, Eric insisted on full control. On top between my legs, not me delicately sitting over him. I tried in vain to hold tight to his hips with my hands in order to restrict him. I had little luck, but as soon as I began to feed, I became lost in the ecstasy of his blood, the passion, my needs being saturated. I could no longer curb the vigor with which he took me.

I should not have allowed him to continue after I had fed; we both had full pleasures from it. Then again, I was so contented, I have little will for no. Just more. Eric knows how to persuade me, even against my will. Eric took over. There were long minutes of his hot open mouth, sucking, licking, until I was squirming and moaning. Still he would not release me until I climaxed again. Then he resumed his position, entering me with all the intensity of our first joining.

It was beautiful, hot, and I did need him so.

Eric paid for it. He was rather beaten and exhausted afterwards. Not only weak from my feeding but the great efforts he put into making love to me.

Eric slept well into Sunday morning, once in a while waking in painful groans. He complained of a sharp pain in his chest and ribs. That worried me more than a bit.

I still have no real proof of the damage to his ribs, if there is a small puncture to a lung. Just my vampire ear to his chest and the educated guess of an ex-nurse.

I felt guilty for his pains. Eric said I was being silly. It was his own desires for me that caused his pain and 'well worth it,' according to him. I babied him the rest of the day, nonetheless. Made him a half dozen eggs, bacon and bagels. Then watched sci-fi movies on my laptop. Eric rested in my arms, face as always cuddled to my breast.

Feel things will be back to 'normal' soon.

Chapter Sixteen

"Margret. Wake up."

Eric is softly shaking me, his hand on my hips. He is lying at my back, face in my neck, nibbling at me. I feel his hardness pushing at my ass. I am sleepy still.

"I need to take a shower. I have to go soon."

I turn half way over, put my arm around the back of his neck, pull him to my lips.

"What? Where are you going?" Groggy. Look to my window for time, sun. "It's full light, I need more sleep." Go to turn over again but he takes my hips, turns me over. Eric crouches over me, kneeling, his open legs tucked around me. Taking me in hand, he brings my legs up far over his back, my butt to his hips.

"I have to go to the hospital; I haven't been there for weeks. Cassie has been texting me and... I am much better, I should go." His face is close to mine and I wake myself to look at him.

"Cassie? Miss her," I say sleepily.

"Yes, she misses you. I texted her, told her that I was ill and couldn't come in. I'm OK now and I should go."

"Why?" I simply ask.

"I like to do something good with my time besides finding you food. It keeps me human." Stresses 'me.'

Never thought of how Eric might feel being saturated in this life, taking care of a vampire and all that. He is still human, and expected to serve me, and still remember his true self as well.

I am awake now and fully aware that he has me nearly folded in half beneath him. He kisses me hard, deep and sweet.

"I need to go," he simply says. His actions are not saying anything about going, only needing. He continues to kiss me, pulling me closer to him. "Quickie? Know that is not easy for us, but..."

His words trail off into my neck. He is naked, as am I. His desire immensely clear.

"I know you are still sleepy, it is only around 11:30, but..." More loving persuasions, both to my lips and now to my heat. His hands caress my ass, find their way around to my heat, rubbing into them. I sigh in sleepy submission. He takes my lower back into one arm, lifting me, the other moving himself into position. Just touching the entrance to me. He gives me a few of his gentle pushes, teasing me. I do love it when he does that. Eric wants me to say yes, plead. I wait for a while, making him apply more pressure, more temptation before I pull my calfs on his back hard to me. That was 'yes' enough for him.

In this position he has full access to me. I am tilted up to him. Eric pushes in to me slowly, and as deeply as possible. It almost feels as if he has gone beyond the capabilities of my chamber. Although he is being very gentle, it makes me gasp. "Too deep?" he softly questions.

"No, never. You are a bit much to handle though," I say with a quiet laugh.

"I love you Margret."

"And I love you, Eric, my keeper."

I run my hand over his hair, stroking it. Kisses over my chest, moves shallowly inside me. Not so quick, very loving. Eventually he needs relief. He sits up right and holds my hips so his thrusts can elongate and become faster. The depth causing repeated gasps as he takes my breath from me. I feel him pull me hard onto him, holding, the warm discharge. Eric falls quickly after into my waiting arms. I kiss his hair, running fingers through it. I want more; he is too hard to let go of. I tighten my body inside and out around him.

He moans. "Margret, I am going to be late. I need a shower. K?"

"You are a bastard." I take a hold of his face, giving him a very persuasive kiss. "And I hate you for making me need you so badly."

Eric's dimpled smile. "Never thought I would want to hear 'I hate you' again from you, but that one wasn't so bad." He give me a quick kiss to my forehead, genially pulls himself out, lets me go. It hurts, this freedom from him. He gets up and starts toward the stairs, still hard. Very difficult to look at when I desire more of him, and he still has more to give. I make an unhappy growling sound.

"Eric." He turns to look at me one foot on the first step.

"Yes?"

"Tell me you know how deeply I love you, how hotly I need you."

He shakes his head and sighs. "What I know is that is exactly how I feel for you. I hope it is for you as well." Air kiss before he heads up the stairs.

Eric still doubts? How can he? The thought makes my heart heavy. How can he doubt my love for him? I decide to go up and make him something to eat before he goes. I am still tired but his love has woken my heart. I want to care for him, feed him.

I rummage through the fridge and cupboards. Supplies are low as he has not gone shopping for a while. Luckily he also hoards food so I can come up with something. I hear the shower upstairs. Try to make sure his food is ready by the time he is done.

Can of chicken noodle soup and a grilled bacon and cheese sandwich. Extra bacon, of course. I just finish plating it as I hear him coming down.

"Who's cooking?" He is in the front room, soon standing at the doorway to the kitchen. Blue jeans and a black dress shirt, hair damp. Beautiful.

"You are always hungry, for something." I smile playfully at him. He slides his arm around my waist, distractedly kisses me on the cheek. Goes right to the food.

"Thank you, you didn't need to, I was going to stop." He sits at the counter. "This looks much better." Dives into it, consumes it all quickly. He was very hungry. I know how that feels too well.

Eric's leather is over the chair, he puts it on. "That was great, thanks." He gives me a warm kiss. "You'll be OK, yes?" At first I don't understand what he means, he has left me for hours, days before. Then I realize he means to leave me here alone unchained while he is gone for the first time.

"Really?" I smile brightly, hopefully up at him. Jumping like a child. He squeezes me tight.

"Really," he states. "It is day, and I think I can trust you." He pulls my face up to him by my chin. Eyes close. "Yes?" I kiss his face happily.

"Yes! Yes, you can. I swear I'll be a good vampire and sleep, and listen to music. Promise!"

"OK, OK." Dismissing my overexcitement. "I'll text you; if you are awake, call me back. OK?"

"K." He gives me a big long hug before leaves me to myself.

I stand alone in the kitchen. It takes a few moments to register. Alone, free of my bonds. What should I do? I clean up the lunch dishes. Not very vampire-like, human-like. I feel good.

I do have full range of the house, but Eric is right. My bed downstairs is still where I feel most comfortable. So after the kitchen is clean, I only rummage through the movies he has on DVD in the cabinet in the front room. Pick a few oldies but goodies and return to my cubby in the basement to watch them on my laptop.

For so long this space was my torture chamber. The basement, my dungeon. I laid here for so long, lost in fear, doubt, and anger. Oddly now when I look at my space, the place he, they, made for me to turn I can see the care they put into it. Not only for others' safety, but for me.

It is a king-sized bed, two mattresses high, the walls closely frame it. Besides the small ledge in the left side, the wall fits tight to the mattress. There are big oversized cushions, like from a couch along the head of the bed. They are covered by pillows of many sizes. Most are deep greens and blues, soothing colors. Besides the large fat grey feather quilt there are a few lighter throws in the same colors as the pillows. All are soft fabrics. I can see it all clearly now. The walls are thick, bricks covered with drywall, painted a soft white. Yes, there are the chains, two large rings hang from the back wall. One high, the no-movement height, one low, full length, giving me use of my arms. They hang now from hooks away for my bedding.

The chains that were attached to the concrete floor at the foot of the bed are gone. Even the metal plates that they were fastened to are covered now with a cheap imitation oriental rug. Still I hate to think of them, and what happened because of them holding my legs wide so he could... I don't like to remember. If I put myself in that place again, I can grow to hate again. If I remember too well the first days I woke from the lost wild state I was in. Before any memory. His face is there, not the same face I see now, but it is his, Eric's face. The one I hated, who raped me, gave me nothing good to feed on, starving me. Awakened my heart and passions with relentless cruel need. I push it away. I know now why. Still the memory sickens me.

Maybe that is why when I asked him if he knew my love and desire for him, he doubted. Maybe Eric is full of remorse, guilt for what he did to me. Willingly, wanting to do it. Not just the rape, endless seduction of his kisses between my legs till he gained his supposed permission. Maybe for making me this uncontrollable deadly thing I am now.

All that is human in Eric, perverted by this life. He was drafted into service; it was not of his choosing. Now Eric has no escape from what and who it has made him. I can sense the struggle it must be to do both, be both. I see both Erics clearly from here, where I stand at the foot of my bed.

I don't know how long I stood there, looking at my cubby. Funny how I try to disarm these memories by calling it that. Thinking, remembering, until I feel myself grow very tired. Want only to crawl into the fat quilt soft pillows and sleep. Maybe when I awake I can forget again what it really is. The place I was broken, taken and tamed.

Usually when I am sleeping it is like death, lights out, darkness. I have not dreamt yet, although Eric assures me once I am more fully myself, I will sometimes. Today I find myself tossing and turning like a stressed human. Must have been all the disturbing thoughts I had before I laid myself to rest. True deep sleep is eluding me. Not awake enough to watch a movie, not asleep enough to find darkness and peace. I lie half in, half out of the world.

I hear knocking, I think. Can't tell where it is coming from so I pay no attention for a while. It gets louder still, accompanied now by a ringing bell. Not really registering where it is coming from; it continues restlessly until I realize it is coming from upstairs. No one comes to this house unless invited! Never had I heard a knock at the door or the bell ring. Yet it goes on and on.

I am fully awake now. Alarmed, I sit up in the bed, wondering who it could be.

The angry pounding at the door continues nonstop for several minutes. Then abruptly it stops. My heart slows from its anxious beat after a few quiet moments. Glad whoever it was is gone. It is again quiet.

But not for long.

Crashing, glass breaking above me in the kitchen. I sit taller, alert. Someone is breaking into the house! I am unsure what is happening or what to do. I pick up my phone and call Eric. F'in voice mail. I frantically leave a message, not sure how coherent, but he'll get the gist. Some one's breaking into the house. I hear more glass crashing to the floor. Footsteps treading over the broken pieces.

I can discern exactly where the intruder is. First in the kitchen, the cracking glass underfoot, dining room, front room. All the while crashing sounds as chairs and tables are thrown violently to the floor. Whoever it is they are trashing the house. Soon I hear their footsteps loudly running upstairs to the bedrooms. Doors open and slam shut, spare rooms, nothing really in them but boxes.

Must be Eric's room now. Again trashing everything by the sound of it.

I try Eric again. It rings. As it does I hear my name screamed out in rage. I can't seem to focus. I'm in shock. My name?

A voice I know too well. One I never expected or hoped to hear again furiously calling out my name.

Vaguely hear Eric on the phone. "Hey, Margret, you're up." Obviously didn't listen to my message, just saw that I called. Can't focus on him. What I am hearing more clearly, more profoundly, is my husband's voice shouting my name over and over from the floors above me.

"You there? Margret!" I hear Eric now.

"He's here!" I frantically whisper.

"Who's there? What are you talking about?"

"My husband. Joe. He broke into the house! He is here, now. Upstairs!"

"Fuck! I'm coming. Just stay in the basement. Jam the door if you can, I am on my way!" He hangs up.

Eric is gone, but the yelling and smashing continues. Bureau drawers are being pulled out and thrown across the room. My enhanced hearing is doing nothing for me now but frightening me further. I hear only rage, even in Joe's mumbles. All hate and threats for me, and Eric.

"Fucking kill you and your fucking lover! You lousy bitch. You can't fucking leave me for some pink-assed boy!"

I curl up in the corner, cover myself like a frightened child in the quilt. Not as frightened by him, although I am, but more frightened by what I can do, will do, if I see him like this. I pray Eric will arrive before that happens.

The noises subside from the bedroom then I hear Joe bounding down the stairs. Can't breathe, thankfully I don't really need to. Hear glass cracking again under his step. Joe is back in the kitchen. He pounds his fits on the counter so violently it shakes the rafters above my bed.

Repeatedly yelling, "Where the fuck are you? I know you're here, you bitch. Margret! Margret!" Somewhat defeated. "Fuck!"

Finally a quiet minute, only heavy breathing from Joe. Then I hear the basement door handle jiggle, open.

No, don't come down here!

The light is on over my bed, the day in the windows, no other lights. I have no time, or real ambition, to hide myself further. Just the covers nearly over my head. If he wants this, he will have it.

Cautiously descends. Each step closer, creaks more resoundingly through the basement. I don't move an inch, frozen. My mind has two things on it: killing Joe, and Eric preventing me from doing it. Wonder who will get to me first?

He is on the floor now. Clearly hear his adrenaline-laced breath. Joe assesses the room, walks further into it. Seeing the light over my bed like a beacon in the dim surroundings. Still hiding in the corner nearest the stairs. Not until he stands directly in front of the space can he see me. Still he looks over it all, the chains on the back wall his central focus. Only a moment passes before he notices me cowering in the corner.

"That you, Margret?" Anger, no concern for me on his face. "Fuck this." Smell the booze with every word. "Shit! What the hell is going on here? Where the hell have you been?" Joe barks at me.

I remove the covers from my face. Sit up, try to look normal, convincing. "Nothing is going on. I'm fine, Joe. Just please go away." Adding in a whimper, "I don't want you here."

"What the fuck do you think you're doing, taking off like that? We just had a little fight, and boohoo you take off on me!" he hollers.

I of course don't remember the fight or what it was about. A fight was not out of the ordinary for us.

"Out with the girls, bullshit! What a slut, I knew it! Fucking knew it! You and lover boy. Right?"

Oh, that was what the fight was over. I must have been going out more than normal and he got crabby about it. Well, tough. He never gave a damn about me when I was home anyway.

"It doesn't matter where I was; you never gave a shit about me. You never loved me the way I deserved to be loved. You're not capable of it! It's over, just leave, Joe!"

"You're not capable of it."

Mocking me. How I hate that, now more than I did before. He always pulled that one out during a fight, just to make me feel inferior.

Joe wavers drunkenly. "I loved you freaken' fine!" His words slurring now.

My anger is growing too quickly. I stand up, only my robe on. Joe looks critically over me, and my wall of chains.

"Think you found love with this asshole? Crazy bitch." Smirking. "Into bondage now, huh?"

Every word brings back memories I don't want. His tone, his manner, the way he looks at me, full of judgment.

His current drunkenness reminds me when he would go out with his buddies, come home drunk, and want to screw me. So wasted he couldn't even see me, just fuck me. Seemed to be the only time he did want me, when he couldn't see straight. And the women, friends of mine he flirted with so pathetically. I was so embarrassed when he got like that. I am sure now he must have cheated on me. I pushed the idea away then though I am sure he did now.

Joe, a stud in his own mind. I remember so much now just from looking at him. Hearing his voice. His fat neck, big blue eyes, his little beer belly. Out of shape football jock, ego a hundred times the size of his... I truly despise him in this moment.

I am glaring at him, he is glaring at me. Stand off. Moments pass before Joe unexpectedly rushes me. Tackles me like one of his high school rivals. Drags me off the bed. I am face down on the rug before I know how to react.

Suppose I could have stopped him anytime. Something stopped me. He was my husband. I once upon a time loved him. I still feel somehow obligated to him? Fear of what I will do to him? Don't know; just let it happen as if I was powerless.

He is lying on top of my back, pushing his lame dick into it. It makes me cringe.

"Why didn't you tell me you liked it rough? I would have chained you up, baby." His hot breath caustic over my neck. "Anytime!"

"Leave me go! Stop it, Joe! Please." Don't use my full force, but struggle, hoping he will come to his senses and free me. "Please, Joe, stop this!" He doesn't relent.

"You know how long it took for me to figure out where you were? Ugh?" Pushing me harder into the floor. "That is after I cared where the hell you were." He bites hard into my shoulder. "I did have a bit of fun in my time off." Again he thrusts himself into me, holding my arms behind my back, underneath him.

"You remember my cop friend Gary, don't you?" Holding back, waiting for Eric to come so I don't...

Know I can overtake him but I just lie there. Every second feeling more the victim I don't need or want to be.

"I had him follow your fuck buddy to make sure. It took weeks before he caught the two of you going out together, coming back here to screw. Fucking whore! I am taking my fucking wife back where she belongs." Another angry jab into my back. Damn it, Eric! Why are you not home yet?

Shit! His bull crap, the memories, his foul mouth. He is really trying to hurt me, pulling my arms tighter up my back, shoving me harder into the floor with his lame thrusts. Even I have never seen him this way, this angry. Ever.

Rage comes up so strong I can't stop it. No more control-my-new-self acts, even as my old self tries not to.

I flip over, hurling Joe to his back. I mount him quickly, holding him down, pushing his shoulders hard into the basement floor. My covering opens a bit with the maneuver.

Joe's face full of surprise at my new strength. "Fuck, Margret!" Amused, amazed, aroused.

I take him by the neck and pull his drunken face to mine. "I am different now," I say sweetly, hoping I look as deadly as I am. "You can't hurt me or make me feel worthless anymore. Understand?" Joe's eyes thin, afraid.

I have him a bit too tight; he is having a hard time breathing. I loosen my grip, he gasps for air. Still the asshole grabs my ass and grinds himself into me.

"You like this rough stuff, Margret? Come on, fuck me."

I can't believe him, so drunk he doesn't even have sense enough to realize he is going to die now. I lean over, kiss his neck softly. Whisper, "Yea, fuck you." I don't know if he heard the bite in my words but...

I tear into his neck, pulling a chunk of flesh out of him. He screams, struggles to gain control, but I am stronger. Between my rage, my hunger and the powerful feelings from overtaking him so easily, I am in a lethal blood lust as I have never felt before.

Thrust my face into the bloody hole I took out of his neck. Just torn flesh and veins, don't even have to try, the blood just rushes in. Still I do love to suck. He gurgles and weakly attempts to push me off him. His strength to struggle with me does not last long.

The colorful blood clouds are not there, not the same. All grey smoke flowing into black.

I feel no comfort, just hot rage. All my pains avenged.

I can't find myself anywhere, true darkness inside me. Feed lustfully, without limit. My mouth fills endlessly with his hot blood.

Is this who I truly am? What I am?

A murky voice, far away, somewhere in the distance, calls to me. Sense something pulling at me. I hold tighter to my food. The voice becomes stronger. The grip of warm flesh more intense. The flesh in my arms is growing cold; this one is hot and strong over me. Tearing at me.

Clarity. "Margret! Stop, Margret!"

I am done, Joe is done. Toss Joe brutally away. I go black.

Stinging on my face. "Margret! Wake up!"

It feels as if I am coming out of a coma. For several moments I have little sense what has happened, where I am.

Not until I open my eyes fully to see Eric's face flushed red do I come to myself. He is sitting on top of me, restraining both hands over my head. Panting, shock in his dark eyes.

"Margret?" I shake my head, somehow it hurts. "What?..." I know what I did, and I know how Eric is going to react. I lie limp under him. No fight or anger left. Just Eric's presence fills me with shame.

"What the hell did you think you were doing?" He pulls me harshly off the floor to my feet.

"You killed him, and not just killed, you tore into him like an animal, Margret!"

Eric looks down at the mess I made of Joe, shaking his head in disgust. He is frantic, pulling his hands through his hair repeatedly. Eventually he looks at me, revulsion in his eyes. "Fuck, Margret!" Stomps over to the sink, wets a big towel, throws it at me. "Clean yourself off. You're covered in blood."

I have never seen him look at me like this, repulsed by me. I am heartsick. Not so much for what I did to Joe, but for how I must appear to Eric right now. A wild bloody beast.

I wipe my face and hands; it's all over me. I am shocked by the amount of blood on the towel as I clean myself off. Feel myself starting to tear up. I stifle the sound but can't stop the tears from overtaking my lids.

Eric is assessing what I did, how to clean this up, get rid of the body. "Shit, shit shit!" Pacing back and forth next to Joe's body. Again he looks at me angrily. "What the hell happened? You knew I was coming!"

I meekly tell him the whole thing, how Joe broke in, trashed the whole house. I was good and stayed put. Then what happened when Joe discovered me. The fight, how restrained I was when Joe had me down grinding himself into me, hurting me.

"You call this restraint?" Eric yells, pointing to the bloody mess. "Shit,

Margret, you completely lost it!" Eric finds a clean robe by the bed. Forcibly hands it to me, not looking at me. He will not look at me! I feel my tears double. I sit at the edge of my bed and look at the blood- saturated carpet, Joe in the middle of it. I did rip into him as I had never done before, not even thought to. It is so ugly, even to me. I can't look at it for long.

"I tried, I really did." Feel my anger rising, because I did try. I took more than I should have, waited as long as I could! "I am what you made me, Eric, a fucking killer!"

He takes a hard angry breath. Let's it out slowly, trying to calm himself. Shaking his head. "I suppose." He sits hard next to me. Breathing still rapid. "Shouldn't have left you alone, unrestrained." Regretful, still furious. "How the hell did he find you?"

Not going to like my answer.

"His buddy, Gary." I pause, grimacing. Eric is wide-eyed, glaring, waiting for the punch line.

"He's a cop." Gingerly adding, "Does detective stuff on the side sometimes." Eric bends over, interlacing his hands at the back of his neck. Letting out another heavy sigh. Stares at the floor for a minute.

"Crap! Things just got even more complicated." Glares over his shoulder at me. "This is the kind of mess you don't want to get yourself into, Margret." Like a father scolding me.

"You are, for all intents and purposes, a missing person. Now your husband Joe here, is, well, dead. Soon to be missing as well. Shit, and now we have a cop who knows about us! Where we live, and most likely that Joe would be coming here to find you." He rattles it all off quickly, like his harsh breathing. "See why killing is so bad? Not just for your humanity, but for your safety?" He is very cross, worried.

I really fucked things up. But I couldn't help it. "I'm sorry, I really am. I tried to wait, to keep my cool...Please, Eric?"

Beg for some small forgiveness. Eric takes my hand with no real affection, kisses the back of it. Distracted, deep in thought.

"What are we going to do?" I am not only full of regret, but now I am frightened as well.

"Don't know yet. I'm thinking." I quietly sit, wiping away the last of my tears with the sleeve of my robe.

Waiting for Eric to figure out a plan to cover up the murder of my husband. I look at Eric, and the floor, try to avoid looking at Joe. Thankfully his face is turned away, but his torn neck is facing me. I drank him pretty dry, only a crimson trickle from the wound. Hard to believe I did that, tore into his neck like that.

Don't look!

Where did the torn flesh go? I scan the area, see nothing. Don't remember spitting it out, but that's not surprising. Nothing but blood lust in my memory. Still, there is a huge chunk of his flesh missing. Dear God, I didn't swallow it? Did I? I start to gag at the very thought. Eric pays no mind as I cover my mouth and try to keep the blood, and whatever else, down. I frighten myself!

Several minutes pass. "Margret, go get dressed and straighten up the house as best, and as fast, as you can. I'll take care of him." He goes to the carpet, pulls Joe to the edge and starts to roll him in it. Classic.

In my bare feet, I make my way around the glass on the kitchen floor carefully. The window over the sink is broken out, shards of glass all over the counters and in the sink. The stools tossed to the floor. The dining room is much the same, chairs thrown about. I quickly run upstairs, ignoring the rest of the destruction.

Every bureau drawer is pulled out, our clothes scattered everywhere. A few of my dresses are ripped, tossed on the bed, and the bedding, torn to shreds. I sort through the clothes strewn about the floor, find a pair of my blue jeans, one of Eric's tee shirts, quickly dress. My high tops are in the bathroom. Joe obviously didn't go in here. Undisturbed.

I start in the kitchen, sweeping up the glass, filling the entire basket. Vacuum up the small shards. I right the chairs in the kitchen, dining room and front rooms. Glad now Eric has few things here. There are some books and movies he pulled out and dropped to the floor but not too much to contend with.

Eric calls up to me impatiently. I run down, anxious.

Joe, the rug, and hopefully all the other bloody bits encased. Duct tape securing a black tarp around all. Hauntingly familiar. Eric had dragged him over near the bottom stair. He is looking intently at the floor, seemingly not noticing my arrival.

"You know what car he drives?" Eric asks distractedly.

Holds up a bunch of keys I recognize as Joe's.

"He has two, the silver SUV and the red pickup truck." I take the keys he is holding out.

"Well, I don't remember seeing anything parked in front of the house. I better go look around see if he parked it down the street somewhere." He leaves quickly, not looking at me once. I don't like standing here alone with a dead body so I go to sit in the kitchen. Nervously wait for Eric's return.

About five minutes later, he comes back. Informs me that Joe parked his red truck around the corner, we would wait till it was late and then dispose of the body, and the truck. No details. He is exhausted, stressed. Eric goes to the couch to rest, telling me to wake him at 1a.m. It's 7:50 now.

Alternating looking down the dark basement stairs, Joe's body at its foot, and at the clock over the fridge, I sit and wait until the hands read one.

Chapter Seventeen

I have been gazing out the truck window at the lights of the passing towns then farms for over two hours. Eric is hugging the speed limit tightly. Joe is in the back, covered in canvas drop cloths he used for painting jobs, his tool box and a spare tire over him for good measure. Eric hasn't said much, well, anything really, the whole time, but it looks like a lot is going on in his head.

"Why are we going so far?" I wished I hadn't asked.

"I am not in the habit of disposing of dead bodies! Know that may surprise you, Margret." Wow. Stressed! "Even if I was, which I am not, they would have been strangers. You know, not in any way connected to me or anyone I know, or married to someone I have stashed in my basement! I want him and his truck as far away and as hard to find as possible!" Inhales only once for all that.

"Maybe I watched too many CSI shows while you turned, but things are different now. Can't just dump a body and hope all will be well. OK!"

K, shit. I'll go back to looking out the window quietly now.

We are driving downstate to a big park, Starved Rock, I think he called it. Find a place there to dispose of my screw up before the sun comes up. We have flash lights and, of course, a shovel.

There is not much to look at now; we are out where there are no street lights, just long dark roads.

I almost ask Eric if he found the flesh I tore out of Joe's neck, but think better of it. He did clean everything up. Maybe it was on the floor near Joe, or underneath him somewhere?

Hold my tongue; what if I ask and he didn't find it anywhere? He would know that...what human would want a mouth that could swallow a chunk of bloody human flesh? I am making myself sick just thinking about it. Remembering the way his torn neck looked. To think I could have swallowed...no, I couldn't have!

Surprising my feelings are so human, how strong they are. I am disgusted with who I am and what I am capable of doing. I did do it, I killed my own husband; this is me now. The old Margret wouldn't hurt anyone, ever. This is why I have Eric, the purpose of a keeper, I suppose.

If I hadn't had to look at Eric's human face, so upset with me, seen the revulsion in his eyes, felt the guilt it inspired in me, maybe I would have stayed in that dark place. Just let it overtake me. Became a wild vampire. A rogue. Only my need and love for Eric drew me back to my real self.

He slows, pulls into what looks like a service road, or a wide trail. Hard to tell in the dark. He turns the headlights to park, dimming them just enough to see the narrow path before us.

Trees closely line it, often brushing the sides or roof of the truck, making an ugly scratching sound. We drive slowly for a while until the dirt road is nearly gone, no more than a foot trail in front of us. Stops and turns off the lights. It's amazingly dark. Even my eyes take a second to adjust before I can see anything, and I see pretty well. Only the near full moon cracking through the trees above.

"OK, now we walk." Eric wastes no time, already has the gate down and uncovering the body before I have my door open and placed a foot on the ground.

"Margret, come on." Impatient, aggravated. "I need your help."

I doubt that, but it's my mess, I should help to clean it up. I join him in the back; we pull Joe out and place him on the ground. I am inwardly stunned and amazed at what I am doing, what I have done.

"Here's where I really need you." Even in the dark, I can see the annoyed look on his face.

"You need to keep track of where we are going, and how to get back. Use all your senses, your good eyesight. I am going to carry him till I find a good place to dig. K?"

He hands me the shovel and a flash light.

"Don't use it unless you have to. The moon is almost full, go by that unless the forest gets too dark."

Lifts Joe easily over his shoulder, turns to walk into the heavy brush off the trail.

I am trying to pay close attention to everything around us, and the moon above us. We walk briskly and silently for about fifteen minutes before Eric stops. There are many great old trees here. Years of leaves piled deep under our feet.

Eric puts Joe down and starts to clear a spot of leaves. I help him, on hands and knees, pushing the leaves away, making a huge pile in no time. Once we hit soil, he starts to shovel. I sit apprehensively nearby, feeling nothing but dread. Feels like I am watching some old scary movie. A foreboding shadowed figure digging a grave deep in the woods illuminated only by bits of moonlight, corpse lying nearby. This is real, not a movie. Because of me we are out here in the dead of night, disposing of a dead body.

I can't help feeling like someone is watching us. Scan the area. Naturally I don't hear or see anything around us. Only my guilt stands watch over us. Still...

When he is done, I help him lift the body and place it in the ground, cover him with soil.

We scatter the pile of leaves over the grave, add a few fallen branches over that.

We have not spoken or even looked at each other. I know he is still mad, but maybe more concerned about the cop, Gary. No one will ever find Joe out here, I am sure of that.

I reach over and take Eric's hand. It's cold as ice. The night air is brisk now that I think about it.

"It will be OK, no one will find him here." I try to sound confident. Eric looks at me for the first time in hours and gives me a weak smile.

"Ya, let's hope so."

I lead him back without much trouble. I seem to be able to recognize every path, tree or bush we passed. The sun is making itself known. A thin burnt orange light invades the black night, low in the sky.

When we get back to the truck, Eric just sits there for a few moments, resting his head on the steering wheel. I say nothing, although questions are overcrowding my head. He turns on the truck and stars slowly backing out of the woods. It takes longer backing out than going in. When we near the trail head he turns to me.

"Margret, I need you to do something for me."

"Anything. What?"

"Crash the car into that big tree over there for me. Don't total it, we need to drive it to a junk yard. It's already junky, but we need to make it look more junky. K? Try to mess the passenger side up. Got it?"

"Oh, OK."

He gets out, comes around to open my door. Takes me by the hand around to the driver's side. Buckles me in. A gentleman even in the worst circumstances.

"I know you can't really hurt yourself, but no need for you to hit your head if you don't have to. Just go about 25, 30, that should do it. Aim toward the center more or you'll take out the front tire."

After all the instructions, he closes the door and gets out of the way. I back up a bit, and then drive the car into the tree as requested.

I jerk hard forward; the seat belt does stop me from hitting my head. The impact hurts a little, but is gone quickly. Eric rushes to the car, making sure I am OK, more from kindness that any real concern.

The car dives OK, pulls to the right side, drivable as he requested. Eric manages to get it to a junk yard about ten miles from the park. The sun is new but I am already feeling it.

When we arrive, I notice there is no fence, just a huge junk yard in the middle of a big open field. There is a farm off in the distance, but nothing else nearby. It's still very early; no one seems to be around.

The old trailer used for the office is parked by the dirt driveway. All dark, the tattered red and white 'closed' sign still hangs crooked in the door's window. Piles of crushed cars all along the front near the road, rows of broken-down rusty vehicles of all kinds behind them. Waiting.

We drive slowly into them. Looking for just the right aisle, I guess.

By the time I get out and he stashes the truck amongst the hundreds of others waiting to be crushed, I am starting to feel dizzy, weak. I lean on a rusty old black bug, unable to stand for myself. I can't seem to keep my eyes open anymore. Don't know if it's the stress or the light, both maybe.

"Margret, I got you."

I was just about to slide to my ass to the ground when Eric swoops me up in his arms. Even in my weakened state, I feel better just to have him touching me again. I wrap my arms around his neck, cuddling my face into it, kiss him repeatedly.

I feel him snuggle me as I drown myself in his neck.

"I am sorry, Margret. I know this is hard on you, but it had to be done quickly." Staunchly adding, "Don't worry, I'll take care of you."

"How? You can't possibly walk me the whole way home."

"No, just to town, then I'll rent a car."

"You can't, it's too far." My words are starting to slur, like I am drunk. Not able to clearly form words.

"Just sleep, maybe someone will see us and give us a lift. Don't worry. Rest."

I feel his kiss on my forehead. I close my eyes and try to sleep buried in the darkness of his hair.

He walks....

Eventually a car does stop. Eric slides me into the back seat. I'm so tired, sun seems so bright. No idea how far he walked as I was in and out of consciousness. Only know I didn't want him to let go of me. He did, so I ball myself up in a self-made cocoon, smell potato chips and beer. I could vaguely hear them talking, but couldn't focus on the conversation enough to make anything out of it.

Seems like just a few minutes until the soothing movement stops. It wakes me. Car doors opening, close. Silence.

Lying in the back seat of a stranger's car feeling most alone. Too tired and unnerved to move.

Muffled voices. My door opens. Eric pulls me out of the back seat, back into his arms.

"Thank you so much, you really saved us back there."

"No, no, man I don't need that, really." The young man is protesting. Eric must be handing him some money for his troubles. Knowing Eric, a lot of it.

"No problem, just hope she feels better." He sounds kind. I couldn't pull my eyes open in the bright sun to even look at him but managed to weakly say 'thank you'; only Eric could hear me.

Eric conveys my appreciation to our rescuer. "She said thank you. Really, thanks so much."

Eric is genuinely grateful to him. The young man laughs. "All good. You take care." Hear his car door shut, it moves off.

Once again sliding into a back seat, now of the rental car, I suppose. When Eric tries to let go of me, I hold as tight as I can around his neck. Want. "Eric." Pleading softly.

"What, Margret, what do you want?" Impatient.

Kissing weakly over his face, my eyes still closed to the light. "You." I pull at his shoulders, drawing them down to me.

"Margret, I can't make love to you in a Hertz parking lot. We'll be home soon and..."

I stop him.

"No, just hold me for a moment. Please, I need you near me."

I know my words are garbled whispers, but he hears, understands. Surrenders to me. Kneeling awkwardly on the floor of the back seat, he covers me with his chest holding me in his arms.

I want his mouth, pull his head up by the thick waves toward mine. I haven't the energy to give him the passion I wish to, but he gives me several gentle kisses. My body further weakened by each. Finally Eric pulls himself from my demands. I make an unhappy whimper.

"We'll be home before you know it. I'll hold you as much as you wish then. K?"

With the last of my energy, I grab onto his shirt before he gets too far. Eric looks rather confused.

"But do you wish it, Eric? Do you..." Tears begin to come, overflowing, my sight washed away by them. Manage only to quietly cry the rest of my question, "still love me?"

Eric pulls me off the seat, arms fully encircle my body. Holds me tightly. If I had nothing but this.

"Yes, yes. I love you. Nothing will ever change that." Convincing. Yet my heart still feels heavy.

Soothing strokes over my hair. Few moments, Eric kisses my forehead. Know what that means, release. His hand cups the back of my head, lowering me into the seat like a rag doll to my rest.

Neither one of us wanted to return to the basement just yet, and I assured him the bedroom was in no condition for rest. Not without a lot of clean up. We decide on the couch.

Eric is so exhausted he falls into a deep sleep almost as soon as he lays his head on the pillow. I have at best broken sleep all day in the sun. It's around 4 p.m. I am still listless.

Flopped on his stomach over the couch, pillow tucked into him. I curl myself as best as I can around him, managing to rest my head in the small of his back. My arm draped over his legs, my legs tucked up awkwardly to fit the bit of the couch left to me. I have to be near, touching.

Although I am teeming with distress, listening to his peaceful breathing, feeling the restful motion of each breath relaxes me to sleep.

It's near 7 a.m. when he wakes, goes right to shower, only giving me a brotherly kiss on my cheek. I need to change, clean up as well. Eric's white tee I threw on yesterday is filthy dirty and my hair a mess of leaves. I lie there for a few moments then follow him upstairs.

He is still in the shower, the bedroom still a disaster. I start to pick up our clothes, fold them. Notice two of my dresses are torn; the tight red one Eric gave me for our first night out and a long black lacy one I got online, never wore.

I am still at it when he comes out, only a towel around him. I try not to look, be tempted by his body. Fiercely go back to my folding.

"Those my jeans?"

I stop, confused. Yes, I am folding his dark denims. Hand them over, again not looking up. I hear a chuckle from him. Find him a tee shirt and toss it over my shoulder at him.

"Thanks."

The doorbell rings out. I look to him now, probably like a deer in head lights. Who could that be at this hour?

"Calm down, Margret, I ordered a pizza." Grabs his wallet off the dresser and rushes downstairs.

I finish the floor and the bed before I clean myself up, change.

Pull on a comfortable long grey sleeveless tee shirt dress and head downstairs.

Eric is sitting on the floor like a child, coffee table covered in the pizza box. Eating right out of it. Doesn't seem to notice me. Only two things keep his attention like this, sex and food. I get him a large glass of ice water from the kitchen and return to his side.

"Thank you." Drinks most of it immediately. "Didn't realize how thirsty I was."

"No problem. The room is all fixed; I found the sheets in the closet and made the bed." He just nods, finishes off another slice. I sit quietly and watch him devour his pizza, slice by slice.

When the box is empty, he cleans it up, makes a huge fire. He, we are not talking much, or looking at each other much. Eric sits on the stoop near the fire, gazing into it, watching it grow stronger, just as my uneasiness grows stronger with every silent second that passes between us.

Had I angered him so that he didn't want me near him? Was he afraid of me? I must have looked like a monster, half naked, covered in blood. Joe's neck torn to shreds. How could I do such a thing? Yet I did. Shamefully loved it in the moment.

Maybe Eric should be afraid of me? That thought brings me horror. I love him, need him to love me.

I know he is concerned about what happened, what will happen next as well. Still I am not used to him paying me so little attention. I can't help but fret, dream up all sorts of dismal thoughts.

Eventually he comes and sits down next to me. Noticing my pouting he pulls me to rest on his shoulder. It is hot from his nearness to the flames. Just his touch relaxes me, well, a bit.

"Margret, I don't think you should go out of the house for a while, maybe a long while." He squeezes my shoulders and gives me a quick kiss to my head. "I am sorry, but I can't risk you being seen right now. And I am afraid to make any sudden moves. I think we, I, should go about things just as if nothing happened...then we'll see."

Obviously just as full of thought as he seemed.

I look up at him. Eric attempts to smile at me; he is too worried to really pull it off. No dimples, just a half-hearted grin.

"What do you think will happen?"

"Depends, if that cop friend of..."

"Gary." I interrupt.

"Yea, Gary just saw us together and has no real proof, like photos, then maybe only a few questions. If he's got pictures, well, still no real proof Joe was here, but adds to the look of my guilt."

His guilt? I am the one who is guilty. I am the one who killed him! Oh, right I am 'missing.'

"Maybe Joe didn't tell him he was coming here, maybe he did. Now Joe is missing and the last thing Gary knows is he told Joe his wife was shacking up with me. Doesn't look good. Gary is going to be snooping around, even if no one else believes him. He is going to try to prove we, well, I, did something to Joe."

He thinks for a minute.

"Margret, you didn't tell Cassie about us, did you?" Forgetting that I've forgotten.

I sit up, turn to look at him. His face firm in my mind. Squeeze my eyes closed, trying to think, remember. Dammit!

"Eric, I still have..." I open my eyes, Eric still nowhere in my recollections.

"You don't remember me at all, do you?" Eric's voice sad, disappointed. He looks away from me. I touch his face, the face I love so much now but can't bring any memory of it to my mind.

"No, I don't. Sorry." I add hopefully, "Sometimes things feel familiar. Like déjà vu. But no real cohesive memory of us, you know, before."

He sighs.

"Well, I do know you well enough to know you wouldn't have told anyone other than her; can't be sure you didn't tell Cassie but. She has questioned me often about you, where I think you might have gone. Never let on that she knew anything though."

"She is my best friend. Even if I didn't tell her, admit it to her, Cassie knew me. I am sure she sensed I had a crush on you, feelings...or something." I smile meekly at him. Crush seems like such a silly way to describe how I feel for him. "She always knew when I found a man attractive, teased me relentlessly about it. No matter how I brushed it off, she would know. Never let it drop till I admitted it."

I like to think about her, but it makes me sad at the same time. I miss Cassie most from my old life, her bright blue eyes, short cropped red hair, her laugh. Giggled like a little girl when you got her going. I could talk to her about anything no matter how stupid or deep.

I feel Eric's hand brush my face. I'm crying. He smiles sympathetically. "Sorry."

"I'm OK," I reply weakly.

"I'm scheduled to go in tomorrow afternoon, and even though I hate to leave you alone, I should go. Everything needs to look normal. Plus I can gossip with the nurses, see if someone suspected something. Somehow it got to your husband. That's what bugs me; how did he know to come here? We, well, you were so careful, at the hospital, more so when you came over here." Mystified. "Can't figure out how he knew about me." Looks off into the fire, ponders some more.

"You are afraid to leave me because you think I'll go crazy again? Will you chain me?"

I add quickly, apologetically, "I'll understand if you need to."

Pulls me gently by my neck with both hands to meet his face. "No! I am not going to chain you Margret." He kisses me, a real kiss for the first time in many hours. I feel myself weaken, heat throbbing. I want him. Know I will not feel better until I have him. But I keep my cool until he lets go of me.

"I don't want to leave you, ever, but especially now. I know you are upset about what happened. I understand why you did what you did." I fall into his arms, hugging him close, my warm forgiving Eric.

"Only wish I was home to protect you from him, from yourself."
Sounding disappointed in himself.

"But I wasn't. It's over, now we need to deal with it as best we can." That tender protective kiss to my forehead.

"Things are going to be a bit lean for you, if that cop starts watching me, and I know he will. I can't exactly go looking for drunk homeless people to bring home for you, or stray dogs for that matter. I am sure that would look odd." He laughs a little, it sounds good. "Maybe I can catch you a possum in the yard." His tone playful.

"Very funny, yuck possum." I rib him, bit too hard.

"Hey that still hurts, at least when you do it," he complains.

I lie on his chest, hear his heart, look into the fire. I wish this was all I really needed, just this. Still I know my hunger will come again, too soon, grow till I can't think of anything else but its burn. Then Eric will be the one in danger.

"How will you feed me? I can't take too much from you. I'd die before I'd hurt you." I could take too much from him weaken him, even... I can't think of it, not even a shadow of a thought.

"You know that isn't true, maybe me, but not you." He ruffles my hair playfully, as if we are not talking about me starving to the point I can't control my feeding, drinking him to his grave.

"Let's not let it get to that, OK?" He hugs me, pulling my legs over him. My dress has a long slit up the side; it falls open when he moves my legs over his. Not unnoticed by him. Slides his hand slowly up my thigh to rest it comfortably there.

"I'll go to the boy bars; I shouldn't have any problem getting someone to come home with me. They may have to stay the night then I'll take them home in the morning." Thinking. "Karl keeps texting me; suppose I could arrange a date here soon."

"Who is Karl?" He chuckles at my question.

"I believe you called him Blondie?"

Oh yes, Blondie, think I heard Eric call him by his name in the morning as he helped him dress but I was too 'drunk' to remember it.

"After he recovered from a mysterious bug he got after our night together, he started texting me, wanting to see me again. So he may work for one or two nights with little effort."

Eric moves the leg he holds aside. Slowly runs the backside of his fingers up the inside of my thigh, then over my heat. I groan in need, craving his touch.

"You have been a very good girl tonight, Margret." Whispers into my ear. His fingers maneuver their way into sodden flesh.

"Good girl?" Inquisitive. Long lost little dimples retuning. I run my hands through his hair, happy to see his smile.

"I know you have been in need several times since we got back," Eric says most sincerely.

"You know I will not deny you, yet you still let me rest and eat."

He is playing with me. His master.

"Mmmmmm..." Find it nearly impossible to form words as his fingers massage me, it's all I can think of. "You were hungry," I moan out.

He presses his mouth to my ear, breathing into it, runs the tip of his tongue along it. Makes me shiver when he does that, and Eric loves to make me shiver. "I still am, very hungry." Thrusts his fingers deep into me.

Sliding himself from under my legs, to his shoulders in between them. He moves my dress up over my hips, pulls me down by them. Eric has that concentrated look on his face. One thought, this thought is only of me. He rips his tee off, tossing it nearly into the fire. I slide my hands back into his waves and pull him down to meet me. Each second like minutes of wanting, waiting for his kiss.

I sob at the first touch of his lips, already so inflamed. Encircle him in my legs, waiting for more. He continues to softly kiss over my yearning, only jabbing his tongue into me briefly. Teasing me again and again.

"Eric," I plead. Not enough pleading. Move my legs higher over his back. Eric merely giving me a few longer passes with his tongue in response. I know what he wants and have no ability to fight with him tonight.

"Please, Eric." I beg him for more.

Knowing, still he asks. "Please what?" I want to hit him, but just tighten the grip I have on his hair, pulling at it harshly.

"Give me your full deep kiss, you're torturing me!" I grunt in feeble anger. I can't force him to me. He will not concede to me no matter how I try to pull at him with my legs, or at his hair. His incessant teasing continues.

"Haven't you tortured me enough?" Breathless, frustrated.

"If this is torture, then no, I can never give you enough." With that he submits. Penetrating, eager. His mouth couples with me. Eric's kiss underneath his open mouth makes me insanely hot. I grind myself to him.

After his teasing, my hours of quiet unanswered desire and his intense kiss, it doesn't take too long before I climax. He never stops after it; he wants it, the climax, most. I squirm and moan, still Eric holds tightly to my hips. Drawing my heat into his mouth until I can't stand it any longer.

I force him to get him up. Tearing at his jeans, demanding his hardness. I need him to be one with me. Eric takes me forcibly in hand, turns me to sitting, yanks me to the edge of the couch. His expression wicked, lustful. Rips his jeans off, retuning to me quickly, kneeling before me. His dark eyes roam over my body with lustful concentration.

The fire our only light, and it does him great justice. His body so hard and strong, like no man I have ever touched. The fire hugs his every muscle hotly, as do my hands, caressing him as he kneels before me. He leans to me, our mouths lock, secures my legs around him at the same time.

"Margret you are so beautiful."

He pulls my strap down, exposing my right breast, falls on it greedily. I hold him hard to me. It goes right through me, the intense needy sucking. As if my nipple has a nerve singular in its intent. An invisible path from my breast to the center of my body. Pooling briefly there, full of wild butterflies. Still committed to its destination deep inside my core, it moves down. Calling my need to have him even more acutely than his touch. The hot desire it forges will only be quelled when he is one with me.

"I love you so much." Scarcely able to enunciate, his mouth still buried into my breast. Though I hear every lovely word, passionately crushed to my heart he is so near.

With that he brings himself to me, pushing, waiting. My need for him is so powerful. I love how he lingers, makes me wait to fulfill it.

Eric makes love to me as he did on the vanity. Slowly appreciating every inch, every second of our joining. Coveting every moment of it until he cannot hold himself back. Only then does he deeply fill me. Bringing us both to the deepest surrender.

I love him beyond love.

Chapter Eighteen

The morning after we disposed of Joe, a man came to replace the kitchen window. Eric wants everything resolved and cleaned up before any real suspicion begins. He left for the hospital locking me securely in the basement to rest. I was to call him if I heard anything but to stay put. Hopefully even if Gary broke into the house, he wouldn't be able to get into my space. He kissed my sleepy lips goodbye and left me around one. For a while after he left, I lay awake, worried, but soon felt the sun and fell into black sleep.

Nothing happened all day. When Eric returned it was full dark in my window. Night comes early as fall on us.

When I hear him unlock the door, I fill with relief.

He has a takeout bag in his hand as he crawls into my bed, kisses me hello. Settles in front of me, legs crossed, bag nestled in them.

"You don't mind if I eat here, do you?" Looks up over his thick lashes, face down, ready to dive into his dinner.

"No, of course not, eat. How did it go?" I ask.

He unwraps a huge sub and a bag of chips, only adds before his first bite. "Interesting."

"What do you mean, interesting?"

As always I have to wait until he has consumed enough to divide his thoughts between food and speech.

"Well, I did do some snooping, subtle, hope it was subtle. Cassie wasn't in today but Beth and Laura, and what's her name? The meek one," thinks, "Carol, were all on. When things were a bit slow around dinner, you know everyone who can eat is eating, I pulled a little info out of them about you, and Joe. Made it sound like I wondered if you had taken off on him, things like that." More bites and then he wants water.

Impatiently I wait for him to return from the kitchen.

He continues. "Well, came out that about three weeks ago Joe came on the ward, afternoon shift. Drunk off his ass and started yelling at the nurses on duty. Harassing them about where you were. What they knew. Being a real asshole. They all were there but Beth, Cassie was on shift. Though she never said anything to me about it, rather strange that she didn't, but. Anyway sounds like someone, none of them would be clear on this, but someone told Joe that you and I were friends as well. Maybe I knew something. Most likely they just wanted to get him off their backs, deflect his rage somewhere else...That probably started it." He takes his last bites, drinks the rest of his water. Shakes his head.

"I may have been followed for days, weeks. I didn't think to look. Never noticed anyone, but, the night we went out for dinner," looks rather anxious, "I remember, now that I think about it. There was a car across the street, started just as we got in ours. It was loud, had a bad muffler. It drove behind us for a while, getting out of the neighborhood. It didn't look like anything suspicious to me at the time. Didn't think to keep track of it. May have been that Gary guy, maybe nothing." Shrugs his shoulders. "Don't know."

"Shit. Do you think he got pictures of us together?"

"Well, depends if he was doing a good investigation for Joe or just a quick favor to get him off his back. Time will tell. He is a cop; either way, there will be some questions asked. He'll be around, checking on me. I have no doubt about that part." He is not telling me something. I heard it in those last words.

"Eric?" Looking at him crossly. "What is it? What are you not telling me?"

"OK, think I may have seen that same car outside when I came home just now." He looks passively at me, waiting for my reaction.

"Now! Just now? Gary is outside the house now?" Unbelievable, seems too soon to be stalking.

"Think so. So if you need to feed, it's me or a really late night deer." Smiles apologetically.

He takes me reassuringly in his arms. "Don't fret, Margret, all will be well. I'll take care of you, at all costs."

"Don't like that all costs part, Eric." I settle into his arms. We lie quietly for a long time, both in our own thoughts and worries.

Several uneventful days passed. Mid-week I grew hungry, not desperately, but hungry. Eric warned me not to let myself become desperate as he may not be able to accommodate me if he was being watched at the time. I did not want to take from Eric but I may really need to, so I will wait.

Early Thursday morning, about 3 a.m., he snuck me to his car. Ever careful just in case, and drove me to the park. My head in his lap the whole way. Couldn't resist a bit of teasing, only got my hair roughly pulled for it.

I was already starting to feel cooped up, I had just gained some freedom and now, well, now I have none again. I did find a deer, drank all of it. I felt much better. Eric let me roam. I walked, and walked for a long while in the dark night through the woods. Just being free, alone. Two things I did not get much of lately.

I did roam rather far, the deer and the walk relaxing me. For the first time in days, I forgot for a while the trouble we could be in, the mess I'd made. I was grateful for that. When the morning started to make its most subtle appearance, I found my way back to him, the only human heart I could hear. My Eric looked like a vagrant wrapped in his long wool coat, asleep on a park bench waiting for me. I think it's mid-October, time and dates still mean little to me. Just day, night. He was cold but sleeping when I returned to him.

We returned home, thankfully unnoticed.

When Friday came, one full week after Joe's early morning burial in the woods, things started happening. At first Eric noticed the car again outside during the afternoon before he left for the store. Had to shop, there was no food not in a can in the house. Obviously Eric couldn't take me with him, so I stayed, well instructed, home. The drapes are always drawn, no peeking out. No noise. Keep my phone with me at all times. Eric bought the phone for me after I was made, trashed my old one somewhere. It's under his name as well, so even if they traced his calls, it would just look like Eric calling Eric. If I heard anything, to call him immediately. If Gary tried to get in the house, go out the back window, hide in the neighbor's garage. Lots of instructions and worried hugs before he left.

It was just Gary in his personal car, no other cops. He was the only one who knew anything tangible. Joe worked construction, his own company. Joe's employees of course, would notice he was not coming in, not answering his phone. Hopefully think he was in a drunken stupor or something. Maybe a friend would call, unreturned, not too unusual. For now only Gary would be genuinely concerned. Suspect something might be wrong.

It's day, should be full of sleep, but much too uneasy to do so. So I sit on the couch and listen to my iPod. They say music soothes the soul, well, it helped.

It was over an hour before Eric returned. He filled the island and all the counters with endless bags of groceries. Making several trips back to the car. Shopped for a zombie apocalypse. I helped him put it all away. Not much conversation, mostly where to put stuff, pantry shelves, fridge, freezer. I was putting a big jug of milk in the fridge when he unexpectedly came up behind me and pulled me to him in a warm hug. I stood there looking into the overflowing fridge, cold air escaping from it, and melted.

"You OK, Eric?"

"Yea, just, well, he followed me. No doubt now that I am a suspect in Joe's and, I'm sure, your disappearances. At least by Gary. Soon he'll have the whole force after me."

I close the door to the fridge and turn to take him fully into my arms. We hold each other tight, both worried yet finding comfort at the same time.

"Margret, you need sleep." Squeezes me a bit harder. "Where?" scooping me up into his arms as he asked.

"My room. Please." He gives me a soft understanding smile, takes me downstairs. Lays me in bed. Eric is hard, feel it. Still he makes no move to relieve it. Just my kiss to my forehead, the gray quilt pulled over me.

I am really tired. As long as Eric is near there is safety, comfort. Fall into darkness quickly.

I wake alone, smell food, not cooking, cooked. Burgers, I think. All is quiet, dark. Only the one light over my bed is on. No sounds from above, not even the TV he sometimes falls asleep to. I see a note on the ledge from him.

Margret,

I am sleeping upstairs, but if you need, want me, want is underlined, *you know where I am. Come get me. Especially if you hunger, take from me tonight. Don't let yourself need anything.* Again, 'anything' clearly underlined in his fine hand. I like just to look at it, his writing. *'Don't worry about things, ok? It will be all right. I will let nothing keep us apart, nothing! You are the love of my life, all of them.*

Your keeper, forever,

Eric

Why is this sweet note bringing me a tear? Begrudgingly I will let him sleep. Eric has too much to deal with. My endless desires for him, his blood, feeding me, protecting me. He is exhausted by it all. Admittedly just his written words make my heat throb for him. Seems I cannot have him enough. Eric is my one true need.

What to do without him? I have my music and laptop. Movie? Not in the mood. I have not read from Markus's journal for quite a while. It does overwhelm me sometimes, as with my fit, fearing Eric would want death and leave me. I do still fear that, but know if Eric wants death, I will go with him. No other, ever!

Pick the leather journal up off the ledge, search for the page I read last. Markus's writing style takes up a page quickly, beautifully. Read the opening lines again, the 'Dearest Margret,' just to remember it is special, for me.

As you are now just coming to yourself, there will be many challenges, fears. Your absence of memory will add greatly to this. Nothing will feel true, real to you for many weeks ahead. You will feel most uncertain of everything you feel, and want. That is, I assure you, quite normal.

Changing is a process. Days and nights maybe lost to you, only as you grow stronger will your mind clear enough to hold on to thought, remember your past.

Even though every organ in the human body is complex in its purpose and design, none come near the complexity of the mind. All its intricate workings, the memories, and deep emotions that reside inside it. This is why it is the last to fully turn. The last to fully wake. It is, for now, an empty place inside you, needing to be filled with who you are. Thus making it so much the harder to adjust to your new self.

I do promise you, Margret, this condition is not permanent. Some memories may be lost, but most return.

So even as you assuredly don't remember your time with Eric as you read these words, believe me please when I say you are Eric's true love, as I believe he is yours.

Trust him.

I expressed to Eric more than a year ago I desired a true death, although, I think I stated before, I knew I was near this before him. We all fight death, even immortals. Though I was certain by the time I took Eric, he would be my last, I was unsure of the years we would share. Eric was unaware of this, continues to be unaware. I knew I didn't have the heart for another.

As I finally convinced him of my wishes, he began his pilgrimage to find a new master to keep. Eric searched, courted many in that year, to my great impatience. He wanted, no, needed to have someone who loved him. More importantly to Eric, one he chose.

I do love him, but ours is, was, much different from what it will be for you. Much different.

Eric and I were very close friends before I took him into my service. I am a very old and powerful vampire, selfish and, admittedly, arrogant. I wanted him in ways he would not have accepted so I took him into my service most unwillingly. Righteously Eric despised me for longer than I care to remember. Eric only grew into love after many years, too many. Although after breaking him, he was always loyal to my needs, served me well. Still, as his master, I longed for his love, not just his submission to me. Thankfully he grew to love me, has for many years now. I cherished it more than I can express on any page.

All of these memories, feelings, and emotions factored into Eric's choice.

You, even if you feel right now that he strives to tame you against your wishes, are unique.

Eric was your first human feed. As I stated before, he will always saturate you more completely with life, calm you, and arouse you like no other.

You, Margret, are very fortunate in this. Countless vampires have had their first blood reclaimed by their makers. As Eric is now mine, their first blood belonged to the maker, his own keeper. Unattainable to them. The keeper is only there to assist in turning, never belonging to them. Regardless, vampires will always lust for the taste of their first blood.

Often a human sacrifice is first blood. It is an uncontrolled feed. Always fatal to the mortal. In this case first blood is never to be savored again. Many of us believe this is the better way as it is only one feed. Not weeks that the keeper's blood is savored, we all know nothing tastes, feels or is more desirable as the blood of your birth. Ever.

My own maker shared his keeper with me for several months. Until I tamed, became more of my true self. Eventually I, with his help, had to find my own.

I had little ambition for it; I only wanted, loved, craved my maker's. Still love her to this day. Alas, I had to find my own and leave them both. No human, though some have reminded me of her, has ever tasted as sweet to me.

As I am going to find true death shortly, Eric is now yours. For as long as you both wish it, your giving and feeding will be most powerful. Again, Margret, you are very fortunate in this. Your connection before you were a vampire coupled with this gift. I pray you don't bleed each other into the dirt in your lusts.

Remember my warnings, heed them. Your regret if you take too much from Eric, Give too much, will be greater than any. I can image it, but it is not mine. It is yours.

You are thoroughly cautioned, Margret!

Eric is very strong and experienced keeper. I believe he will control this, not without reservations. I know now how deeply he feels for you even before you have your full power over him, it will double, if not more.

I know not how quickly you read these pages, how closely you are to your true self. How many bondings, how deeply you have taken each other. I do know you must, for the both of you, accept who you are now, remember who you were. Understand Eric's role and accept his love for you if you wish any peace in the endless years you have ahead of you, Margret.

Any anger you may feel for him at the moment is only a small part of your story together. You must let it go. My desire is that these writings will assist you; if need be convince you. Go forward, you are not as you were before, that is the past. You are a very powerful being now. I made you, fed you well from me. My blood and my power are forever yours. As is my beloved Eric. Take good care of both.

A last note to you, Margret. As I write these thoughts down, Eric is finally asleep, restlessly, but asleep. Like a frightened child clinging to me. His disturbed dreams I am sure are of you and the lonely weeks ahead. It is now early morning and you have finally worn yourself out and are quiet for the time being. I know he wants to be your keeper more than I could have ever seduced him to be mine. Eric chose you. My last concern is that you take him into yourself and love him as he loves you, Margret. He may well die if you do not.

I regret I shall never see the beautiful Vampire you are now. That I shall never embrace my beloved child with more than these writings and the hopes they have for you.

Markus

Find that I am weeping over the loss of a man I do not remember. A man I will never know. Weeping for my immortal father, the man who gave me Eric to love forever.

My desire is inflamed as well. Markus, who I find myself secretly competing with, jealous of, writing of how deeply Eric loves me.

The sun arrives soon, hope Eric has rested. I break my commitment to leave him alone to his sleep. Crave him like blood.

Chapter Nineteen

"Eric, may I ask you a question, or two?"

"Yesss." I can tell he is not eager.

It's Saturday evening. We are sitting on the floor near the fire in the front room. The floor is covered in the soft gray comforter from his bed, extra blankets, many pillows resting against the couch. It is warm and comfortable for us both. I like it here, better than my cubby, but only if he is near.

"I was reading the journal last night, and, well, I wondered about you and Markus. You haven't told me about it." Approaching the topic as demurely as possible.

"About what part of, it?" Noticed my tone when I said 'it' clearly.

"That, uh, how did he put it," feigning some forgetfulness, "he took you unwillingly into his service?"

"Oh, that." Not happy. I am going to have to pull. Eric removes his arm from my shoulders and sits forward.

"I'd like to know what happened. I feel like I know everything and nothing about you at the same time."

"OK, OK," he barks. "Just not something I like to think about, let alone talk about. It was so long ago and I like to live in the present. Can't change anything, so... Guess I should tell you more than I do." He is aggravated already. Looks wide-eyed over his shoulder, raising his brow.

"Sure you want to hear..."

I quickly trample his question. "Yes, I am sure."

"Just don't ask a bunch of questions I don't want to answer. Just listen, K?" He hates my need for details.

"K."

I am looking at the back of his head, I have a feeling I will be for a while. Can't resist a stroke over his hair, he leans into it. Contently rests his head in my palm for a moment. Reluctantly begins.

"It was 1944; I was a fireman on the near south side of Chicago. And no, before you ask, I didn't always live here. Markus and I lived all over the place." Silent for a second.

"Just wanted to come home now." Finally he sits back next to me, but still his eyes to the flames.

"Anyway I was 28, been in the department for eight of those. I loved it even though it was a tough job. I liked helping people. We got called for everything, in those days there weren't many cops on that side of town, just us. Anyhow, we got this new rookie in, Markus Wood." Weakly chuckles, shaking his head.

"Wood, seems such a stupid last name for Markus. His real name is Markus Lazarus Castellanos." Trails off for a moment. Stalling.

"Markus was the new guy so we all picked on him, gave him every crappy chore there was. Did it to all the rookies. Most of them hated us for it, did it but bitching the whole time. Not Markus; he was always ready, happy to do it. Seemed like a really great guy. Didn't take long before we became friends."

Eric stops again, lost in memories.

"Uh, so, I was single, just broke off an engagement, just wanted to drink, and we did, many nights after work. He was a fun, good to talk to, or not talk, if you know what I mean.

Of course almost everything he told me about himself was a lie. Simple manipulations to gain my friendship, trust. He soon had both. I would have run into flames to get him out, died for him. 'Course, that is the way we all were, but Markus undeniably became the best friend I had.

"I was a pretty straight-laced guy, honest, soft-hearted. Kinda open-minded for the times, about most things. Knew my own right and wrong, tried not to judge others. Markus used to tell me how much he admired me, my strength, my heart, never really understood why." He takes a big gulp of his wine, finishing off the glass.

"Need more for this next part." He leaves to go into the kitchen. I wonder what recollection requires more wine.

Returns with his full glass, a fresh bottle in hand. Stands facing the fire for a few moments. Only a pair of black silk lounge pants hangs loose over his sharp hips. Have to fight with my lusts to look at him. Drinks another ample amount from his glass then puts both on the coffee table next to our bedding. Eric sits back down next to me, noticeably a bit farther away now. Breath anxious, as if he does not know what he wants to say next or if he wants to say it at all.

"We went out one Friday after our shift; neither of us were on the next day so we really tied one on. Ate, drank, went to the next bar, drank some more. Picked up girls, had a bit of fun. I drank myself sick that night, literally. Didn't do that usually. Know it was near morning when I finally passed out in the passenger seat of my car. Markus drove, never seemed to get as wasted as I did. I know now he drank, went to the bathroom, puked it up. Very dedicated to his cover, though I never really saw him eat anything. Stupid, never suspected a thing."

Shaking his head, rather disappointed in himself. How could he have known, guessed? It's absurd.

"I woke up the next day, still drunk, head swimming. I was in a big dining room, looked to be some old mansion. There was a huge fireplace, the kind you could walk into, nearby. Didn't know how I got there, no fucking idea where I was, or what happened. Like I said I still felt drunk. Like when you drink so much even a night's rest can't ward off the amount of alcohol you have in your system. Anyway, for a long time, I couldn't get my head around what was going on. I knew I was naked, barely covered by a throw on my lap. My hands behind my back tied to the leg of a long wood dining table, and my ankles tied together. Only the huge fire to keep me from the cold."

I dare not talk, though many questions and strange feelings are rushing around my mind. Like a crazy dust storm swirling in my head. Eric is in a place, not here, back in a place that disturbs him. It is disturbing me as well.

"Eventually he came in, all dressed up. Long black, like a smoking, jacket but all the way to the floor with a fine white dress shirt, black velvet vest, trousers. The finest of gentlemen, so much so at first I didn't even recognize him."

Chuckles quietly. "Markus had really crazy curly hair when it was short, but he, the Markus I knew, always put a ton of hair oil or some shit into it to smooth it down. Never worked too well really, hair was always escaping the lavish amount of oil, popping out everywhere. This Markus let it be as it was, light brown curls. He looked so strange to me...but when he spoke, I knew the curious gentleman was Markus.

"He introduced himself most courteously to me. Markus Lazarus Castellanos. Explained rather coolly that he was a vampire of some 300 plus years. Of course I thought, yea right, a vampire, sure. Markus tried to calmly explain where I was over my swearing and shouting at him.

"Didn't hear much at that point, just thought it was some kind of sick joke. Pay back for all the times we made him clean the crappers with a toothbrush. Just couldn't figure...my head was still foggy at best. My anger soon cleared that."

Eric pauses, takes another ample drink, assembling his thoughts before he continues.

"I remember Markus placed a huge embroidered armchair in front of me. Lifted it in one hand like it weighed nothing. Sat down, again most proper, then he started to explain the whole vampire keeper thing to me. Who he was, why he needed me. How dearly he felt for me. I wouldn't hear any of it. I cursed him at the top of my lungs, pleaded with him to let me go.

Nothing moved him a bit. He sat stoic. Repeated all of his arguments over and over for hours it seemed. Well after I was sober.

"All his persuasions lost on me. Offered me drink, food. Markus's attempts at kindness only angered me further. By then I couldn't be convinced he was anything but a sick human being. Thought he was insane. I didn't believe one word. Finally he stopped trying to persuade me. Just sat there silent for a long while somberly looking off into the fire.

"Eventually Markus rose from his chair, looked rather disappointed at me. Actually thought he was going to let me go when he knelt on the floor next to me, but that wasn't what he did."

Eric shakes his head as if in some new disbelief. "Instead he slit his wrist."

Eric looked over his shoulder at me for the first time since he started.

"With the same giving ring you use now." An ironic tone to this remark. Turns his glance away, words nearly a whisper.

"He forced me to take it, feed. Held my nose and mouth closed with his bleeding hand, remember blood dripping over my chin, down my neck. Eventually I had to breathe. As soon as I opened my mouth to take a breath, Markus pushed his wrist into it, held me very firmly to it." Weakly adds, "He was unnaturally strong."

I rub my hand over his back in a vain effort to soothe him. His muscles are like stone, pulled so tight I don't know if he even felt my soft touch.

"I had to drink to breath. Every breath came with a mouth full of his blood. Held it there, forcing my mouth open, forcing it down my throat until it stopped. Then he made me keep it. I was convulsing, gagging on it. Forbade me even to puke it out. His fingers pressing my nose closed, his other hand on my forehead, tilting my head back, so even if I did threw up it would be forced back down or I'd choke on it. I felt the blood heat right way. I was confused by it, hated it, him."

Half a glass of wine in one gulp. I have never seen him drink so quickly; he may drink a lot, but over a whole evening. He is going through the second bottle of red fast.

"Then it got even stranger, worse. Markus began to kiss passionately over my shoulders and neck, bit at them softly. Trying to seduce me with his words, his unwanted affections. I of course struggled to get away from him but couldn't go far from the table I was bound to. He was so strong, held me like I was just a child having a tantrum. Nothing I said, shouted, not anger, not pleading discouraged him. Markus's blood was in me, had its effect and he would take advantage of it."

Eric stops again, full of memory. Memories he obviously had not allowed himself for a very long time. Drinks his glass dry, generously filling it again.

"Markus took me...in his mouth. That was the first time. Ever."

Eric pulls every word reluctantly out.

"I never had, well, oral; none of the nice woman I had courted had ever done it to me. Even my recent fiancée wouldn't do it. Said it was too dirty. Anyway, I didn't have many women before, but..."

He takes a deep breath, his shoulders rise with it. "I remember the conflict. I hated that it felt so good, his mouth on me. Amazingly good." Nearly inaudibly whispers, "Couldn't help myself."

So familiar, his story. I felt much the same not so long ago. Forced to climax by tenured tongue. I am starting to understand so many things about my Eric. Why it was so important to him that he waited for me, courted me as he says in his sweet old-fashioned way. Deep inside there is still somewhere the Eric of 1944. A young man still searching for his true love, rather innocent, trusting. Believing his future would be bright. All taken from him.

He is quiet. Resting his mind.

"How long until you felt about Markus as you do now? It's clear to me you love him, miss him. How, when he was so cruel, forced you?"

He weakly grins at me. "Was I not cruel to you, in your estimation?"

"Yes, you were, very...but that was different. You were a straight man, forced to..."

Don't want to say it aloud; he was raped, just as I was. From the sounds of it for a long time. Still Eric had no lost memories of love to regain. Only broken. "You didn't love, want him, that way."

I can see he appreciates my rationalizations. "You had your full faculties, unlike me, a wild amnesiac."

I put my arms around his shoulders, kiss his cheek softly. "You loved me before, and I loved you, so I've heard." I try to disarm the moment, to no avail.

His mood quickly shifts from melancholy to umbrage. "You did love me, I insisted on it!" Each word said with great force. "That you said it. That you loved me, before we changed you. It was the only way I would do it. You choosing me." He looks at me, aggravated.

"Markus would have changed you before our first kiss if he had his way. I had to hide it, how crazy I was about you, he was so anxious to be done with my searching." His tone quiets. "We had never fought like we did over you, never."

Our roles reversed, yet so much the same. I decide to leave the many questions I have swirling around my head to ask only one.

"What happened after that night?" He seems to be affected by the glasses of wine now. Tired eyes. Maybe it is the strain of the memories, not the wine that weighs so heavy on his mindfulness.

"It was the better part of a year before he completely released me from my bindings for more than my human needs. Even for sex for a long while. I had so many wild experiences I never thought I'd have. Never even in my most private thoughts. He gave me women, many beautiful women. Only so as I entered them he could enter me. Break me further." Somehow still bewildered.

"The first times Markus took me I was bound over the long dining table near the fire place. Always a fire raging in it. I had little sense of day or night. Just the dining room and the fire. My ankles strapped to the heavy turned wood legs. My arms bound over my head. Markus knew it was too much for me, physically, mentally; it didn't deter him much. I screamed, fought, sobbed. Every time, struggled. It hurt, as well as made me full of shame. Markus would force me to feed before, not much, just enough to ensure my cock was hard."

"I was taken care of after. He lavished me with hot kisses in places I never thought I'd be kissed. Drank from me. Inside of my legs was his favorite. That didn't change much... always he bled me in the back of my shoulder when he was having his way with me. Hated him for it, more for how I responded to it."

"After a few weeks, I think, weeks. Anyway, he started to bring me women. To remind me my manhood was still intact more than anything. I wasn't the kind of man who just screwed women. I cared deeply for the few lovers I had before, but his blood, his bleeding me, his unwanted attentions. It changed me. I greedily took them all. Then he got what he wanted from me. Less fighting that way. I had more women in a single week than I had my entire life."

Eric pauses to drain his glass yet again before he continues.

"The women were all willing for the sex. Only after when the woman was weak from our attentions and a few too many glasses of wine, he would feed on her. Never to death. Always instructing me how to keep watch over his feed. How long he should feed, to rouse him if he lost himself. Teaching me how to be his keeper. Never knew what he did with them after, just knew they were alive when he took them away.

"I learned my role. Had no choice. Although to this day, I doubt he needed me for much really. Just human companionship. Very few times in all the years I watched over his feedings did I have to make him release. Only when the human had something different, intoxicating to him. Blood, scent, features, who knows? Just didn't happen much."

Sheepishly ask, "When did you start to change, to love him?" He lies back to hold me now, pulling my legs over his. Rest my head in his chest, his heart beats harshly in my ear.

"That, took a long time, about five years. Markus fully broke me within a year or so. I did what he wished. We had women mostly, a few men in our bed. For me, I am sure. Though he often fed on men in the bars and streets. I helped find him food, though he needed little help with that, his seduction was perfected. Mine, well, I was a work in progress. He taught me how to read people."

Drinks from his glass, taking a moment's rest from his unwanted disclosures.

"Markus lavished me with every possession he could imagine I would want or need. Handmade clothes, dinners at the best restaurants, concerts, museums. Fine parties we were not invited to, anything to seduce me. Any woman who caught my eye was mine. Markus was very handsome and exceedingly good at seducing people. Suppose it was his years of experience, he always knew what a woman, or man, needed to hear."

Eric clutches me a bit harder. "He did love women, make no mistake. To this day I don't know if they were his preference, or if he had one, you couldn't tell. He just lusted for heat, love, and of course, blood. Never mattered the sex of his feed; it was the person he desired most. They were his."

"How did Markus react when after all those years of hating him, that you didn't, you loved him?" I ask.

Eric pulls my legs over him higher so I am curved completely around him. Wraps his arms tighter. Feel his need for closeness, comfort.

"Do you remember how I reacted when you told me?"

I do remember his tears pooling in that place where my neck and shoulders meet. Feeling the warm sweetness of them weep over my shoulder. The heat of his body over me. Yes," I whisper.

"Much the same." He tilts my face to him, brushes his mouth over my lips. Open, yet not yielding, tender kisses.

"Thank you, Eric. I know that was hard for you, but I feel like I understand you better. Why..."

He cuts me off sharply, mood shifts radically. "Understand what?" He seems angry at me, not sure why. "That I was taken, raped, forced into a life

I didn't want?" Pushes me back to look at me face to face. "You understand why 67 years later I did the same to you? Did exactly what Markus did? To the woman I love?" Violently shaking his head. "Just like him."

His eyes fill with angry tears. None fall but his dark eyes are nearly over-whelmed. "Just like him," Eric repeats. His anger is at himself, not me. "I did and worse. I took your human life from you."

Eric closes his eyes, forcing the pool of tears to stream down his cheeks. There is so much pain and remorse on his face I can barely stand it but I am afraid to touch him. I have never seen him like this. Not sure what's the right thing to do.

"I know full well what I did to you, Margret. How it felt for you those first days of wakefulness. No memory of me, of us. I know. I am so ashamed that I could, did...after what I went through. Yet I still took you, wanted to, needed to, not only to arouse your memory, your heart..." Eric's mouth moves to my ear, nibbling as he knows I love. Hotly whispers over it.

"Admittedly I loved your surrenders to me." His voice wickedly seductive, unlike any note I have heard tonight. Eric pulls away from nuzzling my ear to look at me again. His eyes are dark and lustful.

His moods are shifting so quickly I can hardly understand one before the next is inflicted on me. I must be patient, understanding; I asked Eric to tell me this tale. Realize now why he endeavors to live solely in the present. Memories are too painful and clearly antithetical to the reality he desires them to be.

In a severe voice, Eric confesses, "I am not the man Markus took anymore. Still here, somewhere, full of regret, yes, but I have to forget. I couldn't deal with the things I've done, the person I've become ..." He falls into me, kissing and sucking at my breasts, wanting to be nurtured, needing my embrace.

I lie back, pulling him over me. Forcing him to continue his hold on me. My legs crushing his hardness to me. He makes no move to free himself. His need is reassurance, comfort. Maybe forgiveness.

Eric holds my hips firm, stopping my grinding to gain my attention. Looking somberly into my eyes.

"I did love you, deeply loved you when you were human, Margret, even more now. But I selfishly wanted to continue being young, strong. Have the powerful sex, the nearly immortal life I had. Maybe I should have left you as you were. Because of me you have done things that you could never have thought of. I can't, I am so..."

Silence his confession covering his mouth with mine, knowing he was going to say he was sorry. I don't need to hear it anymore.

No pain, no circumstance, no amount of time will keep me from him.

I have waited for this love, dreamt of it. Believed it was impossible, this deep connection. It is mine now and I will guard it with all I have. Destroy anything, everything, to protect it.

Finally my grinding is answered. Eric is mine now.

Chapter Twenty

The night was long and difficult for him. Eric's lovemaking was just like his moods. Forceful, sad, gentle, angry. He took me well beyond his normal, albeit considerable, abilities. His need to bond with me was uncontrollable. I gave to him; finally that satiated his hunger for me. He became more of himself after and slept content in my arms well into the daylight. I understand him and love him more dearly when the morning breaks.

Currently I am trying to rest in our makeshift bed on the floor. Eric is full of nervous energy, cleaning, vacuuming. Making a lot of noise. I suppose I should go downstairs, but am too lazy to get myself up. The heavy curtains are always closed so the daylight is minimal. Still not as dark as the basement, so I pull a pillow over my head to block the light and the noise. Try to sleep.

I hear the doorbell ring. Sit up, alarmed, don't think it's the pizza boy. Eric comes in from the kitchen, looks at me sternly.

"Stay, don't move." Cover my head with the blanket, curl myself up small into the pillows. The bell rings again. Eric unlocks the bolts on the door.

"Good afternoon. Are you Eric Campbell?"

"Yes, I am. What can I do for you?" He is polite, calm.

"I'm Gary, uh Officer Gary Blonski." Gary is a street cop, must be in plain clothes. It is Saturday, most likely he is off duty, on his own time.

"Mind if you show me your badge, Officer?"

"No, not at all." I hear Eric open the storm door to look at it.

"Chicago? What brings you out here to the burbs, Officer, Blonski?"

"Well, just looking for someone. Missing person... persons. You ever seen this guy around?" Obviously has a picture of Joe to show Eric. "His name is Joseph Thomas, went missing about a week ago."

Eric takes his time, pretending to look closely at the photo. "No sir, never seen him before. I don't get out much, but sure I don't recognize him."

"How about this woman?" Again he pauses but answers quickly.

"Ya, Margret, she worked at the hospital with me. Nice lady, haven't seen her for a few months though."

"Well she, Margret, is missing as well. No proof that she met with foul play but Joe here is her husband. Just odd they would both drop off the map like that. Don't you think?"

"Yea I suppose but, I just volunteer at the hospital. I knew her yes, from work. Had a few lunches in the cafeteria, didn't know much about her, never met her husband." Amazing how good he is at lying, has me convinced.

"You sure about that, Mr. Campbell?" Gary sounds less certain. Knows he is not telling him the truth.

"Very sure, why are you asking me? Like I said, we hardly knew each other."

"Well, just checking all the possibilities. Joe here is a friend of mine, asked me to look into his wife's disappearance. He thought she just left him, but after a while, it really started to bug him. Ya know, where she was, so..." He wonders off into silence.

Shit, I hope he doesn't have any real proof that I am here, with Eric. I am so nervous Eric will be caught. I can't let that happen. There is long stretch, neither having anything more to say, but Gary still stands there.

"Anything else I can help you with, Officer Blonski?" I hear the storm door slowly closing; Eric is done with this conversation.

"Nope, just keep an eye out, let me know if you see or hear anything. Here's my card." Gary sounds irritated, but obviously has nothing else to add.

"Will do. Have a nice day, Officer." Eric closes the door, locks and bolts it. I don't hear him move, I don't move.

"It's OK." I look up; he is looking out the peep hole. I hear Gary's car, yes bad muffler, loudly drive away. "He's gone now."

"Eric?"

"Yes?" He is doing laundry now; I am on my bed reading.

"When do you think will we move to the Chicago place?"

"Don't know, not for a while. I don't want to make any sudden moves. I will look suspicious if I take off, and it might be hard to get you out of here unnoticed." I can hear him loading the clothes, starting the washer.

"Did you live there before here?"

"Yep."

I know he hates when I get all curious and start with the questions. "How long did you live downtown? Where did you live before that?"

Nothing. I look up ready to repeat my questions to see he is standing at the foot my bed. He looks so sweet, grey loose-fit jeans and tight long-sleeved blue shirt, his hair a mess of waves. It's been raining all day, the dampness makes his hair crazy, near curly. I smile.

"You and your questions." Flops on the bed next to me. Lying on his side, elbow bent, resting his head in his hand.

"Not everyone is good at living only in the moment as you are, Eric. So, tell me?"

"Before here, I, we, lived in Napa."

"Wow. Napa Valley?" I ask, hoping.

"Yep. Markus bought a small, well, small for Napa, winery several years ago. It was a beautiful place. You know, the rolling hills filled with grape vines, driveways lined in apple trees. It was really something. Big house. Had this beautiful slate terrace that overlooked the vineyards. Great over-sized chairs, ottomans made of natural tree branches. They were really comfortable. I used to love sitting in them, just hanging out. Some days I barely moved, read, drank great wine, listened to music. Enjoying the view till the sun was low. Then I had to serve Markus's needs."

Sounds like he liked his alone time. Time when he didn't have to be the keeper, just Eric.

"Anyway, when he told me I had to go on without him, either change over or find a new master, or I suppose just go on, that, well, can't really go back to a fully normal life after 67 years being a vampire's keeper. Not a real option." Shakes his head, looks up at me with an awkward smile.

"I just wanted to come home for some reason. Wanted to be back here in Chicago. So he, well, the real estate agent, found us an amazing place here. We still have the Napa house; Markus rented it out. The winery was always run by a family, Sandos; they live in the house now. For a very reasonable price, I might add."

He scooches up closer to me so I can play with his hair and he can play with my breasts. Just affection but will quickly turn if I am not careful, and then no answers, again. No wonder I never seem to get back to all of my inquiries; he deflects them too easily.

"So what's the Chicago place like?"

"Spectacular." He looks up, eyes wide. "It's the on the top of this old building on Michigan Avenue. Built 1890 something, it was an old part of the skyline even when I lived here. Great view of the park, the lake, the city, lots of big windows and glass doors that go out to the roof. You're going to love it. The city has grown so much since I was here last. Loved Chicago back then, even more now. Missed it, you know, home." Stops his nuzzling, eyes smiling up at me.

"Wanted whoever I found to be from my home. Stupid, I guess, but how I felt."

"That's not stupid. Sweet, sentimental, but not stupid." Can't resist playing with his hair. He gives me a sweet look, knows I am possessed by it. More so now that the damp air has had its way with it. He is getting too affectionate, snuggling his face into me. Suppose so am I.

I sit up, taking away his distractions. Disgruntled, he too sits, arranging the pillows behind him. Well away from me sitting in the middle of the bed.

"You rent it? That must cost a ton."

Waving his hand. "No, no, Markus bought it outright. He sold a few big estates in Europe in the last few years, made a bundle on them."

Shakes his head amazed.

"You know all those boxes and files in the spare room? All his papers. I realize now he tried to get me to pay attention to his finances. Made me go with him to his solicitors, as he called them, so I would pay attention. Probably for now, when he is gone and it's all mine. Didn't care as much as I should have. Markus organized them all over these last months, gave me his address book with all the names of real estate places he worked with, lawyers, lots of them. Financial places, advisors, forgers, crooks, you name it. I spent a lot of time looking through it all, trying to make some sense of it, but there's just so much. Gets frustrating after a while and I give up. I really have no idea all he has, just know it's a lot. A lot of money in banks, property and possessions. He amassed much over the years."

Shit, money, possessions, property, never thought to even want it. Really just wanted to be happy and loved. What a bonus, both. I can't even get my head around it. We are still living in this simple house, me hardly out of the life I had. A penthouse at the top of the Chicago skyline seems like a fairy tale. Think I'll believe when I see it. Still a part of me distrusts, I guess.

Chapter Twenty-one

Monday, he is gone to the hospital. I rest as much as I can but my hunger is getting too loud. I haven't told him, yet. Know I need to, so I text him, not the best way but I feel so demanding of him, and this way I don't have to see his face reprimanding me for how long I have waited to tell him. Just a short note. 'Hi, I miss you! :-) Starting to get hungry, very. Love, me.' Let's see what response I get to that.

Just sitting in my cubby listening to my iPod and looking through catalogs; we are getting plenty of them now, after my online shopping spree. I browse, Stevie Ray in my ears, as loud as I can make him. Circle things I like, may order. Wait for my phone to ring or make that text sound. Nothing for a while.

He calls, I pause the song, want to hear it after.

"Hey. How's it going?"

"Margret, why do you wait so long?"

"Sorry."

"I can't tell how long my blood will sustain you, you have to tell me! OK?" May not see his face but hear it well in his tone. "I am here till 4, I'll see what I can do. K? If not you'll have to take me again."

"Eric I just took you, I'll bleed you to death this way, no. I will not. I'll do another deer or...something."

"I'll call if I am going to be any later that 5ish. I gotta go."

Someone must have interrupted him he broke off so quickly.

We'll see what he can arrange. Looking for and bringing home vagrants to me is almost impossible. Gary is often following him now. Seems all his spare time is going into his desire to nail Eric for Joe's, and my, disappearances. There have even been a few black and whites outside, stopping for a bit and then circling the block, reappearing in front of the house. Local police, but all cops are friends. Gary is pulling in favors. Watching Eric even when he can't. It's nerve racking for Eric. He has never been so closely tied to a murder as this. The one I caused. Even if he had been involved with something Markus did, it was a stranger, not tied to their lives. Easily disposed of in the great numbers of missing persons, killings. This one is on his doorstep.

Gary obviously has no real proof of me being with Eric, I don't think. He would have brought him in already. I hate the waiting most. What is going to happen next? Just want it to be over with and move to the Chicago place, go on. Leave the old me here.

After an hour or so, Eric calls again.

"Hi." I know it is him even without the name on the screen; he is the only one who has this number.

"I called Karl, he works at the bar at night. Mondays they're closed so he was good with coming by tonight."

"Great, thank you."

"Sure, just try not to drain him before we can have some fun with him first, OK?"

Eric may need me most, but I do think he misses sex with a man after too long. It is what he was used to, maybe not his preference but still enjoys.

"You miss having men, don't you?" I hear an exasperated breath.

"What do you want me to say?" Getting testy with me. "I'll get him drunk and do nothing with him if that is your wish, Margret."

"No, I am OK with that, that you may want a man... my fingers probably don't satisfy you as much as a man can."

Another more exasperated breath. While kissing, loving his firm behind, I have pressed my fingers inside him a few times. He seems to love it when I do it. Still, a couple of timid fingers doesn't amount to much.

"Your fingers are, fantastic, just, yea, once in a while…" He doesn't finish his thought. I know what it is anyway. "This is not a conversation I want to have, Margret, let alone on the phone. You good with this or not? I don't want to be surprised by you later. Just tell me what you want." Know he is referring to the unexpected fit I had over him making out with that girl at the bar.

Besides, the first time he brought Blondie home, I was still, well, not myself at all. Didn't love him as I do now. Eric seems a bit leery of my jealousy.

"No, I am OK, really I will be good and we'll have fun. Promise." Not sure what I am agreeing to, just want to be agreeable.

"Good, just need to know."

"Know that I love you."

"Love you, see you around 6." He hangs up. Managed to piss him off, again. Thank God he is so forgiving, or is it needy? Forgets quickly his anger with me.

I decide to shower, dress in something sexy and easily removed. A dress. Search the closet. Find a low cut black one, casual, cotton. Still looks nice on me. Get the front room ready, bring down the quilt and place it on the chair in case we want it.

There is a case or two of beer in the basement. I'll put ample beers in the fridge to get them cold before the get-together.

Wait. Six twenty before his car drives in. Another set of lights right behind him. Hope that's not Gary.

Hear the voices in the driveway, Eric and Blondie, well, Karl. Wasn't sure if I was supposed to be here but I am sitting at the kitchen island when they walk in.

"Hey Margret." Eric comes to me, kisses me lightly on my lips. Karl follows. "Nice to see you again." Another kiss, sweet on my cheek.

"Have some cold ones in the fridge, anyone?"

Eric looks gratefully at me. "Yes! Karl, you?" Eric pulls Karl into a half hug.

"Sure, I'm good for a few." Karl seems a bit bashful tonight.

Eric gets two beers out. Karl questions my lack of beverage and I assure him I will drink tonight but I am a lightweight and will start later so I don't get tipsy too fast. Little does he realize my drink will be him.

We relocate to the front room. I have a fire going and many candles along the mantel. Again Eric gives me a look of appreciation.

Karl sits next to me on the couch, Eric in one of the side chairs so he can make eye contact with us both. Fall into a somewhat awkward conversation. Karl is drinking his first few rapidly. I make sure they are readily refilled. They have their effect. Karl seems happy enough, light conversation for a bit, but soon he gets into his personal life. Seems to be a difficult one. Both parents are alcoholics. His father killed someone while drunk driving, now in jail. His mother's drinking only worsened after that...finances horrid. Works the gay bars at night and in an office during the day. No siblings. Lives with, supports, his mother.

His manner is rather odd, but he seems sweet. I have never got to know my food this way. Well, Eric, but that is different. Seem strange that I am feeling affection for him and wanting him to quiet so I can feed off him at the same time. Decide to excuse myself for a bit. Eric's charm will work quicker if there is less conversation. I excuse myself to go upstairs to the bathroom. I don't, of course. I sit on the steps, well away from sight and wait.

Doesn't take as long as I expected. Soon silence, just heavy breathing. I still wait, unsure of when I should return. I hear Eric very softly say my name. Muffled but hear it.

When I return, I see Eric is fully undressed. Karl's shirt is on the floor with Eric's clothes, his pants undone. Eric is biting his nipples and stroking his hardness, causing our Blondie to make the most pleasant moaning sounds. Eric is on the couch next to him where I sat so recently. I just stand there and watch from the doorway for a bit.

Karl gets up and removes his pants, revealing his rather impressive hardness. Falls on his knees before Eric. Takes him vigorously into his mouth.

Eric looks over to me and motions for me to come near. I am a bit apprehensive, but go to him.

"Take off your dress." Knows I have nothing underneath it. I toss it in the pile of discarded clothes.

His hands firmly guiding Karl's head, he only lifts one to motion to me to come closer.

"Come here, Margret." Reassuringly whispers to me.

Not sure what he wants so I kneel on the couch next to him. Eric takes my leg and moves it over him so I am straddling him. My ass touching the top of Karl's blond hair.

Not what Eric wants. He lifts me up by my behind to his waiting mouth. I am very distracted by what Karl is doing to him, yes, even hot from it. Though now Eric's mouth is loving me the passionate way he does, sending me into fits. Eagerly holding me over him, passion in every kiss. Slip my hands into his hair, pulling much more gently than I want. I look behind me, want to see Karl energetically working on Eric stiffness.

Soon Eric breaks this coupling. Lays me on the floor. Eric kisses Karl quite deeply before they come to me.

I know why he did that now; at the time was clueless.

He tries to move him in between my legs; Karl resists. Says something about not doing women any more, but Eric persuades him to just try. Eric's deep kiss was full of my heat.

Karl's mouth is most conservative at first but quickly changes. Not near the affections or need I feel from Eric, but nice. Just as I adjust and relax, Eric demands another position. Guides me to rest on my side, my blond lover in front of me, Eric at my back. Both hardnesses grinding on me, making me crazy with want and need. The blood heat is so strong as they lie near, I nearly forget what is happening.

Unexpectedly Karl enters me. Not at all sure I want this but go with it. Hold Karl in my arms affectionately. Knowing Eric will tell me when to feed. Maybe now as he is so engaged? It feels good, but right now my focus is blood. Only Eric's love can distract me from that need.

I feel Eric rubbing himself between my cheeks, pressing. At first I pay no mind to it, his kisses and soft biting at my neck and shoulders more interesting. He has rubbed himself on me like that before. Karl's thrusts are pleasantly slow.

Eric pushes harder at me, entering just a bit. I struggle, he soothes. Going no deeper. Coaxing me gently.

"Eric." Hope he can hear the pleading and questioning in just his name.

"It's OK, try. Just a little more." With that he enters me a bit deeper. I know his hardness, the length of it. Not nearly as deep as he can give me. Still it hurts, the slow shallow thrusts more than I can handle. I feel them both pushing themselves into me. Both too well endowed to make this pleasurable for me. I clench my behind, again plead.

"Eric, please." Immediately he removes himself.

"I'm sorry." Feel his sweet kiss on my neck. "Take him now," he whispers into my ear, not without a soft bite.

Mine not so soft. Our Blondie makes no resistance at all this time. Eric moves around to Karl's back, takes him with all the force I denied him. I feed. Karl is full of passionate moans, encouraging words. Inside me and Eric inside him. His delight clear.

I am lost in my bloodletting. I feel Karl but the need, well, the blood is my central focus. Hear Eric's loud moan with his release. I know it well.

My feeding on Karl, maybe his 'feed' on me, seems to have much effect. He remains hard even after his climax. Eric pulls him from my mouth, not allowing me take too much. Offers himself to Karl, quickly taken. I am in my contented place, but have my wits enough to watch as he slides himself slowly into Eric. Admittedly now I am most envious; not jealous, envious.

Love Eric's firm ass so much but probing my fingers into him can't compares to this powerful joining. Find I am wishing I could have him as Karl is. Eric's pleasureful moans make me want it even more. I kneel behind

Karl and embrace him with my full body. Locking myself into his back. Move with him. Touching them where they join. I vicariously have my Eric in his lunges.

I bleed Karl once more before the two of them are done. Now quite enough to send him to rest. Most likely a few days of weakness.

I am well fed.

Still I feel disturbed by the evening. More lovers. Suppose I will have to rid myself of that part of my humanity. That part of Margret, who only wanted one true love.

They both sleep. Eric lies on his stomach between us, Blondie's arm and leg over Eric. Eric much the same over me. As they rest I look into the flames, fading now, and wonder who I am becoming.

Chapter Twenty-two

"I have to go." Spoken softly over my neck. I am back in my bed, full day in the window.

"You going in?" Still so sleepy.

"Yes till 5." Eric kisses over my shoulders. Every time he has to leave, he wants. Seems he is too late for even a quickie.

"Just rest."

"I love you."

"You too." Snuggle back into the pillows, tuck his into me.

I hear his car leave, put my phone near my head, go back to sleep.

Don't know how long I was out but hear that buzzing noise my phone makes when I have a text. Clear my head enough to read it.

'Gary and uniform here talking to Cassie. She looked mortified to see me walk in on them. Both cops asked me more questions...details when I get home.'

Crap! I wish this would just go away. I have had many hours of regret for killing Joe. Markus warned me. Yes, an asshole, but didn't deserve death for being an ass. I gave it to him so violently as well. This is, as Eric said, too close to us, our real lives.

Why doesn't Eric just get us fake identities or move us to Chicago?

I know he has his reasons. Most importantly that my change, still in progress, reminds me of my human nature, not more shock me. Don't know what would happen if we took off to Rio, but he seems unwilling to move anywhere.

Maybe the trauma of Markus's passing, (still have not heard all of that story) and my changing. Maybe, like he said, Eric just wants to be home.

He did tell me after Markus took him away, they never came back here, not once in 67 years. Markus may have worried that Eric might remember too much of himself, become unruly or difficult. He just refused Eric's wish to come home even for a visit. Not until he wanted death and Eric had to go on without him did he relent.

Whatever the reasons, he will not even take me down to the city penthouse yet. Will not, because of me, because of Gary, because...well, I don't know why. Just not now; 'soon' I am told.

So Cassie is talking to the police, so curious. What is she telling Gary, the cops? How I wish I could remember if I confided in her. If she knew. Eric has said she has not let on that she knows anything. Maybe, just because we were such good friends? Without me ever actually confessing to her?

I am up and full of worry again. Hunger too. I may have to bleed Eric tonight. I am in need, and don't really feel like another deer. Karl is out for a week. Eric's ability to do his usual stuff is greatly limited by the police watching the house at night. Gary in his every spare minute. I feel for his wife and son. He can't be home much, seems he is always here or nearby.

Finally I see the lights of the car, hear the door to the house opening. Only a glass of ice water from the fridge before he comes down to me.

"So?" I jump with questions before he sits on the bed.

He gives me a brief kiss, guzzling down his glass of water. "Hi to you as well."

"Sorry, just anxious. How was your day?" I coolly kiss him on his cheek, making him laugh.

"Shit, Margret, you don't have to go to right into suburban house wife." Sassy. "My day was great. How was yours?"

"Emm, sorry, just all nerved up," I squeak.

"You're nerved up? You are not the one who has the cops on your ass. Watching your every move. Hoping to prove your some kind of serial killer or something." Finishes his water and puts it on the ledge. Notices the journal. "You done yet?"

"Yes. Not important now. Tell me what happened!"

"Ah, OK. Like I texted, when I got on floor, Cassie was talking to Gary and a local cop. Went about doing my thing, went to the play room, no one was in there so got some crayons, paper, books, the usual. Went off to see Kevin first. Before I got to his room, they stopped me. The local cop asked me much the same questions about you and Joe that Gary did. Same pictures. I told them I had not seen you since that Friday we were on shift together. Never knew you well enough to even know what Joe looked like... never saw him before. Think I was convincing. After they took off, I went on to visit Kevin. I was in there for about fifteen, when Cassie came in. Did her nurse thing and...well, I couldn't let it go. I followed her out, confronted her a bit."

Tone, hearing something more in his tone. What doesn't he want to confess?

"Mind if I get a beer?" Deflecting, stalling.

"Yea, go ahead." I wait with more questions swirling in my head until he sits back down before me. I am resting on my pillows, he is sitting cross-legged in the center of the bed. Suspiciously well away from me.

"Don't get pissed." Not a good start.

"Just tell me!" I bark.

"Cassie was always, well, you know Cassie, flirting with me. I know she is engaged, but well, we flirted. I did a bit with everyone. Everyone but you, really. You were being careful not to give wrong signals, I suppose. No big deal, nothing to it. Though after you went missing, Cassie got a bit..."

Aggressively interrupt him. "A bit what?"

"Ya know, more than flirting, more like hitting on me."

She was a wild thing, more so than I ever was. Even when I was single, I never behaved as loosely as she did while engaged.

"I never did anything about it. Actually backed off completely after that.

No flirting or, anything. Seemed pissed about that. Then she tried again a bit harder." Takes a huge swig of his beer.

"What the hell is that supposed to mean? Harder?" I do realize I am gone to her, and she never knew about Eric and I, maybe suspected, but never knew. Still, my best friend hitting on my lover does not please me.

"Well, brushing up against me like there wasn't enough room to get by, but there was. Touching me anytime she could. Waving her cleavage in my face whenever she could. She asked me out for drinks after work all the time. Lunch. Whatever."

Looks kinda worried at me. "Cassie was the one who put Joe on to us, maybe just a suspicion, but enough to have Gary look into it, and ..." Doesn't finish his thought.

Seriously? My best friend casting suspicion on Eric and hitting on him! Starting to feel the vamp Margret coming to the surface.

"What did she say to you? Huh? After she talked to the police?" He takes a long deep breath.

"Only that she was the one who told Joe we were close, friends, didn't mean anything by it....bla bla bla. Said she was sorry that they were asking so many questions about me, had them on my ass. Maybe she figured the only reason I wasn't responding to her was because I was with you. Think she may have been a bit angry with me for not, you know. "

Cassie is beautiful, really beautiful. Body to die for, full breasts she rarely hid, even at work. I witnessed Eric ogling them a few times myself.

"Fucking her?" I am in pissy Margret mood now.

Eric has that dad-like disapproval on his face. Doesn't stop me.

"Suppose you would love to," my words growing more caustic. "fuck her."

Shakes his head, confused. "Margret, where are you going with this? That is not what we are discussing!"

Hear his annoyance with me and my moods.

"Well, why not? You forced your best friend into our bed; suppose it's only fair I let you do mine." I bite more than I intend, maybe not. My feelings are getting away from me, again. Don't know why I said forced, just came out that way.

He sighs heavily, his head down.

Feel that sick foreboding feeling churning inside my stomach again. Felt it for days, at the moment quite acutely. Not sure what it is.

"I have never touched her! I know what you are thinking, but we have much more important things to deal with than your confused fantasies! I have told you, only what you want, nothing more nothing less. I would never cheat on you. I have no need to!"

The volume lessens considerably.

"What you have witnessed is all there is. No others without you. Cassie is lovely, but she is your best friend. I have stayed well clear of her."

I have done it again, angered him, frustrated him. I am still unsure that I can fully trust him. Know I have to, want to. Yet all this is so strange to me, Margret. He wanted to bring me back to my true self. I dig myself in deeper.

"But you would love to screw her. Watch us do each other."

Eric's face goes red. "Done, I am done with this conversation!" He stands, goes to leave, stops near the stairs, turns to look back at me. His expression miserable, angry. He has one last thing to say before he leaves.

"I love only you. Sorry if I have more sexual partners than you can deal with. Believe me it was never my life's intention, just who I became. I will take no other and be very happy to do so if that's what you wish." Mumbles the rest. "I should have left you the human woman you were." Turns away from me. Under his breath. "I do what my master wishes, nothing more." Laced with resentment.

"Eric," I plead, sorry I pushed him so far.

Ignoring me, Eric disappears upstairs.

His master? Markus is his master. Suppose I am technically his master now. Eric has called me his love many times, prefer it, but never his master. I do not want to be his master, still feel Eric is mine sometimes.

'Left you the human woman you were' No confusing the remorse in that.

This turning thing, well, it's not easy. So confusing. I was never this emotional mess before, weak, needy, possessive. I had no one to need before, really need. No one I could trust with my weakness, or my most possessive desires.

Only Eric.

Arguing makes me nearly as crazy as I get when I have not fed. And I have not fed.

I want to go to him. Love him, bleed him. Am still too full of confused anger and doubt. I have been feeling weird, uneasy ever since the other night with Karl, and this fight is not helping.

Chapter Twenty-three

Eric went to a local gay bar, two-for-one Wednesdays, sure he could find someone to bring home for me. Gary was outside; Eric didn't care if he followed him. I watched, eye to the peep hole; he did. Both gone, all quiet.

I dare not put a fire on, in case he, or some other cop, came by. Impatiently wait in the dark until Eric comes home with our guest. Or shall I say my food. Listen to music to pass the time.

Eric left late, comes home much later. It is near 3 when he rolls in. His friend not quite coherent enough to know where he really is. Eric looks at me rather apologetically. I can smell weed and the booze all over him as he walks in the back door. He's kinda crazy, falling all over the place. Eric helps steady him.

"Pour us a shot of scotch will you, Margret?" Moving him slowly toward the front room, Eric's supporting hug around his waist. I find the bottle, such a waste, good 18-year-old scotch. Well, Eric will appreciate it.

Our guest is an older man, not the young hot lovers he is accustomed to. Has a ring on his finger. 'Straight' married man, out to explore his secret passions. Taking chances he should not. Not unattractive, 45ish, I think. In fairly good shape, bit of a belly. Tries too hard to dress 'gay.' Purple sweater, dark blue pants, a bit tight, for him, anyway. His hair is short, no real style, thinning in back. Still he has handsome green eyes, and round lips. Must have been a killer.

May have just come out, or may have done this as badly as he is now for many nights before. Can't tell, and he is too wasted to really talk. I am glad of that. Don't need to know all my food as well as I do Karl.

Eric is overly affectionate and laughing too hard. I hand them the shots, they toast to new friends. I'd like to laugh, enjoy the crazy display, but I am much too hungry to glean even the smallest amusement from it. Eric smiles sweetly up at me. "Another please?" Holds his glass up; I take them both back to the kitchen, taking my time to fill them again. Reluctantly return to them, refills in hand. Our friend is trying to tell Eric how his wife doesn't understand him, his desires. His speech is slurred, but he attempts anyway.

"I've asked herr, ya know, to doo stuff..." He falls off, reaches for his shot, eyes half open.

"Thanks."

I smile. "You very welcome." I sit down at the far end of the couch, looking impatiently at Eric.

"You are a lucky mann to have a beautiful wooman who understands you." Smiles drunkenly towards me. I return it. "She is a beauty, don't know what you would want with the likes of me when...you... "

Drowns his last words in the shot of scotch.

Eric gives me a look that tells me how sorry he feels for him. I excuse myself, go to the dining room. Hide. Standing near the archway to wait for Eric's word to feed.

"I know, Bruce, women can be hard to understand sometimes. You just have to listen to her, love her, give her the affection she needs. Then she will do the same for you."

Good advice, lost on him in his current state.

Silence for a moment and then a few soft moans from Bruce. I can't help myself but to look in. Eric has him in his arms. Bruce, lying his head on Eric's shoulder. From the looks of his movements, Eric is stroking Bruce. Not so sure he can be fully hard, but still seems to love the affections.

After a short minute, he looks back over the couch, knowing I am there watching. Not a word, only jerks his head for me to enter. I return to sit on the other side of Bruce. Eric's hand is working kindly over him. No, not limp, but not fully hard either. Bruce has turned his head into Eric's neck, attempting to kiss it, not managing much passion. Seems not to notice me.

"Hey, everything's going to be OK," Eric assures him. Nearly gone to the world.

He looks to me. Softly says, "It's time." Eric continues to stroke him, though even Bruce's attempts at kissing cease.

I take my mouth to him, looking up at Eric before I bite. "He'll be OK, just feed."

Dig my teeth into his shoulder, slower bleed than the neck. I can go longer this way, get just as much but feel the connection to the life, to the blood, longer.

For a while I am lost in the feed, let the dark come, then the wisps of color. Then somehow I feel this man's sadness in his blood. Read the un-answered need in his life. I feel his pain, desire for more. This is the first time I have felt this, powerful emotions flowing inside my feed. It distracts me from my bliss.

Eric hand moves to my face, pushes gently for me to stop. I do without needing further prompting.

I look up to him, questions in my eyes.

"What is it, Margret? You OK?" I feel sad, lonely. Not mine, Bruce's feelings.

"Yea, OK." I know I don't sound too convincing. "Take him home now," I add, stroking his head. "Be careful with him."

"All right. I will." Sounding confused. Eric finds Bruce's wallet and keys. Looks to his license for the address. "Not too far." I am righting Bruce's trousers. "Sure you're OK?" Eric asks again.

"Of course, fine. Just get him home before he is in too much trouble with his wife," I say curtly.

Eric's dimples grow deep, he seems oddly happy.

"You are so much your true self right now. Your concern, your..." grabs me, kisses my forehead, "your innocent kindness." I feel his love permeating me, the air around me as he holds me to his lips.

I see why he loves that part of me so. Margret is a sweet sap, full of empathy and innocence. Eric needs it to return him to a bit of himself as well. That is what he really needs from me. Not the sex, not the blood, the innocent me he has endeavored so hard to bring back. An immortal to give him back what he lost so long ago?

I tenderly kiss my feed goodnight. Eric smiles kindly at me then takes Bruce up into his arms. I open the back door. Thankfully no Gary at 4:00 a.m.

The glow still in his eyes. "I love you." Standing in the driveway, a full grown man in his arms. Eric looks up at me with a child's eyes.

"I love you," he says just before I close the door. Go down to my basement. Full of pensiveness about the evening.

Chapter Twenty-four

My legs are tightly wrapped around Eric. Lying on our sides facing each other. He bends over, bringing his mouth to my breasts, I arch upward to assist him. Caress his long hair, loving his hot mouth running over me.

I feel another's soft kiss over my back. Smoothly traversing from my neck longingly down my spine. Sometimes wandering to the front of my ribs, or nibbling at my hips. Still Eric keeps my attentions to him. The hot kissing continues on my lower back, ending on my full cheeks. Bites, gentle, yet aggressive. They feel good. Still I feel uneasy about the strange dark lover behind me.

Eric enters me. I moan at the quick depth. The other moves his full body to lie close behind me, hardness pushing at the small of my back. More loving kisses on the back of my neck, breathing rapidly over my skin. Eric's hands move soothingly over me, finally resting on my backside. His hands grow firm, pulling me apart.

Pressing between my open cheeks, the pressure on me increases. I resist, but they both continue. Eric holds me tighter, the other holds fast his hardness to me, trying to gain entrance. I don't want this. Just want Eric. The dark man's penetrations are strange, painful, unwanted. No, not this!

Eric is moving slowly inside me. The other gradually, painfully, gaining entrance. I look to Eric and plead, "Eric, please, stop him." He seems to not see me, hear me. Eyes dark, foreign, lost to me. His hands still firm, holding me wide. Again I protest, struggling harder against them. Shoving Eric away.

"Let me go!" Trying in vain to pull myself tight, forbidding the other's access. Eric takes my free arm by the wrist tight in his grip, bringing it behind

my back. My right arm is useless, under him, secured with his weight into the bed. I have little ability to fight them. Both so strong, they have my arms and legs firmly in their possession, restraining any ability I have.

Then the hard painful thrusts, his full length deep inside me. The penetration causing me cry out in pain. He is too much, Eric is too much. I feel the fullness of them both inside me. Their coordinated thrusts only brings pain. I feel torn apart. I beg for them to stop. Their thrusts only quicken. Then I feel a sharp pain in the back of my shoulder...

Black.

I bolt up in my bed. My breath and heart rapid. Try to clear my head of sleep and the... dream? I feel as if it just happened it was so real. My whole body, my mind, still in those moments. Yet I find myself alone in my space, safe. Late afternoon light in the window. Reality comes slowly back to me.

This is the first real dream I have experienced. Had wisps of recollection, visions before. Never amounted to even a full memory. Just disjointed pictures before I wake. Like a slide show going too fast to recognize any of the pictures, even if they are my own.

This dream only adds to the foreboding feelings I have been having for the last week. Something deep, nagging at me. Shrouded, obscure, hangs over me like a dark cloud. It is not the difficulty we are having with the police, killing Joe, or any of the effects from it. Something else, and now this unexpected dream exacerbating my inner dread.

I want Eric, need him to calm me.

I look to my clock, on my iPod for real time now. 3:47. The TV is still on in the front room.

Find Eric is lying on the couch, watching an old movie. Nothing but his loose silk pants. Just the dim light from the TV on his shoulders. The shadow and light over his firm muscles. I desire, want to run my mouth over them. Contain myself.

"What you watching?" I ask, much more lighthearted than I feel.

He looks back to see me standing behind him. Happy to see me willingly upstairs.

"Hitchcock, Rear Window." Raises his hand, waves for me to come to him. "Come on, lie with me."

I snuggle in happily next to him. He tosses the couch cushions behind us, giving us more room to lie together comfortably. He tucks sweetly into my back, arms around me. His legs closely mimicking mine.

Eric's hand goes to my breast, warmly cups it, softly embracing me. Lie my hand over his, hold it dearly to my heart. Yes, it could turn into sex, but now it's only need is a loving embrace.

My heart melts in his gentle hand. Surrounding me in tranquil safety, love.

I feel a painful bliss. Covet it. Fear this will somehow be lost to me. I close my eyes to the movie. Want only to feel his hand sweetly holding my breast, his body full and warm against me. His hardness, seemly unnoticed by him, pressed to me. No sex, just all I want to think about tonight. That he really loves me, Margret.

Chapter Twenty-five

Hear the shower upstairs. Daylight's impression on the thick curtains. I am still lying on the couch we shared all night. Eric covered me in a warm knit throw. Sleepiness weighs on me, but need to go upstairs, to Eric.

Lie on his bed. I hardly ever ascend this far during the day, excepting the times he coasted me here. I wait anxiously for his shower to end.

Water running, brushing teeth. Human things I no longer have to do and he hides from me. I am again reminded, Eric is a human.

"Margret, you're awake." Surprised to see me curled up on his bed.

"I am. Sort of."

He goes to the dresser, pulling out boxers, socks. Closet, dress shirt, pants. Seemingly not noticing me.

"I have to go to the city; I have a meeting with my lawyer. Just to keep them abreast of what's going on."

Drops his towel to the floor, boxers in hand. Eric's round dimpled ass facing me.

He will not leave me before I have him. I lunge. Before he knows it, I have pushed him over, plunged my face into his firm cheeks. Biting, kissing. Submissively groans.

I have never been this aggressive, really. I feel very aggressive now. All the hours of tenderness last night has made my love for him very powerful this morning. He is mine and I will have him.

"Margret. I have to go." His protest weak, regretful.

It is me that now who pays no attention to resistance. I want, need. Don't know what time his meeting is and I don't care.

I pull his cheeks wide and deeply kiss the most private parts of it. Feel him weaken, knees bend, nearly lost to him. Push his thighs farther apart, causing him to fall over the dresser for support. My tongue probes, Eric groans in pleasure. There is nothing about him I do not want, nothing I do not love.

Gently suck the loose round flesh into my mouth while using my fingers to fill him. I feel his pleasure, hear it. My needy kiss travels back to the space between. This spot where his hardness hides so deep inside his body. I love this space. Try to draw his veiled manhood from him. Harder and harder my mouth sucks at it. Thrust my fingers deep into him.

"Oh, Margret, that feels so..." groaning every word, nearly lost in pleasure, "good."

I feel the urge to bite but resist it. Take his hips and turn him to face me. Position him to nearly sit on the dresser. I want all of him. He allows me for a few moments to consume him but then pulls me off, taking us to the floor.

Quickly enters me. "You're going to kill me," hotly whispers.

Always when he takes me this hard, there is a bit of pain, sweet new pain. I am unchanging.

Eric is inflamed by my affections, feel it in each concentrated thrust. The force persuades a profound core orgasm from depths unknown to me. My body permeated with his heat, love.

Rapid, breathless into my neck. Eric's kisses start, the slow comforting kind. I know he needs to go. I cling harder while I can. Unwilling to feel the coldness of separation just yet.

Contently murmurs, "You may not think you are so experienced..." His lips touch, hotly speaking into my ear. "You're naturally passionate, Margret, real passion. I feel it in every..." Grateful deep kiss over my mouth. "Nothing could be more beautiful to me as feeling how much you love me, want me."

Eric squeezes his arms around me tightly, pulling me up with him. Hugs me intently before he goes back to dressing himself.

I lie on the bed, happy, I suppose. Still I hate that he is going to leave me. I want more, always more.

Eric pulls on black boxers, they hug tight to his cheeks. Before I can get too aroused again, black dress pants cover my temptation.

Buttoning his fine white shirt, Eric turns to me, smiles. Eyes full of mischief.

"Next time, try to let yourself go a little, ya know, loosen up a bit." Sweetly sarcastic. His little dimples as deep as they can be. I giggle like a shy girl; he is embarrassing me. I am happy my lust pleased him. He finishes his shirt sitting next to me on the bed. Looks from the buttons to me.

"Besides the sharing." His innocent smile. I know he means the blood sharing. "Maybe I have missed loving a woman this much as I had once intended, but you..." His voice low and serious. He leans over to kiss me softly on my lips. "You have made me happy. Mortal and immortal. You're so beautiful." Hear a pang of remorse. "You are my true love, Margret."

Eric looks blankly down to the floor. I can only imagine the thoughts, regrets and pain he may be feeling. All the things I have learned about his past trials. Eric's struggles with turning me. Killing Markus. I have brought too many memories he endeavors to bury deep to the surface.

I do know he is mine and I am now most willingly his. We are all that matters now. I sit up, my knees around his hips, press myself into his back, arms tight around his shoulders, bite playfully at his neck. Eric groans, half with desire and half with the realization he has to leave me now.

I whisper into his ear., "I love you." All I need to say.

He looks out of the corner of his eye back at me sweetly. "I gotta..." Reluctantly I release him to go to his meeting.

Eric tucks me into his bed, forcefully. I feel strange, want to go to my room but he will not hear of it. Won't even allow me to see him out. Knows I will return to my basement if I go downstairs.

"You rest here, in a real bed like a real..." kisses my forehead, holding himself there for a moment, "woman. No more chained dungeon."

He brings up my music in case I want to listen, again ensuring I won't go downstairs and never return.

For a long while after I hear the back door close, his car leave, I can't calm myself. I worry that something will happen while he is gone. Maybe Gary will try to break in to get information, or something else bad will happen. My uneasy feelings have not lessened though they are something else altogether. What, I can't say. They linger deep inside. Much like my past life, so close to recollection. Still eludes me.

Music may help ease and distract my mind. I snuggle into Eric's pillows, pull the covers high over me. I smell him there. I listen to the melodies that will wrap me in comfort much like the pillows I cling to until I find sleep.

We are lying next to each other; Eric takes my legs around his hips and pulls me onto his hardness. Fills me quickly, deeply, nearly lose my breath from his force. A warm body behind me, hardness pushing at the small of my back. More arms surrounding me. Hot kisses on the back of my neck. I am surrounded in rapid breathing and many hands running over my skin. Eric's hands move soothingly over me, caressing my backside. His hands grow firm, pulling my cheeks open.

Chapter Twenty-six

"Margret, wake up." Eric near, his arms trying to coax me to wakefulness.

Turn over, force my sleepy eyes to open. His sweet face near mine. His smile lifts my heart. I was starting to have that dream, the one I had a few days ago. I didn't like it. Grateful he woke me before it went any further.

As soon as I regain my head, I sit up, contently squeeze him. I am so happy, excited.

"Well, you sure seem happy, having a good dream?"

"As a matter of fact, no, I wasn't," I say, distressed. My mood quickly switches. "I do have something I want to tell you though." Endeavoring to contain my excitement. Eric's eyes grow curious.

"OK, do tell." He should tell me his news first then I will share mine.

"No, not yet. Boring lawyer stuff then I'll tell you." Already he is growing distracted, nibbling at my collarbone, hands roaming over my back. "Eric!" His smile is playful, I guess that is a good sign. He seems to be in a good mood as well.

"OK, boring lawyer stuff first." He sits against the head board, legs stretched out long in front of him. I sit, cross my legs, facing him. I want him as much as he wants me, just do a better job of holding my mind...well, I pretend to. Gazing at him in his fine white dress shirt and black jacket, thinking of how hot he looks in his rather conservative suit. When doesn't he look hot to me? I take much energy denying my arousal.

"Well, Markus was a very important client. Now I guess I am. They gave me the royal treatment from the moment I walked in the door. This way, Mr. Campbell." His vocal impressions of a woman leave much to be desired. I laugh anyway.

"The receptionist took me down this long hallway lined with the most beautiful paintings. I swear the huge one in this lawyer guy's office was a Klimt. Anyway, his office was amazing. Floor-to-ceiling windows looking out over Michigan Avenue, the lake. Spectacular view. Sleek black leather furniture, huge wood desk. Reeked big-time bucks."

Eric shakes his head incredulously. "The secretary brought me coffee, mimosas, and some cakey thingy on a silver tray while I waited for the boss. I didn't wait long.

"I had met this guy before, after we got back to Chicago. They handled all the penthouse legal stuff, some funds transferred from Europe. Don't know all of it, didn't pay as much attention as I should have. All goes..." Eric's hand swoops over his head. I laugh, know what he means.

"The lawyer, Jonathan Mercer, 'but please, call me John'— you know, the brilliant type who wants to seem down to earth— greeted me like I was very important. I thought I'd just see one of the grunts, but I got the boss."

Eric brushes his hand over my hair and looks so kindly at me. Somehow I think this simple fantasy he has here with me suits him just fine for now.

"Yea, OK, so? You're the king, what did you tell them?"

Eric exhales slowly, bringing himself back. "Well, told him all about our friend Officer Blonski. That he was visiting me on his off-duty time, questioning me...following me. Irritating the shit out of me! I didn't say that but I did explain how you and Joe went missing, Officer Blonski was a friend of yours and decided to look into things himself. John took notes, listened while I explained the situation."

"Did you tell him about me?"

"Yea, 'course not that you're a vampire I had chained up in my basement." Sarcastic, smiling.

"I said that you were a good friend of mine, didn't expound. I offered to hide you from your husband when you wanted to leave him. 'Course I made your situation sound more desperate than it was. Made it clear that you are afraid of Joe and didn't want him to know where you were. Told him I didn't think anyone knows that you are staying with me, but can't be positive about it."

Eric pauses. "Said that Gary must have suspected me because of our friendship at the hospital…blah, blah, blah, you know, Cassie. Mostly the truth, well, some of it." He looks up comically at me. "Left out the part about you drinking Joe to death, unmarked grave in the woods, all that stuff I omitted."

I hit him in the arm. "Not funny!" Only his playful smile.

"He only asked me a few questions. If I had ever met Joe before, had any confrontations with him in public. No and no. Really the truth about that. Told me he would look into a restraining order but if Gary had not been threatening, he couldn't do much about a police officer sitting in front of my house."

"So, what? We can't do anything?" Frustrated.

"No, Margret." Impatient with me. "I knew that before I went in but if something happens, I needed to have a good lawyer who knows what's going on with all this."

I sigh, rather unhappy, wish there was a way to get Gary, and all the others, off Eric's back. I know it causes him so much stress. Attempting to feed me, hide and protect me while under such close watch. I can't go to jail, not even for few nights. God only knows what I would turn into under the stress of those conditions. Without Eric, my hunger, no human would be safe near me. Still I know I won't be the one locked up. If, only if, it came down to that, Eric would confess…and I would go just as mad as if I were in a cell myself without him.

"What would happen, you know, if they were to find out somehow, put you in jail? I couldn't go on, Eric." My happiness is well forgotten for now. I am near tears just at the thought of it.

Eric grabs a hold of me, pulls me onto his chest. Runs his hands soothingly over my hair and back. "I will never let that happen. I told you nothing will keep us apart. If it does get messy I'll, we'll, just have to start a new life. Again." He said 'again' very disheartened. He has done this before?

"What do you mean 'again'?"

He pulls me off him, his hands on my chin. Looks intently into my eyes. Determined. "You know, I don't want to talk about it really. But yes, I have been Eric this or Eric that, new city new home, new name." His brow crinkled. "I just want to be Eric Campbell again, who lives in Chicago with the woman he loves." His voice almost angry.

Yet another can of worms I have accidentally opened. More understanding of him, his wounds. I decide this is a good time to switch to my more pleasant news.

Whisper to him. "Eric."

"Yes?" Reluctant. Afraid I may continue questioning him.

He has both of my hands wrapped gently in his. I break one free to get my iPod. "Listen." Handing it to him. Eric takes my headphones, places them over his ears. I have the song ready, just listened to it, again, before I fell to sleep.

Hit play.

This song was new to me, didn't remember it buying it before. When Eric gave my music back to me, I found a playlist unfamiliar to me. The first time I heard the new songs, I seemed to remember them somehow. Brought back not one solid memory, but a soft familiarity. One made my heart melt, the next wanted to joyfully dance. I know now they were songs that I was familiar with because of him.

His face looks concentrated as he listens. Then the dimples, growing larger. His eyes close to the world, deep in recollection and the music. This recollection seems to bring him much happiness.

Moans melodically. "Yes, I remember it." His eyes open, gleaming with love for me.

His brow crinkles. "Do you?" Questioning my remembrance.

"Tell me," I softly insist

"NO! You." Teasing.

"Eric! I want to be sure, please tell me..." I need his confirmation. He grins and makes a soft grunt. Kisses my hand.

"OK. I'll tell you." Compliantly. "You and I were out dancing with people from the hospital, at Scoobies."

I remember it, nothing fancy, just a bar near the hospital we would all go to.

"A bunch of us were on the floor dancing to a fast, you know, fun song. Everyone was bouncing around, dancing with each other. Having a great time. Anyway, after a few songs, a slow song came on, so everyone started leaving the dance floor. This was the song that came on."

Holds up my iPod and looks at it as if the echoes of that night resound inside it.

"I actually asked the DJ to play it, you didn't know that but...anyway, you were nearly off the floor, I grabbed your hand and pulled you back. Pleaded with you to dance with me. You resisted for a moment, or two, but I laid on the saddest eyes I could manage."

I know full well his manipulations, his dark irresistible eyes.

"Begged you to stay, dance with me." His sigh full of pleasant reminiscence. "You finally agreed. I pulled you close, real close. I had never held you like that before," softly chuckles, "and I took full advantage." His grin grows devilish; know that one as well.

"At first you were a bit stiff but soon you melted. We held tight to each other. I had longed for you so." Shakes his head. "It was sweeter than anything I had felt for a very, very long time. The innocent desire. The need in it, for us both. I prayed it would go on forever, Margret."

"YES! Yes!" My eyes fill with happy tears. I do remember him! I throw myself at him. Eric laughs at me. Grabbing at his sweet long hair and kissing over his face as if I had not seen him in years. As if my heart had missed him so painfully for all these months. It did. My beautiful Eric returned to me.

Finally I calm, a bit. Look into his smiling face.

Deeply sighs, relieved. "You remember me?"

Again I see wet eyes, these finally from joy. Softly suck the tears from them. They taste nearly as intoxicating as his blood. Eric holds dearly to me.

"I do! I remember, not everything but more than enough to know that I loved you." Take a deep breath, try to speak clearly, calmly. Try, but rattle off at full speed. My joy overtaking me again.

"Like when I first met you, how hot I thought you were, and you were so damn sweet. How kind and gentle you were with the children. Coloring with them, your silly jokes. You were just so frickin' perfect. Your kindness made you even more handsome, beautiful... I wanted you so damn bad. Long before I ever..." I trail off to force my open mouth over his, grind myself into his hips. Too excited to contain myself.

Confessing all my forbidden desires for him.

How I secretly lusted after him, eventually conceded to him, loved him. My relief so great. Yes, I have in my blank new heart and mind loved him, accepted him, but he was my keeper. No other could love me as I am now, care for me as he does. Want me as I am now. Yet to finally remember the forbidden heat I felt for him. The excitement I felt every time he was near me. To remember I did love him as a human woman. I am overwhelmed.

Eric is being nothing but patient with my wild emotions. One second I want to have him, the next recall more of my memories, the next so happy I can't be held. He responds lovingly to each shift in my emotions.

No other memory that has come back has meant as much to me. Me, my choice to love him, yet again in my past life.

Eric appeases my every mood. Holds me tightly, kisses me deeply, laughs at my wildness. I have not felt this whole since...maybe ever. This was the one missing puzzle piece that could complete me. Placed now in its rightful spot, the dubious whole that was in my heart.

Finally at his limit, he takes me firmly by my shoulders and flips me to my back. Happy snort- like laugh.

"Margret!" Grabs my attention. "Do you remember the end of that evening?" Firmly over me, still dressed but his hardness seems to be exceeding the limits of the fabric trying to constrain it. I can hardly breathe in my excited state.

I close my eyes to him. Forage in the mess of thoughts and feelings, like a tempest in my mind. Locate the memory, grab ahold of it.

"Yes." My eyes pop open. "You walked me out to my car. Said it was too late to ..." I am lost in memory and exhausted from the energy I have spent in my excitement.

"You, you said I had to know how you felt about me, how you wanted me. I remember how I backed myself into my car. I am sure you thought I was pulling away from you, but really my knees were so weak, Eric."

I kiss him softly. "I was afraid I would lose them."

His eyes are closed. He smiles sweetly at me, waiting.

"Then you said I'm sorry. Apologizing in advance for the forceful kiss you were about to give me. I wanted, well, thought I should resist you, but I couldn't. I never wanted a kiss so badly. Yet I was so afraid of you. You pressed me hard to the car, encircling me tightly in your arms. Then forced your mouth over mine, sucked my tongue into you until I gave it willingly. No timid soft first kiss, it was so passionate, so hot. I had never felt a kiss like that, Eric. I had to force myself to stop it."

I look tenderly to him lying over me. Eric chuckles.

"I had waited long enough; there was no timid in me by then. I knew I had maybe that one chance to make you feel it, how much I cared for you, wanted you."

"Oh, you did." Run my palm affectionately over his face. "The whole drive home, I felt drunk. I was drunk, from your kiss." This time it is Eric that stops me, in need of a gentle kiss.

I continue. "Oh God, how I throbbed, wanted more of you. I had a husband at home waiting for me. I couldn't do what my heart wanted." I pause, trying to catch my breath. "I wanted to turn around, return to your arms so badly. Nearly did a few times, but my guilt keep me from it. When I finally got home and into bed, it took hours until I could sleep. I ached for you. Ugh." The memory bringing the lustful aching back so vividly. Eric hears it clearly.

He does not leave me but undresses as best he can while staying close. I have nothing to release myself from. I hold to him, kiss him wherever I can. Only making his attempts at undressing more difficult. Finally Eric lays his warm body fully over me. His skin, his heat. I grind myself into him. Embrace him with every limb.

He does not take me, with all my crazy teasing, he gives me only slow tender kisses. Love for me.

Must be late day, my time for rest, and I do feel it. The emotions, excitement, the light. Weak. Eric knows, but also knows I need to be one, have all of him.

Eric enters me so slowly, surely waiting for my bite. I resist demanding more of him. Let him softly thrust himself into me without answering my other need as long as I can. Hot kisses and lustful hands move over me. All sweetly needy. Sense his relief that I finally remember him, that I loved him in every touch.

Eric, the real Eric, has been lost for so long. I know this from his reluctant recollection and confessions. Even the evil ones. I need to love him. As Markus said, 'He may well die if you cannot.'

Eric comes to his forearms, deeply thrusting inside me. I break our kiss to take my mouth to his thick bicep, bite into it. Immediately his thrust becomes more forceful, elongated. Pull my legs high over his back, tightly hold him to me. Slow repeated groaning, sounding as if he is in pain. I know he is trying to hold himself until I have fed long enough.

The beauty of this complete oneness. All of Eric rushing into me, all lustful needs satiated by him, impossible to describe.

Only my love for him can stop me. My orgasms from this coupling are so intense, as are Eric's. When he releases hot inside me, I reluctantly stop without prompting. Licking the last drops greedily from his arm. The wound heals with my kiss almost as if it never happened.

My need to keep him alive, overwhelming love for him, are the only things that can save his life. In more ways than just this one.

Eric holds me for a while after, both trying to calm our breathing. Then pulls himself off me to caress my heat with his sweet mouth. His intimate kiss full of desire. I pull him into me more forcefully than I have ever done before. My hands locked into his hair. Eric groans deep into hot flesh.

Not sure if it was feeling his intense desire for me, his blood rushing inside me or his precise attentions. "Eric!" I yell out as he brings me to yet another breathless peak.

We hold tight to each other, unmoving for a long time. I know one thing clearly now, I will die only when Eric wants to. Eric's Master? No. I am his greedy lover, and he is my beloved keeper.

My heart is so full, my new love for him, my past life's love for him. I can barely rest I am so overwhelmed by him.

We are loving most of the rest of the day into the night. Eventually we fall into a broken sleep. Always needing each other, even in our exhausted darkness. Our hearts reach out to each other with our limbs. Every turn in our sleep wakes the other a bit, calls out to each other. Needing a hand to hold. An arm rest over each other. Our legs always trying to entangle. Cannot separate ourselves even for a moment's rest.

Chapter Twenty-seven

For the next few days, nothing could bring my mood down from the high I was on. Not stalking Gary, or the police cars driving by the house. My dreadful nagging feeling, all but forgotten.

I remember so much more now. Each new recollection brings relief, happiness.

I remembered how I avoided Eric at the hospital for a week after he kissed me that night. He was professional, never trying to pursue me at work. There was a new hopeful glimmer in his eyes every time he looked at me. I was so conflicted, married, my vows to Joe, well, they were vows. Guess I was once in love with Joe, long forgotten now. Secretly unhappy, I even attempted to keep it secret from myself.

Never felt the passion I felt in the kiss Eric gave me that night. It was nearly all I could think of. Eventually Eric's relentless, albeit vague, texts to talk resulted in our first 'date.'

Not out. I was too afraid that someone would see me with him. Even though it would have looked like nothing more than drink with a coworker I'm sure, but my guilt and desire for him made me paranoid. So I stupidly met him at his house, just for a short drink to discuss things in private.

I had every intention of telling Eric that I was very flattered but nothing could come of it. I was married and that's that. How I could be so naive? Just the thought of him made me throb, my mind swim. I had been very attracted to him all along. So damn handsome. Loved his dark eyes, his long wavy hair from the first second I laid eyes him. Even the slight bump on the bridge of his otherwise perfect nose was endearingly attractive.

His kiss, well, that set me perpetually on fire. Why I stayed as clear of him as possible at work. Although Eric made that nearly impossible. Seemed everywhere I turned, his beautiful face, dimpled smile, eyes full of mischief. It was unbearable. So I caved, agreed to meet with him.

A full week later, Friday night, I arrived at his house. Eric was cool and polite. No hug, no kiss, when I arrived. Controlled distance though Eric had a fire going, candles everywhere and vodka tonics chilling. Romantic, to say the least. Clearly I was doomed before the conversation even started.

He took me to the kitchen to fill my first glass. I stared at the dark marble counter top, nervously tracing the white veins, avoiding his eyes. Always feeling his intense gaze over me while we engaged in small talk about work. Finally he took my shaking hand in his and guided me to sit on the couch in front of the fire. Eric kept a gentleman's distance. Though he didn't wait too long to start his persuasions. Told me how beautiful I was, how crazy he was about me. He couldn't stop thinking about me. I didn't want to hear it; every word out of his mouth was weakening me further. Melting me into the cushions like a helpless ice cube on a hot summer's day.

I made a good effort to tell him no, I couldn't. Repeatedly.

Seemingly discouraged Eric went to the kitchen to get me another drink. My nervousness causing me to drink my first way too fast. When he returned he sat my glass firmly on the coffee table and knelt, knelt before me. He took both my hands in his. Held one he tightly in my lap, buried his face in the palm of the other, covering it with kisses. All the while nearly begging me to heed his desire for me.

I remember how lost I felt, confused. My heart beating out of my chest. My emotions so overwhelming, I began to cry uncontrollably.

Distraught, I yelled, 'I can't do this!'

Eric stopped, took me in his arms, draped my legs over his lap, held me sweetly while I wept into his shirt. Didn't try to kiss me, didn't try anything. Just held me close while I purged my guilt.

After I calmed down, I realized how tightly I had wrapped myself around him. I stiffened. Eric gently pulled my head back to look up at him. Firmly said, 'Don't.' I knew he meant don't pull away. His eyes were so sweet, understanding. I didn't, just returned to the shelter of his undemanding embrace.

We sat for a long time in silence. I listened to his heart beating rapidly. No matter what his secret desires making his heart beat so, Eric only held tightly to me, stroked my hair tenderly. Asked nothing more of me.

When I had to leave, he reluctantly helped me to my feet, saw me to the door. No mention of our feelings, of being bound to each other by them. We said nothing at all. I couldn't look at him, kept my face down, avoiding his longing gaze.

Then Eric slid his hands around my neck, back into my hair, gently pulling me closer to him and said, "I'd like to tell you that I am falling in love with you, Margret," his smile shy, boyish, "but I don't want to scare you away."

The kiss he gave me that night was slower and sweeter than our first. The effect on me was the same though, drunk from its passion. I recall driving home, shaking so violently I feared I would swerve off the road. I was going to have an affair, with sweet Eric Campbell.

Chapter Twenty-eight

Eric?" I hesitantly ask for his attention.

He is lying over the couch, legs draped over mine, watching another old movie from when he was just himself. This one irritates me. Dracula with Bela Lugosi. Don't know if he finds this amusing or just loved it in 1931 when it was released but, really? I take the TV control and turn the volume down.

"I am growing hungry. Distractedly so." I look over to him; he is so comfortable now, after my remembrances. I swear he forgets what I am. What he made me.

"Oh Margret, I am so sorry. Between the cops and, well, being so happy... I will find you something." He kisses over my face apologetically.

I have fed off him. It does quiet my need longer than any other feed. Still...

"I wish I didn't need so much, but..."

Eric cuts me off. "No! You are very strong, Margret. Your feeding from me keeps you for a long time, and well, Markus was strong, he gave you his power. No, for as new, as young as you are, your needs are not nearly as demanding they should be."

Eric shakes his head, angry with himself. "I will go to the bar tonight, find you someone. OK?" His eyes beg for my forgiveness. I grab his face and kiss him hard.

"You are my keeper, Eric, and you keep me well." He smiles and hugs me briefly before he rushes upstairs to shower and dress for his hunt for my food.

I turn the movie off, find a show about the solar system on Discovery channel. Anything is better than a vampire movie. All wrong, stupid, and still so disturbing that I am, well, a vampire myself. Don't feel nearly as disturbed, as strange, about it as I should. Know that is only because of Eric. How he shields me, delicately feeds and protects me. This simple haven we have made for ourselves to hide in.

He comes down after a while looking so hot I nearly forget my burning hunger. White poet's shirt scarcely laced, black leather pants. God, how I wish I didn't need to feed! His long hair over his shoulders, the loose blouse draped over the muscular body that lies under it. Looks like a cross between a gothic novel and a porn movie. Looking diligently for his keys.

"Shit, Eric!" I say almost angrily. Takes his eyes from his searching to look up at me...

"What?" he replies distractedly.

I pounce; in one leap I am on him. Grabbing at his hair with one hand, his leathered ass with the other. Biting soft over his neck. Wild with heat. Eric laughs.

"Maybe I should have dressed in the car?" I have bled Eric far too many times to take from him again tonight. I had to give to him today just to regain his full strength.

Preoccupied with his mission, Eric pulls away. Only his loving kiss to my forehead before he retreats into the kitchen searching for the misplaced keys. I pursue him closely. Eric spies them on the island almost covered by today's junk mail. Relentless, press myself hard into his back, slide my hand around, groping him.

"Margret." His tone impatient. I continue rubbing at his bulging leather pants. Eric moans as I stroke my hands needy over him. Again I bite playfully. Kissing the back of his neck and shoulders, grinding myself into him.

Eric realizes he will not get out of the house unless he appeases me.

"You win." Whispers, frustrated.

Quickly lifts me, sits me firmly on the high counter chair. Moves my dress over my hips. He looks severely at me while his frees himself. Pretending to be perturbed with my demands on him. This one I think he loves. Blood lust forgotten at the moment. Just lust now.

Places his hardness firmly to my yearning but doesn't enter. Frustrated I pull him closer, my legs high around his back. Need to have him. I hold tightly to his wrists gripped under my thighs. Pulling.

Finally he gives me a bit of himself, pulls back. Again and again. He knows full well my intense desire for him. Still he continues to agitate and coerce me. Until...

"Eric please!" I yell. Still nothing. He wants more. Weak, beg. "I want you." He leans over to bite hard at my breast covered still by my dress.

"I thought you wanted to feed, my love," he teases coyly.

I wrap my arms tight around him. He loves to tease me when I am in such a state. Usually I do as well, but am growing impatient with it. "I want you more," my breath nearly gone, I whimper, "want you inside me." Pulling at his arms with my cries.

Finally my desperate pleading is answered. He thrusts himself fully into me. His restraint seemingly as hard on him as it was for me. Gives himself to me with passionate force. Nearly knocking me and the chair underneath me to the floor. But for my one hand hard set on the counter, the other firm over Eric's shoulders, he would have.

After we are fully gratified, Eric holds me in his warm embrace, regretful he has to leave me.

"I love you, Margret." A hot whisper over my ear.

I draw all my strength. Pull myself away, let him go. Only so Eric can bring me what I need now. Blood.

After he is gone, I lie on the couch near the dying fire. Endeavoring to ignore my burning hunger. My veins are quickly turning to fire. All I can do is wait for Eric to bring me someone to cool it.

In my pensiveness I begin to wonder if Eric's teasing is maybe more than just what it seems. A playful desire. Maybe he needs to hear me desperate for him. Begging for him. It wasn't so long ago, I pleaded for him to stop.

I have heard his remorse, yes, for what he did to me, but also for his willingness to do it.

Reviles himself involuntary, so unwilling. I think this is clear now.

My eyes grow dark along with the decreasing flames.

Wake to my phone ringing. Startled, I hunt for my phone. It's on the table. The bright panel reads 3 a.m.

"Hello?" I say, sleepy. Expect Eric's voice, but it's not Eric I hear on the other end.

"Is this Ms. Margret Cooper to whom I am speaking?" I am in shock; no one has this number but Eric. Excepting a few misdials, no other voice but Eric's. This man's is unfamiliar, so formal, at 3 a.m. no less.

Tentatively answer. "Yes, this is Margret Cooper."

"I'm Jonathan Mercer, Mr. Campbell's lawyer."

Why is he calling me? At this hour? My heart is pounding, something must be wrong.

"Mr. Campbell asked that I call to inform you that he has been arrested this evening. Seemingly under some suspicion of Joseph Thomas, as well as your, disappearances." My breathing stops. I am too stunned to respond. How could he be arrested? Mr. Mercer continues before I can get my head around this news.

"There is nothing I can do at this hour, but I will be at the police station first thing in the morning to take care of the situation. I assure you they have no..."

I cut him short. "Where? Where is Eric being held?"

Mr. Mercer clears his throat. "In the city, 20th precinct, I believe." Yawns. "I'm sure the police arrested him this late in the evening to intimidate Mr. Campbell, make him spend the night in custody. As I was about to say, I don't believe they have anything to hold him on."

I am shaking, angry. "What time will you be there?" I ask tersely.

"Six is the earliest I can be there. I'll know more in the morning after

I speak to the police and Mr. Campbell. I will call you when I have any news." I can hear his impatience to end the conversation.

"OK, thank you for calling."

"Goodnight, Ms. Cooper." Mr. Mercer hangs up. Blankly hold the phone to my ear for many moments after.

What the hell am I to do? Whatever food Eric had for me, well, it's not coming! I can't just wait here and do nothing while they have him in custody. Because of me!

Think! Clearing my head is nearly impossible when I am this hungry.

Clearly I have to feed; I will be in no condition to do anything if I don't. My hunger exacerbated now that I know nothing is coming home with Eric. Eric is not coming home at all!

Decide to get dressed and go to the park. Hopefully a deer will give me enough strength to be in the light and around mortals. Not so sure about that, but I have to try. I am going to the police station in the morning; put an end to my 'disappearance' once and for all.

Discreetly take all alleys, tuck into the darkest spaces on my way to the park. Unwilling to let myself be seen or to see anyone. Very aware of what I am, and what my uncontrolled hunger can do.

Silently search the woods for my food. There is a soft snow over the ground now. Don't like my footsteps being so clearly marked. Strive even in my pursuit to obscure them. Silly, but I am afraid I will be followed somehow.

I feel so alone, and not the pleasant alone. When I know he waits for me, near me. Without Eric my mood shifts so easy to anger, fear. I can't let them take hold of me. I have to feed, need to be strong, need to help Eric.

Eventually deep in the woods I spy a deer. Golden mother, two delicate fawns near her. She is big, but I take her easily. Her fawns wait for a second, confused, then bolt into the brush. The cold, or maybe her hunger, she does not give me the struggle I am used to. Taking her life makes me feel better, but I was already so hungry. Still feel the need for more.

I walk on; my thoughts drift to the two fawns. They may not make it through the winter without their mother. I feel oddly sad at the thought of them alone. Eventually the thick woods uncoil into a deep marsh. Long grasses and cattails reach upward toward the night sky.

The snow deceptively covers the soggy ground below. Stepping into it I quickly realize how muddy it still is under the fallen snow. Still I walk fearless into the dark grass, a place I would never have roamed before I became what I am now.

Just a sliver of the moon shows in the night sky. Obese wet snowflakes begin to fall, catching every bit of light there is. Sticking readily to every furry tail and the long dry leaves of the reeds. It is beautiful. The wet flakes quickly cover Eric's leather jacket as well. Thought I should at least have a jacket on a night like this. Just in case someone saw me walking in the cold night air.

I walk then bolt like the fawns, freeing myself of the dense marsh.

A railroad track bounds the reeds and wild grasses. Make my way up to the spur, regard both directions. The tracks disappearing into the darkness oddly attracts me. Decide to walk along the spur for a while. My iPod in hand checking the time, 4:26 am.

I want to stay out for as long as I can. The cold night air clears my head. With any luck I may come across another deer as well.

Something about tracks causes an oddly comforting loneliness in me. Different from the one I already have. Nevertheless determined, I continue my excursion alongside them.

A train is coming. The dim headlight piercing the darkness far ahead. Becoming brighter and brighter as it quickly approaches.

Fearless I stand dangerously close to the tracks as it speeds by me. The rush of air whips my long hair around my head like a wild lasso. The deafening clatter, the might of the locomotive so close. Its power vibrates through me, the force nearly shakes me off my feet.

I love it!

I feel a strange connection to the train rushing by. Somehow trying to take me away on its journey. Going who knows where, just away into the blackness ahead. Somehow that seems very appealing at the moment.

The last of the cars passes by, sounds fading. The earth under my feet stills.

I stand unmoving for a moment, calming my exhilaration. My mind forgot everything but its seductive force. Now slowly returning to reality. Eric in jail, my loneliness, my hunger. Yes, my hunger is still too hot.

Don't know exactly how long I continue to walk but I must be near some major road as there is a long overpass ahead. I am tired, morning is near. Yet I am drawn to go on by the dim lights of the bridge cutting into the dark.

When I grow near, I hear a faint beat, not that of a deer's heart, but a human.

Cautiously I creep into the broken light. A dim buzz from the bulbs that still struggle to give light echoes in the cement tunnel.

A lone figure is curled into the shelter of the supports midway in. It is very cold out tonight. Here they are guarded somewhat from the cold, the blistering winds. As I draw near, I see it's a man covered only in a dirty jacket, a familiar blanket over him.

I kneel before him, tightly balled into himself. Shielded from the winter's bite by the inadequate blanket. I pull some of its protection from his face. A scruffy beard, long peppered hair.

Yes, my feed from many weeks ago. Maybe this is where Eric found him, right here in this very spot. He lies here still, again in my company.

The man does not realize I am here. Nearly frozen, sleeping, maybe even drunk. Unable or unwilling to see me.

Sit myself down next to him, the cold ground immediately penetrating my jeans. Lift my dirty friend into my arms to hold him. He gives no resistance. I lie with him for a while. My embrace gives him some warmth and comfort. I know he has felt neither for a long while.

His unruly hair, I stroke. His weak body, I hold. His feeble moans I pray from comfort not fear. I can hear his heart, slowly beating. I hurt for a moment. My heart literally aches inside my chest.

I need Eric, my keeper. I must have the strength of this life to do it.

"I am sorry, my friend." Almost in tears.

Tilt his head back, delicately press my teeth into frigid flesh. An outpour of warmth gushes from his neck into my mouth. I feel only a strange relief, odd comfort flow into me. Is his blood whispering to me? Quickly drink him until I feel the last of his warm breath on my face. I am thankful he gave no struggle. The blood feelings, I am grateful for them as well. Kiss him gently, like Eric does to me, on his dirty forehead.

Know I can't leave him here like this but worry about the street overhead and the light from it. I slip my arm around his back, flop his arm over my shoulders and lift him to standing. We walk away from the overpass. Pray if spied upon, we look only as if I am supporting a drunken friend. Until we escape the light completely, I keep up my charade.

As soon as we are fully in darkness, I lift him effortlessly into my arms. Surprising myself with the ease that I take his weight, I run swiftly back down the tracks to the marsh. My guilt already making noise. I feel my every move conspicuous, observed by someone. There is nothing but darkness, not even a rodent's heart beat nearby. Still I am quickly becoming submerged in guilt for my deed.

I rush into the deep reeds. Lay him in the snowy mud, covering him with the blanket Eric left him with. Not the burial he deserves, but...

The snow is growing deeper. Falling quickly now. The wind whipping the white flakes wildly about.

I make an effort to sink him further into the mud and snow. Push him down until he sinks into the muck. Pray he will be as forgotten in death as he was in life.

It is near 6 a.m. I run all the way home.

After a quick shower and calling a cab, I dress and wait anxiously near the kitchen door. Mr. Mercer said he would be there around 6 a.m. I will not arrive till near 7 at this rate.

Chapter Twenty-nine

The city police station is as expected, red brick, tall old wood doors. My cab leaves and I walk reluctantly inside. A light snow spitting out of the gray sky. I am thankful for the dreary sky. Greatly helps me feel strong, as did my human friend. I feel much better than I expected to.

"Hi, I am looking for Eric Campbell. He was arrested last night. I believe he is here?" The young uniformed officer behind the reception desk looks through some papers, looks up at me blankly.

"And you are?" Seeming uninterested in my response.

"Margret Cooper Thomas," I state simply.

His attention caught. Phone, guardedly speaking into it. I can hear every word of course. "There's a woman here, says she's Margret Thomas. Doesn't Blonski have a guy in for questioning? Just let a lawyer back there about a half hour ago?"

"What? Send her back." The voice on the other end reeked of suspicion.

He hangs up and looks skeptically over me. "You can go back. Through those doors, straight down the hall to the end. Someone will meet you there."

I nod and say thanks under my breath. Head to the dark wood doors and down the hall lined with windowed offices. Detective's names on each. At the end of the hallway are two doors with glass framed windows. Police officers, many others mulling about behind them.

My heart is racing. As if leaving the house alone, a long worried ride down here, getting the guts to enter a police station full of humans didn't have it fast enough. Now, accelerated by the knowledge that I will soon be near Eric. Not sure how he, or the cops, will react to my unexpected visit.

236

I take several long deep breaths, think only of Eric somewhere behind these doors. Resolute, I open them. A rush of noise meets me. Overwhelms me, much like opening the doors to the night club did. I close my eyes to it for a second.

Soon after a plain-clothed, and I mean plain-clothed, officer greets me. Only the badge on his belt and his gun give him away.

"Uh, you Margret?" Polite smile. "Margret Thomas?"

"I prefer Cooper Thomas, but yes, I am." Smile sweetly, belying the heat I feel from all this humanity. No Eric to calm me or shield me from it.

"This way." Outstretching his hand to direct me to follow him through the maze of desks.

Another hall, this one short, small rooms with large windows flank us. Some occupied, but I am too distracted to notice much inside them.

The officer opens the last door on the left, keeping me well behind him. Pokes only his head inside, softly introduces me. Again as if I can't hear him, suppose I shouldn't be able, but I do.

"This woman says she's Margret Thomas." Hate that, just Cooper now. The blinds are near closed on the windows, hard to see anything or anyone inside.

Gary's demanding voice. "Bring her in!"

The officer politely stands back, motions for me to enter the room. All I want to see is Eric.

Gary is right in my face as I step in, anxious to see me, I suppose. Another man sits on a steel-topped table with his back to me. He obscures much of my view of the two people sitting in front of him. He turns as I enter to look over his shoulder at me and Gary.

"Margret! Glad to see you are OK." Gary makes an awkward attempt at a hug. "We were so worried about you." I only smile.

The other officer stands, clearing the obstruction. Eric and, I assume, his lawyer are staring wide-eyed at me from their seats. Eric's face is nothing less than shocked. Both of them seem astonished that I'm standing here.

Clearly Eric didn't expect me to do something like this. I meet his glance, my heart fills. Pull back, looking down for a moment to regain myself. His lawyer rises to greet me as well as the other officer.

"You're Margret?" The officer is short and fat, balding in front, blue ill-fitted suit. Looks as though a cigar should be forever hanging from his plump mouth. I reach out, shake his hand firmly.

"Yes, I am Margret Cooper," reluctantly add, "Thomas."

Eric's gaze still riveted on me, not a word but his eyes say enough. Mr. Mercer is very tall and slender, 60ish, gray full well-kept hair. His suit looks to be worth a year's salary as a nurse. Gracefully he walks around the table to take my hand.

"This is quite a surprise, Margret, we weren't expecting you." Sounds a bit annoyed to see me. Didn't realize before I walked in they were both in full denial of where I was, or any relation to me other than at the hospital. That deception over now.

Gary politely pulls a chair up, smiling uncomfortably. I refuse it for the time being.

"No thank you. I'll stand."

Mr. Mercer resumes his position sitting next to Eric. I walk over behind Eric, softly asking as I pass. "Are you OK?"

Eric turns to look severely over his shoulder at me. Disapproving father-look if I ever saw one.

"Yes, thank you, Margret, I am quite fine." What he really said was, 'Why are you here? I can handle this.'

I don't give a shit, want this mess resolved now. I feel strong, bitchy and needy. I missed Eric. Didn't realize how much until I see him. Still in his poet's shirt and leather pants, looking quite out of place amongst the cement walls, barred windows, oh, and the suits.

"So," the short stocky officer begins, "I am Officer Carlton." Slightly bowing his head. "Greg, please. You said your name is Margret..."

Gary interjects, overstepping his superior officer. "She's Margret Thomas, I know her."

A harsh glance relaying 'stay in your place' from Officer Carlton. Not a word, just a 'shut the f up' look. Gary does, taking a step backward.

I stand still behind Eric; our eyes cannot meet, as I wish. He will distract me, and I'm on a mission.

"What brings you here, Mrs. Thomas? We were under the impression that you were missing, maybe in some kind of difficulties...." His smile bites at Eric. "I was told no one knew where you were, yet here you stand." His query full of suspicion. Continues, not waiting for my answer.

"Officer Blonski here thought he saw the two of you together, but as you can see from his photo," pauses only to shake his head, "not so good." Greg holds up an enlarged photo of Eric opening the car door for me in the driveway at the house. My head is turned to the side, my red dress. Our first night out. Gary obviously didn't follow us the whole evening. By the looks of it, took this with his phone.

They have nothing, and anyway I am here, fine.

Eric runs his hands nervously through his hair. Mr. Mercer waits impatiently for something to jump on. Fingering at his yellow note pad, irritated.

"None of this is really a problem, Margret," Greg looks first to Eric and then up to me, trying to look intimidating, "until we get to your husband, Joe. Officer Blonski tells me he informed your husband of your suspected whereabouts."

Police talk, so annoying. Rest myself against the wall, unwilling to put myself in Eric's line of vision.

"With Mr. Campbell," pointing at Eric as if I don't know to whom he is referring. Greg sits with half his round behind on the table, one short leg hardly touching the floor, leaning over Eric. I don't think he can intimidate Eric, not sure anything can. Think my presence is more agitating to him than anything Officer Carlton can throw at him.

"Seems after that your husband went missing, poof gone. Hasn't answered a call, or made a call...his phone must be off or destroyed as we have been unable to track it. Hasn't been at work." He looks over his ample brow at me. "Think maybe your husband showed up for a little visit. Maybe things got heated? Maybe your friend Mr. Campbell and your husband had it out over you? Things got a bit out of hand?"

Gary is annoyingly shaking his head in agreement. Eric is fidgeting nervously in his chair. I wish he wouldn't do that, makes him look guilty. Suppose Eric may be worried that I will do something really stupid, like confess that I killed Joe. That's not going to happen. We are going home, together.

"Happy, very happy to see you, Mrs. Thomas, safe and sound, but where is your husband?" His smile chubby with false sincerity. "Just like to know the truth, Margret, about the two of you, and where your husband went after he found out about it."

His eyes narrow full of suspicion. Now for me as well as Eric. "He hasn't been seen or heard from in weeks," he adds confounded.

Gary has driven this, his cop hunches and theories. Detective Carlton is making a great effort to support this scenario without any real evidence. Don't see how they could have any evidence of anything really.

I am near the end of my ability to be silent. My emotions have been kept well in check the whole time. Chiefly anger, plenty of it, fear of being found out. Need to hold my Eric, all must be controlled. I look ahead as blank and emotionless as I possibly can.

I know Eric. He needs to regain himself, the self forced from him. We will clear him, and Eric will live a long life, as long as he wishes, here in his home town. I will be his love, he my beloved keeper. No one will obstruct me.

Greg seems to be done, finally. Unnecessarily clear my throat, dramatic reasons only.

Everyone is quiet, staring at me. Gather my thoughts; they wait for me to respond. I stand up straight and slowly walk around the table to face our accusers closely. My back to Eric. I don't look at him as I pass, just firmly into Gary's and then Greg's eyes.

"Well," I am a bit too close to Greg, still leaning on the table. Hopefully my blouse, unbuttoned just one too many, will add some distraction, "Officers, that is a very fantastic theory. I assure you nothing like that happened. I have no idea where Joe is." Again I stare harshly at Gary. "I haven't seen or talked to Joe since my disappearance." Acrimoniously assert my innocence.

"And honestly, as long as Joe stays away from me, I don't care where he is. He has not visited me, or for that matter, Eric." Greg uncomfortable with my nearness stands, moves a few steps back.

I soften my demeanor considerably. "I will tell you one thing though, when I was at the end of my rope, Mr. Campbell," couldn't help the sarcasm, "took me into his home," add in a contrived painful whisper, "the mess I was."

I look down at the table, run my hand over the sharp steel edge. Speak softly.

"My husband could be, well, very harsh sometimes."

Gary is silent, Greg's expression still suspicious. Endeavor to convey the obedient tortured spouse. "When I finally had the courage to express my desire to leave him, Joe became very angry, violent." I know if Gary knew him at all that this was at least plausible to him.

"I was quite frightened of him. As I said, I was at the end of my ability to handle Joe, my work, everything." I look up sheepishly at the two of them. "I needed to get away; Eric kindly gave me a place to get away to." Let a few tears I have persuaded from my bogus emotions silently drop.

"My husband did not even know about my friendship with Eric. They never met or had words. I never even mentioned his name to Joe. Nothing! That is why his house was the safest place. Joe had no knowledge of my whereabouts. So if Greg did tell Joe that he saw us together, he never acted on that information. As I said I have not seen him and I would like to keep it that way!" My fear clearly pronounced.

Greg looks judgmentally at me. "You and Mr. Campbell here are nothing more than friends?"

I have put myself fully into this deception. Although even in its falsehoods so close to the truth. The best lies always are.

Impatiently snap. "What does it matter if I was, or am, currently anything more to him? Eric helped me, took me in. Protects me from Joe by hiding me, even from you!" I yell at them.

"Joe can never know where I am..." I trail off, as if he is still alive, still a danger to me. Think I have them. "Eric is the only one I trusted." I finally turn around to stand next to Eric. Look down into his eyes, meaning every word. "Eric keeps me safe, he is my dearest friend."

Eric looks up at me, smiles. I see he is proud of my performance. Taking the hand I have placed on his shoulder, Eric kisses it tenderly. Ouch! I want to hold him so badly. I quickly turn back to Greg and Gary. See if that worked as well on them as it did Eric.

Both fixed on me, Eric, and our affections suspiciously.

I grow tired of these games and just tired. I want Eric home, my beloved keeper in my arms.

Finally Eric's lawyer interjects. "Officer Carlton, from what I have seen and heard, you have no proof of any foul play by my client. You don't have any idea where Mr. Thomas is. This is all speculations and fairy tales. Mr. Thomas could have driven his car off a bridge, or be in a bar somewhere drinking himself to death for all we know." Mr. Mercer stands to make his point clearer. "You have no reason to hold my client any longer!" he states forcefully.

Greg and Gary exchange glances, clearly irked. Silently convey something to each other.

"Margret, would you please excuse us for a moment." Greg's smile saccharine. Opens the door for me to leave the room. I walk out, not looking at anyone. Stand in the hall near the window.

"Just wait here, we'll only be a few minutes."

Leaning on the window frame, I look wearily out at the busy city street below. I wonder why they asked me to leave? Listen with my vampire ears.

Mr. Mercer aggressively barking, "This is all conjecture...false arrest.... police intimidation...Officer Blonski following my client in his off-duty hours..." His tone getting louder with each point. Blah blah blah. I am so worn-out. Hope this will be over soon.

My attention returns to gaze out the dirty window. It must be near a shift change, uniformed police pepper the street below. The two lanes near a standstill, waiting for pedestrians as they cross willy nilly in front of the cars.

Seem so strange that I am standing here surrounded by police, now a three-time murderess. Right here in their midst, unnoticed for who I really am.

Wonder if I should tell Eric about my adventures last night? Overfeeding, to put it nicely. Probably not, his stress level will go through the roof, and his disappointment... I'll keep that to myself for the time being.

After a few minutes, the door opens.

"Margret, you can come back in now." Gary, red-faced, looking disappointed.

Eric is standing next to Mr. Mercer who is signing some papers, handing them to Eric to do the same.

Greg gives me a crooked grin over his shoulder. "Seems you two can go home now."

Thank God!

"But please, if you hear from, or by any chance, see your husband, give me a call right away." He hands me his card.

"Of course." Curtly.

After all the papers have been signed, the officers quickly excuse themselves and leave the room. I'm still in the doorway, look to Eric. Relief all over his weary face. "Let's get out of here please." Don't think my keeper liked being in jail.

Out on the street, Mr. Mercer offers us a lift as his driver opens the limo door for him. Eric declines, thanking him for all his help.

"You are most welcome, but I believe it was Margret's unexpected visit that put the final nail in the coffin."

He politely shakes both our hands, assures us that he will assist us anytime we need. As he drives off, Eric finally looks at me directly. For the first time we are alone, face to face. I worry what he will say. Will he be angry, grateful, stern?

"What did you think you were doing in there, Margret?"

Answer is...STERN.

"My lawyer could have got me ..."

Cut him off. "Eric, I am tired of hiding, sneaking around. No more! You are free, and now I am free as well. It's all over!" Smiles, eyes dense with mischief. His sternness was half-hearted at best. He hugs me tightly.

"You are quite the actress, didn't know you had it in you." Kiss his cheek.

"I wanted you back, ya know, motivation." Our faces express the great relief of having this behind us.

Eric hails a cab to take us to his car still parked at the night club, Side Traxx. Finally relax in his embrace. My exhaustion clear in how my body weeps over him. I have given all my strength to my performance.

Eric whispers. "You must be famished by now. I can't believe you were strong enough to come down here, all these people...you need rest as well." His mouth close to my ear. "Take me when we get home." Snuggle further into his neck.

Whisper back to him. "I will have you, but not for food. I am fine, just a bit sleepy, and very needy."

"But you were so..."

Stop him. "I'm all good." Chuckling. "I had venison last night."

Believe that I will be the aggressor. Even my weary state will not inhibit me I want him so badly. Again selfishly demanding after I know he has spent a restless night in jail. Worried about me, not his situation.

Wrong.

The back door is hardly shut behind us before Eric has swooped me up into his arms, taking me to the front room.

The coffee table may never recover. Eric kicked it out of the way, clearing the floor. Lands on top of me as soon as my back hits the carpet. His knee spreads my legs wide, grinds himself hard into me. Grasping at my thighs, roaming to my breasts. Caressing all of me desperately. All the while, his mouth barely leaves me but to take a much-needed breath. My hands roam perplexed as to what they want to hold to. His behind, his back, shoulders, arms, of course into his hair. After a few minutes, he abruptly stops, goes to his knees, aggressively pulling my pants from me. Tearing my blouse off me, delaying only for a soft kiss as he does so.

His clothes come off even faster.

Honestly I don't know what we are striving to do to each other. Both of us are all over the place. Finding one position, only to have the other force something else. Both in such a fervor for each other. We kiss as if it has been weeks not hours. Maybe it was the mere threat of weeks apart that has us so.

Eric presses his fingers inside me then strokes the wetness over my breast, licking my heat from my hard nipple. Repeatedly returning inside me, filling them again. Unexpectedly he rubs his wet fingers slowly over my gasping mouth, hotly kissing me after. I want the same, strive to bring his drops to my lips, instead he assists my desire, rubbing his thumb over his dripping head to bring it to my eager mouth to suck on. I try to force myself down on him, but he will not let me go just yet.

As he often does, Eric takes charge after too many minutes of loving mayhem.

Pushing his hand hard into my hair, he looks intently into my eyes.

"I want to suck your heat." His eyes gleam. "And I think you want me as well?"

"Yes." I weakly mumble.

Compromise.

Eric turns, his legs wide over me. Pulling my open legs up behind his arms.

I can reach his long hair falling between my legs, his broad shoulders. Grasp his hard chest, rippled stomach, thick arms. Run my hands over all of him greedily. Hold to his strong back, muscular legs straddled over me, I pull them hard to me. All the while I kiss, gently bite and suck over him, loving every inch my mouth can access. Want all of him at once.

We have been in this position for a long while before. Making out, you might say. Understand when to hold back, the sweetly bitter drops telling me to turn my attentions elsewhere. There is nothing I don't longingly take in my mouth. I only pause when Eric's affections are way too distracting. His hot attentions bringing me to climax more than once already, but I refuse to give Eric his for a while.

I do want to take his release but I know no matter how he pleases me, or I him. Until I am one with him, I will not be fully satisfied. Want more time to consume him with arms and kisses. I think he may be too tired for a marathon. Though I would bet my life on two.

I extend him as long as I can.

"Margret, please, do it." My affections finally too much. His groans grow almost agonized as I continue my tongue's deep probing. Know what he wants so I move down to his hardness. Pulling only with my lustful mouth to take him. Wrap my arms around his hips, pulling myself closer. Gently press my fingers deep inside him, rubbing. Soon intense spasms tighten around them. Eric groans as his passion finally bursts inside my mouth.

His abrupt transition takes me back. Eric mounts me before his taste has left my tongue.

I expect hard, but get soft. He is tired, as am I. Either he knows my need to join with him, or his need is as strong as mine. Only slow enduring thrusts.

"Margret," softly in my ear, "I need you, your love so badly." Sighs. "I have been..." takes himself nearly out of me, presses slowly back to full depth, looking into my eyes, "lost without you."

Whisper over his sweet lips. "I know." Realize he is not referring to the short hours we have been apart. He is referring to the many years his heart longed for me. Kiss him deeply. "Keep me, always." Cling tightly, unwilling to let even a sliver of space between us. Quiet tears full of love, need, and desire overwhelming me. His manhood still locked into me.

I know only his love can shield me from what I am because everything disappears in it.

Eric resumes his gentle movements and soft kisses.

Our love is stronger than I could ever have imagined before him. More passionate than my hottest dreams.

<hr />

I wake long before Eric. Know I should be sore from the hours of love-making. I am not. One of the many benefits of my new self. My beloved, though strong and virile beyond belief is still very much human. He is sprawled out over his bed, quite spent. Well, our bed now. I am banished from the basement I am told.

Afternoon's golden sunlight streams into the room. The mounds and folds of the brown quilt have become a vast mountain range in their disarray at the foot of the bed. A sheet scarcely covers Eric's dimpled ass, his bare back, thick arms resting over his head...I must let him sleep!

Restless, I slip out to make him a meal. Know Eric will be ravenous when he wakes. Besides, I need something to do other than lust over his beautiful body lying beside me.

Scrambling, browning, frying, toasting. Thinking.

I had that disturbing dream again before I woke but will not let it spoil my mood. One cloud has been lifted, I hope for good. I will let the dream quietly hang over me, unattended to for now. Eric's meal needs all my attention at the moment. I hear him up in the bathroom; luckily all I have to do now is somehow fit all of this food on the tray to bring to him.

Find him in some state of wakefulness when I arrive.

"Oh good, food!" The smell brings him quickly to attention. "Thank you, my love."

Place the tray on his waiting lap and sit on the bed. He manages to kiss my cheek before he dives in. I make no attempt at conversation for several moments. I do enjoy watching him eat.

"So tell me what happened before I got to the police station?" I ask.

Still too focused on eating his half dozen eggs and sausages.

"Tell me!" I insist. Mouth full, waving me off until he swallows. Laughs, always amused, or irritated by my questions.

"OK, OK. My lawyer and I were denying any knowledge of your whereabouts, as they said. I hadn't seen you since July sixth." Looks over at me, nodding his head. "That was the night..." Back to his food for a few bites. Will assume he means the night they turned me. His food prohibits a complete sentence.

"Anyway, Gary said Joe got a bit crazy after a few weeks...missed your cooking, I guess." I hit him playfully, we both laugh.

"Asked him if he would look into it. He did, went to the hospital first, asking questions. Sounded like before Joe went in and freaked everybody out. Odd, I never heard about either visit," he adds. "Between the two of them, they thought I was the best bet. Must have been when Joe came here." Eric looks mildly irritated.

"John and I were both silent while Gary went through his theories and accusations. Then Carlton started questioning me, accusing me of having something to do with your disappearance. Like I kidnapped you or something."

"Well, you kinda did," I interject.

Ignoring my comment, he continues. "Then you show up just as we had them nearly convinced." Eats the last of his eggs. Impatiently take the tray and put it on the nightstand.

"Sorry," I say, a bit offended. "I didn't know what to do. Didn't know what the cops knew or what they were holding you on really. Besides, like I said, wanted it over. I wanted you home." Smiling at me. Knows my impatience for him.

"It all turned out fine. I was just astounded you showed up at all, but it was daytime, Margret. Didn't expect that in a million years. You surprise me." Kisses my cheek softly. "I love that about you."

I hold my tongue. Still don't want to tell him about my kill. My third in so few months; I fear what the future would bring without Eric to care for me.

Chapter Thirty

The next few weeks we lay around making love endlessly, resting in between. Seems like we watched a thousand movies. Many nights we danced in the front room as we did when we were dating. Only when I grew hungry and had taken too much of my beloved did we venture out.

It was wonderful to be free again, although something still hung over me. The many weeks of hiding, the sunken nagging feeling that held on. Something felt threatening to my freedom, my happiness. I made great efforts to dismiss it; after a while, I succeeded.

I often fed after hours of dancing at one of the many night clubs in Chicago. Always someone too drunk to even notice my attack.

As it was last week. We decided to stroll along Lake Michigan. Enjoying the lights of the many buildings on one side and the glistening reflections on the black waves on the other. Cold but so beautiful. Eric nearly froze but saw my pleasure and endured it for me. I was in need so, at the end of our long walk, we found a bar nearby in the park. Waited outside until the last of the patrons were leaving. Predictably a drunken man, not so attractive, was leaving dishearteningly alone. I approached him in the dark lot behind the bar. Found he was easily seduced into my arms. As always, Eric took as much care of my feed as he does me. Tucked him in the back seat of his car, left him to recover from me and his drunkenness without worry.

I am seeing now that between the craven, the drunk, the forgotten and the just plain strange, there are more than enough people to feed on. Unnoticed by anyone. I feel nothing but grateful, caring for even the least of them. Eric always keeps me away from evil people. Especially now that he knows I often sense their true selves in my feeding. The loneliness that drives their pain, the strange behaviors, or the chances they take with themselves. For now, never to those, and I know there are many, whom I may want to give death to. The ones I could despise for their own evils.

Eric Keeps me well, guards me from my own devils. Brings me the weak, forgotten, those my human heart will find some empathy for. I remember in each what it was like before, when I was human. When I had fears and pains, loneliness of my own. I no longer need to fear death, sickness or physical pain. Things I was surrounded by in my past life. And loneliness... how could I feel it when he is with me? Gives me all of himself without limit.

I am comfortable with myself and my needs with Eric by my side. We are happy, and he tells me we will soon be moving to the Chicago penthouse. I can't wait!

Chapter Thirty-one

My legs are tight around Eric's sharp hips. His eyes loving as we lay on our sides facing each other. He bends to bring his mouth to my breasts, I arch myself up to him. Caress his long hair, loving his hot mouth on my skin. His hands run softly over me.

Then I feel soft kisses on my back, traveling from my neck, longingly down my spine. Sometimes wandering to the front of my ribs, nibbling deep into my hip. Still Eric keeps my attentions to him.

Hot kisses in the nape of my back, on my full cheeks. Bites, gentle, yet aggressive. They feel good, but still I feel anxious about the dark lover with us.

Eric enters me, I gasp at the thickness and force of him. The other brings his full body close to me. His hard cock nestled in the last of my spine. Breathing rapidly into my neck. I feel Eric's hands move soothingly, quieting me. Caressing my backside as he continues his slow penetrations. Eric's hands grow firmer, pulls me open.

I resist, but they both continue. Eric holds me tighter, the other holds fast his hardness to me, trying to gain entrance. The pressure on me increases. His hard cock held fast...the force increases. The obscure man's penetrations strange, painful, unwanted.

No, not this!

Eric is moving slowly inside me. The other gradually, painfully, gaining full entrance into me. I look to Eric and plead. "Eric, please, stop him." He seems to not see me, seems not to hear me

"Please, stop!"

My Eric dark, lost to me. Still his hands hold tight. Again I protest, strug-gling harder against them. Now pushing Eric away.

"Let me go!" Trying in vain to pull myself tight, forbidding the other. Only making his unrelenting efforts more painful.

Eric takes my free arm by the wrist, tight in his grip brings it behind my back. I look to him, his eyes do not see me, meet mine. I continue to beg them to stop. His eyes are black, seem unaware of me, my cries, or any feelings he has for me.

My right arm and leg are useless underneath the weight of him. Pressed firmly into the bed. I have no ability to fight them. They have my free arm and leg securely in their grasp. Restraining me, forcing me.

Their full lengths thrust deep inside me. Both penetrations making me cry out in pain. He is too much, Eric is too much. I feel the fullness of them both inside me. Their coordinated thrusts only brings agony. I feel torn apart. I cry, pleading over and over for it to stop. No one hears me. Their thrusts only quicken, seemingly enjoying my inability to gain release. My pain and loneliness too much, I can only sob as they finish. Then I feel a sharp pain in the back of my shoulder. Greater even than the forced coupling...an evil darkness in its kiss.

I wake, covered in sweat; I don't sweat. My heart exploding. This was the most vivid, powerful dream I have had yet. Eric's bedside clock reads 5:28 p.m. Dark as midnight already. I pull all the covers over me, hide in them. I fear this recurring dream more than I can understand.

I wait, allow my breath slow, my heart to slow.

Panicked. "Eric!" I yell at the top of my lungs. I can hear the washing machine, dryer, the TV. He is doing his chores. Still he hears me scream out his name. Hear Eric running up the stairs to me.

Peeking out of the covers like a frightened child. Eric rushes to my side, cradles me in his arms.

"What's wrong, Margret?" Holding me close, kissing my head, face full of gentleness and concern. "You look like you have seen a ghost." A common expression, I hope I have not.

Take a long deep breath; I still seem to need them.

"I have been having this dream, for weeks now, not a pleasant one."

Cling to him as if it is my last.

"It only gets worse every time I have it," I whimper into his chest. "It was the first real dream..."

Eric cuts me off. "Why didn't you tell me?"

I look up at him. "There were more important things to deal with than a stupid dream!" I say irritated. "Doesn't matter, it has been getting worse, more detailed, vivid every time!"

Eric looks curiously at me. "OK, tell me about it."

I tell him, every intimate detail. Can't help but notice his eyes go from mine down to the quilt. They never return as I relay the totality of my dream.

Somewhere I know.

"Eric." Demanding. "Tell me what this is. You know, don't you?"

I have heard many sighs from him. This one heavy with dread.

"Yes, I know," reluctantly whispers. "That's not a dream, Margret, it's a memory."

Moaning over his last words, "Oh God, oh God. I knew it..."

Knew it in my heart! Denied this memory because I wanted to, needed to. Prayed it was only one of my disjointed thoughts. My heart devoured. I feel it crush under the weight of realization...not a dream, not a dream. I feel like a thousand swords are piercing me. Eric betrayed me. Let his master rape me, helped him do it. He took Margret's body and soul that night. I saw no love in Eric's eyes for me, only his perverse duty to Markus.

Hold my anger tight inside. I have more questions.

Calmly, betraying the hot rage that is erupting in me. "Eric, tell me the truth, no bullshit, tell me what happened that night," I demand.

Eric's eyes still fixed on the quilt. I am watching him closely. Notice his hand mildly shaking as he fidgets with the covers.

"You know what happened, I told..." Angrily stomp on his words.

"NO! I don't know what really happened that night! You were at best vague when we talked about this before. I remembered nothing, not even myself back then. Advantageously you left out the part about forcing me to fuck you both! Raping me!" Screaming at him. Eric looks up over his thick lashes sheepishly.

"Now!" I insist.

His heart clearly heavy, he starts.

"Markus was growing very impatient with me. I insisted we wait until you told me you loved me. You DID tell me, but I didn't want him to know. Maybe I was having second thoughts. I don't know, but Markus was always near, watching us, listening by then. I couldn't hide how I felt about you as hard as I tried. He insisted we turn you right away after he heard you," gasps for air as if he is drowning, "tell me how much you loved me."

Eric goes silent, fighting with his tears.

"Markus wanted that one night with me and you before he found true death. His keeper and his new child. So when you came for our Friday night date, he was here. We talked, drank, even danced together. You and Markus...got along well." Clears his throat nervously.

"After a few hours and a lot of affection, we persuaded you to come up-stairs. I know you didn't think anything big would happen. I knew you. We seduced you into bed with us. You only wanted to be with me, but..." Eric looks shamefully at me.

"I was his keeper, Markus wanted you; we both wanted you." Stumbling over his words.

"Regretfully I did what Markus desired over my feelings for you. I couldn't stop him, not even sure I wanted to. At the time, making love to both of you... Margret, you have to understand, my sense of reality was so perverse, distorted." Eric eyes ask for some understanding. My eyes, restrained hate. He reads them well.

"I'm ...can't even say I'm sorry or ashamed. I am, but it seems so insignificant now. I know it does." Feebly conceding.

My anger over this betrayal, my hate, so amazingly powerful. I pride myself for containing it until Eric finishes his pitiful excuses.

"I should have told him no before it even started. I knew it was wrong, still I was torn between my love for you and for Markus...my duty to him."

Eric, always the devoted keeper.

"So tell me the details, after I blacked out. What, you were fucking me, Markus was fucking me, what happened next?" Spitefully ask.

My rage as restrained as I could manage, still painfully clear. He holds his head low, so full of shame.

Good.

I continue. "I seem to remember you saying you stayed with me?"

Almost inaudibly answers. "Yes, I did. Marcus told me that it would bind us if I was, with you." Pausing to regain his deceitful tongue. "To be with you while he bled you out, and while you turned...you would be one with me and..."

"You mean you still fucked me while he bled me to death? You still fucked me?" Astonished.

Surprisingly Eric quickly shifts from shame and regret to red hot anger.

"NO! I CAN'T FUCK YOU, MARGRET, I LOVE YOU!" he screams at me, so enraged. Unlike I have ever heard. "Yes, I stayed inside you. Held you. I have never been as frightened or miserable as I was that night." Crumples over into himself. I can barely hear him as he mutters, "Markus said you wouldn't remember any of it, it was too close to your turning." Sorrowfully weeps.

Throw my arms up in amazement. "Oh, that's OK then! I wasn't supposed to remember it. So yea, sure, as long as she doesn't remember, go ahead, sodomize her." Sarcasm ripe with my contempt for him. "Rape her, Master, whatever you wish!"

Oh the sweet tears of his guilt. Eric's remorseful tears. I have no sympathy for him. Every drop of his regret, the scent of each tear, feeds my vindictiveness.

He said he loved me, human Margret. How could he do that to me? I actually understand his need for me as I am now, his vampire companion, lover. It's all he knew for 67 years, to be a keeper. Maybe even for Eric to *stay* with me while I changed, as disgusting as that is. Can actually forgive that, but what I can't understand is why it was necessary to force me to have Markus, take them both! To rape me, both of them. NO! I didn't want it, begged for them to stop. They took me regardless of my tears.

My head and stomach churning, sick. I am as confused and tormented as I was when I woke to this nightmare. Certainly as enraged, only now there is sense to it.

Just hours ago I held him, pulled him into me, so full of love and passion. Somehow that has become the dream. A sweet fiction of my innocence. His betrayal devours everything.

In their sick selfish lusts, they killed me, they raped me, and I have had my fill of that!

Eric looks destroyed. Only now fully realizing the fullness of what he did. That 'the moment' is not always all that matters, the past sometimes holds greater weight. His guilt is consuming him, and I am not here to help. Want only to deeply salt his wounds.

I take a long slow breath. "So, let me get this straight. You'll correct me if I am wrong." Sardonic.

"You and Markus got me drunk, seduced me to believe you only wanted to share some affections with me. I do remember myself well enough now, Eric..." I bite at him. "I know how far Margret could be seduced." Push him harshly away from me, nearly knocking him off the bed. I am disgusted at the sight of him. He looks surprised at my physical behavior towards him. "Then you, Eric, you forced me to screw both of you while he drank me to death? Is that about right?"

Eric groans out a harsh breath, looks up over his thick lashes at me.

"Margret, please." He whimpers, "You know me. Everything that is important about who, what I am. I have no excuse for what I have done, none you don't already know. I am sorry. I never meant to hurt you, ever. I only hope you remember how I have loved you. How I need you, more than anything, anyone."

I am unmoved. "I suppose my stupid fantasies of true love are just as distorted as your sick idea of love." I get up, want my room.

"Don't come down, talk to me, fuck me! Never pretend to actually love me again, ever. I am far too strong for you to force your deceitful lovemaking on me again! Just do your job, keeper, bring me food!" Tears are running silently down Eric's face. He looks up to fully meet my hateful gaze. I have never seen him look so fragile. His eyes red, the dark specks overtaking them, pleading.

"Margret, please, please! I can't take it back, I was wrong to let him... but that doesn't change everything else. Doesn't change how much I have loved you!" He is grabbing my hand, arm, trying to pull me back to him crumpled on the edge of the bed. I shake him off like he is vermin.

"Oh but it does change everything, Eric. You chose Markus's pleasures over my trust, my love for you! I pleaded for you to stop, begged. You loved him, not me. I believed you, but everything you've done..." I choke back tears. Unwilling to give him even a drop of them. "I was right months ago; you have no idea what love is, Eric!"

I have forgotten everything before and everything after. Nothing at this moment matters to me but Eric forgot me, betrayed my trust. I feel such awful pain not only his deceitful act, but all the hate I held dear for weeks after as I turned returning with a vengeance. My hatred of him is all I remember now.

I spend the rest of the night howling in such deep agony. Too loud to hide from him somewhere above me. I only hoped each cry caused him as much suffering as it was me.

I am as he wished, remembering my human self. I am changed, yes, my sense of morality very much distorted now. I have too much under my belt to pretend I am the same person, but I remember my human self clearly now. Suppose this is the most painful type of growing pain. I do remember Margret, even if I am not exactly her anymore. And the man she loved so deeply, trusted...I can't bear to think of what he did to her.

Cry until light is blaring in the windows. Until I have nothing left. Until human tears die, only crimson seeps from my eyes. Only bloody tears left now.

Exhausted I finally sleep. Thankfully without dreams.

Chapter Thirty-two

Two days go by, my hunger grows too hot ignore any longer. I have cried and moaned from all of it relentlessly. My lost humanity, the people I have killed, the rapes, the betrayals. So much pain and remorse. Seems I am to be forever lost in it. Time means nothing until my hunger grows so desperate it overtakes everything.

Scream up to him. "Eric, I hunger!" He briskly runs down the stairs.

Eric looks like shit, eyes red and swollen, unshaven.

I am pleased to see pain carved in his physical appearance. No matter how much I cry or am unable to rest, I will look as beautiful to him as always. Unchanged.

"I hunger. Bring me someone, here. I am in no mood to go out," I angrily demand.

Standing the edge of my bed, Eric looks sadly at me.

"Margret, please...you know that I love you, know me, better than..." Cut him off. No more!

"Stop saying that! I don't know anything about you! You are full of deceit! I will hear none of your lies."

Eric looks disappointed that my rage has not waned. Clearly he hoped a few days of crying would result in my missing him, maybe a bit of forgiveness.

"Bring me a young man I can fuck while I feed. No disgusting vagrants! I want to screw while I bleed him." He looks as horrified as I had hoped.

"Margret?" Perplexed. "You never talk that way and..." At a loss.

"Don't address me that way again, Eric!" My eyes red hot, burning into him. "You will call me Master from now on! Never use my mortal name again, ever," I command.

"Please, Margret, stop this! This has gone too far. I am sorry. It was a selfish, horrid thing I did to you. I had forgotten...forgotten myself. You have to understand... I told you, everything...I was his, Markus's keeper!" Breathing rapid, heart beating just as much. "I should have tried to love you as you were...as a regular human man. Lived our lives, grow old."

Can't complete a sentence in his hasty entreaties He finishes in a low moan. Eric knows I understand him. He fails to see I no longer care about his pains, his lost life. I have my own.

The tears he is desperately trying to confine silently overwhelm his lids.

"You can't forget my love for you, our love. Giving to me, feeding from me..." Urgently adding, "I am yours, only yours. Your first. You must feed from me!"

I can't believe how pathetically he is begging me to feed from him. Most likely thinking my lusts will not be limited to his blood. Seducing me even now to return to his arms.

I have filled myself with such rage that this display, the feelings he is trying to arouse in me, only anger me further.

"NO! I will never feed from you again, Eric. Or you from me! Do as I wish, as you are charged to do keeper. Bring me what I ask for, what I need."

His expression transforms; desperation to shock.

I whisper bitterly, "I don't want you anymore." Fight my own tears.

I believed Eric could look no worse than when he came down to me. Shed no more tears than I have already elicited from him.

My declaration has sent him into a new depth. He can no longer stand upright. Eric's knees leave him, his head falls onto the edge of my bed. Hear his stifled sobs; he tries to keep them close, though his back and shoulders give all away, heaving in pain. I have fully rejected him. Rejected my keeper. I wait and watch with no pity until Eric recovers himself. After many minutes of sobbing, he stands unsteadily. Already the sadness seems to have aged him.

"All right, Master, I will bring you..." his breath so labored he can barely speak, "what you want."

Unable to fully cope with my complete and total rejection of him, he stumbles up the stairs. I hear the back door slam, car race away.

Eric is gone. Now I am truly alone. In a way I have never felt before, as I demanded to be.

❦

He is very young looking. Must be at least 21, as Eric finds them mostly at bars, but looks, well, younger still. Tall and thin, as most young boys are. Hope he will be able to keep up. Although I do this only to torture Eric, maybe I can glean some enjoyment out of it besides my feeding. My loneliness already grows heavy.

He is high on something, only smell beer. His manner is rather aggravated and confused. He comes to my bed eagerly, without question. I have only a black lace gown over my nakedness. His long black hair is inviting, I pull him down on me by it. I see Eric go to leave us as the young man starts to pleasure me.

"Eric." Sternly bark. "Stay. Watch over us, so I don't lose control." Taunting him. Eric is frozen in place.

"Keeper?" Questioning his obedience.

Eric's expressions is nothing less than abysmal.

"As you wish, Master," he concedes, sits on the floor in the dim light beyond my bed.

My feed is hastily licking at me. Honestly I hardly notice his efforts. My eyes fixed on Eric. Though I relax after a bit. Nice, but unnecessary. Want his blood. I turn him quickly to his back, suck his long cock, hoping Eric is full of raging jealousy and desire for me. My human's moans are loud and full of delight. His release even more pronounced. I spit him out, a taste I no longer desire. As soon as he is able, I drive myself onto him. Taking him inside me in long slow motions. My restraint more about tormenting Eric than any pleasure.

I look back over my shoulder. Eric's eyes are fixed on the floor in front of him. I will have none of that.

"Watch me! I want to feed now." Maliciously instructing my keeper.

My young friend hardly noticed. I am well versed in teasing a man now; I kept him going as long as I could. The longer I ride him, the harder it is for Eric. Hear even Eric's most stifled exasperations. Watching me take another as I deny him this, everything.

That thought alone brings me such an evil pleasure, but when I finally sink my teeth into my young friend, Eric's agonized groan is closely matched by my young lover's. Confirming how much pain I am inflicting on him. How he misses my love, feeding from him as I am doing now to a complete stranger.

Eric's lusts must be uncontrollable, yet he has no choice but to control them. He is forbidden from my bed. May only watch me give my body to another, bleed another. It will be the first of many.

I do so love the suffering I am causing him.

I drank until Eric wordlessly pulled me off him. A soon as Eric touched me, I stopped and roughly tossed him aside like the trash he was to me.

"Take him home now," I demand without looking at Eric.

I drank much from my lover. Eric's dark uncaring mood, my anger, hunger...really, he is lucky to have drop left in him. Uncaring, I cover myself, turning my back to them both. Eric dresses his limp body; I know he will take him safely home to recover.

As soon as I heard his car leave, I start to sob. What am I doing? Becoming? I had no thought for the human, his sex, his life! Even my feeding was more of a performance for Eric. Sure I would have gladly killed him if Eric hadn't stopped me.

I am a vampire, but when Eric was one with me, I felt like me, like Margret. Remembered my human feelings. Now there is nothing but hate and blood lust. Haven't felt the need for blood this fiercely since my first incoherent weeks. My hunger is nearly all I can think of, well, besides my rage.

I realize now just how much Eric has kept me, tamed me. I have chosen to let my evil free by rejecting him, my keeper.

Except for the black whole of sadness consuming me, I feel nothing.

Not until I hear his car return do I force silence on my misery.

Chapter Thirty-three

I have let nearly three weeks go by. I have not fed from Eric, or he from me. I only see Eric every couple of days when he brings me a human to feed on. I have insisted on all being men I could have sex with. Cruelly forcing Eric to watch over them all. Although now the need for him to stop me from killing is inevitable. No control left in me, only rage and darkness.

I inflict as much pain on Eric as I can. He looks worse every time I see him. Which is not much; even when he is near, I avoid looking at him. I am miserable, lost to myself.

Need to get away from this hell. Need to go out tonight. I dress myself, black jeans and the sexiest top I can find. Pull my hair back, don't bother with makeup.

"Where are your keys?" Eric looks like shit, lying shirtless on the couch like an old rag, watching TV. I turn my head away. Eric's shitty is still more beautiful than I can stand to look at.

I miss him. Even my dreams are spitefully betraying me. Slipping into remembrances I don't want.

All of our courting, as he calls it, comes back to torment me in my dreams. The nights we danced before romantic fires, laughed, ate pizza. I even dreamt of the first night we made love far too graphically.

Eric was so romantic, so patient, understanding. Yes, I was already cheating on my husband but this was different. Giving myself to Eric. I was scared to death. I had only made love to Joe before. Eric soothed and held me, kissed me until I had no resistance left. He was so beautiful, so hot. I honestly don't know how I ever stopped myself before.

Remember it all too clearly now. I try to fight the memories, but they just keep coming. Always when I am near rest and am too exhausted to hold to my anger. Before darkness overtakes me.

I am so depressed. Still I can't seem to let this burning rage go. Even if I fall to sleep crying for him, I wake in anger.

I want to leave this house! Too much here.

"Margret, you are too wild to go out alone. I will take you wherever you want but not..."

"I told you not to call me that!" Divulging too much as I sounded pained in my demand.

"I am sorry, Master." He bows his head to me sarcastically. I don't like it. I continue to demand anyway.

"Give me your keys, now!" Weakly add, "I need to get out, just drive."

"Let me go with you," he pleads.

"No, why should you?" Sarcastically add, "I'm a big vampire now." Eric picks up the local paper on the coffee table, holds it up for me to read.

The headline, from a few weeks ago by the date, "Body Found in Community Woods Park." Scan the first few lines, dead homeless man...most likely died from exposure...found near a trail...badly eaten by animals.

"What did you do?" Clearly accusing me.

My anger rises. How dare he question me? I did what I needed to do. What he made me to do.

"I had nothing to do with that!" I lie. As always, Eric reads me too well.

"You are full of shit, Master!" Eric may be weak, but his derisive tone is still very clear to me.

Eric knows it was me who killed this man. Think he has put two and two together. Only a deer gave me the strength I had that day at the police station? Hate that I can't hide from him.

Still I am confused. I didn't hide my feed anywhere near the trails, I left him deep in the weeds. Who could have found him, moved him? Why? Briefly remember the feeling of being watched that night but let it go. I don't really give a shit right now; I just want to be far away from here, from Eric, as I can be.

"Just give me the keys, or I will take them by force. Pick!" I stare darkly at him.

Reluctantly Eric gives up the discussion and digs his key out of his jeans, angrily throws them at me.

"Please, please don't do anything stu..." auto correct "you'll regret. Just drive, stay away from people, stay in the car. Please. And don't drive like a maniac; remember you don't have a license anymore."

I manage to retain eye contact for the moments he begs for my good behavior. Eric's full of concern.

Whisper. "I just want to get out, alone." I turn and run quickly out the back door before one of us stops me.

When the black Escalade reaches the foot of the driveway, I stop. Right or left? Where am I going? I look at the house I am finally free of. Eric is gazing out the window, looking like a concerned parent letting the teenager take the car for the first time.

I go right, like a bat out of hell. All puns apply.

Drive directly to the freeway, I can go faster here. Although I still stay within the unwritten ten miles above the speed limit. It's Thursday, I think. The car's clock reads 1:13 a.m. Roads are quiet. Turn the radio on. Eric's fancy car has that radio thing where you can pick a station that plays different genres. Eric loves fifties music, I have learned to love it as well. Many of the songs he swung me around to in the living room were fifties songs, favorites of his. Probably shouldn't but. Press the station anyway.

"Bye, bye love
Bye, bye sweet caress
Hello emptiness'
I laugh out loud. Turn it up louder.
'I feel like I could die
Bye bye, my love, goodbye."

Irony. Laugh until I am in tears. Quickly they become sad ones.

Like the song gods are salting my wounds. I angrily turn the radio to contemporary rock.

Don't know where I am going just yet. Even so I find myself decisively turning off the highway at the next exit.

Cheap little town, Walmart. Dark rural roads...

There are no bikes in the parking lot, just a few cars. Too damn cold for even a fool to ride now. I park in a dark place near the woods at the edge of the gravel lot. Turn off the car, the lights and sit. 1:42 a.m. Bikers slowly trail out to their broken-down cars.

No Mark. I will wait until the last car is gone before I give up.

1:55; three cars remain. The door to the bar opens. Mark. My blood lust rushes like a waterfall over me.

Control myself.

Laugh to myself. It looks as if he has not changed his clothes since last I saw him. He gets in his car and drives off. Wait a few second before I follow. Don't know what I think I am doing, but I do it anyway. He turns right out of the lot, the opposite direction I came in. Use only my parking lights and stay back as far as I can. Not a lot of turn offs, but I don't want to lose him either. Even as I am following him, I have no idea what I intend to do, or why I am doing this.

Finally he turns down a dark two-lane road. I try to turn off the head lights but this damn new car always has them on. I hold back further. About a mile down, I see his car turn, disappearing into darkness. I pull over to the side of the road and turn the car off. Quickly run to where I saw his car disappear.

By the time I run up the twisted wooded drive, I see lights going on inside a double wide trailer. I smell water nearby, the rich earth, smell of the woods surrounding me. I sneak around the house to investigate the property. Yes, a small lake, maybe about 100 yards from the trailer. No other houses nearby, just trees.

Now or never. Boldly I walk up to the door and knock.

Nothing. I knock again louder. Finally Mark opens the door, unsteady, leans on the doorway for support.

Good; already a few sheets.

"What are you doing here at this time of night, little lady? You lost or something?"

Don't think he recognizes me so I quickly explain I am the woman who was with the jerk he beat up a few months back. Margret. Nods, opening the door for me.

"Yea, yea, I remember that...Sort of." Rubs his head.

"I wanted to buy you a drink but by the time I got to the bar it was too late, so I followed you home." Meekly add. "Sorry it's so late."

Mark happily lets me inside.

"Jack OK?" he asks, clearly intoxicated.

"Yea, sure."

Motions for me to sit at the small round kitchen table. Two mismatched chairs to sit on. A bottle already in the middle, shot glass waiting. Seems he was about to have a night cap.

"Sorry about this, I know it's late but..."

Mark is shaking his head as if it's no bother. Gets a glass out of the barren cupboard for me.

"We just had a big fight, ya know, real bad one. I just took off and before I knew it I was out here and..."

"Where ya from?"

"The city." I simply state.

"That is a waze." Mark slurs.

I feel a bit uncomfortable then remember who and what I am. I toast him, drink down the shot. Burns like hell, tastes like acid, but I get it down.

Remember what Eric told me about Markus. How he would drink, throw it up afterwards. If Markus could do it, then so shall I. I pour us another, mine only half. It won't take long till I am sure I can take him without any struggle. Glad he has already had a few or he might find this situation as strange as it is.

We both drink our second shot back. I pour another, but I'm not going to drink it, can't. Mark has it to his lips already.

"I need to go to the bathroom." Two seems my limit.

"Yea, sure, right there after the fridge, you'll see the door." His speech slurred. I need to get this shit out of me!

The tiny pale green bathroom is not so surprisingly filthy. I turn on the water on and lean over the toilet, standing as far away as I can. Only have to press under my breast once and it comes up. Blood with it. Burning all the way up as badly as it did going down. I take a dirty glass from the sink and pour water over the splash of blood I got on the seat. Wasn't touching anything in here. Seems some of my human delicacies are still strong if nothing else.

When I emerge he is already dozing in his chair. No need to wake him from his peaceful slumber.

Walk over to stand next to him. Looking down at his unshaven face, I vividly recall Mark kicking the shit out of my keeper. The cracking sound as his heavy boot landed in Eric's ribs.

How crazy with rage it made me. Clearly see the bruises over Eric's body, the weeks it took him to fully recover his strength.

I grow angry and very, very hungry. I lean over and snuggle my face into his neck. He wakes a bit, tries to embrace me, thinking I want him. Even if I did want more than his blood, does he really think he has anything to give me tonight? Such egos men have.

I take what I came for with ease. Mark falls off his chair but my teeth go with him. His few struggles easily overcome. Straddling him I feed enthusiastically, no Eric to stop me tonight. My head fills with a mix black and gray smoke, no colors. Sizzling blood flows rapidly into my needy mouth. I see, I feel, nothing of Mark in it, just life's energy flowing into me. Finally I hear the last of his heart, feel the last of his breath. I let go.

I feel so powerful, stronger than ever. Feel nothing for the dead man at my feet. I pull him uncaringly by his leather jacket to the door. Quickly dragging him outside, over rocks and branches down to the lake as if his body weighed nothing.

Stop at the dark water's edge to gaze at the moon's light as it reflects on the mirror stillness. It's so beautiful, the black silhouettes of tall trees lining the dark mass. The moon's reflection on the still water.

Abruptly pick him up and toss him as far as I can. A loud splash pierces the quiet night as his large body hits the lake. I watch the moon kissing the silent ripples as they move away from his final resting place until all is still. Glass and moon light again.

The fantasy I had that long night while I held Eric's beaten body in my arms, to drink Mark to death, now fulfilled.

<hr />

When I arrive home even as I am well fed I am as full of darkness as ever. I find Eric where I left him, TV still on. I stand over him, despising Eric for all that he has done to me. What his love has made me.

"Margret, please." Softly moaning, imploring me. I grow impatient with him. I have told him repeatedly not to call me that! I am just about to chastise him for his continued disobedience when Eric rolls over. Clearly fully asleep.

I stand frozen. Again I hear him restlessly call out my name. Eric's dreams are filled with pain and need for me. An agonized throbbing grows in my chest. My legs weaken.

His back facing me. The random light of the television flickers over his dark hair, over his shoulders. I admire anew the hard muscles along his back. His loose jeans revealing the upper mounds of his round behind. The sweet spot where his spine ends into them replete with hot shadow.

For a moment I am enticed to bury my face in its darkness, kiss him, bite into the tight muscles. Want him, his body, his blood.

STOP!

Urgent to get away from my temptation I run down to my dark bed. Cover myself completely in the fat gray quilt. I lie there breathlessly for a few moments. Try to calm the rising desire. Focus my mind on my rage.

I fail.

Shamefully I give in, begin to pleasure myself. Thinking of Eric's passionate lovemaking, the warmth of his beautiful body. His kiss.

I miss him, want him so badly. My heart and heat throbbing in odd union. I am crying in pain even as I bring myself to climax. Just the thought of him tears me apart, seduces me. I can't go on like this! The temptation to return to his deceitful arms, to fail in my righteous hatred, my rejection of him. As long as he is alive, I will see him, smell him, know he is near. My resistance obviously grows weak at just the smallest incitement.

I have to decide.

Chapter Thirty-four

I make no sound for several days. Do not ask for food, don't want to see him even for a second. Still my hunger grows hotter. I fight with it incessantly. Finally it grows too strong to ignore, to control.

Fear what I may do to satisfy it.

I hear his few movements. A shower, rarely in the kitchen for food, the TV on constantly. His only companion I suppose. Not a word from him. My need for Eric is growing stronger than my hatred. I will either have to drink him dry or fail in my rejection of him and all he has done to me. Need to eliminate the snare of his arms. My need for my keeper, to feed from him, have him inside me as cardinal as the burning need for blood.

One of us must be defeated.

Growing near insane with need. Burning lava resurfacing. Every moment more of the wildness that overtook me when I first awoke. Finally I relent.

Scream angrily through the rafters. "Eric, I hunger! I want to feed!"

Sheepishly he comes down to me, each step reluctant. Head depressed into his chest.

"What do you need, Master?" Whispers. Every week without me has aged him. His eyes dark, face drawn, seemingly slimmer. Is it the pain or lack of food, blood? Regardless he looks pathetic, weak.

"Come, feed me." Demanding.

I realize I am hunched like a tiger. Wild and naked, ready to leap off my bed. Obediently he comes to sit near me, waits for my move. I grab his arm, look up scornfully, warning.

"Don't move. Don't even think to touch me." Each softly uttered, still only a shadow of my abhorrent heart.

"Yes, master, drink, all you wish." He gives up his arm like an obedient pet. My teeth violently sink into his wrist. Even my indecent bite does not induce the slightest sound from him.

The sweetest blood rushes hotly over my eager tongue. Succulent. I have forgotten the exquisite taste of my keeper. How he completely saturates, satisfies me.

With great abandon I drink from his vein; nothing will stop me. Tonight I will take all I want of his sweetness.

Wispy clouds saturated with every color overtake the darkness that has filled my mind for weeks. Feel his blood moving from my mouth, seeping into my veins. An electric pulse, reanimating every cell. My desire for it is insatiable.

My lock on his arm unbreakable. Eric calmly lies down, giving up completely to me regardless of any pain my zealous bite causes him. Not the slightest struggle.

He must know I mean to kill him. Yet no plead for mercy escapes him. He makes no protest. I feed and feed, feeling him weaken as I gorge on the blood I lust for over all others.

Soon my keeper will be no more. Stone dead, as I have longed for many times in the past.

Yet as my victory draws closer, my body begins to ache. My heat pulsates distractingly. My desire for oneness is becoming as powerful as this salacious feeding. God, how I want to fully bond with him!

Struggle with my desires. Still my core vibrates so distractedly I can't even taste his blood anymore! My mouth craves his kiss. Even as the most desirable blood fills it, I am craving his lips pressed to mine!

I scream from the overwhelming pain, my need for him. Releasing his vein to set my anguish free.

Only now does he utter a tormented groan. Curl myself up in a ball, weeping in anguish. Cry uncontrollably. Eric makes no move to hold or comfort me. Only drags himself off the bed to the foot of the stairs. I crawl to the edge of my bed, pursuing my lustful desires.

Eric is drained, maybe near death? I don't know how much I took from him!

Feebly he manages to lift himself up, using the banister to assist in his efforts.

Eric's blood is molten glass in my veins. As my hateful heart cools, it breaks into sanguine shards. Flowing rapidly through me. Ripping every fiber of me into bloody pieces!

"Why didn't you finish me?" Weak whispers. "Why didn't you end this hell, Margret?"

With the last of his strength, he pulls himself up the stairs leaving his vampire master alone with her suffering.

Not since I was a virgin vampire have I felt this out of control. I tear at everything within my reach. My bed is tossed into shambles in seconds. The covers, the pillows, ripped to shreds. In my rage I rip every page from Markus's journal that I cherished so into tiny pieces and toss them about like confetti.

I howl, I scream, I cry. Even begin to hiss like a wild cat. I have no control. Torment and pain rule me. I tear at my wrists. Violently scratching into them until they are torn and bloody. I know I can't even release myself from this hell; no matter how deeply I dig into them they will heal!

Why is he not coming to me, comforting me, controlling me? Only a foreboding silence above me. I drown myself in the torn quilt, weep with great abandon, the grey fibers unable to keep up with my tears.

Somewhere deep inside I hope for him.

Where is he? Why doesn't he try to calm me? Why doesn't Eric control me, chain me? Seduce me restrained in my bindings as he did before? Take me until he gains my concession to him. Force me to be his again.

Rape me until I remember my love for him! Why?

STOP THIS!

I pound my head into the thick plaster wall next to my bed to relieve the agony. Beating all thought from it. Endeavoring to alleviate the extreme pressure of my desires. My need to have him.

Over and over. I feel the impact, feel it alleviate too soon. So I pound my head into the wall faster, and faster, so there is not a second of healing, a second without pain. Flagellating myself until I am hemorrhaging and chunks of plaster crumble onto my bed. Finally I stop, frightened of myself. Blood dripping from my wounds over my face and lips and down my neck.

After months of relative peace with my new self, tonight I am acutely aware of myself and what I am. Frightens me more than it has ever before.

I want to run wild. It takes every bit of Margret left in me not to. I remember Eric saying as I turned 'You are an animal, uncontrollable, you would have the innocent, kill anyone.'

Tonight I know Eric's words truthful. More clearly than the night he first spoke them. I would kill anyone. I just tried to kill my beloved keeper!

I fall weeping into my blood-soaked bed.

Why isn't he coming to me?

The dark basement seems colder, the artificial light in the windows dimmer.

I feel isolated. Vampire, human. Both lost.

A hushed loneliness covers me finally. It seems there isn't a sound in all the world to be heard.

The stillness nearly as disturbing as the violence.

Is Eric is upstairs dying, as I lie here wishing that I could?

Chapter Thirty-five

I lie blank in my bed for the rest of the night and the next day. Even my pain is muffled. I am in a very dark place. Hiding myself, hiding from the world, from him. Don't feel my hunger. All I feel is loneliness, isolation. Self-inflicted.

Every time I close my eyes, I see him struggling off my bed, pulling himself up the stairs. Eric's face seared into my mind.

I need to end this.

Looking through the shambles of my bed, I find the ring. Place it on my thumb, forcing myself to get up. Blindly I make my way up the stairs, turn the glass handle, freeing myself.

Eric lies on his back on the couch. Shirtless, loose jeans, as he came to me last night. Only a throw over him. The TV is on, but no sound. Scatter bits of accidental light eerily move throughout the room.

I am grateful he is still alive. His heart weak, but beating.

Sit on the coffee table to face him, unsure of what I am doing. What I am going to say to him. He looks sadly over to me, pulls himself up a bit. His eyes swollen, not leaving mine for a second.

Does he hate me now as much as I do him?

I breath in deeply, hold it unnaturally long, exhale. Eric's eyes still riveted to me, waiting.

"You look like hell." All I could bring to mind.

Eric's gaze moves down to see the giving ring placed on my thumb. He sharply looks away, groaning as if he was punched in his stomach.

"Margret," growling, "please." Rubs harshly at his eyes as if his head is exploding. "I deserve every bit of agony you are putting me through. And make no mistake, I am in agony." Painful whispers seeping from him. "Drink me dry if you wish. I hoped you would last night." Sighs, beaten. "Wanted you to. But I will not feed from you. I can't."

"Why not?" I angrily snap.

Shakes his head. "It is giving. And you no longer wish to give me anything but pain. Well- deserved, I suppose, for what I did to you, all of it." Eric hides his face in his hands. I see nothing, smell salt.

"But I cannot, will not, endure feeding from you, Margret, without..." He pauses. "My pain is too great already." His agonized refusal.

"It's all you want! What you really need from me, isn't it?" Refreshing my anger, my doubt.

"NO! What I want is your forgiveness, what I need is your love, Margret!" He makes no effort to hide his tears any longer. His eyes piercing into me.

"If I can't have either, then I'd rather join Markus." Eric's defeat clear.

That will have to be enough. I can't hate him any longer. It will kill us both.

"I don't know how to stop it, Eric." Finally weeping.

Not a move to touch or comfort me.

"Stop what?"

"The pain! I don't know how to..." sobbing into my hands, "stop this terrible pain. I do know you are in agony, I wanted you there! Now so am I. I hurt, I hunger for you. I have been digging this great hole of rage and I don't know how to stop." I crumble on the coffee table, wanting him to rescue me.

"How do I climb out of this, Eric? Please," I sorrowfully ask.

"I have begged for your forgiveness, even as I know I don't really deserve it. But, Margret, you must remember the love we have shared. Our connection to each other. No one knows, understands...no one could love as deeply as we love each other."

He grabs the hand I have tucked into myself in his. With great effort he leans forward, brings it to his lips, softly kisses it. "I am so sorry for everything I've done. I know I deserve this. I didn't know who or what I was anymore. I should have left you human, loved you. I didn't think I knew how to be human anymore..." Kisses hard into my palm, wrapping my hand around his face like a safe blanket. Holds it dearly to him.

"Please forgive me, Margret," he begs. "I love you more than I thought possible, always have, always will..."

I sit up, marvel that even in his unkempt state, I find him as beautiful as ever. More. His love and need for me sink deeply.

"You must feed," I whisper. Move to sit next to him.

"If you wish, Master."

Forcefully cover his mouth with mine, draw the very breath out of him. Grab his tongue, sucking the word Master from it.

"Never call me that again, just my love, as you used to." Whispering over soft kisses. "Remind me every minute of your love for me. If you don't, I will fall, be lost as I am now. You are my keeper." I cling hard. "Force it, sustain it but... keep me safe in your arms! Your love is," I weep into his neck, "all I really need. I know that now. My life is yours to keep, Eric."

He grabs the back of my head, bringing me to his kiss. I know Eric's passion well, he is too drained to give me all he desires.

I move myself to lie over him. Softly kiss over his face, run my lips over his mouth. Too frail to caresses me with his passion, but he tries to hold me as best he can.

"I do need to feed, but I don't think I can love you as my heart desires to." Just our conversation has fatigued him. "I only want to heal you, help you regain..." He gently squeezes my hips. "I want to be near you, please." Regretful. "Even if I can't..."

I know what he wants. I remove his jeans, see his limp manhood. Honestly, only seeing him in this condition when I have had him to his limit. He is always is some degree of desire otherwise. I have nothing on so lie delicately over him. Eric moans so painfully sweet, like he has never felt my flesh on his before. Admittedly it feels the same to me. Like the first time I felt the heat of his skin. Both starved. I hold him, gently kiss him for many moments before I sit up. I am afraid for him. But I have to feed him or I may well lose him. The nurse in me is well aware of his condition; heart beats, but his pulse is weak.

"Margret, only once." Eric cautions. "I know you need as I do, but I can't be strong, control this tonight. I am too near death, if you..." I bend over to swallow his fat lips in a slow kiss.

"Promise. I will think only of you, no matter how you make me throb with desire. OK?"

Unhappily grunts. "That's supposed to make me feel better?"

We both chuckle lamely, knowing this is not really funny. Our urges during bleedings are hard to control even when we have already saturated ourselves in each other.

I pull him up to sitting, turn him to rest on the back of the couch. Although I crave even a rub, I keep my heat well back over his thighs as I sit over him. I press the point into me, worried that I will not be able to protect him from my lusts. My body is starved for Eric, as he is for me.

Eric makes no move to take me into his mouth even as I start to bleed. His kiss is always on top of my hand, eagerly anticipating the flow. He is too weak. I lift his head to my bleeding nipple. Hold him tenderly to it.

I cannot help it normally, but now? As I have denied myself his love, his warm body for weeks? The neediness of Eric's sucking draws my passion through me. Finally sinking like a great weight into my core. Reverberating painfully in its emptiness. Groan incessantly from the excruciating desire.

Eric holds as tightly as he can to me. It further underlines his weakness. As I heal, everything in me wants to cut again, feed him more. Maybe another will make him hard and I will have all of him.

No, I can't! If I do, I risk killing him. Fear my vampire blood will strive to turn him in his frail state. It will kill Eric for sure.

My breast still in his mouth, I force myself to lie back, taking him with me. His grip on me little improved. Eric lies close beside me, releases my nipple like a satisfied baby. His head rolls back into my arm. He sleeps.

Even if I wanted rest, my heat is throbbing with a relentless pressure. Building until, even in his arms, I can no longer ignore it.

I move my hand between my legs, find my hood, and tightly circle it with the motions of my fingers. All I need is the thought of him, his warm body touching. My muffled climax nearly immediate. Still unsatisfied, I continue.

He stirs; I stop, embarrassed.

"Don't stop, Margret." His hand softly covers mine, holding it to me. "Please."

Reluctantly I continue to pleasure myself. He kisses my ear, breathing hard into it.

"My heart wants you so badly, Margret."

Still his body is unable to comply. His mouth travels slowly down my body, finding rest on my hip, his hand loosely over mine the whole time. Eric watches me pleasure myself.

Gently he kisses the top of my hand, licks slowly down my fingers pressed into my folds. I wait.

"Don't, stop," he repeats. He sucks at my fingers as I rub over myself. His hot breath driving me mad with desire. He continues sucking and licking over my wet fingers until finally he pushes them aside. Covers me, drawing my burning into his mouth. The succeeding kisses make me quiver. Running both hands through his long hair, I pull him into me, give him my climax.

Shivering, now weeping, Eric pulls himself up, encircling me in his arms, his head buried between my breasts.

"You OK, Margret?" he asks.

"Yes, just..."

He raises his head up to look at me, attempts a smile. "Just what?"

"You could give me a thousand orgasms, but until I am one with you..." Tearfully trail off. He knows.

"I'm sorry. It's not from lack of desire." Apologetically.

I gently push his head back to lie on me, run my hands through his hair. "I love you, Eric."

My gentle strokes quickly send him to rest.

Eric sleeps like a corpse for the next seven hours straight. Most likely the first real sleep he has had in weeks. I spent most my time fondling, clinging to him. Listening to his heart grow stronger. Think about the hell I put us both through.

I do know him, understand him. Eric is a keeper, mine now. He would do nearly anything I asked of him. Hell, he brought me more lovers than I care to remember. Gave them to me, yes, to feed on, but really just to torment him. Willingly. He didn't have to; I would have taken anyone, anything, but he did as I asked. Could have restrained me again while I slept, fed me dogs until I grew mad with starvation, but he didn't. He endured my punishment, watching me take all of them as I forbade him everything he desired.

Hard to believe I could be that vengeful hateful thing I was.

And the life I took, out of my rabid anger. I am glad that Mark had told me he was divorced, no children. I regret killing him enough, if he had a family.... I have done so many horrid things already. Fear what I would do without Eric grounding me, calming my devil.

I am not justifying anything he did, it was wrong, all of it, he knows it. Just didn't realize how wrong it was anymore. As he has said many times, he was lost. As I was. We have found each other, and ourselves in each other. I will not let anything tear us apart again. I know full well what will become of me if I do. Know what will happen to Eric.

Forgiveness is a much better option.

Sneak out of Eric's arms to make him something to eat. Even in his deep sleep, his stomach is loudly growling. I have witnessed many times the amount it takes to keep him going. He has not been eating nearly enough.

My body feels cold and barren as soon as I let go of him. I tuck a pillow into Eric's side hoping he will not miss me until I have his breakfast ready.

The sun is bright in the kitchen window. I focus on the loving chore ahead.

Steak and half a dozen eggs. I know there are frozen hash browns, some toast. Juice, water. I work quickly, want it all ready before I wake him.

"Margret, where are you?" Sleepy. "You cooking?" Should have known the smell of food would rouse him.

"Yes, you have to eat. It's almost done." Hear him trying to get up.

Yell to him. "Don't move! I'll be right in with it."

Everything is done but the eggs. I pour them into the hot pan.

Hear Eric whisper, "I miss you." I smile, happy. I miss him.

"I'm coming, Eric." Rushing.

I bring in the first plates, place them on the coffee table in front of him. A huge steak on one, mound of hash browns and toast on the other.

Dimples smiling up at me. God how I have missed them. Takes all I have not to suck them off his sweet face but I only kiss his forehead and rush back for the eggs before I burn them.

"Shit, this is a ton of food. Smells good."

Eggs done, plated. I place the eggs down with the other dishes before he has lifted a fork. Smiles up at me again. Glad to see the boyish glimmer in his eyes. "Wow. Thank you." Gratefully kisses my hand.

"Just eat," I order. He sits forward and I slide behind him, encircling him in arms and legs, rest my head between his shoulders. He will have to eat with me clinging to him. I have already hit my limit of separation for the moment. Eric rubs his hands over my arms tight around him, pulls them into him, understanding my need to be near.

"I love you," he whispers.

"And I love you."

After he has consumed nearly all of it, he wants to shower. I offer to help him, still weak from my zealous feeding, but he refuses. He needs to have his human time and I think also fears he will not be able to handle my lusts. Correctly so.

I busy myself with the dishes and cleaning up the kitchen. Feels good to feel 'normal' again.

Still not down so I make a fire, straighten up the front room. Then sit and wait, fidgeting. Seems like hours. My desire has not waned much, still feel its incessant throbbing.

Finally I hear him on the stairs. I have covered myself in Eric's disregarded shirt I found on the floor. It smells like him, comforts me. Eric looks much improved. Hair still wet, wavy. Only a pair of black cotton lounge pants on. His hard chest and stomach bare; I wish he had covered them as well.

"You OK?" I am still concerned.

"I feel better, full, but better." He sits down and pulls my legs over his, lifting me to sit in between them. Takes me tight into his arms. Happy to hear his heartbeat is strong as is his grip around me.

I try to calm my lusts but after a few short moments, my mouth starts to wander over his chest, sucking his nipple hard. I hear him groan. Not sure if it's painful or wanting. I force myself to stop. Look meekly up at him.

"Sorry."

"Don't be. You have no idea how much I want you." Eric takes my hand and moves it between his legs. "If you think your need is painful..." Feel the bud of hardness beneath the fabric. Not yet flush with blood. "I want more than I can give." My hand strokes gently over him.

"It's OK, you are still too weak."

He grabs the hair at the nape of my neck and pulls me back. Covers my feeble protests in the deep hot kiss I have longed for.

Soft, hard, forceful, gentle, how can it be all of them! It is. Eric continues to give me his mouth. No kiss is as lovely, as passionate as Eric's. Again I find myself shivering as if I am freezing in his arms. He only tightens his hold over me. I pull my hands through his hair, grasping for more. Eric tries to wander off few times but I force him back, passionately giving into my desires each time. I have no idea how long we are locked into each other's mouths but finally he forces me down to the floor. Opening my legs with his knee, he lies between them.

"Ooow." A agonized moan escapes me. "Eric." The strength of his hardness crushes into my mound. "Now. I need you inside me now." I whimper, "Please." His pants are gone quickly, my grip on him so tight I am amazed he could move. I wrap my legs under his backside and pull his naked body tight to me. Pray that he will not make me beg. I am begging already.

"Margret, tell me." His cruelty knows no end!

"What?" I weakly snap.

"Tell me." I twist and turn in my frustration, attempt to force him inside me.

"I love you, I need you. Please!" Mutter atop my kiss.

Pressing firmly to my hot yearning, still he will not. Eric has to want me as badly as I do him! He forces me to look at him. See sadness. "No, tell me. Do you forgive me, Margret?"

Like no man possible. I am dripping wet for him, begging for him. Yet he wants my forgiveness before he will give himself to me? My loving confession, my lust not convincing enough? It breaks my blind passion for him. Take my hands from digging into his back to gently caress his face. Look sincerely into his brown eyes.

"What the hell does 'I love you' mean, Eric, if not I forgive you? Forgive everything you have done, everything you will do. It means nothing, just empty words! I do love you, Eric, with all my heart. I can't endure being without you." Softly moaning into his mouth. "Yes, I forgive you... I hope you will forgive me."

I did try to kill him after all.

"I deserved it." Thrusts himself hard into me. I gasp as if I have never taken a man before.

"Just don't do it again, I couldn't live through it." I feel his smile pressed to my face. "You are my true love, Margret."

For several moments Eric enters, reenters. He has done this many times before, but slowly teasing. This is different. His shallow thrusts are breathtakingly rapid. Confesses hotly into my neck that he loves to feel my body give into him. After a while he penetrates me as far as he can. The rhythm of his thrusts, his hands over me, like a hot dance. I violently succumb to them, my convulsing forces Eric to join me.

"You're so... hot. I needed you..." His breath labored, he can hardly speak.

A question pops in to my head. Even in our loving state, I can't help it.

"Am I hot? Not cold like they say a vampire is?" He rolls to his back, taking me with him, laughs sweetly. I am glad to hear it even if he is laughing at my unexpected question.

"You're back, my beloved Margret." He chuckles. Crushes me into his chest. "No, you are not cold; maybe not as warm as a human, but not cold. But your," he pauses knows I hate trashy words, "well, being inside you is as hot as any mortal woman. Your special blood fills it, and it's very hot blood, my love."

"Good. I don't want to be cold...I feel hot when I'm with you."

"Believe me I feel it, inside and out."

Receive his sweet kiss to my forehead. Can't believe how much I have missed this simple tenderness. Unexpectedly I start to sob. His kiss prompted it but maybe more from our reunion.

"It's OK, I've got you."

"Don't let go of me, Eric." Wrap myself tighter around him.

"I won't, not ever again."

I can sense his need for more rest. I help him to the couch and pull him over me. Even Eric will need days to recover from my feeding. Hopefully I can give to him again soon. No matter, I have his warm body around me, his heart beating close to me. His love for me. All I really need.

Chapter Thirty-six

We are going to the penthouse! Well, soon. I am so excited. Can't wait to see it. After three full days of recovery from my attempt to kill him and several reunions, Eric is again strong. Finally he decided it was time. I can't wait to leave this house and mourn it at the same time. No need for it anymore. Time to start over.

We have been cleaning up, packing the few things we will take with us. Eric fixed the bloody mess I made of my bed and wall without question. Well, not audible questions, just a raised brow and a worried fatherly look. He doesn't really want to know anyway. He burnt my bedding, caked with blood, in the fire place. Mended the hole in the wall, my torn mattress out to the trash. I didn't need to tell him, my manic distress written on all of it.

I have not been able to let him go very far from me. Leaching on him constantly. Every time I let him free for too long, well too long for me, I cling. They are unexpected, these feelings. Overcome me. I have distracted him often. Sinking myself into his back as he makes his lunch, or endeavors to pack a box. My hands go from holding to groping quickly. Starts only needing a hug, but soon my touch begins to roam, landing on his hardness, and well... He is patient with my needy mood swings. Although I know he has them as well. His sleep is often broken, pleading for near immediate entrance into me. His mind still wounded by my total rejection. I will deny him nothing now. I have denied him quite enough.

We could have, would have, been out of here already if it wasn't for our constant distractions. I have hurt us both with my rage. Now we are trying to reassure ourselves that it will never happen again, never feel the painful separation we just endured. So we don't separate much.

"Margret what is this bag of your clothes. I got you boxes and suitcases." Testy.

"I am not walking into a six million dollar penthouse with trash bags full of clothes!" Six million? Shit! "Those are to give away, my old things!" I snap back.

Eric shakes his head, smiles. "Sorry, I'll get them to Goodwill." Think this move is worrying him somehow. Well this is, as simple as it may be to him, ours. The good and the bad are ours, this house ours. He fears moving me away from it.

The car packed to capacity. "I'll take this downtown." We worked all night, sunlight oozing into the sky.

"I'll go with you." I insist.

"No, sleep. I'll take you later. I want it to be perfect when you get there." Kisses my head. "You'll be OK, just sleep. I made you a nice fire." Persuading me.

I can't let go of him, I mean to, but cling. Burying my face into his neck, kissing and gently biting it.

"Margret, you should feed when I get back." This sidetracks my desires. I have not fed from him, not since I nearly bled him to death. The thought makes me physically shiver. Eric pulls me tighter.

"I'll wake you when I get back and then we can, OK?" I am shaking my head into his shoulder, digging my fingers into his back. His hand strokes soothingly over my hair. "You need to be strong, and you may not want to leave the penthouse for a few days. It's best if you are satisfied. K?"

I groan. "No. I don't..."

He cuts me off. "No, you do, need to, want to."

"No!" Stubborn.

"Don't be afraid, Margret. You don't want to kill me anymore, do you?" His tone playful.

I don't feel playful. I fully realize what I attempted to do. After reuniting with him, his feeding, our lovemaking; each drove fear of the horrid thing I nearly accomplished deep into my heart. Like nails into it. How could I even think to kill him? My love, my keeper, my stability?

Yet I nearly did. If he was a normal mortal, he would have surely died from it.

"No, I don't, but know I could, Eric. I nearly did. I drank so much from you, I couldn't stop. I'm terrified I won't be able to stop myself from consuming you if I taste you again."

Eric pulls my face from its hiding place and gently kisses me. "You can, and you must. I will make you full and happy as nothing else can. You need me."

As he needs me to.

"I do, but alive." My head tilted back, tears start to fall over my cheeks. His hot mouth softly sucking each one dry.

"It will be OK, Margret, promise." I allow him to pacify me, still my fears worsen.

"Do you still have the silver cuffs?" I open my eyes to find his near.

"Yes, packed but..."

"Find them, bring them. I will not feed from you unless you have them in hand to protect yourself from me."

Runs his lips over mine, speaking over them. "Nothing can protect me from you, my love." Crushes his mouth over mine, sucking me into his. Demanding. So much like our first kiss. My heat goes into overdrive. He lifts me up and takes me to lie on the couch.

"Save all that passion." Soft kiss on my forehead. "I'll be back soon. Rest."

Winter's imposition slowly relents. It's 6 p.m.; dusk. He has been gone since just before 6 a.m. I have slept, fed the fire, waited frustrated for hours.

My texts unanswered. Worried me until I heard his phone vibrating on the dresser in his room upstairs. Forgotten. Not like him, but he is distracted. I shower, I walk around the house impatiently in circles. None of the furniture will come, it is all rather tacky.

Finally I hear Eric's car arrive. I try to restrain my anxious excitement. Hold my legs close as I sit on the couch, looking into the fire.

Eric rushes into my arms, encircling me, pulling me over him. "God I missed you," he whispers into my breasts. Grabs the back of my head and kisses me passionately. "It's all done, all the construction, furniture in, all ready for you." His eyes are full of happiness. Still I sense his fatigue. He has not slept as I have.

"I can't wait to see it!" I say, giddy.

"Well, you have to for a bit longer." Sighs. "You need to feed," he adds firmly.

Reluctant, I pull back. We silently stare into each other's eyes for a moment before I protest.

"I am afraid to Eric."

He reaches into the back pocket of his jeans and pulls out a silver cuff. "I have it, as you wanted. Now take off your clothes." His determination clear.

Unhappily groaning, I stand and slowly undress for him, slipping off my black jeans, pulling his white tee over my head. Even in the dim light, I can see his pants filling, making a fat mound my mouth is craving as I undress.

I stand naked before him, the firelight behind me. Eric hums..."You are so beautiful, Margret, so beautiful."

"Now you," I demand.

His dimpled smile as he unzips, unleashes. Just a glimpse of his thick manhood peeking out of his jeans. Control my desire to fall over it. Eric pulls his shirt over his head, slowly pushes his jeans down over his thick legs, revealing himself to me. For a few seconds, we both look over each other, craving.

"The cuff?" I demand.

"I have it! Now take me," Eric demands.

I want him, always like I have never wanted a man before. I bring myself over him. Immediately he positions himself to my heat, sinking it in my folds. Pulls my head down to his kiss. "Hold me." I answer his request, gripping him tightly. Eric's hands smoothly roam over me. Mine grasping him into our kiss. Grind ourselves into each other as we lock our mouths together. Grinding is good, pushing better. Eric takes hold of my hips, steadying them and pushes in a bit. His kiss still hot and needy. My hands roam over his shoulders, arms, always returning to run through his hair, pulling him deeper into my mouth.

"Margret, feed." I abruptly stop and pull away from him.

"I want you on top, in control, the silver cuff in your hand." The cuff rests on the couch next to us, still not close enough for me.

Shaking his head. "Margret, why do you resist what you want? What you need?"

"I need you, fear what I could do..."

Pulls me back into his chest. His arms feel so safe and warm around me. "I will protect you, I am your keeper."

"No! No, you are my love, yes, keeper, but...my heart beats inside you... you are more than a keeper to me, Eric. I'm not human anymore, I am a killer. Even you are not immune to it!"

"Margret, please, you didn't kill me when your heart was full of rage. You won't kill me now. Feed." He insists.

Eric's confidence does not dissuade my fears much.

He throws me to the floor more forcefully than he would a human woman. Mounts me with as much force, taking my breath from me. Holds himself deep inside me. Whispers, "When I die, I want it to be in your arms. You cannot do any injustice to me even if you drain me now. Now or a hundred years from now."

His body collapses into me. I envelope him in arms and legs. His warm breath like a draft of summer's heat over my shoulder. I need. Eric's thrusts gentle. His arm comes up to cradle my head, the thick muscle presses against my lips, seducing me. Open my mouth over it, still I hesitate.

"Bite. I want you to." Demanding whisper in my ear. I give up, sink my teeth into his smooth skin. Eric loudly moans. Not from any pain, but the pleasure of giving all of himself to me. Hold the hot rush of blood so it makes my mouth full before I swallow the sweetness. I am more aware of his complete bond with me than ever before. My core filled, his slow undulations rubbing against my walls. Every inch of his skin melting into mine. My mouth sucking like a baby, filling over and over. My orgasm intense, unending. He pulsates, explodes, filling me with liquid fire. I have all of him flowing inside me; still I want more. Only my acute awareness of his human heart passionately beating stops me from continuing the intense pleasure. I wait until his throbbing stops, release his arm from my greed.

Eric's mouth quickly covers mine, tasting the last of his blood with his deep kiss. I start to sob, from the beauty of him, from the pain of releasing him.

"I love you, Margret." My tears increase.

"I'm sorry, I can't help it. You overwhelm me, then it just erupts." Turns to his back, pulling me onto his chest. "I suppose Markus never cried like a baby." Eric takes my wet face in his gentle hands. Looking deep into my eyes.

"Markus was more like, just sex. You, you are an experience no one truly deserves to have. Yet you are mine, my love, my Margret. Nothing compares to the beauty of being one with you."

Chapter Thirty-seven

"Why is everything you buy me skintight?" Fidgeting with the charcoal colored cashmere sweater dress he brought home for me.

"Because you have a beautiful body, so if you're going to be dressed, I want to see as much of your curves as I can."

"If I would have known you were going to make me immortal, I would have lost ten pounds," I complain.

"Stop that! You're perfect, curvy and full in all the right places. Don't like shapeless sticks." He goes to grope my breast with one hand, my behind with the other. I push him away, perturbed.

I was in fairly good shape, always on my feet as a nurse. Worked on my abs a bit, though nothing like he is.

"You're so, well, perfect," I say exasperated. "Were you always like that?"

"Sort of. I do work out, helps with stress. Don't think I can change much, though. My metabolism from all the givings..." Words fade, softly grips my hips, pulling me to him. "Don't ever doubt this. You're beautiful, Margret. I love you, want you as you are."

Gratefully kiss his cheek. Eric's truth, all that matters.

He is impatient now. "Let's go. If we leave now, we should be downtown before sunrise, and you want to see the sunrise over the lake, Margret, it's amazing."

A feeling unmistakably similar to leaving the basement for the first time washes over me as we close the door for the last time. Locking this life away with the turn of a key. I am excited to move, anxious to move on. Somehow sad at the same time.

My past life, my future life wildly conflict.

I grow impatient and a bit bored on the drive downtown. Decide to take advantage of our confinement.

"Can I ask you a few questions while I have your complete attention?" The *look* casts my way. I meet it with an innocent smile.

"Nothing serious. I don't want to talk about anything that's sad, bad or will cause an argument." His displeasure reverberating in the car.

"Well, that leaves out everything!" We both chuckle, his touched with reluctance. I have him trapped and he can't distract me while he is driving. So I proceed, his requirements narrowing me to few.

"All the days you left me alone, where did you go? I know some to the hospital but not all."

Nodding his head.

"Often it was to the penthouse, overseeing the final construction. Did a ton of shopping, furniture, curtains, all the things we need." His eyes fixed on the road ahead.

"I thought you said you and Markus lived there?"

"Not in the penthouse, a few floors down. The place was pretty much a blank slate when Markus got it. Not much more than a few empty floors with walls."

"Oh. You shopped for curtains?" I ask suspiciously.

"Yes, I did. I have great taste, not that you could tell by the house."

"Your bachelor pad?" Can't resist the sarcasm.

"The things I put up with to get you..." Chuckling under his words. "Markus had already purchased a good deal of the furnishings but I canceled them and bought things I liked better for the place. Think you will as well."

"Like what?"

"No spoilers, you see it soon enough. OK next; that can't be all, not from you."

Think, have so many floating around.

"Did you ever work at a real job or just do, I don't know...what do you do? Just take care of Markus, be his keeper?"

Nodding his head. "That's a good question. I have done many things besides being his keeper. Which is quite demanding enough sometimes. I like to have something to do with myself, something that keeps me connected to normal life, real people. It's easy to get lost in all the travel, fine places, rich people. Not real, if you know what I mean. So if we were settled somewhere for a bit, I would find something to do, something to keep me real." More than a note of sadness. Seems he may feel like he has not always been so successful at the real part. Know he struggles to keep the sweet fireman from Chicago alive somewhere. After a moment of thought, he continues.

"I worked...let's see, I was a high school teacher for a bit." He adds rather proudly. "Art history. I was an orderly, volunteered at senior homes, a few day care centers, soup kitchens. Stuff like that. Markus would do whatever I wanted to keep me happy. If I asked, he would make it happen, like I opened a gallery when we were in Napa, before that an Irish pub, even had a book store many years ago. They were all fun, didn't last for too long, a few years. I met a lot of interesting people because of them. Didn't matter if the business did well really. Markus couldn't have cared less. They all did, though. Markus would want to move on or we may have had to move on. Things." He finishes with a clear note of I don't want to talk about it.

I wanted to broach the subject of their moving 'because we had to'. Remembering Eric's dispirited comments about a new name, new home. Thought that may be pushing the envelope too far. Besides we are on Lake Shore Drive now. Questions cease. My attention soaked up in seemly endless buildings. Lights in scattered boxes gleaming in each tall figure like a new crossword puzzle waiting to be filled in.

The lake still blanketed in darkness. Only a hint of morning and the unnatural luminescence of the great city allowing its perception. Soon the long curves wind into Michigan Avenue. Now the light grows stronger. The street lined with fancy stores, tall brightly lit windows full of every beautiful thing a mind could imagine to want. To look straight down the center of the street is like looking at the very heart of Christmas. Red and green traffic lights on every corner as far as my eyes can see. Even at this early hour, cars, taxis, people rush down Michigan Avenue.

The avenue's median is overflowing with every early spring flower and newly budding tree you can think of. My excitement grows with each mile we drive.

Over the Michigan Avenue bridge, the art museum, diners old and new, the park....

"That's it." I have not even noticed his heartbeat until now as his voice wakes me from my fascination with the city. Eric is anxious to show me our new home. I look over; even though his focus is on driving, I see the excitement on his face.

After we round the corner across from Millennium Park, we make our way into a dark garage, winding our way up several floors to find our parking spot. As soon as we pull in, Eric is at my door opening it while I try to gather myself.

"These two are ours." Pointing to the black and white metal sign that reads Reserved for Penthouse-Nineteen. Two small arrows point down to the slots tucked next to the elevators. We just parked in one of the arrowed spaces; in the other is an old red Mustang convertible. Pristine, like new. I was so lost in thought I didn't even notice it as we drove in. I don't really get into cars, but an old Mustang... I love old cars. This one of my favorites.

"Shit, Eric it's beautiful!" Running my hand over the shiny finish. A bright red lipstick color. Seductive overpowering red. Smooth metal under my fingertips.

"Like it?" he asks needlessly.

"It's beautiful, what's not to like, but who..." Before I can finish my question as to who has parked in our spot, I see he is holding up a key dangling from a gold heart. "Yours."

"NO! No way! Really?"

"Yours." Tucks the key into my hand and kisses it. "From Markus." An ample smile on his face, still touched with a bit of melancholy.

I jump up and down like a child receiving the most desired gift on Christmas morning. Almost unable to get the key in; finally I sit in my new car. A car! I have another freedom, this one will blow my hair back, fill my lungs with speed as I drive it anywhere I wish. I have nearly forgotten the penthouse. My hands linger over the steering wheel, imagining driving down lake shore at speeds I know I could never get away with in Chicago traffic. He touches my shoulder after a few minutes of my pawing over the dash and black leather seats.

"I knew you would like it. The sun is coming and I don't want you to miss it." His hand extends, I reluctantly take it. "We'll take it out soon, Margret." Kissing my forehead, leads me quickly to the elevator.

After we get into the building and make our way down a hall, Eric uses a key card to access an elevator. Small, the bottom lined in dark wood panels the top wood framed mirrors. He hits 20, the last floor.

He is not holding my hand nor does he have even a loose arm around my waist. Seems oddly nervous to show me my new home. As if I wouldn't like it?

Thirteen.

Looking at the elevator doors. "It's two, well, two plus floors, nineteen and twenty. Our bedroom can only be accessed by the stairs," he whispers. Feel like I could pee my pants; can't but feel it just the same.

Seventeen.

"Why the twentieth floor, not nineteen?"

Takes my hand, squeezing it. "You'll see."

Nineteen...twenty.

"Close your eyes." I comply as I hear the rolling sound of the old metal doors slowly opening. Eric guides me onto the steady floor for several steps. Gently pulling me along until he stops.

"OK, you can open them." A last tight grip to my hand, he slips it loosely behind my back.

The grandeur of the room fills me so quickly. I am glad to have his strong arm around my back to steady me. We move a few small steps into a great room unlike any I have ever seen. Before me, to my right, my left, surrounded in tall arched windows. Three windows in each marbled wall, leaving scarcely a space between them. All flanked by ionic columns, the tight curls adorning them like a fine wig. Two deep in each window. They must be at least fifteen feet high. Resting atop the columns, a deep sweeping arch that is adorned in boxed rosettes in matching rows.

Eric stands close to me as I take in the majestic space that surrounds us. The night is still in the sky. Only a soft light hiding in the thick moldings that finish the towering walls casts a fall-like glow into the room. The floors a white grey-veined marble, so finely polished they reflect nearly like glass the sepia light from above. Changing their natural colors from white to golden. All the front windows are French doors. I walk to the center doors, take the handles and pull them open.

The great surge of wind rushes over me like the power of the locomotive I stood so near, its unexpected force taking me back a step. I recover, step out onto a narrow balcony. The waist- high railing is tightly woven with cement balustrades. White curvaceous figures rigidly stand in long rows against the night sky.

I feel a warmth slide over my stomach, Eric's arm wraps around me. The brisk morning wind whisks my hair about at will. Caresses my skin as I look over the lights in the park below. The sun weakly intruding into the dark horizon, yet every second brings her closer. My eyes burn, unwilling to blink even as the powerful winds dry them into deserts. Morning grows more demanding. Forcing itself into the line between heaven and earth.

Eric pulls himself closer, wraps his arms tighter around me. I hold his arms dear to my womb, knowing he will be my only child, my only friend, my only love. His steady hot breath on my neck, his warm embrace in such deep contrast to the cool winds that caress me as well. As beautiful to me as nature's. He is silent as am I. Our hearts blended in these moments of the day's birth.

Rust light spreads over the grey waters, reflecting not separating save a thin line nearly imperceptible. As the silver arch pierces the glow everything changes. The dark waters become grey blue, then royal blue. The buildings of the city like dry sponges take on her light. Everything awakes. More cars, more people, more noise. Not even the sounds of the city can drowned out the birds happily tweeting in the park below me. I hear and see it all as I never have before, maybe never could. All of it overwhelmingly beautiful. Human life rushing at my feet, nature's renewal rises before me.

I tug at Eric's arm, bringing him around to hold me fully. His head never leaves my shoulder, tucked with his soft lips resting on me. Shielding me from the winds, he presses his face to mine. His hand grips my hair, holding me in place. Hot breath like August's gentle breeze amidst the cool storm encircling us. I look out at the day breaking through holding what I love dearest to me. The sun's breast arches into the sky bringing with it a new day I know is mine. A new life, unsought, but mine now. I will embrace it as tightly as I do Eric, my beloved keeper.

Chapter Thirty-eight

After my tour of all the beautiful rooms that make up our new home, we return our master bedroom. It sits atop the ballroom, as Eric called it, smaller but just as grand. The top-most point of this old building.

The ceilings look to be a story and a half high. Long rectangular windows monopolize the three walls, exposing the city and the ocean-like lake at its shores. Centered above there are large porthole-like windows encircled in beautiful rosettes, much like the ones in the ballroom below, only these are massive flowers surrounding each glass. Long pleated gold draperies fall in pools over the marble floors. Each tied aside by thick silk rope, wound in red, gold, olive; heavy tassels dangling from them. Inside the draperies hang antique lace sheers that wisp in the breeze like ghosts trying to gain entrance into the room.

I am sure when drawn the heavy curtains will ensure my rest even on the brightest day.

Our kingly four-post bed is tucked in the left corner in front of an opulent bath. Harmoniously the quilt and pillows are patterned in earthy reds, pure golds, deep olives. All as plush as I have never seen.

It calls to me to rest in their many flowers. I eagerly flop on the soft velvet and silks of our elegant new bedding. Eric is standing on one of the many Persian rugs that are scattered over the marble floors, seemingly rethinking the layout of the dressers, chaise and armoire.

He is exhausted, still wanting to appease my excitement. Eric patiently took me through every corner of our new home.

I try to grab his attention, provocatively slithering over the bedding. Nothing.

"Eric!" Finally his gaze meets mine. I smile; his smile still somewhat distracted. "Lie with me on our new bed. It's so damn soft." I curl myself into a ball, taking a fat pillow under my head. Eric gives a last glance to the room before he comes to cup himself into my back. Warmth, comfort, bliss.

I debate with myself. I could rest here until he sleeps as I know he needs to. Or I could turn over and seduce him to give me the crown of the day.

I don't debate for long. Flip over, mount him as I pull my long dress over my head in one swift movement. Eric groans unhappily. I will soon change that.

Keeping myself composed I unbutton his shirt. Kissing newly exposed flesh with each unfastened inch. I sense his reluctance, his desire for rest, but my needs will not go unanswered.

I slowly relish the taste of his sweet salty skin. Too slowly, it would seem.

"Margret." Gentle plead for mercy. "I'm so tired."

"You don't have to do a thing. Just be hard. And you are hard, my beloved." I stroke my hand over the thick rock he cannot suppress. Again his sleepy moans. I hump his muscular thigh as I run my breasts over him. My kiss again travels from his neck to his shoulders. He grows even thicker in my tight grip. Chest biting, stomach licking. My needy mouth teases him. Eric groans, expressing his unwilling pleasure. Still I take my time to love him in every deep dark place until my need to be one is too great.

Positioning myself on his stiff pillar, I press down only enough to break into me. Eric's eyes closed, his weak grip on me. I want to gain his full attention. My kisses arousing and relaxing at the same time. I wait, unmoving. I let myself down only a fraction. His sleepy hands on my thighs begin to wake, trying to pull me fully on to him. I hold firm, refuse to admit him.

Under his breath, "Margret, please I want you." Struggles to lift his hips, force himself into me. I rise, forbidding him each inch his thrust endeavors to gain.

"All of you," he pleads. I see now why he likes to tease me so. His desire for me, the need it arouses in him, only makes me burn hotter. Eric's eyes tightly closed until he senses I will not concede. After several moments of my teasing, our eyes meet. Eric's stern look. Yet the playful glisten in them.

"Pay back?" Irritably groans. I laugh. He has teased me this way far too many times.

While he has me so engaged in the lure of his gaze, he takes firm hold of my hips, swiftly gains the depth he desired.

"I can't take any more of your seductions Margret. You have been at me for over a half hour my love. Yet you still want to tease me further? I am too wasted to handle your unending lusts."

"I said you didn't have to do anything," I answer coyly, smiling down at him.

He flips me to my stomach, quickly pulls me to cup the edge of the bed.

Hotly whispers into the back of my neck, "You just want to torment me." His forceful thrust corresponding to my long enticements.

"I will take what I desire, my love." As he always has. "You might be stronger than me now, but not when you are hot..."

He is right, I gladly give into him.

❦

Eric is sleeping soundly; he has been up for 48 hours. I lie next to him, awake, feeling a peaceful joy just in his unconscious nearness to me. So many worries lifted from me. My anger, fear, pain, remorse agonizingly relinquished. I have fully accepted who I am, who Eric is. Learning to live in the moment as he does...not without lesson, but without remorse. Holding on to everything I have been through will only bring us unnecessary, and unending, misery.

Our connection, regardless of how it came to be, is more powerful, deeper than any I could have dreamt of in my human heart. No man could love me as he has, care for me as he does. Know me, both human and immortal as Eric does. I know that. My rejection of him, separation from him I see now was necessary. A growing pain I could not circumvent. I needed to see clearly what would become of me without him.

Eric's ability to love, give of himself singular. Why Markus wanted him so. Even as I am jealous of Markus's love for Eric, Eric's love for him. Hate what he did to Eric to make him his. I feel an incomprehensible gratitude to him. Markus laid my greatest love in my lap, gave him to me without request.

Yes, I suppose Eric and I are enhanced by our uniqueness. Even so all that Eric has lived through, all he has left behind...Even if he left me a mortal woman, I know his love would be greater than any. I know it because I remember it. We are truly made for each other, me literally!

I will take all the years he is able to give me. Maybe when several human lifetimes have passed, he will want death. Nothing will make me embrace death closer than the thought of going on without him.

Eric sleeps his head resting on my thigh, arms around my leg as if I were his pillow. As I look down at him, run my hand over his hair, I know if I have him all will be well. Without him Margret will die. If this body lived beyond that loss what I would become would only be a shell. My body, but not me.

Chapter Thirty-nine

Run my hands over the beautiful black marble fire place, lounge over the old-fashioned tapestries of the wood framed sofa in the living room, sit at the head of the long dark wood dining table with it's eight tall chairs richly carved in winding flourishes, look into every cherry wood kitchen cabinet stuffed full of fine china and crystal... only then do I long for the ballroom. Our living quarters though beautiful, do not serve my needs as well as the ballroom at the center of the three floors of our new home. The grander of it captures my deepest desire. Freedom.

There are two sitting areas on either side of the towering entrance. European sofas with graceful curves framed in intricate carved woods. Cream leather fastened with nail-head trimmings. Soft striped and flowered pillows on each in natural browns and creams. The wing back chairs closely mirror the colors but the glistening chenille is covered with embroidered floras.

Though the two groupings are tucked into the back wall, nothing obscures the beautiful views in this expansive room. Only there to quietly sit and take in the overwhelming span of the sky and the lake beyond.

Want to sit on them; I want to dance over the marble floors.

I hear Eric is awake above as I walk slowly up the iron-rimmed staircase to the middle floor.

"Eric, you awake?" I call up to our bedroom. The arch and the gold light inside beckoning; although the cast iron railings that continue on the other side of the room hugging the wall, curving upward, beckons me to meet him as well. The black iron paisley patterns swoop up to our bedroom above just like the one that comes up from our living quarters below.

Only the towering arch to the ballroom and the beautiful views beyond can seduce me more.

"I'll meet you," I weakly holler up to him, caring little if he hears me. I turn to the ballroom entrance. It takes me a second to register; there is a tall black figure standing on our balcony. I take a few cautious steps into the archway. My eyes are not playing any tricks on me. A man stands looking out over the lake just as I did hours ago. A long dark coat whips in the uncontrolled winds.

Transfixed on the shadow-like figure of the intruder, I stand frozen, only hear Eric's descent behind me.

"Sorry I slept so long." Eric kisses my forehead, hugs me. I stand stoic. He believes my gaze is distracted by the grand room and sweeping views. Snuggles into my neck affectionately. Only when Eric senses my rigid stance does he lift his head to see what has me so engaged.

Eric's eyes still full of sleep, he pulls me silently into the room. Seeing but not seeing. He stops abruptly when we reach its center most point. The hand he has tenderly in mine tightens almost painfully.

"No...no, can't be." His words only for himself. Wide eyes full of disbelief. Fixed like glue to the strange man. Eric's reaction only adds to my foreboding.

Who is this strange man, and why does his presence frighten me so?

The figure swiftly turns, pushing the two center doors open in a great fluid motion. Forceful winds swoops in with him, filling the room as does his presence. He tucks his hands firmly into the pockets of his long black coat, restricting the windswept fabric from getting too far ahead of him. No entrance I have ever seen in a movie more impressive. His bright green eyes catch the last of the day's light, a thick brow above them. Windblown child-like light brown curls cover his head. Rather long oval face, mouth shaped like a kiss. Strikingly handsome.

We are both hypnotized, only the firm grip we have on each other reminds us that he is not the only one in the room.

His long graceful gait brings him quickly before us. Only now do I sense Eric's shaking. Only now do I realize who I am looking at.

"Ah, there you are." Friendly, only a slight British accent remaining in his English. Reaching out to cup Eric's face, roughly pulling it to meet his kiss. "My beloved keeper."

Eric is speechless. Frozen. I hear his heart racing, breath nearly nonexistent.

"Markus." His utterance not a word but a gasp. "How?"

Markus laughs under his breath. His smile deceptive, as is the rest of him. He looks very young, maybe 22, but the intellect in his eyes, the powerful way he moves, refutes the smoothness of his skin.

Almost chuckling. "Yes, how?"

He has not looked at me once, his attention set on Eric. "Well, my beloved, it seems that for the first time in all our long years, you have failed me."

He walks around Eric's frozen body to whisper in his ear, "Gravely failed me, if you will forgive the unintended pun." There is no mistaking the controlled malice in his tone. I feel him slowly walk behind me. Just the inch between us so hot it is as if he is touching me though he is not. Again no acknowledgement of me, returns to stand over Eric. His few inches seemingly exacerbated by his powerful presence.

"I did as you asked. I deeply cut you, bled you out, buried you in silver." Each word harsh, yet breathless.

A soft condescending laugh escapes Markus. Staring into Eric's unwilling eyes.

"No. Not exactly as I asked, not as I instructed you. As I remember, my instructions were to remove my head, not sever it."

Eric looks questionably at Markus. "I couldn't do it, remove it....you were no more than skin and bones. Bled out, dead."

Markus runs a sympathetic hand over Eric's face, lifting it to look into his piercing eyes.

"You failed me," he simply states.

His eyes grow angry but his voice remains cool. "It took weeks just to move my boney limbs out of the loose silver you bound me tightly in when I had flesh and muscle. Every slight movement a painful triumph. For many days after that, I pathetically dug my way out of the black earth grain by grain. Every second in such agony, agony I have never felt, dreamt of in all my centuries combined." He makes a moment's glance at me, yet does not see me.

"I had every rodent and animal I could call to me as my head broke the ground before I could fully free myself of the soil. Not even my turning was so painful, the profound hunger incomparable." Again a spiteful chuckle under his breath. "Unfortunately the park seems to be cursed with a wild animal, most likely a bear, the authorities surmise. Several hikers have gone missing...." Markus lets his insinuation trail off into silence. No real question about the fate of the hikers.

"Nonetheless my anguishing hunger was nearly unaffected." Again he grabs Eric's face in his long thin hand and pulls it near to his. "This, my dearest Eric, the endless suffering I endured is forever seared into my mind and body." Like a threat he recalls his torments. "The months it took me to regain my full strength," pauses smugly smiling, "and beauty."

"I am so sorry, Markus. I didn't want to cause you any pain, I didn't want...certainly not that..." Eric trails off, not knowing what more to say. How to ask for forgiveness.

"I suppose it is of my own making. I shielded you too much from the cruelties of this life. Babied you..." Runs his thumb slowly over Eric's bottom lip. "Your temperament, and your sweet fat lips, always like an innocent child's to me." Markus roughly releases Eric.

Only now does he turn his attention to me. Soon wish I was as invisible to him as the moment before.

"And my new child, Margret." Addressing me with barely a glance at first. "You are such a beauty, and so passionate, in love, and your rage. I have spied them both. Impressive." I feel a great uneasiness. Markus has seen more than he is saying, more than I want him to know. He slips his arm around my waist, pulling me into him, my hand still locked in Eric's. Kisses hotly over my rigid lips with his open mouth.

"I look forward to sharing both your passions." That angers Eric enough to break the trance of disbelief he has been captured in.

"No, Markus!" Although he has let me go, Eric moves himself protectively between us. Markus's laugh so loud and evil, echoing in the great room. He takes a few steps back and starts to circle us like a predator. Slow thoughtful steps. Still quietly chuckling to himself. Eric takes my hand again in his, now cupped into his back as he stands in front of me. I tuck myself into him, yet I will not hide my eyes from the unbelievable sight before us.

Filling the space around us in a forceful voice. "So now we have a problem, my dearest ones. A rather big one. It is, of course, not unheard of for a master to engage two keepers. We do as we wish; many want both sexes to serve them. However, for one keeper to have two masters, well, I am sure you can see the many conflicts that would arouse. We only share during a changing, and then only for a few months at best." Markus, now in front of me, looks deeply into my eyes with contempt.

"You can imagine the strain, Margret, on a simple mortal endeavoring to please two vampires. Not even our beloved Eric, as strong as he may be, could keep up with our demands. I do know what great demands you ask of him...as you did earlier today." Markus was here? Watching us? Watching me, for how long? "Even his many physical abilities would be unable to keep us both satisfied."

Eric starts to object. "Markus, please, Margret is my..."

"Quiet!" Booming. "I know full well what Margret is to you! How you love her." Belittling us.

"I know more of her secrets than you. Both of your secrets. You have no say in this, Keeper." I can't believe the tone he has, as if Eric is a thing, not the beautiful man he loves.

"You are mine," he says decisively. "Only when I no longer walk this earth will you be released from me!"

This is not about love, it's about possession, of Eric. Markus continues his oration. Eric shadows every inch of Markus's movements.

A disdainful smirk fastens to Markus's face.

"For now we will do as best we can. I need no keeper for my feeds. I take all I wish, as I have for months now. Yet admittedly I have missed the familiar comforts of my keeper's arms. The pleasures I found there." Still speaking as if Eric is a thing, a possession. Markus now faces the gray sky filling the tall windows several feet in front of us. Whispers offhandedly, "We can't have two uncontrolled vampires feeding in one city, now can we?"

My mind can't absorb what is happing, what I am hearing. My maker, Eric's Master, stands alive before me, trying to take him away from me!

Even though he is not engaging us, Markus holds us both in an inexplicable grip though I feel some small comfort in Eric's constant hold, his protection. Even though I know there is little he can do without risking his life. Markus is obviously a rogue. Not the Markus Eric spent many decades with. He has become 'a wild soulless thing' as he once warned me I would become without a keeper. Markus has been without for many months now.

Markus's dark figure turns, saunters back to face us. Green hypnotic orbs staring into my eyes. "You will have to be tamed yet again, my child, and Eric retrained to suit our new conditions." Artlessly wicked.

My uncontrollable fear, turning to anger, to protective rage. Ours eyes link into each other's. My fury ascends like oil in water, unstoppable, although I struggle with all I have to stop it. Fear what will become if it… my whole body reeking of it. Eric tightens his grip on my hand, pulling it into his stomach, encircling it with both hands. As always he reads me without a word, knows. Markus spies our embrace. With a false sympathy, Markus runs his hand gently over my head, softly grasping my long hair, tracing his hand slowly over my shoulder, bicep, forearm. Reaches for my hand woven into Eric's. In a firm gesture full of meaning, he forces his between us, breaking our grip. Eric grabs Markus's arm. Markus seizes Eric wrist and effortlessly snaps it. I hear cracking bone and Eric's cry simultaneously perforate me. Eric, still in his grip, falls to the floor in pain; Markus's eyes boring into his keeper.

Eric's soothing hold gone, my rage flows free. As Markus looks down at his once beloved keeper crying in agony on the floor, I leap over him. Pound on him with angry fists. Rip into him with all my fury. I am so lost in my struggle to hurt him, I take no notice of his stance for several moments.

I am only an irritation he allows to prove himself. Standing tall, unmoving, as I unleash every bit of my strength and rage on him. Unaffected. Finally he grows impatient with my display. Taking both hand over his head to grab onto me, he effortlessly flings me across the room. I feel myself fly through the air, a few painful bounces on the marble floor. My propulsion only stops when I forcefully hit the farthest wall of the foyer many feet outside the ballroom. Again I feel all the pain of each impact, but gone quickly so I can feel the next.

"Markus, please stop." Eric's groans ring in my ears. I leap back into the room. Hold him protectively. Markus lets out a sarcastic laugh. Knowing neither of us has the power to overtake him. Mocking our love for each other.

Both of us well chastised, cowering together at his feet.

"I am well aware of all your misbehaviors." Saccharinely.

Both of us look up at Markus from our lowly position.

"So, if you would try to deceive me, disobey me, overtake me, certain information would become known to the police." Hotly stares into my eyes. "Your unfortunate husband is no longer where you left him." Chuckles to himself, casually strolling around us. "Not too far from where you buried me, Eric." Sighs, full of thought.

"Just as I removed that vagrant you killed from the reeds, the dreadful biker from the pond, I also moved your husband," snickers, "to a safe place I know of. Nevertheless its safety depends on your willingness to cooperate."

His not-so-veiled threats continue.

"If either of you cause me any difficulties, not only, as I think you both understand now, will I correct you, never doubt that I would take your lives if need be." Pompously grinning.

"On the other hand, maybe it would be better to keep you both alive and forever separated. I have the power to have Eric incarcerated for your, shall we say, indiscretions."

Crouching down to closely stare into Eric's eyes. "Margret can watch you grow old, literally rot behind bars without being able to do a thing about it, and she will go insane without you."

Again he stands tall over us. Pretentiously purrs, "I made you, Margret, and I know Eric, quite intimately. Neither of you can hide from me. So you will do as I wish, both of you!" he spits.

With that he quickly strolls back to the open doors and leaps out like a hawk into the early night sky.

-*Epilogue*-

Lying in our beautiful new bed, embraced in Eric's limbs, apprehension and fear saturating us both. We silently imagine the torturous hell Markus will put us through. Both of us uniquely bound to him.

I rest my ear to Eric's heart, its distressed beat not slowing much even in rest. Kiss the small estate between his breasts, trying to soothe the heaviness I know lies inside it.

After Markus unexpectedly leaped into the sky, I brought Eric up to our room to attend to his broken wrist. The only sound he made for many long minutes were painful cries as I set it. I wrapped it tightly, not a cast but the best I could do.

The only spoken words he has managed... 'I'm sorry' and repeated 'I love yous', both accompanied by regretful kisses over my face or hand.

Shock has taken every expression from him. Both realize that our future together does not look as bright as the sunrise we shared just a few hours ago.

Time impossible to hold, changes everything in just a few short measures of it.

I find myself missing the tight walls of my cubby. Safely holding me, hiding me inside them. My bindings have changed, though Markus's bonds are as firm and foreboding as were those that held me when I woke a vampire.

As impossible to break free of.

For now.

My Keeper

www.ingramcontent.com/pod-product-compliance
Lightning Source LLC
Chambersburg PA
CBHW070221260626
47160CB00002B/628